"Part fantasy, part mystery, and part suspense story. The authors have done a great job balancing the three elements and braiding them together into one exciting read." —Blogcritics

"A contemporary mystery thriller with elements of *Oliver Twist,* a caper story, and a dash of the supernatural—namely ghosts, Victorian magic, and steampunk . . . Spectacular." —*Fantasy Book Critic*

"A modern, supernatural take on *Oliver Twist* . . . Golden and Lebbon paint an evocative portrait of London, present and past." —*Fangoria*

"*Mind the Gap* starts off with a bang, throwing you right into the story, and once it takes off running, it doesn't let up. . . . It's moody, highly atmospheric, and pulls no punches in involving the senses as it creates the hidden world of a forgotten, decaying, buried London. . . . A series worth watching." —SF Site

Praise for THE MAP OF MOMENTS

"Urban realism meets dark fantasy in this spine-tingling second collaboration between authors Golden and Lebbon . . . as they merge the repercussions of Hurricane Katrina with New Orleans' terrifying ghostly past. . . . Golden and Lebbon have far outstripped their past efforts with this wonderfully creepy thriller of a ghost story." —*Publishers Weekly* (starred review)

"Golden and Lebbon vividly evoke the rich, enduring character of New Orleans, as well as spinning a compelling fantasy yarn." —*Booklist*

"Draws from the aftermath of a tragic moment in recent history, telling a dark, gripping story set in a shattered but unbeaten New Orleans . . . Part ghost story, part thriller, it doesn't pull any punches along the way, putting the hero through a physical, mental and spiritual ordeal even as it paints an honest, stark picture of a city just starting to recover from a near-fatal blow. . . . A hell of a harrowing tale [and] a great read, illuminating a time and place in American history that should not be ignored or forgotten." —SF Site

"*The Map of Moments* is set in post-Katrina New Orleans, and it's as much a love letter to the city and its people as it is a lamentation for what has been, perhaps irrevocably, lost. . . . Not an easy, comforting read, but it is an alluring, engrossing one, and a wiser, truer book than something simpler could have been."
—*The Green Man Review*

"Christopher Golden and Tim Lebbon have crafted a love letter to New Orleans in *The Map of Moments*. . . . Fans of unconventional urban fantasy will enjoy following this map into some very interesting places indeed." —SFRevu

"*The Map of Moments* is a truly haunting look at the dark history and magic to the underside of New Orleans and the ghosts they hide." —*The Mad Hatter*

"Golden and Lebbon do a masterful job of presenting the chase and the discovery of the darkness lurking in New Orleans's history. I ended up reading much of the book at night when the house was quiet, and I think that really lent itself to the overall experience. So if you can get somewhere quiet, with darkness all around, except for your reading lamp, *The Map of Moments* is a wonderfully creepy experience down streets littered with dead and dark things." —Blogcritics

THE
SHADOW
MEN

CHRISTOPHER GOLDEN
AND TIM LEBBON

BALLANTINE BOOKS • NEW YORK

A Spectra Mass Market Original
Copyright © 2011 by Christopher Golden and Tim Lebbon
All rights reserved.

Published in the United States by Spectra, an imprint of The Random House Publishing Group, a division of Random House, Inc., New York.

SPECTRA and the portrayal of a boxed "s" are trademarks of Random House, Inc.

ISBN: 978-0-553-38657-8

Cover design: Jae Song
Cover art: burning book © Tony Hutchings/Getty Images; buildings © Jim West/Alamy

Printed in the United States of America

www.ballantinebooks.com

9 8 7 6 5 4 3 2 1

Spectra mass market edition: July 2011

For John McIlveen and his girls
—C.G.

For Scott, Kelly, and the girls
—T.L.

Reality is merely an illusion,
albeit a very persistent one.

—ALBERT EINSTEIN

Us of Lesser Gods

1

J IM BANKS had never seen this view of the Boston sky-line, because it did not exist. Hundreds of low-rise buildings stood silhouetted against the starry sky, some of them softly lit by sweeping chains of lamps lining the haphazardly arranged streets, and more than a dozen tall church spires spiked at the night. He opened his eyes and the dreamscape remained, painted onto his bed-room ceiling by a memory that was already fogging the view. The sense of dislocation remained.

He could switch on his bedside lamp—Jenny hated when he did that, but she never complained—and sketch the basics of that view. But he knew that even if he managed to re-create the shapes and silhouettes, the many church spires and unevenly pitched roofs, the feeling would fade away. Wakefulness was already stealing those disturbing dream visions, swallowing them down into his subconscious. There was only one way that he could retain the flavor and tone, the strange light and shape of that fleeting vision of a Boston he had never known: he would have to paint.

Jim sat up and slid his feet into his slippers. Goose-bumps formed on his arms. *Damn, it's cold. Winter's on its way.* Jenny mumbled something and turned over, sighing gently. Jim stood and stared at her vague shadow for a few seconds, making sure he hadn't woken her and enjoying this private moment. He relished watching his wife sleep. It was a precious time, and as an artist, he could not help wondering what secret things she dreamed. He always looked for a reaction when she viewed one of his new skyline paintings—images that unsettled him so—but her attitude toward them was ambivalent at best.

He walked to the bathroom, closing the door and leaving the light off. Light would wash away more of his dream. Every second that passed diluted it, and he was keen to get up to his attic studio and start painting as soon as possible. But first he needed to use the toilet, and if he didn't slip on his bathrobe, he'd freeze to death up there.

Up there on those low roofs, he thought, *trapped in a roof valley when the first snows come, listening to the hourly chimes from so many church bells—because they all ring on the hour, though there's no way I can know that. Watching the pigeons flit from roof to roof, listening to the sounds from the street below, the people passing by and the cars, and the lilt to their voices that I can't quite place because . . .*

"Because I've never really heard it," he muttered, and the memory of his dream faded a little more.

He hurried across the landing, glancing in at Holly as he passed her bedroom. She was snoring softly beneath an avalanche of cuddly toys, surrounded by the trappings of a little girl's life—pink walls that he'd decorated with Disney characters, books about fairies and imaginary lands, posters of puppies and horses and a landscape from Oz. He smiled, heart aching with love for his daughter. Then he went up the narrow staircase to his studio, closing the door behind him. Jim always painted to music, and he knew how annoyed Jenny would be if he woke them up.

It was three a.m. He'd get no more sleep tonight.

He switched on the lights, and the studio was reflected back down at him from the wide roof windows. He loved this space. During the day the east- and west-facing windows let in the best of the light, and the south-facing balcony at the gable end was often where he took his lunch and coffee breaks. Sometimes Jenny came up to eat with him, on those rare days when she wasn't teaching, and they'd chat quietly as they watched the world go by below. There were at least half a dozen people he waved to regularly—he didn't know their names, but routine gave them the opportunity to acknowledge each other. He didn't *want* to know their names. Unusually for an artistic type, routine was important to Jim, and to discover their names and perhaps become friends would be to move on to something new.

But now all the light was contained—an even white illumination from the expensive system he'd had installed a few years before. His midnight painting sprees were not that common, but he often found them the most rewarding.

He turned on the music system and ran his finger along the three full shelves of CDs. Chance usually dictated what he listened to while he worked, and sometimes a subconscious decision based on what might influence a current painting. His forefinger slipped across a case. He saw his daughter's name—*No, it says Flogging* Molly— and he slipped the CD into the player. As the first strains of mandolin and fiddle slipped from the speakers, he stood before his working plinth. The current canvas was an advertising design for a new chain of pubs in Boston, part of their forthcoming Christmas campaign. He took it down carefully, set it to one side, and mounted a blank canvas. The *dreaded* blank canvas. He was confident in his abilities but also acknowledged that every new project began with fear.

Jim closed his eyes, trying not to think too much, music passing through him, breathing deeply and trying to hang on to the last vestiges of sleep. Later he'd have coffee, perhaps even sitting out on the balcony if he wrapped up warmly, but that would be when he was properly awake. Now he had to begin. He breathed slowly, deeply, letting that mysterious skyline swallow him, and when he opened his eyes again the canvas was no longer blank.

He picked up a brush and began to transform his dream into reality.

"What time did you get up?" Jenny asked. Jim had heard her moving around half an hour ago, and when her feet trod gently up toward his studio he was already sitting in one of two comfortable chairs, ankles crossed and relaxing as he stared at what he had done.

"Hey, babe," he said. "About three."

Jenny smiled and shook her head. Her gorgeous auburn hair hung free, obscuring one eye and swinging across her face in a way he found unbelievably alluring. She wore her long bathrobe and fluffy pig-faced slippers and carried a tray bearing two steaming coffee mugs and a large plate of pancakes and crispy bacon. Her eyes were still swollen from sleep and her hair a mess, and Jim loved her dearly. Eight years of marriage and no sign of an itch yet.

"Slave to your muse, as ever." She set the tray on the small table between chairs and slumped into the one beside him, reaching out to squeeze his hand.

"Yeah, but I'll ride that bitch till she obeys my every command."

Jenny raised an eyebrow and one corner of her mouth, playfully stern. "I'm not even going to dignify that with a response."

"You look good enough to eat," he said, glancing down pointedly at her long legs.

"Bacon and pancakes," she said, yawning.

"I was thinking you might rather have sausage."

"Jesus, it's obvious you had a little too much wine last night."

Jim smiled and shrugged, picking up a coffee mug and inhaling the warm aroma. He always seemed to be horny the morning after a night of drink. Sipping coffee, he looked back to the canvas he'd been working on for almost four hours, and any other thoughts faded away.

I have no idea where this comes from, he thought, but it was not the dreamy origins of these scenes that worried him. There were at least a dozen such canvases in his storage room at the other end of the studio—of this strange Boston, and another that had also never existed—and three more hanging in Boston's Rose Gallery, part of a permanent display from local artists. The thing that disturbed him was that he didn't know *why* they disturbed him. If it was only him that they affected that way, perhaps he could have attributed it to some feeling from those dreams that lingered in his painted representations—a subconscious fear that was given life in his strokes, blocking, and shading. But Holly didn't like these skylines, either.

To Jenny, they were simply strange. "This one's a bit different," she said.

"Well . . . they all are." He glanced sidelong at his wife, watched her regarding his night's work over the rim of her coffee mug. She seemed to be hiding behind the steam, as if that would protect her from something.

"No," she said, and then fell silent again. She was examining this painting more closely than usual, her slight frown remaining in place even as she put the mug down and picked up a pancake. She took a bite and chewed, never taking her eyes from the painting.

It's not finished, he wanted to say. *It's just blocked out, really. There's shading to do and the sky's wrong. It's dark enough, but not heavy enough; there's no depth.* But he held back, because he always found himself striving to defend his work. He had a strange relationship with his art: he was utterly confident in his abilities and talent, yet never content with a finished piece.

"I know what it is," she said through a mouthful of pancake. "It's more detailed. Closer."

"Closer." For a moment he wasn't sure what she meant. It was still an unknown skyline—although it *was* Boston, he'd insist to anyone who doubted him, *always* Boston—this painting was more real, more *there* than any he had ever done. "Yeah . . . ," he said, then the studio door opened.

"Can I have ice cream for breakfast?" Holly asked.

"Morning, sweetie!" Jenny said, standing and sweeping their daughter into a hug.

Holly squeezed her mother tightly and smiled over her shoulder at Jim. Jim smiled back, then made a face, sticking out his tongue and waving his hands beside his head. Holly did the same back at him.

"Hey, what're you up to?" Jenny asked, leaning back to look at her daughter. Holly giggled, and the sound warmed Jim inside. He and Holly often indulged in secretive stuff—silly faces, name calling, silent singing—and she called it their special time. Jenny knew what was going on, of course, but that didn't matter.

"Nothing, Mom," Holly said, giggling some more. Then she saw the remnants of breakfast and her eyes went wide. "Yay, pancakes!"

Jim snatched up the last pancake, folded it around a piece of bacon, and stuffed it into his mouth.

"Not fair!" Holly wailed.

"Jim," Jenny said, smiling and shaking her head.

"Ony hut ons for oo," he mumbled, and a blizzard of crumbs settled on his chest. Holly squealed with delight, and as Jim chewed the huge mouthful and raised his eyebrows at Jenny's mock sternness, he reveled in the moment.

Jim had just hit forty. And realizing how far through life he was, he'd started to concentrate more than ever on the here and now. He'd always been an ambitious person, rushing around to make sure tomorrow brought what he most desired . . . and the todays were often lost with him barely noticing. In his darker moments, he would berate himself for the way he sometimes treated Jenny. She never complained, and he loved her for that, but she had always been the contented one of the partnership, able to cruise through life and appreciate the moment rather than constantly looking ahead. Jim always seemed to be somewhere else.

And then one day, one moment, walking in the woods in Breakheart Reservation up in Saugus with Jenny and seeing Holly leaping from a fallen tree into a muddy puddle, he'd had an epiphany: he was luckier than most. Beautiful wife, gorgeous child, good friends, a nice home, and a job he loved. He'd done his best to hold on to that truth ever since.

Living for the moment had become his new, unspoken motto, and he'd done his best. If Jenny had noticed a change, she hadn't mentioned it, but for the past few months he had felt a calmness to their relationship that he hadn't noticed before. They had never had any doubt about their love, but sometimes there was a distance around Jim that love strained to cross.

"What are you trying to say, Daddy?" Holly said through her giggles.

Jim swallowed and picked up the empty plate. "I said, only hot ones for you. Come on, honey, help me make some more pancake mix. And I see blueberries in our future."

"Cool," Holly said, but she had become distracted. "Where's that?" she asked, looking at the new painting.

"Just somewhere from my dreams."

"What's wrong with it? It's one of those wrong places again."

"What do you mean, honey?"

"I don't like it."

"Daddy hasn't finished it . . . ," Jenny began, but the girl seemed to cling tighter around her mother's neck.

"Well, at least we don't *really* have to go there."

"No, we don't," Jim said. "The only place we're headed is the kitchen. Pancakes. Blueberries." Holly's smile returned the instant she looked away from the painting.

"Yay!" she squealed, and it was as if the smile had never slipped.

What's wrong with it? she'd asked.

It's closer, he thought.

Jenny gave him a quizzical look, though she couldn't hide her pleasure. "Hey, I don't mind if you need to stay up here for a while," she said.

He stood, leaned in close, and kissed Holly, still clinging around Jenny's neck. "Nah," he said, and he gave his wife's behind a squeeze. "I'm done here."

"Well then, maybe Holly can watch some TV after breakfast," she said, turning and giving him a glance over her shoulder that made his knees weak.

Jim whistled as he gathered up the coffee mugs and plate. At the studio door he looked back at the canvas.

Viewed from this angle, with morning sunlight slanting across it from the sloping skylight, the painting retained its potency. *Closer,* Jenny had said.

"Maybe tonight I'll dream of somewhere else," he said aloud. The echo of his voice was the only reply.

Holly helped him mix more pancake batter, spilling half of it across the counter and the stove, and by the time they'd cooked and eaten several blueberry pancakes each it was almost nine o'clock. It was a Saturday, and Jim's agent, Jonathan Morris, was due around ten for coffee and a chat. Jonathan had been his agent for longer than Jim and Jenny had known each other, and he was one of their best friends. When it came to the business, he was beyond compare, and much of what Jim had achieved was due to Jonathan's expertise when it came to corporate negotiation and contracts. But for the last year, Jonathan's private life had been a mess, and the Saturday visits had become a regular occurrence. They were never really about business.

They cleaned up in the kitchen, then Holly cuddled on the sofa with Marv the Moose, her favorite stuffed toy, and Jenny led Jim upstairs to their master bath. They showered together, making love against the cool tiled wall. Afterward, they soaped each other down. Jim watched the soap swirl from their bodies and spiral down the drain, and he could not avoid seeing patterns and textures in the spinning bubbles. His artist's eye rarely rested.

"Wow," Jenny said. "You *were* horny."

"Can you blame me?" he asked, rubbing soap across her breasts. Before he met Jenny he'd been an ass man, but the first time she took her bra off for him, he was converted.

"What, these old things?" she said, looking down.

"Jonathan's going to be here soon," Jim said.

"I feel so sorry for him, but I'm starting to think some people just aren't meant to spend their life with one person."

"I thought he and Philip had it made. Such a sweet guy."

Jenny shampooed her hair and Jim massaged it in, working with his fingertips. She sighed in contentment, then opened one eye. "Did you know Philip has a huge dick?"

"Eh? No. How would I? Who told you?"

"Jonathan, of course! Not something he'd tell you, I guess."

"Guess not." Jim laughed as he adjusted the showerhead, then started rinsing Jenny's hair, watching the bubbled shampoo spill across her neck and shoulders. In his art, he liked to catch movement—the flow of water, the drift of clouds, the smear of light on a darkened landscape—and his observation of movement was often different from most people's.

"Nine inches."

"Okay, I don't think I need any more information," he said, and he moved his hands down from her hair to her breasts.

"Wow," Jenny said, eyes closed again.

"Good?" he asked, because it certainly felt good to him.

". . . nine inches . . . ," she purred.

"It's not the tools, but the craftsman," Jim said, drawing her close.

Jenny ran her hand across his stomach and found him again, eyes opening in surprise. "Oh!"

"Yeah." Jim leaned in and kissed her, and they embraced, relishing each other's familiar nakedness. Their lovemaking was always passionate, familiarity only adding to the excitement they still felt for each other. "I figure we've got ten minutes."

Jenny turned around. "Better get busy, then," she said.

"Hi, sweetie!" Jonathan said as Holly opened the front door for him. He bent down to give her a hug and handed her a candy bar, making a great play of saying it was their secret. Holly looked back at Jim and Jenny, giggling and slipping the bar into her pajama pocket.

"What?" Jim said. "I saw nothing." Holly ran into their living room, and cartoon voices shared her secret.

"Hi, guys," Jonathan said, smiling. "I brought Dunkin' Donuts to go with our coffee." He brandished a large, flat box.

"Then, young Jonathan, you may enter," Jim said, sweeping his arm toward the kitchen. Jonathan was ten years his senior but had always looked younger than Jim.

Jenny and Jonathan sat at the breakfast bar while Jim ground coffee beans and loaded the machine, making small talk. Jim could hear the hurt in his friend's voice, a shadow of sadness that made him sound more tired than usual. But for now none of them mentioned what had happened so recently—Philip's final departure, after so many stormy months. *Maybe now you can move on,* Jim thought, but he knew how insensitive that would sound if he actually said it aloud. Jonathan was heartbroken, and moving on was the last thing someone with a broken heart wished for. All he wanted to do was move backward to when it had all been good.

"I wanted to take you and Holly out today," Jonathan said to Jenny. "Lunch in town, then maybe we can look around for something I can buy Holly for Christmas."

"That's two months away!" Jim said.

"I like to be organized," Jonathan said. "How do you think you get all those fine deals I make for you?"

"Sounds good to me," Jenny said. "We don't really have any plans for today, do we, Jim?"

Jim shrugged. No plans, though he had been thinking about just hanging around the house as a family, watching a movie, maybe getting takeout later. Jonathan smiled at him, and the sadness had infected his eyes as well. Jim realized that he just wanted to be out doing something, in company he felt comfortable with, and he really couldn't blame his friend for that. If he ever lost Jenny . . .

"Jim's been up all night painting, anyway," Jenny said.

"Really?" Jonathan said. "Not working on the pub thing, though . . ."

"One of my cityscapes," Jim said. The rich aroma from the coffee machine was filling the kitchen now, and combined with the smell of donuts, it was almost heavenly.

"Is it . . . ?" Jonathan began. He'd never liked those paintings. He said they weren't salable, and it was one of the few times he and Jim had disagreed about his work. *It's not all about the money,* Jim had said, and Jonathan had thrown a fit, offended that Jim even had to say that. *I've always supported your art,* he'd said, and that was the truth.

"It's different," Jenny said.

"Still needs work. Needs finishing. I'll do it today while you're out."

Jonathan nodded, then flipped open the box's lid. "Anyone mind if I have first dibs?"

"Help yourself," Jim said, pouring the coffee. So, that was today laid out before them. Usually the idea of spending a few hours on his own, working in the studio with music blasting and lunch on the balcony luring him on, would have filled him with delight, but now he felt painted out. Four intense hours had done that to him, and the revelation of his faded dream on canvas had left him with a familiar sense of dislocation. Maybe all dreams born were meant to die, but he'd had the same feeling after painting each of those unknown cityscapes—the one today, with low roofs, and the other unknown Boston, with high buildings and a never-seen silhouette. If he was left alone at home, he'd more than likely end up puttering in his studio for an hour or two, then coming down to the living room and falling asleep in front of the TV.

"So, how are you?" Jenny asked.

"I'm okay," Jonathan replied.

Jim placed their coffees in front of them and took a seat. Jonathan was smiling sadly and looking down at the table. He picked up a crushed blueberry that they'd missed and examined it on the end of his finger, then raised an eyebrow and tasted it. "You had pancakes and didn't leave any for me?"

Jim looked at the box of a dozen donuts and burst out laughing.

"Hey, comfort food!" Jonathan said. "I've just suffered a very traumatic separation, and considering I haven't had a drink or a smoke in years, what do I have left?"

"Hard drugs," Jim said, still chuckling.

"They don't agree with me," Jonathan said, arching an eyebrow.

"So, donuts it is."

Jonathan bit into his donut, sugar speckling the stubble across his top lip.

Jim could see already that Jonathan's spirits had lifted in the few minutes he'd been here. Jenny had always had that effect on him. She was one of life's calm ones, and she seemed to be able to pass her gift on to anyone who needed it, whatever the circumstances. They chatted some more, shooting the breeze, and Jim refilled their coffee mugs. Jonathan laughed a lot, and mostly Jim could tell that it was genuine, though sometimes it was not. It would take him a long time to get over Philip, tempestuous though their relationship had been. Once when Jim had asked about it, his friend had replied, *I just love loving someone who's so fucking alive!*

Jenny finished a donut and went to take Holly upstairs to wash and dress. The two men waited in companionable silence for a couple of minutes—the sort of unpressured quiet that only good friends or lovers could ever maintain. Jonathan rested his elbows on the counter and kept his mug pressed to his lips, looking into the middle distance.

"Dude, nine inches?" Jim said. "Dude" was a word he only ever used when the subject was a little uncomfortable; it softened the blow.

Jonathan looked at him, mug still in front of his mouth. He raised an eyebrow. "Better believe it, dude."

The two men laughed again, and when Jonathan left with Jenny and Holly, everyone seemed happy, looking forward to the day. Even Jim. He'd resolved to stay out of his studio, spending the time instead catching up on some reading, and if he drifted off to sleep, well . . . he'd welcome it.

He kissed his wife good-bye at the door while Jonathan strapped Holly into his BMW.

"Have fun," Jim said as they hugged.

"Will do," she said. They both squeezed a little bit harder.

"Love you."

"Love you more," Jim said. He watched her walking down their front path to the car, then closed the door, breathing in the silence.

When he awoke, the house felt empty. Not just silent or still, but *empty*. He sat up quickly, gasping as if startled awake by the phone or doorbell. But there were no echoes, and his phone was on the carpet beside the sofa. *Christ, me and these fucking dreams!*

Jim rubbed his eyes and looked around. The large living room seemed different, and he couldn't quite place why. Something appeared to be missing, but recognizing things that had gone was not as easy as seeing things that shouldn't be there. He frowned and shook his head, resting it in his hands for a few moments while he gathered his thoughts. He glanced at his watch—almost five p.m. Jenny and Holly had left with Jonathan over six hours ago; he'd had no idea that they would be gone so long.

Picking up the phone, he expected to see a text, but there was none. That was weird. Jenny usually kept in touch when she was out, especially when she was going to be home later than expected. They'd never lived in each other's pockets. They both had space to spread out—he with his art, she with her teaching and wide circle of friends—but they both understood the limits of their relationship. If Jim expected her and Holly home at a certain time and they were going to be late . . .

He opened a new text and keyed in, *Hi sexy, got an ETA?* Then he scrolled down his contacts list, missing Jenny's name, pressing the red button by mistake, and having to enter the list again. *Damn it,* he needed to get up, stir himself, have a strong coffee and a shower.

He smiled at the memory of that morning's shower. Her deep sigh as she came, her leg hooked around his.

The warmth as he soaped her down. Her look of surprise when she'd found him hard again so soon . . .

Her name wasn't in his contacts list. That was weird. And then he frowned, because he couldn't remember her mobile number. He'd never had to; whenever he called or texted her, the number was already entered in his phone.

"Fuck it." He stood and stretched, and all the while his eyes were darting left and right and *something felt wrong.*

"Hello?" he called, because the silence was becoming oppressive. But no one replied. He hadn't expected them to, because if they *had* come home earlier and found him asleep, Holly would have leapt on him, bouncing on his chest until he woke so that she could tell him about her day, the shops they'd visited, what she'd had for lunch, and the jokes Uncle Jonathan had told.

He began to stride from the room, blinked, then froze.

There was a picture missing from the wall beside the flat-screen TV. His and Jenny's wedding photograph—unobtrusive, yet one of his favorite images of them together. They'd spent almost a thousand dollars on an official wedding photographer, but this snap had come from Jonathan's camera, capturing more of their love and happiness than any amount of posing could ever find.

And now it was gone.

"Okay," Jim said. "Okay." He glanced around the room. The TV looked different—same size, same sleek black shape, but . . .

It was a different make.

"That's just—"

Just before he'd fallen asleep, he'd noticed Marv the Moose sitting on the floor in front of the TV. *Night, Marv,* he'd said, smiling because it made him think of how Holly cuddled the thing the same way every single night, snug under her left arm with its face pointing up at hers. But now Marv had vanished as well.

"Okay," he said again, then snapped his phone open again and scanned down for Jonathan's number. He called, and as the ringing tone whispered in his ear he shoved aside his unsettling thoughts. He was still tired and confused from his afternoon sleep, his legs hadn't woken properly yet, and maybe he'd dreamed something weird again—something that still impressed upon him without him being able to remember anything.

"Hey," Jonathan said when he answered. "How's it hangin'?"

"Less than nine inches," Jim said.

"What?"

"Nothing. Are Jenny and Holly still with you?"

"Who?"

"Jenny. Holly. They must be still with you, because they didn't take our car. I was just wondering when they'd be home."

Jonathan was silent for a few seconds. Jim heard his agent breathing softly, and he listened for Holly's conspiratorial giggle as she watched her uncle Jonathan playing a joke on Daddy.

"Say that again. What are you talking about?" Jonathan asked.

"Jenny and Holly. Where are they?"

"Who the hell are Jenny and Holly?"

"Jonathan, stop screwing around. I was going to get takeout tonight, and I need to know when they're coming home so that—"

"Have you been drinking?" Jonathan asked.

"No." Jim frowned, looking around for an empty glass or bottle. *Have I? No, that was last night, because I always get horny the morning after a drink and . . .* He remembered sex in the shower, and the taste of Jenny on his tongue.

"So who are Jenny and Holly? Did you have one of your weird dreams again?"

"Okay, that's enough. I'm tired and cranky and—"

"*You're* cranky? The love of my life has left me, my liver's about to call it quits, and *you're* cranky?"

"Jonathan?"

"Yes, *dude*?"

"What are you doing?"

"Jim . . . this is just weird. I mean . . . you know what I'm going through here." He fell silent again for another few seconds, his breathing not as light as before. "Jim, you're not on drugs, are you?"

"No! You know I've never . . ." Jim closed his eyes and trailed off, rubbing at his head and trying to contain his anger. Then he opened his eyes again, looking at where their wedding photo had once hung.

"What's happening?" Jim asked. "Where are they? Help me here, Jonathan."

"Jim, I have no idea who you're talking about. Jenny? Molly?"

"*Holly!* My daughter, *Holly.* And Jenny, my wife."

"Riiight . . . ," Jonathan drawled. "Okay. Well, considering you've never been married—"

Jim snapped the cell phone shut. He'd seen something that thumped at his chest, something not there that he'd only just noticed, because things not there were so much harder to see. He closed his eyes and thought back. The photograph had been there forever. *Mummy and Daddy got mallied,* Holly would shout, and Jonathan never failed to comment on his superior photography, and how his talent was wasted as Boston's most successful artistic agent.

He opened his eyes again and walked across the room

to where the picture had been removed. There was no square mark where the paint on the wall behind it had faded over the years, no hook, no nail.

No hole.

It was as if the picture of him and his wife had never hung there at all.

2

Man with No Country

B REATHE, *JIM*. He squeezed his eyes shut, forced himself to take four long, shuddering breaths, then opened his eyes again and looked around the living room. His hands were clenched into fists—not in anger, but in some subconscious attempt to grab hold of the fabric of the world, as if he could clutch it to himself and it would not slip away.

The wedding photo had been just the beginning. His mind had been muddled by sleep and then by irritation with Jonathan, but that empty place on the wall where the photo should have hung—and the absence of any faded paint, any hook, any evidence of a nail—sparked a barrage of tiny epiphanies that paralyzed him. At first he'd thought the furniture had been rearranged, but that impression lasted only a split second before he realized that the room around him had changed much more than that.

The armchair by the fireplace had been stiff-backed, striped in white and burgundy, but the chair that now occupied that spot was wider and plusher, upholstered in a chalky shade of blue. The end table beside the sofa and the long teak coffee table were the same, if a little more pristine than he remembered, but the lamps were different. When Jenny's grandfather had died, her mother had sold the house and asked them to take whatever they wanted. The only furnishings Jenny had claimed were a set of antique lamps with glass shades hand-painted with red and pink roses. The lamps had vanished, replaced by more modern lighting, including a brass floor lamp Jim could not imagine ever buying.

"Jenny?" he shouted in the empty apartment. "Holly?"

His voice filled the place, giving it a sense of occupancy that felt entirely wrong. His voice alone shouldn't be enough to make the apartment seem full. The very life and laughter of the place had gone from it, and it did not yawn with emptiness the way a home ought to when its people were out.

He glanced at the mirror over the fireplace. He had inherited it from his own mother. It remained, but something caught his eye, and Jim finally snapped from his paralysis and rushed over to stare at the mantelpiece. The two small framed photos that had always seemed to attract too much dust were now missing. One had been a baby picture of Holly, the other a snapshot from a Vermont trip a few years ago when Holly had been four or so, the three of them sitting on an old-time toboggan in the snow. But the pictures weren't there. Neither did he see any sign of the usual detritus that having a daughter provided. Jim and Jenny were constantly picking up small parts of her toys—plastic Barbie shoes, pet bobbleheads, Super Balls, beads from broken bracelets—but the mantel was clear.

These absences hit him faster now, and his gut churned with nausea. A quick glance at the curio cabinet behind the chair revealed awards he had won and small statuettes, knickknacks of a lifetime. Bronze replicas of western-motif sculptures by Frederic Remington were side by side with the carved glass Viking he'd picked up

in Sweden and the crystal ball Jonathan had given to Jim
after he'd earned his first million—"to see the future,"
he'd said.

His face felt flushed, and he leaned against the chair,
staring in through the glass doors of the cabinet. His
hands were shaking as he reached out to touch the knob.
They had built in a magnetic latch to keep Holly from
getting into the cabinet, but the door pulled open easily.
No latch.

Gone were the Lladró figures that Jenny had so loved:
the mermaid, the mother and daughter, the Japanese
woman in her kimono, and others he could not recall.
Gone were the *matryoshka* nesting dolls Jenny had
brought home from St. Petersburg when she was preg-
nant with Holly.

Shaking his head, trembling even more, he backed
away from the curio cabinet until his legs hit the coffee
table. He turned around in circles, a peculiar kind of
anger blazing up within him, fueled by fear and confusion. "This. Isn't. Funny!" he shouted.

You're being ridiculous. The common-sense voice
threw cold water on his panic. *It's a joke. A really horrible, almost unforgivable joke.*

He left the living room behind, striding purposefully
into the dining room. Something on top of the china
cabinet caught his eye. A platter, incredibly detailed,
bone china with blue trim. It had sat in the same place in
his childhood home in Andover, used only on Thanksgiving, a family heirloom that had come down from his
mother's grandmother, and it would have been his, except that on the first Thanksgiving after he and Jenny
had begun dating, she had caught her foot on the carpet
and tripped, destroying both a century of family history
and Thanksgiving dinner in seconds. Jim's mother, God
rest her, had never forgotten. For the few years she had

left of her life, she had tried to make light of it, but Jim had felt the distance the woman had placed between herself and her future daughter-in-law, and he knew Jenny had felt it, too.

In his mind's eye, he could still see the shattered platter and the ruined bird on the floor of his parents' dining room, the shards like the rough edges of broken clamshells.

Yet there it was, good as new, on display on top of his china cabinet.

It broke him. He stood on tiptoes, reached up on top of the cabinet, and swept the platter onto the floor. It shattered, smashed as it should have been, and then Jim bolted for the stairs, not pausing to study the kitchen for the thousand inaccuracies it no doubt contained. One picture hung on the stairwell's wall—him and a gorgeous young woman he did not know, holding hands on a skyscraper balcony somewhere—where there should have been a dozen snaps of him, Jenny, and Holly. He ignored the unknown picture and ran his palm along where the other frames should have been, a cold knot forming in his belly. He passed the door to the guest room, running into his own room. His and Jenny's.

His eyes began to burn with unshed tears, blurring.

She'd left no trace of herself behind.

"Jenny!" he called, like a medium trying to summon a ghost, looking at the ceiling and at the shadowed corners of the room. "This isn't funny!"

This isn't funny. The plaintive wail of a child left alone in the dark by his older siblings.

Slowly he turned to look at the door to the corridor—the one he'd just come through. He took short, sharp breaths and then forced himself to leave his bedroom and walk toward the back of the apartment. If it wasn't a trick, what was it? Had she left him? Could he have done something terrible to her without even knowing it? Something so awful that it could have driven her to abandon him so thoroughly?

No. He'd seen the love and the sweet mischief in her eyes just this morning. They had made love in the shower, as tenderly and as hungrily as they ever had. And if Jenny had left, that didn't explain the apartment. Why would she bother to erase all evidence that she had ever been his wife? How the hell *could* she have done it? It would have been easy enough to drug him this morning, something in his breakfast or his coffee, or in the donuts that Jonathan brought—

Jonathan. He denied even knowing Jenny. And Holly! How could he do that? He had to be involved.

But even with him sedated, could they have changed everything so completely in just six hours? Could he really have been that heavily drugged and not feel any lingering effects now?

He stood in front of the last door at the end of the hall. No, she wouldn't have left. Not the woman he had loved all these years. Not the woman who had smiled at him so beautifully, so intimately, that morning. Not his Jenny. But that opened up another possibility. Had his family been taken? If so, by whom? And again, the most troubling, most impossible question—how?

Jim pushed open the door to Holly's bedroom, a picture in his mind of the soft pink decorations, the princesses, the bookshelf he had built for her, the fairies he had painted on the wall.

The room held only a desk and filing cabinet, an old computer, boxes of books, and an old love seat. On the seat cushion was a dark stain from where he'd spilled grape soda the last day of fourth grade. Thirty years ago.

Jenny had persuaded him to put that love seat out at the curb for trash pickers to cart off when he put his parents' house up for sale after his mother's funeral. It had been taken away within an hour, and he hadn't seen it since.

It couldn't be there.

Jim sank into the love seat, numb and hollow, this impossible piece of furniture that had been left—along with his great-grandmother's platter—in the place of his wife and his little girl.

Minutes passed—he didn't know how many—before he blinked and looked around, as though waking from a trance. He wiped away tears with the back of his hand as he stared first at the boxes and then at the old computer. "What the fuck is this?" he whispered to himself.

Then he was up and moving, because he knew what he had to do.

Jim's building stood on a corner across from Union Square in Boston's trendy South End. The six-story bowfront brick row house was the last on the block. Its upper five stories were split between two apartments, with the Banks family taking the top three, including the dormered attic where Jim had his studio. The ground floor housed Tallulah's, a restaurant and café that specialized in European fare and damn fine coffee. The apartment in between was occupied by a fiftyish travel writer named Carole Levitt and her latest boyfriend, Oliver Chin.

Jim knocked so hard the door shook. He waited only seconds before knocking again, standing in the dim light of the stairwell landing.

"All right, all right!" Carole called from inside. Jim heard the lock slide back, and then she opened the door, irritation creasing her brow. "You don't look like you're on fire. What's the—"

"Have you seen Jenny and Holly today?" he demanded, jaw set, daring her to say no.

A bemused smile lit Carole's eyes, and she leaned against the door frame. "Are those the two college girls you had up there a while back? If so, then no, and I'm sure Ollie hasn't seen them, either, because he would definitely have noticed. He sure noticed them the night you brought them home."

Of all possible responses, this was one Jim had not considered. It struck him dumb for a moment, then he shook his head, trying to clear it. "Listen, Carole—"

"Did they steal something? I've warned you about letting these girls you barely know into your place, Jimmy. They see something shiny, and that's—"

"Damn it, will you listen?" he shouted at her.

Carole scowled, stepping back from the door, about to close it. "Why don't you come back when you figure out what the hell your problem is?"

Jim slammed a palm against the door, preventing her from closing it. Alarm flared in her eyes, and he could see her trying to decide if he was secretly a psychopath or a rapist or both.

"Please, just . . . ," he started, forcing himself to calm down, to take even breaths. "You really don't know who I'm talking about? When I say 'Jenny and Holly,' you don't know who I mean?"

Carole seemed to sense his genuine distress at last and take pity on him. "Look, Jimmy, I liked that one girl last year, the one who works in the mayor's office? But it's not like I invite all your flings in for tea. If you want me to try to remember these girls, you could at least describe them. But short answer is no, I haven't seen or heard anyone on the stairs today except for you and Oliver."

A dreadful chill had begun to settle into his bones, and he felt weariness and surrender waiting for him at the edges of his consciousness like thieves lurking in shadows. "Thank you," he said. "Thanks. I'm sorry I . . ."

But he didn't finish. Instead he backed through the door, turned, and ran down the stairs toward their shared exit out onto the street. What could he possibly have said?

Tallulah's thrummed with clinking plates and glasses and the buzz of conversation. The aroma of coffee hung like a thick, warm cloud inside the restaurant; Jenny had always claimed to get a caffeine high just from walking into the place.

Jim walked like a man spoiling for a fight, but he couldn't help it. His hands were curled into fists, and he clenched his jaw, the muscles in his neck and shoulders drawn tight. The hostess, Miranda, had bottle-red hair and a top cut so low her breasts seemed about to pop out and say hello. She smiled as he approached. "Wow, Jim, you look so serious," she said, her voice almost teasing. "Someone key your car or something?"

He almost couldn't get the question out, that cold dread filling him with a terrible certainty. "Has Jenny been in today?"

Miranda frowned. "Jenny?"

"Yes, Jenny!" he said, slamming both hands down on the hostess's podium. "My wife, goddamn it! Have you seen . . ." He faltered, emotion welling up in him, feeling utterly lost. "Oh, Christ, Miranda. Please tell me you've seen my wife."

But Miranda's eyes had narrowed to cold slits. The dozen or so people waiting to be seated had moved to a safe distance, eyeing him warily, but Miranda only stared contempt in his direction. "You never told me you had a wife, Jim," she said, biting off each word. "Don't you think you should've told me?"

He shook his head. "This isn't real. This isn't my life."

Miranda shouted something at him as he staggered out the door, but he didn't hear. He reached into his pocket and pulled out a heavy, unfamiliar key ring, only vaguely noticing that it was different before he bent over a metal trash can and vomited. Blinking, trying to catch his breath, he stared down into the can, grateful that he couldn't tell what it was he'd just thrown up . . . because he knew it wasn't blueberry pancakes.

Spitting on the sidewalk, he turned the corner and hurried around to the back of the building, where the reserved parking spaces that came with the apartment were located. It must have been nearly six o'clock by now. The shadows had grown long and the sky had the strange, ethereal quality of autumn evenings, almost like a dream.

Jim wished he could believe this was all a dream, but he knew he was awake.

Awake, yeah. But sane? He didn't know the answer to that.

He stopped short, staring at the silver Mercedes parked in his spot. Jim drove a six-year-old blue Audi. His hand closed around his car keys, and the unfamiliarity of their shape and heft struck him again. He opened his hand and looked down at the logo on the key ring. Mercedes.

Jim made up his mind then. He gritted his teeth as he clicked the button to unlock the car. The Mercedes chirped.

"Fine," he said as he slid into the driver's seat and plunged the key into the ignition. "I don't care."

And he didn't. The details didn't matter. Only Jenny and Holly mattered. It was almost as if they had been erased from the world, but Jim knew—as sure as he knew that the road beneath his tires was solid and that the Earth revolved around the sun—that people couldn't be deleted from existence. Either he was crazy, or something impossible had happened.

It was time to find out which.

The knot in Jim's gut twisted tighter as he drove over to Jonathan's apartment in the Back Bay. With one hand on the wheel and only occasional glances at the road, he scanned the contacts list on his cell phone, thinking he would call friends, try to find someone who would end the nightmare, tell him it was all a joke. Somehow, he had to fight the growing certainty that it was neither a joke nor a dream, that either reality or his own sanity had been abruptly and brutally altered. Now that he was away from the apartment, he could pretend it was possible that he had been drugged, that someone had come in and erased all traces of her from his life. And though that idea horrified him, it was somehow preferable to the alternatives.

But now he saw that something had happened to his cell phone contacts list. Names were missing—Jenny's best friend, Trixie Newcomb, who had become Jim's friend as well. Matt and Gretchen Kelleher, whom Jenny had met at the gym and who had become their go-to dinner companions—the one couple they really seemed to get along with. The office number for the Atherton School, where Jenny taught.

In place of those listings there were new contacts, names that were unfamiliar to him, and it chilled Jim to wonder who they were and how their information had gotten into his cell phone. If he phoned them and introduced himself, what would they say to him? How well would they know him, these people whose names he did not know?

But not all of his familiar contacts were gone—only the ones he had known through, or because of, Jenny.

A car braked too fast in front of him, and he stopped fast enough for the tires to skid, cutting the wheel and slewing to the right. Another night he would have shot the guy the finger or at least muttered some curse under his breath, but his focus was on the phone instead of the road. The car drove on and Jim accelerated. He had driven this route to Jonathan's apartment hundreds of times. One hand on the wheel, he navigated on autopilot, scanning the list, finding Steve Menken, and hitting CALL.

Menken answered on the third ring. "Jimbo! To what do I owe the pleasure?"

"I need to ask you a question," Jim said.

"Oooh. Sounds ominous."

"It is."

A hesitation on the line. Jim could practically see the smile fading from Menken's face. They had known each other for more than a decade, running in the same circles in Boston's artistic community. Menken worked at Hiram Davis Press in Cambridge, editing nonfiction from biographies to art books. He and Jim had become friends without ever managing to work on a project together—Hiram Davis couldn't afford Jim Banks. They had bonded over a mutual love of beer, old science-fiction movies, and Boston sports teams—common enough interests for men in the city, but not in their line of work.

"You can ask me anything, Jim," Menken said. "What's going on? You sound awful."

"This is . . . this may sound weird. Do you remember Jenny and Holly?"

Menken paused in thought before replying. "I don't think I know anyone named Holly. Are you talking about Jenny Garza?"

Jim went numb. "No. Not Jenny Garza."

"You're gonna have to give me something more to go on," Menken said.

"Never mind, I'll talk to you later," Jim said, ending the call.

He tossed the phone onto the seat beside him. There were other people still in his contacts list—friends and colleagues who knew him well enough to know his wife and daughter—but he no longer had any desire to call them. Another conversation like the one he'd just had with Menken, and he might completely fall apart.

Instead, he drove in silence. No talk radio. No music. No phone. Several times he encountered snarled traffic, but he knew these streets well enough by now to avoid most of it, and soon he was pulling up to Jonathan's Marlborough Street brownstone. He cruised another block before noticing an aging BMW pulling out, and he slid into the vacated parking space.

As Jim climbed out of the car, an unseasonably icy breeze swept along the street and seemed to eddy around him. He looked toward Jonathan's apartment, and a coil of fear encircled him. He could almost picture Marlborough Street as the road to Oz, and he felt a terrible trepidation at the prospect of approaching the wizard. Jonathan had been the last to see Jenny and Holly.

Hollybaby, he thought, missing his daughter so much that he nearly fell to his knees. He practically flung himself across the street, picking up his pace as he hurried toward Jonathan's brownstone, so that by the time he reached the front door he was running. With a quick glance at the intercom, he pressed the bottom-most button. It made a sound less like a buzzer than an old-fashioned school bell. Seconds ticked by, each one an eternity, and he hit the button again.

Crackle. "Who is it?"

"It's Jim. I need to—"

"What are you doing here?" Jonathan asked sharply, the intercom crackling.

"We have to talk," Jim said, hearing the pleading in his own voice and hating it. "I really . . . I'm at my wit's end here, Jonathan. I need a reality check, man. I need a friend."

For several seconds the intercom did not even crackle. And then the door buzzed.

Jim hauled it open, then made sure the heavy door latched behind him. The foyer of the building smelled of disinfectant. He headed past the stairs toward the door at the rear of the foyer. Jonathan lived on the ground floor. He could have easily afforded the view from the top-floor apartment, but he didn't like heights.

As Jim approached the door he heard the dead bolt slide back, and then the door swung open. Jonathan stood outlined in the doorway, the wan light from the hall casting shadows on the lines and hollows of his face. The sight of him startled Jim so much he came to an abrupt halt. At fifty, Jonathan had perfected the aura of a 1940s movie idol trying to hold on to his looks. Always tan, his silver hair always neatly trimmed, he was a man with expensive tastes.

But this was not the Jonathan that Jim knew. This man was a withered husk, his clothes hanging on his thinning frame, his silver hair gone dull and gray, his skin jaundiced and sagging. "Jesus," Jim whispered. "What the hell's happened to you?"

Jonathan's eyes flashed with anger, and he straightened himself up. "What kind of question is that? First that crap on the phone, and now you show up here with your eyes wide like it's your first fucking day on Earth? What's so goddamned important?"

Jim shook himself and took a step forward, frowning. "Sorry. You caught me by surprise."

"*I* caught *you*?"

But Jim barely registered the sarcasm. He took another step nearer, the sadness that already enveloped him growing heavier. "Are you sick?" he asked. Then he shook his head. "I mean, obviously you are. But what is it? How did it happen so fast? Christ, Jonathan, you never said anything."

Jonathan cocked his head, regarding Jim anew. His eyes narrowed. "You're really asking that," Jonathan said, almost to himself. When he spoke again, he had softened. "What's wrong with you? You really forgot I have cancer?"

Jim closed his eyes, shaking his head, wishing it all away. "Cancer?"

"In my brain. I . . . hell, Jim, you know all this. I've got eight, maybe nine months."

They stood in the hallway, those two old friends, and stared at each other.

"So you can't have been at my place this morning," Jim said.

"I haven't been over to your place since Labor Day," Jonathan replied. Then he stepped back into his apartment. "Come in, Jim. Call your shrink. I'm serious. I don't know what that stuff was on the phone before about Julie or whatever—"

"Jenny."

"—but you're having an episode or something. Are you on any medication?"

Jim stood paralyzed in the hall, bathed in that hideous yellow light.

"Hey," Jonathan said, coming out into the hall and reaching for his arm. "Please, don't. I've had enough tears."

Only when Jim tasted salt on his lips did he understand that he had started to cry. Instantly he shut off the tears, wiping them from his cheeks. He pulled away from Jonathan. "I have to go."

"I don't think that's a good idea," Jonathan said. "Come in. Please. Sit with me. I'll make tea and you can clear your mind, talk to me about what's going on in your head right now."

Jim backed away from him, toward the foyer. "I'm sorry. I have to go."

This isn't my Jonathan. This isn't my life. Somehow, the world he knew had been stolen from him while he slept. *Or maybe this is my life, and the rest was just me inventing one that isn't so fucking ugly. Maybe I'm* meant *to be alone.*

But he rejected that instantly. Even with all the hours that had passed, his lips could still remember Jenny's kiss. He could close his eyes and picture her, recall her smell, the perfect way her body cleaved to his when they slid into bed at night. He knew Holly's laugh, the dimple in her left cheek, the silly way she would dance to make him smile whenever he grew too serious for her liking.

They were his wife and his little girl. They weren't inventions.

"Call Dr. Lebowitz," Jonathan said, starting to follow him into the hall but too weary to chase him.

"First thing in the morning," Jim muttered.

"Promise?"

"I've got to go."

Then he was out the door and running for his car, wondering what else would be taken from him today . . . and then realizing that he had nothing else in his life that really mattered.

Jim felt invisible to the world. He drove home in a fog, trying to figure out what to do next. Memories of Jenny and Holly kept crowding into his thoughts. He found himself singing softly in the silence of the car—all those songs he had used as lullabies on nights when Holly had trouble falling asleep as a toddler. No one remembered them. If he called the police, they would probably think he was crazy. He might even end up on some psych ward for evaluation. But what other choice did he have? He couldn't just do nothing. Prayer wasn't going to bring them back. He knew a private detective—a poker buddy of Menken's—who would at least listen without calling him crazy.

Jonathan had been afraid for him. Jim had seen it in his eyes, the sympathy for the artist who had finally lost his mind. But he refused to believe that insanity could summon up the vivid details and the heartbreaking emotions that filled him now. Maybe schizophrenia could produce such delusions, but didn't the very fact that he could so coolly examine the possibility make that unlikely?

"Oh, Jesus," he whispered, gripping the steering wheel tighter as though holding on for his life. Perhaps, in spite of himself, he was praying without even realizing it.

He would search the apartment top to bottom, and much more meticulously this time. If any trace of them remained, he would find it. And if he found no trace, then what? It had all happened while he was sleeping. Maybe if he went back to sleep, he would wake up in the morning and the world would have returned to normal, and it would seem like it really had been a dream.

A little bit of madness had crept into him. Jim knew that, and he welcomed it. He thought he would need it to survive.

Adrift in his own mind, he parked in his space behind his building. His sense of dislocation made even those most familiar surroundings feel surreal. He hurried along the sidewalk beside Tallulah's and turned right at the corner, keys clutched in his hand, thinking of the nooks and hidden corners of the apartment where some evidence might still be found that he did not live there alone.

Music came from the café, acoustic guitars and voices raised in song. He heard it only vaguely, like elevator Muzak, too focused on the task ahead. But a few steps past Tallulah's he heard the music grow louder as someone opened the door, and a voice called his name. Hope flickered and died within him as, for half a second, he thought it could be Jenny. But it wasn't her voice.

The woman had lovely, anguished features and bright pink hair. Everything about her spoke of desperation, from her black clothing to the imploring look in her eyes. "Jim, please say you know me," she whispered.

He blinked in surprise and studied her. "Trix?"

Something burst within her. She let out a sob and rushed to him, threw her arms around him, and held on tight. Trix Newcomb. Jenny's best friend. Thinner than he remembered, her pink, jagged-cut hair such a radical departure from her usual look, she was barely recognizable at first. Now she wept into his shoulder, trying to talk but unable to get words out past the sobs.

"Trix," he said again, in wonder. With some effort, he pried her away from him, staring into her face. "You remember."

Eyes wide, she caught her breath. "I just . . ." She gestured at her clothes, then grabbed fistfuls of her hair. "I *changed*. In, like, a millisecond. I totally freaked. I didn't know if someone had slipped me something or, shit, I just didn't know. I went to call Jenny and her number wasn't in my cell. Yours, either. I was already online, and I went to find it on her Facebook page, but it's gone, so I looked for her blog, only that's gone, too. So I called information and your number is unlisted and there's nothing for her and then I started calling around and . . ."

Her voice stopped working. Her mouth opened and closed, but her lower lip quivered and fresh tears slid down her cheeks.

Jim hugged her again, so relieved to see her, to have her *know* him. He wasn't alone. And if Trix remembered Jenny and Holly, then that meant that Jim wasn't crazy. They had existed. Somehow they had vanished, and who- or whatever had taken them had managed to eliminate them from the minds of anyone who had known them, except for Jim. And now Trix.

"Holly's gone, too," he said. The hardest words he'd ever spoken.

"Where . . . where are they?" Trix pleaded with him.

Jim didn't let her go. Trix had become his anchor. "I don't know," he said. "But we'll find them. I swear we'll find them both."

3

You Won't Make a Fool Out of Me

ONCE, TRIX had dreamed that Jenny loved her. More than that, she had dreamed that they were *in* love, and so fiercely that when she had woken from that dream, it had broken her heart to realize it wasn't real. It hardly seemed fair. She had loved Jenny since college, constantly fighting not to be the love-struck lesbian her friends had warned her she might become, mooning over the straight girl she could never have.

Over the years she had forged her love for Jenny into something sweet and mostly selfless. In the beginning, Trix had wanted to hate Jim, but she'd found herself unable to do it. They had too much in common. They had *Jenny* in common. And over time, Trix had come to realize that she cared for Jim nearly as much as she did Jenny, though in a very different way.

Then Holly had come along, and that had caused a metamorphosis in Trix. All the romance and lustful thoughts she had harbored for her best friend over the years had receded as her dedication to Jenny became a love for and loyalty to this family. Jenny, Holly, and even Jim . . . they were as much her family as anyone related to her by blood.

But sometimes she remembered that dream, and the

love she felt so deeply that waking had broken her heart, and she let herself fantasize about making her way up to the apartment and entering to find Jenny alone. She toyed with the scenario in her mind, a conversation that would finally set fire to the spark between them. They would make love, Jenny discovering a part of herself she had never acknowledged. They would hold each other afterward, and it would feel so natural.

Trix never relayed these dreams to Jenny and Jim, not even in jest. After eight years of joyful marriage, Jenny might not understand.

Now Trix stood outside the door to Jim and Jenny's apartment. She was shaking. Anticipation was part of it—she had found the one person who seemed to accept what had happened to her, and now was the time to see just how much he had changed as well—but the climb up the stairs had shaken her. She never took the elevator, always kept in shape, and three flights of stairs were more beneficial than standing in a moving box held up by a few wires. But since she'd changed, even the way she moved felt strange. She was thinner than before, more wiry, stronger, and the effort she needed to do things was different. Before, she would have walked up the stairs and been breathing a little heavy. Now she had run up and wasn't even breathless. Her heart thumped in her chest, and she could see her T-shirt rippling beneath the leather jacket. When she closed her eyes the whole sense of herself was different—her awareness of limbs, the space her body occupied, and her personal space surrounding her. It was as if she had been removed and re-placed, and the world around her refused to adapt.

It's not the world, chick, she thought. *It's you who's not adapting.* There was an unbearable truth in that—the world was ambivalent, at best—but she couldn't face it right now. She had to believe that she was still Trix

Newcomb, and that perception of herself had changed because of quirks in the world around her. There was the pink hair and the sleeker body, yes . . . but inside, she was still *her*.

Remembering Jenny and Holly proved that. She and Jim couldn't both be crazy, could they?

"Can we?" she whispered, and she slid Jim's key into the lock.

He'd remained down in the parking lot, sitting in his locked, darkened car. No, she'd confirmed, she'd never seen him in the Mercedes, either. He drove a six-year-old Audi. He couldn't face coming up here again, not right now, but he'd asked her to look for a few things.

Entering Jim and Jenny's home, Trix thought of how much her own place might have changed. She hadn't returned there yet. When she had felt this impossible change while out shopping, she had wanted the company of friends, not the silence of her lonely apartment.

Even the smells were different. She pushed the door closed behind her and heard it snick shut, then stood there with her eyes closed for a few seconds. The apartment felt different, smelled different, and when she opened her eyes and took a few steps into the hallway, it sounded wrong as well. She looked around. The large leather sofa looked the same as before, but it was newer, unscuffed, and not smothered with the usual mountain of scatter cushions. She was sure that the big flat-screen TV was a different make, and the Wii game console was gone, along with the slew of game boxes usually piled beneath it.

It could have been a different apartment entirely, but Trix didn't believe that for a second. All the spaces were right, it was just what those spaces contained that seemed so wrong.

"What the fuck is this?" she said aloud, and the apart-

ment swallowed her voice. She'd always been careful
not to swear here in case Holly heard. She walked past
the living room and gasped as something moved to her
left. She stumbled back against the wall, bringing her
fists up, shock surging through her until she realized it
was herself. The mirror was a new addition to the hallway as well, perhaps there to make the space look larger.
She stared into the mirror and only just recognized herself. Her sporty, urban chic style was gone. Her hair was
more spiked and punky than she'd ever worn it, even as
a rebellious teenager. Her face was thin and delicate,
body hard and lithe instead of curvy. She knew her
eyes—the pain and shock there, as well as the subtle
green color that had always been her most distinctive
feature.

"Trix," she said, and the reflection named itself.
"Okay . . . okay . . ." She hurried on, because being
somewhere so familiar and yet so utterly different was
freaking her out. In Jim, she'd found momentary respite
from the nightmare her life had suddenly become, and
she wanted to return to him as soon as possible. But first
there were two places he'd asked her to look, and one
she wanted to see for herself.

She entered the bedroom, and here Jenny's absence
was harsher still. It was obviously a man's room; although Jim's artistic flourishes extended this far, there
were no feminine touches. *Bedside cabinet,* he'd told
her. *Third drawer down, hidden beneath the file of old
newspaper clippings at the bottom. A poem I wrote to
Jenny the day Holly was born. I never gave it to her, because I was embarrassed. Stupid, I know. But I could
also never throw it away.* Trix had nodded, understanding where he was reaching. The poem was entirely to do
with him, and because it had never been a part of
Jenny's awareness, perhaps it would still be there now.

She sat on the bed and opened the drawer. Blinked. For the briefest instant she thought, *They're doing this as a practical joke, maybe they're even filming.* But that idea went as quickly as it had come. In these days of the Internet, she didn't even know that guys looked at magazine porn anymore. She took the magazines out and laid them on the bed beside her. They seemed safe enough, and there was almost a retro feel to the covers, as if they might even show pubes instead of the preferred shaven parts of modern porn. But the dates were recent.

Beneath the magazines was a brown folder. Trix took it out and flicked through the contents. Newspaper clippings, as Jim had said—a variety of stories and features that often inspired him for a painting. And beneath the folder in the drawer . . . nothing. No poem. No envelope or folded paper. She examined the drawer in case it had a false bottom or she'd missed something. Scanned through the paper clippings more thoroughly. Held the magazines up by their spines, shaking them, expecting the sheet of paper to fall out at any moment. But there was nothing, and she didn't even bother placing the items back in the drawer before moving on.

After she had encountered him on the street, Jim had sat in the driver's seat of his car with her beside him, his hands gripping the wheel, his face a mask of concentration as he tried to think of something that would provide evidence of his wife's and daughter's existence. The poem had been one idea, and then as she'd opened the car to leave, he'd reached out, hooked a finger into her belt, and pulled her back inside. Then he'd leaned across the seats, so close to her that for a second Trix had been a little scared. Jim had never unsettled her before, but his breath had smelled of fear, his eyes were wide as a rabbit's in headlights, and she'd wondered, *Am I really on my own after all?*

"There's a painting," he'd said. "It's . . . special. Jenny knew about it, but no one else, not even Jonathan. Not even you."

"Special how?" she'd asked, and instantly felt at ease once again. She was as eager to cling on to Jim as he was to her, because right now he was all she seemed to know. In Tallulah's, the waitress had recognized her right away. No shock at the pink hair, no confusion over this subtly changed woman. *I've always been like this here,* Trix had thought, and the idea distressed her more and more.

"I painted it before I met Jenny," he'd said. One hand rested on Trix's knee, and the warmth was comfort to both of them. "I don't usually do portraits, and this one . . . well, even this isn't quite that. But it's me and a woman, bodies enveloped with storm clouds, sunlight, reveling in the natural. And the woman is Jenny."

"What do you mean?"

"I painted it before we even met." He'd waved his hand. "Oh, there are differences. It's like Jenny how she might have been, not exactly how she is. But it was as if I'd created a vision of my perfect woman, and then two years later . . ." He'd sobbed then, and Trix closed her hand over his and squeezed.

"Just tell me where it is."

So now she climbed the narrower staircase to his studio, desperately hoping that the painting of Jim's wife—her friend, the woman she'd loved for a long time—was still up there.

When she clicked the studio lights on she knew to squeeze her eyes shut. Jim had special lighting there, designed to be as close to real daylight as possible. She waited a few moments, then opened her eyes slowly, letting them adjust as she looked around the room. The fact that the studio appeared completely different was not what surprised and shocked her; she'd anticipated that, and the canvases propped around the place lived up to her expectation. Most of them seemed to be part of one advertising campaign or another, but their style was markedly different from what she was used to seeing from Jim. Before, his paintings had always had a soul about them, some element of tone or mood that she always found moving, whether they were seascapes painted for his own pleasure or advertising images for a new brand of sneaker. He'd always found some way to affect the viewer, and Trix always attributed that to Jim's own sensitive personality. These paintings were different: brash, loud, technically brilliant but lacking in something profound. She imagined that they pleased many advertisers with their directness, and probably earned him a lot of money. But the soul had gone.

She crossed to the rear of the studio where the large storage racking system still stood behind two doors. Pulling the racks out and pivoting them aside, she flicked on the soft light inside the cupboard and entered. There was a mess of old canvases at the back, and he'd told her that the painting of him and Jenny lay buried behind them. Not because it was bad, but because it had always unnerved him. Jenny found it beautiful; he just wondered where it had come from.

Trix moved canvases aside, frowning at the different sense of Jim these paintings gave her. *That's the Jim I know down there,* she had to keep reminding herself. But in that case, where was the Jim who had painted all these? She shivered, shook her head, and started whistling as she searched. But the whistle made the studio feel even more deserted, so she stopped.

The painting was obvious when she saw it, but she did not recognize the place it represented. A man and woman, yes, but like no one she had ever known, their features emphasized and stylized in a strangely cartoon-ish manner, his enlarged penis and her rounded breasts more explicit than anything Jim had ever painted. The sex in the picture was brazen and rich, the figures painted with loving attention, but it only made her feel uneasy. She stared at their faces, but there was nothing familiar there. The man seemed to stare over her shoul-der; the woman glared right back, eyes wide and harsh.

"You didn't paint this," she said, backing away, rolling the racks back in after her, and closing the doors. This was not Jim's studio, at least not the Jim she knew so well. "What the fuck is this?" she shouted again. There was no reply. She wondered what she would dis-cover back in her own apartment, and the thought of going there and seeing unknown things filled her with dread. This place lacked not only touches of Jenny and Holly but the imprint of Jim himself. And yet it *was* his place still.

Trix turned to run from the room, then froze.

On the pedestal beneath the wide windows stood one of her nightmares. Since a brush with death at the age of seven, she'd had disturbing dreams of an unknown city. But since her near-fatal car crash three years before, an-other city had intruded upon her nightmares just as powerfully—different, yet hauntingly familiar. And now here it was. She closed her eyes, fighting the queasiness that swept through her, biting the inside of her lip to pre-vent herself from fainting. When she looked again, she was hoping it would have changed, that she'd imagined it . . . but no, it was still there. And it was the only thing in the whole apartment that she truly recognized.

"I never told Jenny," Jim said. They were sitting in the car together again, Trix panting as she tried to catch her breath. It was fear that had winded her, and uncertainty. "She never liked those paintings, but she thought they were all mine. I never told her that some of them came from *you*. She was weirded out enough that we both saw these two strange places in our dreams."

"Nightmares," Trix said.

"Whatever." He was staring ahead, and she could tell by the set of his jaw that he was fighting hard.

"It was exact," she said. "Just . . . as if you plucked it from my mind."

"But that one was based on *my* dream," he said. "I've done others after talking to you, but that one was . . ." He trailed off, shaking his head. "Last night."

"That can't be," Trix said, but those words seemed weak and ineffectual in the light of what *had* happened. "Maybe you should go and look, see if—"

"No!" he said. "I've finished with that place for tonight." He glanced sidelong at her. "Can we go to your apartment, talk this through? Try and decide what the fuck is going on?"

"My place?" She'd been trying on a blouse in the changing room of her favorite clothes shop, Francine's, when the faint had washed over her. *Something's gone,* she'd thought as she leaned against the mirror, closing her eyes and then snapping them open again when something had twisted through her. That was the best way she could think of describing it—there had been no actual pain, but it felt as if every part of her body flexed and shifted, just for an instant. And as her breath faded from the mirror's surface, a stranger stared back at her.

Somehow, Trix had managed not to scream. She'd smiled in apology—*something's broken the mirror, and I'm looking into the next changing cubicle at a cute-*

looking woman with pink spiky hair and a designer torn top that I like but would never have the guts to wear— and then when the woman returned her smile she'd taken a step back—*I don't know her, she looks harmless enough, but there's no telling just how—* and then the realization as her hands traveled up over her unfamiliar body, her eyes went wide, and every move she made was imitated by the woman in the mirror. Thinner, more athletic; just as she glimpsed the unknown tattoo peering from beneath her sleeve, her palm passed across her breast and felt the piercing in her nipple. "No!" she had gasped, leaning forward and misting the mirror again.

The next few moments were a blur. Fleeing the changing rooms, the browsers and shoppers not staring even though something was terribly wrong, somehow remembering to pay for the new clothes she wore, the clothes she'd never have been daring enough to wear before. And then in the street outside, the instant decision—she was much closer to Jenny's than her own apartment.

She had wandered at first, freaking out, trying to find some proof that she was hallucinating. In a bar near Kenmore Square, she had stopped and had a shot of rum, and then another, but the woman looking back at her from the mirror behind the bar remained the same punky chick she'd first encountered in that dressing room.

At last, not knowing what else to do and needing someone to hold her, to tell her she was still herself, she had gone to Jim and Jenny's. Finding no one at home, she'd waited in Tallulah's for them to return.

"I haven't been back home," she whispered. "Not since . . ."

"Trix," Jim said. He was trying to comfort her, but

there was desperation in his voice, too. She reached out and took his hand, and they sat silently for a few moments. *He knows I'm me,* Trix thought.

"I don't know what I'll find there," she said.

"Maybe an answer," Jim said. He'd leaned in sideways so that he was almost resting his head on her shoulder. Trix felt the drip of a tear, and she squeezed her eyes closed and pressed her lips together. *He's lost his wife and daughter,* she thought. She'd already phoned her father and brother, several friends, and they all knew her. So far as she could tell, the only number missing from her mobile phone was Jenny's.

"Okay," she said. "Have you called the cops?"

"And said what?"

"That Jenny and Holly—"

"Jenny and Holly who no one else remembers?"

"I remember, Jim," she said softly. "If it was just you, then yeah, you'd have to admit that you might have a bit of a problem. But there's two of us. And we can't both have been hallucinating the same thing for . . . however long."

Some people emerged from Tallulah's and came around the corner, laughing and joking as they passed the parked car. One of them glanced inside and looked away again, a nervous smile playing at her lips. *They think we're lovers,* Trix thought.

"Jonathan's dying," Jim said into the darkness.

"What?" Trix knew Jonathan. They weren't the best of friends—there'd always been something between them that made them not quite fit together, as if their personalities abraded each other in all the wrong places—but she knew how much Jim and Jenny loved the guy.

"Remember he was ill a few years back?"

"When he had his scare?"

"Yeah," Jim said. "Scare. It was Jenny who persuaded him to go see the doctor." He sat up again, wiping his face with his hands and drawing his cheeks down, as if to see more clearly. "He'd been having dizzy spells, headaches. Put them down to age, or booze. Jenny talked to him and said he should get it checked out. He did, they did a scan, found the tumor, removed it. Benign. He got better." Jim laughed. "We were drunk a couple of years ago, and he told me he'd once gotten a blow job after showing some guy the scar across his scalp."

"Ew," Trix said.

"I saw him today, Trix. And he's dying. Brain cancer, he said. And he acted . . . *angry*, as if I'd forgotten on purpose. Months to live. Because—"

"Because Jenny never told him."

Jim nodded. "She wasn't *here* to tell him."

"I'm dreaming," she said, and that was the only alternative, wasn't it? She was dreaming, because this was impossible. If she spent some time and started thinking back, she'd reach the moment when she'd fallen asleep, and perhaps that would wake her again. She'd snap back into the world she knew and feel her hair with one hand, blond and cut short, not pink and spiked up. And with the other hand she'd clasp her unpierced breast, and then lift her sleeve to see the smooth, non-tattooed skin of her upper arm. But she could not think back to that moment because it did not exist. Even if she *was* dreaming, she might well be here forever.

"Look," she said, turning the car's interior light on and lifting her sleeve. It was a Celtic band, intricate and beautifully wrought.

"But you hate needles nearly as much as I do," he said softly. He didn't sound surprised.

"Tell me about it," she said. It had been a constant joke between them—one that Jenny always found a little weird—that she'd never liked pricks. She glanced around quickly and lifted her T-shirt. She was braless, something else she'd rarely done before. The light glinted from the ring in her nipple.

"Shit, Trix," Jim said, startled and embarrassed for a moment. Then he saw the piercing and looked up at her as she lowered the top again.

"Fucking *hate* needles," she said. She nodded down at his lap. "Think you should be checking?"

Jim smiled. It was good to see. The surreal, gentle moment of humor amid such trauma lasted only for a second, but that second seemed to clear her head a little, and in that space an idea began to form.

"Okay, my place," she said again. "We can't stay sitting in the car forever."

"Right," Jim said, and he placed both hands on the wheel.

"Er . . . best to start the motor."

"Yeah." But he made no move to turn the key, just staring ahead at the building before them. A couple passed along the sidewalk arm in arm, and Trix watched Jim's eyes follow them. He and Jenny had a strong, safe marriage, and she knew that even though she was sitting here with him right now—the only person he'd found to acknowledge the impossible thing that had happened—he must be feeling very alone.

"It's okay," Trix said, and she felt tears burning behind her eyes. But she had to keep them in, because Jim was suffering more. He'd lost his entire family.

"That's our home," he said.

"And it will be tomorrow. But maybe for tonight it *will* be best to stay at mine."

"What if they come back?" he said. "What if they find their way home and I'm not *there,* Trix?"

Trix had no real answer for that, though she thought: *Wherever we are, Jenny and Holly have never been here.* It was an odd idea, and it shocked her to think that maybe she and Jim had gone somewhere else instead of the other way around. But in some respects it seemed to fit. This was not the exact world she had known a few hours ago—there were differences close to her and Jim, and those changes must stretch farther afield—and she dreaded what she would discover when she arrived home. "Losing it won't help them," she said. "We need to recharge. Think it through. And maybe find someone who can help."

"Someone?" he asked. Trix just shrugged. She remembered everything they had to do, and where they had to go. That is, if the Trix she was now would even consider such things.

"I'll come back later," he said, nodding at the apartment. "Tomorrow. I'll come back."

"Good plan," she said.

Jim started the car and drove them across the city, and Trix watched from the windows. She searched frantically for signs of something being as wrong out there as it felt inside, but the shop names were the same. Dunkin' Donuts wasn't spelled differently, and the mix of old and new Boston architecture presented familiar façades. They passed Monument Square, and the Bunker Hill Monument looked exactly the same as before. But Trix couldn't tell how high it was, nor could she read the inscriptions or identify the face on the statue standing before it.

Boston looks just the same, she thought. *It's just us who are different.* But that wasn't quite true, either.

Jim's agent, Jonathan, was dying. The brain cancer that had been cured due to Jenny's involvement years before had run riot, and soon it would take him. "Because Jenny's not here, and never has been," she whispered.

"What?" It had started raining, and Jim turned on the wipers. They whispered left and screeched right, a rhythmic gasp and moan.

"Jenny and Holly," she said. "I was just thinking aloud. It's not just that they're gone now, but that they've *been* gone . . ." *Forever,* she almost said. But that was too final. "Their past has been stolen, as well as their present."

"And their future?" he asked, voice breaking on the last word.

"I'm going to help you," Trix said. She eyed Jim in the car's dark interior, wondering how much he had changed and where. He seemed a little thinner than before, perhaps a bit more heavily muscled, facial structure more defined. *He's a bachelor; he'll want to take care of himself more so that the women flock to him.* She closed her eyes and breathed deeply, and something about the familiar smells of Boston—wet streets, car fumes, coffee, and a suggestion of Italian food—calmed her. At least the city smelled the same.

As they neared the old townhouse on St. Botolph Street—not far from Symphony Hall—where she had her apartment, Trix sat up and clasped her hands in her lap. She checked out the cars parked along the sidewalks and recognized some of them. She saw a tall, thin woman walking her standard poodle along the street and went to wave. But would Mrs. Wilkinson recognize her with her pink hair and punky gear? *In this world, yeah,* Trix thought. *It's only me who doesn't recognize myself.* She lowered her window and leaned out to put that to the test, but by then they'd passed Mrs. Wilkinson and Jim was pulling up at the curb.

"I'll come with you," he said.

"No, Jim, it's okay, I'll—"

"I'm coming with you!" His tone invited no dispute. She tried to smile, and he reached out and squeezed her hand. "Trix," he said. "Whatever we find . . ." He looked past her at the building.

"I know," she said. "Whatever we find, I'm still me." She opened the car door, got out, and stood waiting on the sidewalk, staring at her apartment's drawn curtains. They did not look familiar. And when she ran up the three steps and checked the nameplate beside her buzzer, she groaned and leaned against the wall.

"It doesn't mean . . . ," Jim began.

Trix went to try her key in the front door, but it had been left unlocked and drifted open as she leaned against it. Inside, she heard music emanating from her apartment. The harsh, thrashy guitars, drums, and growling lyrics of the Dropkick Murphys. You couldn't be young and living in Boston and not know the Dropkicks, but they had always been a bit too brash for her taste. "Jim," she said, "I always open my curtains in the morning."

"Maybe not this morning."

This morning I was someone else, she thought, and she swayed as unreality washed over her. She felt Jim's hand steadying her and leaned into him, and then a horrible sense of anticipation lit inside her chest. *Who am I going to find in there?* she wondered. In her *real* life in the *real* world she hadn't had a girlfriend for over a year, since her last long-term relationship had ended badly. And as Jim's hand rested against her upper arm, a startling, electrifying certainty hit her.

This was a world with different rules. Perhaps here Jenny loved her as much as she loved Jenny.

She headed for the apartment door, already knowing that her thinking was skewed. *No one knows Jenny,* she thought. But no one knew the Jenny she and Jim remembered. Maybe here she was someone else entirely.

She tried her key, and it did not fit.

"Doesn't mean anything," Jim said.

Trix's heart was thumping as she reached for the buzzer, but she held back, kneeling instead and lifting the letter flap. It had a draft shield on the inside, and as she pushed her finger through and lifted it, she closed her eyes, because everything was already strange. *That music's not mine, my key doesn't fit, I smell Chinese and I hate Chinese, and . . .*

She looked into the apartment. "That's not my home," she said. The décor was different, the furniture, and as she watched, a strikingly tall black woman walked naked from the bathroom, across the hallway, and into the living room.

Trix caught her breath. *Perhaps we're lovers,* she thought, but then a man emerged from the bathroom, naked and sheened with sweat, smiling and still semierect.

"Ice?" she heard the woman call, and Trix let the letter flap close softly as she rested back on her heels. Instead of being shocked or upset or disturbed, all she could wonder was how they could still make love with the city falling apart around them.

"Trix?" Jim asked.

"We can go now," she said, standing and walking toward the stairs.

"You're sure?"

She turned to him and was sad to see the hope fading

from his eyes. "We'll look somewhere else," she said. "We need to go to someone who will listen."

"Who?"

Trix glanced back at the familiar building one more time, glad that the rain would camouflage her tears.

"In the car," she said. "We need to leave here. I'll explain then."

4

Rare Ould Times

As Jim drove through the city, windshield wipers battling the rain, he glanced at familiar stores and landmarks. His sense of dislocation had increased, despite the absence of any obvious changes. Every detail of Boston remained the same, at least based on a cursory inventory, and yet somehow it seemed as alien to him as if a tornado had dropped him into Oz. "Seriously, Trix, where are we going?" he asked.

"I told you. State Street. Try to get a parking space near the Old State House."

"Easier said than done," he said.

Trix nodded, peering out the rain-slicked passenger window. "I know. But we only need a few minutes. Double-park if you have to."

Jim jerked the steering wheel to swerve around a taxi that stopped abruptly in front of them. One wheel splashed through a pothole, and he swore. Trix reacted not at all, and he glanced at her, trying to figure her out. Her appearance had changed dramatically, even her body, but she was still Trix.

It should have given him comfort, having a close friend beside him, going through all of this with him. Instead, it scared the shit out of him. It had been terrifying enough to think—as he had at first—that Jenny had taken Holly and vanished from his life intentionally, and then to suspect a meticulous and cruel conspiracy of abduction. And when he had begun to believe that he might be insane, his fear had bloomed into something near enough to lunacy that he might as well have been crazy. But this . . . somehow, this was worse. Trix remembered the world the way Jim did—remembered Jenny and Holly—and that meant that neither of them was crazy. Instead, it meant that the world had suddenly become hideously malleable. Reality had turned fluid.

"You're really not going to tell me what we're doing here?" he asked.

She squeezed her eyes shut a moment, then opened them and turned to look at him. Her new look—the pink hair, different makeup—made her seem more intense, but her eyes were the same as ever, and glinting with unshed tears. "You know how much Jenny means to me, right?" she asked. "Jenny and Holly, I mean?"

Trix loved Jenny almost as much as he did. In truth, he had always suspected Trix was deeply *in* love with his wife, though Jenny had always insisted that whatever feelings Trix might have for her were in the past. Every time Trix ended a relationship with a girlfriend and the three of them would get together and drink too much wine, he would see that old wistful sadness in Trix's eyes, but eventually he had learned not to mention it. Things were what they were. Jenny and Trix had a powerful bond, but Jim had never felt threatened by it.

Trix might be Jenny's best friend, but she had become one of his closest friends as well.

"Yeah. I know," Jim said.

"Then I'm going to need you to trust me for a little while. There's someone we need to talk to—a woman named Veronica Braden—and if I find her and she can't help us, then we'll think of something else. We will, Jim. We're going to figure out how this is possible, and we'll find them."

He laughed darkly. "You sound so sure."

Trix turned to look back out at the rain. "I have to be. And you'll have to be, too." She lowered her voice. "Whatever this is, it can't be the first time it's happened to anyone. I've read Stephen Hawking, y'know? Parallel dimensions and black holes and all that shit. We're going to figure this out, and we're going to get . . . get your girls back."

Silence filled the space between them then, save for the *shush* of the wipers and the rumble of the road beneath his tires. He drove down Congress Street searching without luck for a parking spot. Roadwork took up two long blocks on the right, and the left had parked cars bumper to bumper. As he approached State, he took a chance and turned left onto narrow Quaker Lane, saw a spot, and pulled in.

"There's a sign," Trix said.

Jim didn't respond. He killed the engine and climbed out, cold rain spattering him and drops running down the back of his collar. Trix stepped out of the car, and they both looked at the sign she had pointed out, a list of parking restrictions. She had said they wouldn't be long, but he found he could not care about tickets or tow trucks.

"If you want an umbrella, I saw one on the backseat," he said, slamming the door.

Trix turned her face up to the sky, seeming to relish the cold rain. "Fuck it."

They walked up Quaker Lane all the way to Devonshire and turned right. The rain was little more than a drizzle, but Jim kept wiping it from his eyes. Trix pushed wet hair out of her face, the rain having taken all the punky spikiness out of the pink dye job. When they came to the end of Devonshire, where the Old State House stood on the corner, Trix frowned and glanced around. Then she set off along State Street.

"What are you looking for?" Jim asked, avoiding puddles that had started to form in the warped, uneven sidewalk.

She ignored him, picking up her pace, weaving around people who had just come out of the State Street T station, which was located beneath the Old State House. At the corner, she glanced up at the building's front balcony, then across the street. They'd walked three quarters of the way around the old brick structure now. "There," Trix said, setting off again.

But this time she did not go far, only to a traffic island that jutted into the street. In the island was a wide circle made of cobblestones set in concentric patterns. Trix hesitated as though about to walk across hot coals. Jim could only stare, wondering what she was up to, but then she turned and held out her hand. "Come on."

"Where?" he asked.

"Right here," she insisted. "You said you trusted me."

He stared at her, pink hair plastered to her scalp and face now, rain running in rivulets down her cheeks, and he wondered if he had made a terrible mistake, if whatever sinister manipulations were at work here, Trix was a part of them. But then she pushed the hair from her eyes and he saw the pain in her imploring gaze, and chided himself for hesitating.

Jim took her hand, and together they stepped into the cobblestone circle.

Revelers going into the city for the night maneuvered around them, umbrellas sluicing rain. Hardy tourists gave them a wide berth, though hardly anyone really looked at them, the two nut jobs standing in the rain for no apparent reason.

Trix held his hand tightly, closed her eyes, and began to whisper. Jim leaned in to listen, feeling her breath warm and intimate on his face.

". . . Jennifer Anne Garland Banks and Holly Marie Banks," Trix whispered. "They've vanished and we have to find them. We love them, and our lives—our world—are falling apart. We need your help."

Jim pulled back, staring at her. Sensing his withdrawal, Trix opened her eyes in alarm. "No," she said, tugging him back toward her. "You said you trusted me."

"I do, but . . ." *This is crazy,* he wanted to say. "You dragged me halfway across the city to fucking *pray*?"

Trix gripped his hand harder. "I'm not praying. But right now, on this spot, you've got to ask for help."

"Who am I asking?" he said, eyes narrowed, as he looked around at the rain-swept street and the umbrella people passing by. He pointed at the sky. "Someone up there?"

Trix laughed uneasily. "The way I understand it, you're asking Boston."

"Boston?"

She nodded. "The city. Yeah."

Jim let his shoulders sag. "Oh, Jesus, Trix, you can't believe that. You wasted all this time—"

"When we could have been doing what?" she snapped, her gaze intense. "Look at me, Jim. There's nothing normal about this. We can't hire a private detective or something. Another search of your apartment isn't going to turn up shit. So please, just . . . let me try."

"Who even told you about this?"

Trix took a deep breath. "My grandmother. I'll explain later. But for now . . . I need your help."

He let out a breath and nodded, trying to think of a next step, something he should be doing to try to find his wife and daughter in a world where they had apparently never existed. "All right," he said, a great void opening up within him. Whatever hope he still had had begun to fade.

"You have to ask for help."

Jim tried not to pay attention to the people passing around them, to faces halfway hidden beneath umbrellas, to conversations and cell phones and a burst of laughter from half a block away.

He closed his eyes. "Please," he whispered, his heart breaking all over again as he surrendered to the truth, that he had no chance of finding them himself. "I've got to find them. I can't live without them." The moment the words were out of his mouth, he knew they were true. He would never be able to survive in a world where his two reasons for living had simply vanished, where all that he loved had been taken away. Deleted.

"Okay," Trix said, squeezing his hand. "Let's go."

Jim let her lead him. "Where?"

She looked up at the street signs on the corner. "To dinner."

"Are you serious?" he asked. "I couldn't eat anything right now."

Trix let go of his hand and he saw his own heartbreak reflected in her eyes. "What about a drink? I'm not screwing around, Jim. There's a place we need to go."

Jim exhaled. They should be out searching, but where would they even begin to look? "And over a drink, you'll tell me what this is all about?" he asked.

"I swear," Trix said.

"Then lead the way. Maybe a whiskey will steady my nerves."

* * *

As it turned out, the whiskey didn't help.

Other than telling him where they were going, Trix had been resolutely silent on their short drive to the North End. Jim had found a parking spot across the street from Mike's Pastry, and they'd walked past the strange spectacle of a trio of fiftyish Italian men sitting in lawn chairs in front of a small shop as though nothing had changed in the century since the North End had been the heart of Boston's Italian-immigrant community.

These days, the people descended from those immigrants couldn't afford to live in the trendy neighborhood, but nearly every storefront was an Italian restaurant. The North End was a dining mecca for tourists and locals alike, and the sidewalks were always thronged with people, the streets jammed with traffic. And yet those men in their lawn chairs seemed unmoved by the changes in the neighborhood. They were either Mafia or Mafia-connected, but even the Mob had been watered down tremendously over the years, and they were the only ones who didn't seem to realize it.

They had passed by a dozen more modern restaurants, walking along Hanover Street away from the worst of the crowd. On a block of three-story apartment houses, tucked between a small Laundromat and an even smaller Italian grocery, was a restaurant called Abruzzi's that seemed to make no effort to draw the attention of passersby. There was no sandwich board advertising specials on the sidewalk, no awning, no valet parking—just a menu taped to the inside of the tinted front window.

Inside, Abruzzi's seemed stuck in the 1970s, with red vinyl booths and Sinatra playing on the sound system, photographs of Italian landscapes and cityscapes on the wall, and paper placemats upon which a map of "the boot" had been printed. But the moment they walked in,

Jim's stomach growled, betraying him. He hadn't eaten anything since that morning, and hunger had been gnawing quietly at him, subordinate to hysteria and grief but now making itself known.

Reluctantly, he agreed to eat. Trix ordered pizza.

Now they waited, and Jim watched her as he sipped his whiskey. Glasses clinked. An old man celebrated his ninety-first birthday with what appeared to be three younger generations around a long table. When they sang to him, the whole restaurant joined in except for Jim and Trix, who feigned smiles and applauded politely. And then at last everyone turned their attention back to their own dining companions, and Jim took another sip, relished the burn of the whiskey in his throat, and looked at Trix.

In the car she had fixed her hair as best she could, pushing her fingers through it, but still he knew they both looked like something the cat had dragged in. He had to wonder what the other diners must have thought when they first came in. But then he realized he didn't care. None of these people meant anything to him. They weren't even really of his world. In some unsettling way, because they were only aware of a world where Jenny and Holly had never existed, they felt like the enemy to him. In fact, it felt like he and Trix had snuck behind enemy lines and at any moment might be discovered as outsiders.

We don't belong here, he thought, taking another sip. And maybe that was true. It made him wonder if other people had vanished, too. If there were other people out there who were aware that the world had been subtly altered. He and Trix might as well be invaders from Mars.

She stared at the bottle of Heineken on the table in front of her, passing her thumb over the green glass like she was trying to see something floating in the beer inside. Every ten or fifteen seconds she glanced toward the door.

"Trix," he said.

She blinked, focusing on him like she'd forgotten he was there.

"What the hell are we doing here?" Jim asked. "How is this helping, and what was that crazy shit about your grandmother?"

Trix took a swig from her Heineken and gave him the Cheshire cat grin that he had seen before, whenever she felt stupid or embarrassed. "Do you know the story of the Oracle of Delphi?" she asked.

Jim stared at her. "Sure. The Athenians went to her for guidance. She communed with the gods or something and could give them answers, see the future. That kind of thing."

Trix stared at her beer. Someone came in, and she looked up hopefully, then turned again to Jim, dejected. "I don't know about seeing the future."

"What does this have to do with—"

She cut him off with a glare. "Just listen."

"I'm trying," he said sharply. "You're not saying anything."

Trix sighed. "All right. So, you know my father took off for L.A. when I was little and that after my mother died, my grandparents raised me."

"Yeah."

She started to strip the label from her beer bottle. "When I was maybe nine or ten my grandfather started to slip. Dementia. Alzheimer's. He went downhill fast, and he died the day before my twelfth birthday.

"When I was in the fifth grade, I came home from school one day and my grandmother was a wreck. She totally flipped out. By then there were times when my grandfather had no idea who we were or where we were. He would think it was, like, the fifties again and that my grandmother was his sister Paulette. The neighbors all sort of kept an eye on him during those times. But this one day he'd been doing pretty well. My grandmother had been ironing in her bedroom, watching television, and when she went to look in on him, he'd disappeared."

Jim felt a sick twist in his gut. "Vanished? You mean like Jenny and Holly? You've been through something like this before?"

But Trix shook her head. "No. Nothing like this. He just . . . he wandered off because he didn't know where he was. He barely knew *who* he was. Well, how far can an old man get, right? But by the time I got home from school, six hours had passed with no sign of him and my grandmother had started to freak out completely. She said there was only one person she knew of who could really help, and we got on the bus—she didn't have a car and couldn't afford a cab—and she brought me to the Old State House, to that same spot."

Jim frowned. "But what is it?"

"I'm surprised you don't know. You've lived in Boston your whole life, and you've never followed the Freedom Trail?"

"Maybe when I was a kid. What does—"

"The Boston Massacre. That's the spot, right there in front of the Old State House, within spitting distance of the balcony."

He knew the story well enough—colonials throwing snowballs at British soldiers posted in the city, taunting them until the situation became so tense that there was musket fire, killing five men. It had been one of the events that fed the growing anti-British sentiment that led to the Revolution. "You've totally lost me," he said.

Now when Trix glanced at the front door of Abruzzi's, Jim looked as well.

"What are you waiting for?" he asked.

Trix smiled nervously. "I'm getting to that."

"Fine. So your grandmother took you to that spot?"

"And she asked for help—"

"Why would she—"

"Just fucking listen!" Trix hissed, eyes full of pain.

The dad at the next table gave them a nasty look, but Jim stared him down and he finally turned away.

"I'm sorry," Trix said, taking a swig of her beer.

The waitress came and slid a basket of bread between them. Jim waited for her to walk away, then he took a piece and tore off a chunk. "Go on," he said.

Trix hesitated, looked at the door, and then squeezed her eyes shut again. "All right. Short version. I'm sorry, it's just so . . . Jenny's the only person I've ever told this story, and now when it matters, it's hard to figure out how to explain."

Jim said nothing, just listening. From a speaker set into the ceiling above them, Sinatra sang about coffee. He chewed the bread and found it too dry to swallow, so he chased it down with a sip of water, then more whiskey.

Opening her eyes, Trix seemed to have come to a decision. "I'll tell you what my grandmother told me. She said Boston had an Oracle, like in ancient Greece. This woman knew everything about the city." Trix shook her head. "No, it was more than that. It was like . . . I don't remember the words my grandmother used, but it's like she shares a soul with the city. She knows every brick, right? Every corner. Something happens in Boston, she knows, whether it's a secret or not. You know that saying about when a tree falls in a forest when there's no one there to hear it, does it make a noise? The Oracle would hear. So people go to her. If your kid runs away and is still in the city, the Oracle can find him. If someone stole your car and dumped it, she can tell you where they left it. She knows where all the bodies are buried, literally."

Jim pushed back into the red vinyl seat. "So how are there still unsolved murders?"

"You think the cops are going to ask 'the Oracle of Boston'? Seriously?" Trix said. "It'd be like calling a psychic hot line. They wouldn't risk their careers."

Jim narrowed his eyes, staring at her. "Jesus. And you really believe in this?"

Trix sipped her beer, glaring at him. "I have to. It's our only hope. And it worked once before."

"It did?"

"Just listen. My grandmother took me to that spot, and we asked for help finding my grandfather. Then she brought me here. Her friend Celia had told her this was the place—that you asked for help and then you waited at De Pasquale Brothers, which was the name of this place back then. I cried a lot that afternoon, waiting here. Not my grandmother. Her eyes were red but she didn't cry. The woman looked like her face had turned to stone." Trix shook her head, gazing at the wall as though she could see through it, back across the years.

"And?" Jim said. "Did she come? The Oracle?"

Trix reached up and pushed a matted lock of pink hair from her eyes. "Do you think we'd be sitting here if she didn't?"

The waitress arrived and slid the metal pizza tray onto the table. Jim and Trix stared at each other, both drinking, as the woman served them each a slice and then asked if there was anything else she could get them. They both muttered noncommittally, and the waitress hurried off to her next customer.

"You found your grandfather?"

Trix took a swig that drained the remains of her Heineken. "He'd been a tailor in Chinatown in his thirties and forties. He was walking up and down Harrison Avenue trying to figure out why the business wasn't there anymore. He thought he was late for work and had gotten turned around."

"And that was where this Oracle woman had told you he would be?"

Trix glanced at the door. That was answer enough for Jim.

"This is nuts," he said.

She bit into her pizza, chewed, and swallowed that first bite. "If you have a better idea . . . if you have the *first clue* what the fuck we should do about this . . ." She laughed a little crazily and touched her hair. "Please share. Because I don't think calling Missing Persons is going to bring Jenny and Holly back."

As Trix ate, Jim stared at the pizza cooling on his plate. Perhaps two full minutes passed before he picked it up and started to eat, feeling with every bite like he was somehow betraying his wife and daughter by feeding himself. He should have been out on the street, visiting every place they had ever been, or back at home waiting for them to return. But inside, he knew that was foolish.

Trix caught him staring at her. "What?" she demanded.

"Just trying to adjust to your new look."

Trix shook her hair back. "Me, too. You know, I'm not the only one who looks different."

"What, me?"

She tapped her eyebrow. "Your scar, from the night you and Jenny went to the U2 concert? It's gone."

Jim reached up and ran his finger across the place

where the scar ought to be, but he couldn't muster shock or even surprise. He'd earned the scar in a quick exchange of fists with an asshole who'd groped Jenny's ass at the concert. There had been blood in his eyes—the guy wore a ring with a Celtic design—and by the time he'd wiped it away they were all being thrown out. But that had never happened, so there was no scar.

"You're in better shape, too," Trix told him. "Leaner, maybe a little better built. In the car, when you hugged me, I could tell."

Now that she mentioned it, he did feel different. For several seconds he studied her again, then he flagged the waitress as she went by. "Another whiskey, please."

"Do you want another Heineken, honey?" the waitress asked Trix.

Trix laughed uneasily. "Damn right."

And so they ate and drank and waited, talking very little. There was nothing they could have said that would not have seemed either redundant or ridiculously trivial.

But when the glasses were empty and they'd eaten their fill—and even after they had ordered coffee and the dregs were cooling—no one had come over to talk to them, and no one Trix recognized had come through the front door. The restaurant had a bar that ran its length, right across from the booth where they sat, and from what Jim could tell there weren't even any single women there.

The waitress had brought the check, but they weren't in a hurry to pay, though they could feel her silently willing them to give up the table. He had to fight the urge to be up and out of there, to be doing something— anything—to find out what had happened to Jenny and Holly. What would he do, Google "vanishing people"? He would get crazy Bermuda Triangle stories and Amelia Earhart.

Are you sure? he wondered, and realized he wasn't.

Another twenty minutes went by, and the waitress had obviously become uncomfortable. If he and Trix had been talking, they wouldn't have drawn any real attention, but even the bartender kept glancing at them uneasily because they just sat there, waiting.

"Are you two sure I can't get you another cup of coffee or another drink?" the waitress asked.

Jim looked at Trix, who shook her head. "We're good, thanks," he told the waitress.

But this time the woman didn't go away. She hesitated before speaking.

"Are you waiting for someone? It's just, you keep looking at the door."

Jim stared at Trix a minute, running his forefinger over the rim of his coffee cup. Then he started to stand. "We're going," he said. "I'm sorry we took up the table so long."

"No, no," the waitress said. "No one's waiting. I just wondered if you needed anything."

"Jim," Trix said, staring at him. "Let's . . . please let's just get another cup of coffee. A little while longer, okay?"

He glanced at her and then the waitress. "All right," he said, sitting down. "Decaf."

Trix asked for a cappuccino, and when the waitress left them alone, she slid back her chair. "I've got to use the bathroom," she said.

"Hey," he said as she started to walk away. "One more cup and then we go."

Trix froze, looking back at him. "And then what?"

Jim stared at his empty cup. "Maybe we wake up in the morning and it's all back to normal."

"Like Scrooge?" Trix said, and it was obvious she did not believe it for a second. "Yeah. Maybe."

She headed off toward the back of the restaurant, where a sign painted on the wall pointed the way to the restrooms. Jim fiddled with his cup until the waitress came and refilled it with decaf. As she walked away he poured a little cream and took a sip, flinching at the burn of the hot liquid.

"May I sit?"

Jim glanced up, startled to find an old woman standing beside the table.

She smiled. "I'm sorry. I'm always doing that. My friends tell me I walk on cat feet. I didn't mean to make you jump."

"No, no, I'm fine," he said, studying her.

Once she would have been considered tall for a woman—especially in her youth, which must have been sixty years gone, at least—but now age had stooped her so badly that she had lost several inches. Deep wrinkles lined her face with the gentle scars of time. And yet her eyes were a kaleidoscope, hazel flecked with gold, bright and alert and full of humor. She wore her white hair to her shoulders, unlike so many women of advanced age.

"Can I help you with something?" he asked.

She smiled. "Quite the contrary, Mr. Banks. May I sit?"

Jim frowned and glanced toward the bathroom, then focused on the woman again. He was unsettled now. "What's that supposed to mean?"

Now she looked . . . cross. The perfect word for the disgruntled expression on the old woman's face. "You're being quite impolite, James. Or is it Jim? Yes, I suspect it is. Didn't your mother teach you any manners? It's rude not to offer an old lady a seat, Jim, especially when she's already asked for the courtesy."

He shook himself and half stood, nodding. "Yes. I'm sorry, please sit down."

Quite the contrary. Did that mean she meant to help

him? He stared at her as she settled into the spot Trix had vacated in the booth.

She laughed softly. "Ah, yes. Now you're thinking, 'The old hag doesn't look especially magical.' Or something like that. Though perhaps not 'hag.' Not from you."

He started to protest and glanced toward the back of the restaurant again.

"Don't worry. Trix will be along in a minute or two. I'm so sorry to have kept you waiting, but it couldn't be helped, I'm afraid. It's been quite a busy day. A young man in Jamaica Plain needed to prove that his great-great-grandfather had never deeded a piece of property to the city that . . . well, never mind. I had to guide the young man to the original deed, and the hundred-year lease, which was all the city had."

Part of Jim wanted to laugh in her face. It was such a cliché, wasn't it? The wise old woman, like some kind of Gypsy fortune-teller. But she wore a jacket and skirt ensemble that must have cost seven or eight hundred dollars, easily, and her haircut hadn't come cheaply, either. This was no sideshow crystal-ball gazer.

A scam, then? Had Trix set him up somehow?

But the instant he had the thought, he pushed it away. Trix's anguish was genuine, and so was her hope. Which left only one possibility.

"Jesus," Jim whispered, staring at the woman. "You're for real."

When the Oracle of Boston smiled in delight, it took a dozen years off her face. "Oh, excellent," she said. "It's refreshing to meet someone who just dives right in. Saves time as well." She held out her hand. "Veronica Braden."

Jim shook her hand, not at all surprised by the firmness of her grip. He took a ragged breath, only then realizing that he had stopped breathing for a moment. The hours that had passed since this afternoon when he had woken from his nap had been a long nightmare, but Trix had been right to chide him for his doubt. The impossible had turned his world upside down and ripped away all that he loved. He would waste no more time with what was possible and what was not.

"You make it hard enough to meet you."

"I enjoy the . . . *tradition* of the process."

"So, can you find them?" Jim asked, a heavy question. "Do you know where they are?"

"Ah," Veronica said, arching a brow, kaleidoscope eyes alight with secret knowledge. She smiled, and Jim knew she harbored secrets. "Those are two different questions. Finding Jennifer and Holly is not the same as knowing where they are."

Jim put a hand over his mouth as though afraid the wrong words would come out. The waitress arrived with Trix's cappuccino. She glanced at them oddly, but Jim gestured for her to put the cup down and she did, casting a curious look over her shoulder as she retreated once more. "I don't understand," Jim said quietly.

"You will." Veronica touched his hand, and her hand was cool. Then she picked up Trix's cappuccino and drained half the cup in three long sips.

"That was—"

"She won't have time to drink it," Veronica said, sliding her chair back. "Come along."

As the Oracle rose, the illusion of vitality dropped away. She moved stiffly but with a kind of imperious air; perhaps she had earned it. Her hand shook as she gestured toward him. "Pay the bill, dear. And leave a nice tip for your server. New girl. Only been here a few weeks, and she needs the reassurance as much as the money. Terrible job, having to smile at people all the time."

Jim obeyed, sliding the cash from his wallet and tucking it into the faux-leather binder in which the bill had arrived.

"And here she is now," Veronica said, her voice an aged rasp.

As Jim put his wallet back into his pocket he looked up to see that Trix had frozen in the middle of Abruzzi's, staring at Veronica. Other diners had started to turn to watch the scene unfold. Jim noticed that some people—staff and regulars—seemed to be very studiously avoiding looking at them at all. He wondered how many times they had seen Veronica Braden arrive here to help people in need. People in pain.

"You came," Trix managed, fighting back a sob. Tears slid down her face, and she did not bother to wipe them away. "I wasn't sure you were even still alive."

"If not me, then someone else," Veronica said, ignoring the eyes upon her. "Now, come along, Trixie. We don't have all night."

5

Cruel Mistress

"IN THE old days," Veronica said, slipping into the Mercedes' front passenger seat without asking Trix if she minded sitting in the back, "we'd have had to wait until morning. All the shops closed at a decent time then. Life was less frantic. Now people want twenty-four-hour everything. TV, takeout. Clothes shopping. Things are changing."

"What do you mean?" Jim asked. He held the passenger door open, watching as Veronica made herself comfortable and then sat motionless with her hands folded in her lap. The only real sign of effort was the woman's subtle sigh.

"Shopping," Veronica said. She looked up at Jim, eyes twinkling, then glanced over his shoulder at Trix. "Oh, you're coming, dear, aren't you?"

"Of course," Trix said. She got into the back of the car, glancing at Jim and trying to communicate something with a frown, a sharp nod.

"What shopping?" Jim said, and he thought, *Is she really just a crazy old lady after all?* Out here on the busy Boston street, the woman seemed somehow smaller than she had in the restaurant, and less convincing.

Veronica closed her eyes briefly, resting her head back

against the seat as if asleep. But the frown was not at home on a relaxed face. Her hands twitched a little in her lap, and Jim leaned sideways to look in the rear window. Trix, sitting in the backseat, was watching Veronica with her mouth slightly open, whether in awe or fear he couldn't tell.

Veronica opened her eyes so suddenly that Jim took a small step back. "Copley Place," she said. "There's a mime artist on the library steps as they pass. Holly wants to stop and watch, but Jenny's in a hurry to get into the mall and find somewhere to eat. Jonathan holds her elbow and whispers something to her. Something Holly can't hear. *I think she's a little spooked.* Jenny's missed that. *What kind of a mother am I?* She puts one arm around Holly's shoulder.

"But Holly's fascinated by the mime, and his silently moving mouth. She rubs her ears, as if she's been swimming and maybe got water in them. But she can still hear the pigeons and the traffic, and a bunch of children across by the church are singing a song she hasn't heard before. The mime opens and closes windows in thin air, as if he's peering through from somewhere else, and he smiles at her. She smiles back. He's not so scary."

"What is all this?" Jim asked. "What are you *doing*?"

"I'm giving you what I can of your wife and daughter before they went," Veronica said. "Now, if you'll just . . ." She raised and lowered one hand, an almost dismissive gesture.

"Trix, I don't like—"

"Jim!" Trix snapped from the backseat. If her voice had been angry or impatient, he might have argued. But Jim could see that she was crying.

"Jenny's hungry. She's got lunch on her mind. But Jonathan sees what Holly really wants. He knows even as they pass the bookshop, and Holly slips away from her mother, pressing her face to the window. There's a display of fairy books there. She already has some—she has three of them—but there are two others she's always wanted. *I'll get us a table*, Jonathan says, and Jenny smiles at him and nods. *I won't be long.* She follows Holly inside. The smell of new books, coffee from the Starbucks upstairs in the shop, the sound of gentle conversation at the counter. Pages flip, books thump closed. Holly is already past the counter and at the kids' section, and she has a book in each hand, deciding which to read."

Veronica fell silent and her expression slowly changed. Gone was the gentle smile as she relayed Holly's supposed behavior earlier that day. In its place was something like resignation.

"What happened next?" Jim asked, because he did believe, really. It wasn't that he knew the story, but the subtleties were accurate: Holly's delight at the fairy books, Jenny's eagerness to get her daughter fed before shopping, Jonathan's surprising perceptiveness for a guy who'd never wanted kids. She couldn't be making this up.

"A book falls from the shelves," the old woman said. "Jenny reaches for it, wonders, *Why the hell did that one tumble, there's no one to push it, there's no reason—* And then . . ." Veronica looked up at him again, and for a second there was a smile in her eyes. "Jonathan is back at home. The falling book is on its shelf, and your wife has never touched it."

Jim breathed heavily, trying to process what she had said, and what she was still saying. "I don't understand."

"We must go there," Veronica said. "That's not always essential, but it can help. You need to *feel* the place to know it."

"Copley Place?" he asked. The old woman nodded,

and in the backseat Trix was looking at him expectantly. Jim pushed the door closed and stood alone on the street for a moment, cold, getting damp again from the fine rain. *It's where they were headed when I last saw them, so why the hell not?* he thought. But as he got in and started the car, he knew there was more to it than that. He would go because Veronica had suggested it. And she knew.

The old woman sat quietly beside him as he drove, hands still crossed in her lap, and he adjusted the rearview mirror so that he could see Trix.

"You all right?" he asked. Trix caught his eye and nodded. She even offered him a smile that said, *Yes, fine now.* He thought of standing on that traffic island pleading with the patterned cobbles for help, and the rain, and the long wait in the restaurant while Veronica dealt with some other city emergency.

"So what makes you the Oracle of Boston?" he asked. He heard an intake of breath from the backseat.

"Long story," Veronica said.

"Well, it'll take a few minutes to—"

"And private."

"Right." Jim pressed his lips together and flicked on the wipers. The rain was growing heavy again, and Boston's evening streets demanded his attention. Dueling taxicabs jockeyed for position as they took couples and friends out for the evening. Other cars lined up at traffic signals, pedestrians dashed across the streets, and horns erupted here and there as impatience settled and tempers flared. *You must first have a lot of patience to learn to have patience,* he'd read somewhere once, and he leaned on the car horn for no reason.

Veronica turned to look directly at him. "Breathe, Mr. Banks," she said. "I'll do all I can."

"Why Copley Square?" Jim asked. "Are Jenny and Holly still there?"

"Nowhere near. But you know that."

"Then we should be going where they are!"

"You understand, Jim. You're just trying hard not to."

"Then fucking *make* me understand!"

"Jim!" Trix said from the backseat, but fear and anger had Jim now, and such emotions combined brought out the worst in people.

"Learn patience, Jim," Veronica said, as if she'd known what he was just thinking. "I need to see where they *were* before they went, even if you do not. I need to . . . taste the air. It will help me pin down their location."

Jim scoffed but said nothing. Tears pressed against his eyes and throat, and he did his best to swallow them down. They were as useless as drops in a rainstorm. "But you'll help me find them?" he said finally.

"I have every intention of setting you on the right path."

Jim nodded, and a tear streaked down his right cheek. Veronica saw it. He didn't know how he knew that, but the air in the car seemed to soften. But perhaps that was just him. The trials of driving through a busy Boston possessed him for a while, and each time he looked in the mirror he saw Trix, light splaying across her bright hair, eyes sad, face shadowed with confusion and grief. *We've both got to hold it together,* he thought. *And so far, she's done more than I have to find Holly and Jenny.*

"Thank you for helping," he said softly, glancing across at the old woman. "And I'm sorry about . . ." He shrugged.

"Oh! A thank-you. Well, that's an even better start."

It took another ten minutes to wend their way toward Copley Square. They passed Boston Common, rolling along Beacon Street, then cut left along Clarendon, finding a parking space opposite the First Baptist Church.

"It's Borders, on the corner," Veronica said. She was breathing more heavily now, and Jim noticed that her skin had taken on a sickly pallor.

"Are you okay, Miss Braden?" Trix asked, leaning over from the backseat.

"I'm fine," the old lady said. She took a few breaths, seeming to gather herself, and then offered Jim a small smile. "When there's a trauma to the city, I suffer a little myself."

"A trauma to the city?" he asked.

"I'll explain when we're there."

Jim glanced at his watch. Almost ten p.m. "It'll be closing in a minute."

"Not tonight," Veronica said. "Tonight it will remain open until almost ten-fifteen." She checked the side mirror, then opened the door, standing up with an audible groan.

"Jim," Trix said as soon as Veronica let the door swing shut, "you've got to give her a chance. You *must*! Believe me, this is the only thing—"

"We're here now," he said. "This is where they came. And the things she said about Holly, those fairy books . . ." He shook his head. "She couldn't know that."

"So you'll give her a chance?"

"It's what I'm doing, isn't it?" It came out harsher than he'd intended, but when he and Trix got out of the car he smiled at her, and she nodded. She knew him so well, and even with everything that was happening, she'd know that Jim would struggle to hold on to reason. Though an artist, he was also a pragmatist, an atheist, and a skeptic when it came to the supernatural or anything associated with it.

"She'll amaze you," Trix said. "Come on. She's going."

They followed Veronica along the street, and Jim was surprised when Trix clasped his hand. He took great comfort from the contact, and as he realized it was because she was afraid, he acknowledged his own fear as well.

Entering the shop, breathing in warmth and the familiar smell of new books, he wondered what they would find.

It was almost as if he had walked this way before. He had, of course, many times in the past. He and Jenny were both big readers, though their tastes differed—she loved thrillers, historical novels, and real-life stories, while he preferred biographies and science fiction. When they came into town they often spent an hour in one bookstore or another, enjoying watching Holly browse the books, buying a couple here and there, maybe progressing to the café for coffee and a shortbread, and sitting to check out their purchases. But this time was different. Veronica had said only a few sentences about Holly and Jenny being here, but the picture conjured in his mind was complete. He was walking in his missing family's footsteps.

Breathing deeply, Jim moved past the counter and approached the children's section.

Trix had let go of his hand as they walked through the front doors. Perhaps she'd felt the tension growing in him, or sensed that his mind wasn't quite in the present as he tried to relive that moment, following Jenny and Holly's path.

"Here," Veronica said. She'd gone ahead, and as if following a guide of some kind, Jim and Trix had stayed a few steps behind. Now he saw her swaying slightly, and he reached out hesitantly, not wanting to touch her but worried that she was about to fall. *If she drops dead here, now, just what the fuck will that mean?* But she didn't fall, and when she looked back at them he saw a strength in her eyes that he hadn't noticed before. Something was affecting her, challenging her. But she was fighting back.

"I'm not sure," Trix said. A strange thing to say.

"Do you feel it, Jim?" Veronica asked.

He frowned and looked around at the book stacks— the splash of colors and textures, words and names jumping out at him, the spines of children's books hinting at the stories inside, and books faced out tempting with elaborate and enticing covers. "No," he said, not understanding what she meant, but even as he closed his mouth again he *did* feel something. He felt . . .

Someone passed him by, but there was no one there.

The front door closed softly, and he heard the distant jangle of keys, but when he looked back it stood open, warm-air curtain shimmering his view of the rain-slicked sidewalk outside.

It's all so wrong! he thought, and a nightmare he used to have when he was young struck him for the first time in decades. It used to plague him when he was sick, and he'd never been able to describe it, not even to himself. It was an impression of terrible space, so wide, so endless, that it lessened him where he stood at its heart, smothered him, crushed him down with enormity and possibility. And now it impacted again, because everything he saw and felt around him seemed, for a moment, an infinity away.

He gasped in air that was too far away to breathe. Book titles on the shelving before him blurred, and he closed his eyes to the cold, staggering thought, *They mean something else!* He stepped back and Trix stopped him, hands on his waist and her chin resting against his shoulder. He heard her breathing hard, felt her heart thudding against his back.

"What *is* it?" she asked Veronica, voice loud in Jim's ear.

He opened his eyes again, and the woman was staring at a bookshelf. It was four rows above the floor, a selection of hardback books for children—atlases, natural-history books, histories—and as she slowly lifted her hand and moved closer, Jim knew what she was doing.

"This one," she said. She touched the spine of a book called *People and Places*. "It fell, but not here. It only fell *there*."

"Where?" Jim asked. Anger flared and faded again just as quickly, because now, through the fear, he only felt a desperate need to know. "*Please* tell me, where?"

"Where they went," Veronica said. "They slipped through into another Boston, and this is where it happened. Here." She tapped the book's spine and looked around again, ignoring an inquiring look from a shop attendant. "It's all closed up again now, though. The In-Between has receded; the wound is mended. But there are always scars."

"I don't understand any of this," Jim said.

Trix held him tighter. "I think I'm starting to."

Veronica froze, and it was that sudden stillness that made Jim realize just how alive she seemed. Even while sitting beside him in the car she had been a formidable presence—a person whose gravity was greater than most—and he imagined her being the sort who could command a room upon entry, if she so desired. But for that brief moment she became more immobile than he believed any living person could.

"Closing time," the shop assistant said.

"Yes," Veronica said, turning and breezing past Jim and Trix. "Good. It's gone now. Come with me."

"Where to?" Jim asked, pleased to leave that place. *They were here and then they weren't,* he thought, and there was something cold about that shop, and distant, and he wondered why the assistant didn't seem to feel it. She smiled indulgently as they exited the store, and he heard the jangle of keys as she closed and locked the door behind them.

"Somewhere special," Veronica said. "I can tell you more in the car. Hurry."

As the rain stopped, a siren wailed in the distance. They walked back to the car. It took Jim a couple of seconds to identify the sensation rising inside him.

It was hope.

They slipped through, Trix thought. She was sitting in the backseat again, heart thudding, and as Veronica lowered herself gently into the front passenger seat, Trix said, "They're somewhere else."

"Yes, dear," the woman replied. Jim was walking around the front of the car to the driver's side, and for an unsettling moment Trix felt complicit in something of which she had no knowledge.

"But you can help us find them?" she whispered.

"I can help you."

Jim opened the door and climbed in. He slipped the keys into the ignition and placed his hands on the wheel, ten to two. "So will you start telling me now?"

"I will," Veronica said. "Now that I know for sure, I will."

"Good. Where to?"

"The North End," Veronica said. "Home."

"We're going to your house?" Trix asked.

"Like I said, dear. Somewhere special."

Trix stared from the window and watched Boston passing them by, and thought about who they were with and where they were going. For some reason she'd never imagined the Oracle of Boston even *having* a home. Her grandmother had told her that story when she was barely into her teens, and the Oracle had taken on the hue of someone mystical and mysterious, one of the city's own shadows, a breath of Boston's unique air, a ghost. The story had been remarkable and felt very real, and Trix had always believed it was this, more than a thousand childhood dreams and a love of books, that had given her the open mind she had grown up with. She'd toyed with various prescriptive religions before settling into the comfortable embrace of her own beliefs. She'd once heard a ghost, and remembered the way sadness had settled around her for a brief, shattering moment as the wraith walked by. And now here she was in a shiny new Mercedes with the woman who knew Boston, and whom Boston knew.

"A long time ago, there was a man called Thomas McGee," Veronica said. Her voice had changed somewhat, as if she used different tones and inflections to relay stories, and Trix felt herself settling in to listen. "He was the Oracle at the end of the nineteenth century," the older woman continued. "The first Irish Oracle, in fact, since the Boston Brahmins had dominated up until then."

Trix frowned. "Brahmin" was such an outmoded word to describe Boston's first families and their English Protestant ancestors. She wondered how old Veronica really was, and how long she had been the Oracle.

"By all accounts McGee was a proud man," Veronica continued, "an older Irishman who'd seen his countrymen struggling toward equality against a background of bigotry and resentment. Since the middle of that century they'd filled most of the unskilled-labor jobs in the city, household domestics and the like, but as the years went on they became the backbone of Boston's industrial boom. Yet they were still looked down upon. They lived in squalor in the North End and other areas. The all-Irish neighborhoods housed whole families living in single rooms. McGee grew up through that, and after he took on the mantle of Oracle he became more determined than ever to ensure that his people lived better lives in the future."

"But as Oracle, weren't all Boston's people *his* people?" Trix asked. Maybe she had a rose-tinted view of what being Oracle meant; maybe she'd set Veronica on a pedestal higher than the position justified. Just because it was a little beyond and outside the perception of most normal people, did that mean that being Oracle implied perfection?

"Of course," Veronica said. "But McGee . . . well, no one becomes Oracle without maintaining hold of his or her earlier experiences. We are a product of our experiences after all. He was as human as I, and I'm as human as you, dear."

"So what happened?" Jim asked. He was driving quickly, paying close attention to the road, hands gripping the wheel tightly. He'd moved the rearview mirror back to its original position, and Trix had to lean to the left to catch sight of him now. But he was no longer glancing back to see if she was all right. His focus was elsewhere.

"The longer he remained Oracle, the more he witnessed events in the city around him, the more determined McGee became to ensure that the Oracle of Boston was *always* Irish."

"Are you?" Trix asked.

"No," Veronica said. "My father was English, my mother Italian. I do have *some* Irish in me, many generations old. But if Thomas McGee were alive today, he'd view me as his . . ."

"Enemy?" Trix finished for her.

"Perhaps," Veronica said, smiling enigmatically.

"What does any of this have to do with Jenny and Holly?" Jim asked. Trix knew that tone; he was barely holding back his impatience. She'd heard him like that a few times before—usually when Holly was being difficult and deadlines pressured him into being a lesser father than they all knew he was.

"Plenty," Veronica said. "Didn't I say I'd tell you what was happening?"

The car was silent, and neither of them responded. *And she shut down his rising anger just like that,* Trix thought, seeing how much more loosely Jim sat in his seat.

"Well, then," the woman continued. "Thomas McGee spent a long time planning how to pass on the responsibility of Oracle. It's not a title, as such. It's not a position that you can interview people for, or place an ad in the newspaper for when you feel your time in this world is coming to an end. The Oracle is you, as much as you are the Oracle, and it makes decisions through you."

"It's something separate?" Trix asked.

"Yes and no. The Oracle shares the soul of the city. It exists within me just as my own soul does. Though the city does not control the Oracle, it influences." Her voice was lower, darker. "It becomes a corner of your own soul, when your soul has no corners.

"McGee was the city's heart and soul for over forty years. In that time he saved countless lives, settled hearts, calmed ghosts, protected the city from dangers. He was, as far as I can tell, a good man. But he also spent a long time studying magicks that no Oracle should ever need. Druid ceremonial chants, Native American magic, Chinese and Eastern European spells, and much, much more. He accumulated a whole library of texts and parchments, purchasing them when he had to, procuring them by other means if he could. Though he could never leave the city, he sent people out to fetch what he sought. He studied and planned, and made it his aim to secure the Irish lineage of Oracles from his life forth."

"He wanted Boston to remain Irish forever," Jim said.

"Yes. He witnessed the Italians flooding the city, lessening the Irish majority, and though he was the Oracle, I believe there was always a small part of him that was still too much of what he had been before. He'd suffered hardships and discrimination, and that twisted parts of him that not even being Oracle could completely erase."

"I've never heard of him," Jim said.

"Have you ever heard of *me*?" Veronica asked.

In the backseat, Trix smiled. That had been a question she'd asked her grandmother, all those years ago. *If the Oracle's so awesome, how come everyone doesn't go to her?* And her grandmother's answer had stuck with her forever: *She's there to help people who come to her with open minds and open hearts, and who are truly in need. Others will never believe in her, and if they don't believe, they'll never find her.*

"Fair point," Jim said. "Which way?"

"Left here. Five minutes. I'll show you more then, but for now all you need to know is this: McGee tried something that no one had ever tried before, and he failed. And his failure had dire consequences.

"He performed a ritual to try to secure Boston for the Irish, to make sure the influence of Irish culture would remain and that the Oracle would always be Irish. But he toyed with magicks far beyond his capacity to control, and his meddling splintered the city. No one since has discovered just how he did this, because everything he used in the process was destroyed. But his ritual created a schism, splitting Boston's reality into three distinct paths: one where a Brahmin Oracle would exist, and the city reflected those influences; one where an Irish Oracle persisted; and one, this world we know, where the Oracle is chosen by the city, as was always intended."

"What happened to McGee?" Trix asked, though she thought the answer was almost inevitable.

"I believe he died," Veronica said. Trix hadn't been expecting that. *Doesn't she know for sure?* she wondered.

"And these Bostons," Jim said, gesturing at the windshield as if to indicate all three. "What are they? *Where* are they?"

"They're here and now, but beyond the reach of most," Veronica said. "Alternate paths. Histories, presents, and futures created by McGee's dabbling. He smashed reality and replaced it without most people noticing. It's possible he changed things—thousands might have ceased to exist, and thousands more been dragged into existence, though there's no way of telling."

"But how could he do that and not change the whole world?" Trix asked. "If he changes Boston . . ."

"They're alternate paths, and in the other Bostons the worlds beyond are subtly different, too," the old woman said. "But only insofar as they're affected by Boston. He split this city into three new worlds, but Boston is the heart of the change. Its differences seep into the wider world. He made it one of the most important cities ever, and most Bostonians don't even know."

"Jesus Christ," Jim muttered. He stopped at traffic signals and glanced back over his shoulder, and Trix expected to see his weary cynicism souring his face. But he looked excited and hopeful, the emotions sheltered but definitely there. She knew him well enough to see that.

"You think Jenny and Holly have slipped through to one of these other worlds?" Trix asked.

"Our world, but an alternate path," Veronica said. "And yes, that is what happened."

"How?" Trix asked. "Why? In that bookshop? How come no one saw, or raised the alarm? Why them? What happened to them, do they know, will they . . . Will they be scared?"

Veronica turned in her seat, shifting sideways so that she could look comfortably at Trix. Jim glanced nervously at her, as if expecting her to do something terrible or unexpected. But the woman simply remained there, staring at Trix as something changed in her eyes. *She's seeking,* Trix thought, unsure where the idea came from. But it seemed to fit. Veronica was in the car with them, but part of her was elsewhere as well.

"Trix, you were cold and wet and alone," she said. "You tried to grab the branch, but it was slippery, wet from the rain and slick with moss. You tried for a long time, kicking against the current. Kicking against the depths pulling you down."

Trix suddenly felt very cold. She gasped, shock stealing her breath.

"Every time you grabbed the branch you held on tighter, but when you tried to pull yourself out, it always slipped away. Because you *weren't* grasping tighter, you were holding on *weaker*. You were fading. You knew it, but you refused to panic." She leaned toward Trix, almost kneeling on the front seat now. "Am I right, Trix?"

"Yes," Trix tried to say, but it came out as little more than a breath.

"How old were you?"

"Seven. My grandparents told me not to go too close to the river. We were on vacation in Baxter State Park in Maine. They were in the cabin getting dinner, and I . . . I went for a walk."

"Too close to the river," Veronica said.

"Yeah." Trix remembered seeing the branch above her for the last time, shattered into a hundred slivers as she slipped below the water and sunlight glancing from the surface rippled her vision. Something grabbed her then and dragged her away, her limbs trailing through plants and weeds growing across the riverbed, though she could not grab hold of anything. She remembered wondering why, with hands so small and strong, nothing would let her hold on. And then after that things were dark and lost, until the sun prized her eyelids apart and her grandfather was crying above her.

"In the other Bostons . . . I don't know if you drowned in that river at the age of seven, or died at a later age in an entirely separate incident. But in both of the other Bostons, you no longer exist."

"Three years ago," Trix said. "I had a bad car crash." A chill went through her, raising goosebumps on her arms. For an instant too short to be measured she felt totally, utterly alone, little more than the memory of a name in the cool vastness of space. Then Jim adjusted the mirror again so he could see her, and his kind eyes brought her back.

"You died there, Trix," Veronica said. "But here you live. And that makes you one of a handful." She turned back to Jim. "You, too."

"Jim?" Trix asked.

"Meningitis when I was six," he said. "My mother always told a story about me fading away and then coming back again. I died, she told me. They brought me back."

"And so they did," Veronica said. "But in those other Bostons, death caught up with you, either that day or some other. You're both Uniques. Most people exist across realities, but not you. And that gives you a certain freedom that those people don't have."

"What freedom?" Trix asked.

"To dream. You're missing over there, but perhaps when you sleep, you know those other worlds."

"The paintings," Trix said, and she saw Jim's gentle nod. The cityscapes that haunted them both were more real than they could have imagined.

"We're here," Veronica said, gesturing through the windshield. "Third house along. Come inside, and I'll show you."

Jim pulled up to the curb and put the car in park, killing the engine. "Just tell me," he said. "Please, just tell me."

"It is possible that you'll see them again," Veronica said. "That's what you want to know, isn't it? But much will depend on what the two of you do next."

Standing at the front door, feeling Jim slip his hand into hers while Veronica fumbled with a set of keys, Trix had a very definite image in her mind of what to expect in an Oracle's home. There would be walls lined with books and framed maps, both old and new. There would be a wealth of artifacts from Boston's past—many of them rare, some perhaps believed lost to antiquity. There would be dark, shadow-clogged rooms with high-backed leather chairs, a liquor cabinet, perhaps, and the carpets would be worn by generations of honored footsteps. Perhaps the place would be slightly run-down, in need of a spring cleaning, but the accumulated dust would be a sign of just how crammed the building was with evidence of a wonderful history. An Oracle was a human as well, and there would be a kitchen and dining area with a well-stocked fridge and pantry. And upstairs, perhaps she slept in a four-poster bed, her window open to the night so that she could hear the pained requests and sad wishes of those in the city who believed.

But as Veronica pushed the door open, Trix realized quickly that her preconceptions were about to be shot down.

The hallway was light and airy, the stairwell rising above them to an atrium window on the third floor. Moonlight flooded in, silvering the walls and dark wooden staircases. The floor was light oak and the furnishings spare: a phone table, a chair, a coatrack with a lone umbrella propped in the stand.

"Please, come in," Veronica said. "Hang your coats. The rack's by a radiator so they'll dry."

"Where are we going?" Jim asked.

Veronica closed the door behind them and smiled gently at Trix. "There's a room upstairs," she said. "I'll lead you. It's where Thomas McGee tried to cast his abominable spells, and where he probably died."

"Probably?"

"It was his library. His study. This whole house." She waved one hand to indicate the building around them, taking in all the rooms whose doors they could see and others they could not. "He could have used any room, but he chose that one. And every time I even walk by the closed door, I know why."

"You sound afraid," Trix said.

"The room . . . fascinates me," she said softly, and

then without further explanation she started up the staircase.

Jim followed without even sparing Trix a glance. *He thinks he's close,* she thought. *He must be terrified that she's lied, or is mad, but he can't ignore the idea that every second takes us one step closer to getting them back.*

Trix climbed the stairs after Jim, and soon Veronica stood on the landing outside a closed door. She was pale, and the effect was not simply moonlight on her skin. The gentle artificial light emphasized the bags beneath her eyes, and the skin hanging on to her jawline seemed to defy gravity's best efforts. Her eyes were wide, and there was a sheen of perspiration across her brow. "You don't have to—" Trix began, but Veronica quickly cut her off, harsh and berating.

"Of course I do!" She reached out and opened the door. "There's a small anteroom, then another doorway. An attempt at privacy, put in by Thomas McGee, I suspect. Just . . . just look for now. Look and see, and you'll believe me. You might not understand . . . but you'll believe. Then come to the living room downstairs, because I have something to give you."

"What?"

"Two letters." Veronica swayed past them and started down the stairs; she seemed to strengthen a little, and a smile crept over her face.

Trix suddenly felt abandoned.

Jim grabbed her hand and nodded at the open door. Inside, in the shadows, she could see a second closed door. A strange smell emerged—old, wet ash, and something less identifiable, like the scent of fallen pine needles but more sour.

"Are we doing the right thing?" she asked softly, and Jim scoffed.

"You're the one who—" But he stopped mid-sentence, his face softening. "Trix, if there's any clue, *any* chance that I can know what happened to them"—he looked at the doorway—"however crazy . . ."

"We have to take that chance," she said.

"Yeah. We have to." Holding Trix's hand, Jim reached for the inner door.

6

With a Wonder and a Wild Desire

As Jim pushed the door inward, he felt resistance, as though the air pressure was different on the other side. It opened with a sigh, a musty breath escaping from within, and he thought of Carter discovering the tomb of Tutankhamen. He entered, and Trix followed a step behind.

The only light came from behind them, providing just enough illumination to make out the ragged outline of a broken chair, and to see that the rough wooden floor seemed to have been blackened by flame. Then Trix made a murmur of discovery and clicked on a light-switch, and a ceiling fixture on the other side of the room blazed to life.

"Holy shit," Jim whispered.

Trix stepped up beside him, and the two of them looked around the room, unnerved. It was not merely the floor that had been blackened by fire, or at least scorched by a blast of blistering heat. Bookshelves had partially collapsed, leaving piles of books on the floor beneath them that looked like little more than ash sculptures. On the shelves that were intact, some of the books looked as though the fire had been a hungry animal, gnawing away the bindings and leaving scorched pages exposed. Others had their bindings intact, but they were only partially legible.

Jim took several steps toward the nearest shelf and saw that, beneath a sooty film, leather bindings on some of the older volumes had crinkled and tightened, but he could make out words in foreign languages he did not speak and arcane symbols he understood even less.

He turned to see that Trix had gone in the other direction. Some kind of sideboard had once abutted the wall there, only the rear legs still in evidence, fused to the wall. Jutting from the wall itself was a pattern of what he first took to be more strange designs, but then he recognized what appeared to be a copper coil, along with what might have been a sailor's sextant and several other strange instruments. They were set into the wall as though it had once been wet cement and the objects had been pressed into the surface before it dried. Yet here the wall looked almost as though the wood had melted and run like candle wax.

The chair between them was actually only half of a chair, burnt so badly that the legs were thin and brittle sticks of charcoal. Beyond it, at the center of the room, the floor was streaked with a grayish white starburst pattern. Jim dragged the toe of his shoe through it and found it greasy and chalky at the same time, like creosote built up inside a fireplace.

Yet the most startling thing about the room had nothing to do with its ruinous state. The starburst pattern in its center was really only half of a shape. The destruction of the premises ended halfway across the room, and the other half appeared entirely untouched by whatever had occurred there.

Over Jim's head hung a light fixture whose metal arms had been wilted by incredible heat. But on the other side of the room was an identical fixture, controlled by the switch Trix had turned on, whose only flaw was a layer of dust. A similar sheen of dust covered the wooden floorboards over there. The bookshelves remained untouched by the event that had ravaged the part of the room where Jim and Trix stood. A small writing desk stood in one corner, a pile of books upon it. One volume lay open on the desk.

Trix came over beside Jim. They stood in silence, shoulders almost touching, the tips of their shoes nearly meeting the line that separated the ruined half of the room from the part that had been preserved. "This just isn't possible," Trix said.

Jim glanced at her. For a moment they searched each other's eyes, wordlessly acknowledging the obvious— that neither of them felt capable of judging what was and wasn't possible anymore. Trix looked away first, shaking her head, then took the initial step into the unmarred side of the room. Nothing happened. The place seemed solid and ordinary except for the obvious fact of its impossible half ruin. "It's like someone cut the room in half," Jim said.

"No," Trix replied, walking over to the writing desk and examining the book that lay open there. "It's like half the room was here for . . . whatever did all this damage—McGee's fuckup—and the other half of the room was somewhere else."

She flipped a page in the book, then turned to look at him, a kind of almost panic dancing in her eyes. "Magic."

Jim flinched at the word. Veronica's story had sounded like some kind of bizarre fairy tale, but the room around them was tangible, the evidence of the impossible undeniable. Now he took a steadying breath and crossed the room as well, heading for the door set in the opposite wall, beside the writing desk.

The knob turned easily and he pushed it open, hope surging in the moment when the hinges creaked and the light from the ceiling fixture spilled into the next room. But beyond the door he discovered no passage into other worlds. Instead, he took a single step across the threshold into a small, dust-coated bedroom decorated with antique furniture and piled with boxes. Two old television sets sat on the floor, abandoned. Across the small room was yet another door, this one partially open, and a small amount of light seeped in, revealing a set of narrow servants' stairs that likely went down to the kitchen or pantry on the floor below.

Jim turned back into the half-ravaged room. Veronica had taken them into a damned bookstore in Copley Place and claimed that his wife and daughter had vanished from that very spot, just slipped into a parallel world, as though talk of such things was ordinary conversation and the existence of variable dimensions was something only a fool would deny. But Jim had gone along with her because he had no other alternative— Trix had led him to that circle of cobblestones by the State Street station, they had asked the city for help, and this woman had heard them. Even so, he had felt as though his every step took him deeper into a nightmare.

This room, though . . . this was real.

"Trix," he said.

She glanced up from the old leather-bound book, looking pale and queasy. Then she stepped away from the desk as if the book might bite her. She turned to stare across the room at the door through which they had first entered. "This is all real."

"You're the one who knew about her," Jim said. "You didn't believe her?"

Trix laughed uneasily. "Finding someone you've lost track of, or the truth about a girlfriend you think might be getting beaten up by her husband . . . yeah, I can wrap my brain around *that*. You can chalk that up to, like, some kind of psychic powers or something. But this— magic spells and splintered cities—seems so crazy."

Jim shut the door he had opened and walked to the center of the room. He stared down at the place where the undamaged floorboards met scorched and glassy wood, and then at the starburst pattern where it appeared something had burned hottest of all, and possibly exploded.

Something like Thomas McGee.

He looked at the charred remnant of what had apparently been the only chair in the room, and then he turned to Trix, surprised to find a smile beginning to spread across his face. "If this is true—"

"Then the rest of it . . . ," Trix said, faltering as if she was afraid to finish the thought. She glanced back at the magic book, then started for the scorched door, new purpose in her stride. "Come on. Veronica's waiting."

Jim took one last look at that spot in the center of the room, then hurried after her.

Trix found Veronica in the front parlor, where she had just set out a tea tray with service for three and a plate of Pepperidge Farm cookies. The elegant old woman glanced up guiltily, as though she'd been caught at something awkward. "I know they're nothing special," Veronica said, "but they're my favorites. And, honestly, I couldn't bake anything edible to save my life."

Trix stopped just inside the room and stared at her, uncomprehending.

"It's all right," Jim said, sweeping past her and perching on the edge of a chair by the coffee table. "We're not exactly invited guests. And we don't have time for courtesies."

Only then did Trix realize that the old woman had been talking about the cookies. Veronica's concern for such a thing seemed surreal in the midst of the nightmare she and Jim were living—an absurd attempt at the ordinary.

"Tell us what we need to do," Jim said.

As Veronica poured tea, Trix stepped into the room. "Hold on," she said. "I need to slow down a second."

Jim shot her a hard look. "You saw that room. I know you were thinking the same thing I was. We don't have *time* to slow down."

Trix sat on the love seat across from him. Veronica poured tea and offered them both cups, and though eager to move on, they both accepted. Veronica took her own teacup and sat on the love seat beside Trix, exhaling as she settled in, staring at her, the plate, and Trix again.

Trix smiled and took a cookie, and Jim plucked one up as well.

"Which one of you will carry my letters?" Veronica asked, sipping her tea as though all of this was perfectly normal.

"I'll do whatever you need me to do," Jim said. "Just tell us how we get to where Jenny and Holly are."

Trix noticed he'd chosen his words carefully. He might have accepted what Veronica had told them as the truth, but he wasn't ready to say it out loud, and she didn't blame him. Not caring whether or not she was being rude, she set her cup and saucer down. "We need to know what we're walking into," Trix said, looking at Jim before she focused on Veronica. "Please, ma'am."

"I've already explained—" Veronica began.

"I know," Trix interrupted. "And I know Jim is ready. This is his wife and daughter we're talking about, and he'll jump headfirst into hell for them."

"And you won't?" Jim said. "You love her, too."

Trix blinked, surprised at the bold acknowledgment from him. His tone made clear he wasn't talking about the love of a friend. She nodded but kept her focus on Veronica. "Of course I'll go," Trix said. "But I just need to understand."

"Understand what?" Agitated, Jim sloshed a bit of tea and it pooled in his saucer. As if only now realizing the cup was in his hands, he set it on the table.

"Why here?" Trix said. "Is this the only place this has happened? And have people crossed over before? Uniques, I mean. That's what you called us, right? Have Uniques crossed over before, and come back?"

As if the kindly-hostess persona had been a mask she could peel away, Veronica's entire mien changed. She sipped her tea again but sat up straighter, her eyes narrowing and seeming to grow darker. "There have been moments in history when reality has strained and splintered," she said, taking an almost professorial tone. "Such moments can create schismatic realities. Usually these revolve around a particular locus, the point of origin of the schism. One took place in Boston in 1890."

Veronica paused, studying them. "You want to understand how this happened? What the other two Bostons might be like, should you enter them?"

Trix nodded. "Exactly."

"I've dreamed of those other places," Jim said.

"Nightmares," Trix said.

"Uniques do tend to dream across realities, I suspect because a part of them is missing in those alternate worlds."

"So tell us," Jim said.

Veronica was the last to surrender her tea. She set it down on the table. Now all three cups were forgotten. Three cookies remained on the plate. "Quickly, then," she said, straightening up. "A variety of circumstances, most prominently the nearness of New York, conspired to prevent Boston from becoming a major center of immigration in the late eighteenth and early ninteenth centuries. In the 1840s, two elements conspired to change that. First, it was determined that the best way for mail to reach Canada was through the port of Boston, making transportation to our fair city from Liverpool and Dublin astonishingly cheap. Second, land evictions and the potato famine sent tens of thousands of Irish fleeing their own country. They arrived in Boston with no money, no skills, and nowhere else to go.

"I imagine you're familiar enough with what the lives of Irish immigrants were like in that era. They filled the city, lived in poverty. But over time that began to change, as the Irish populated the police force and worked their way into Boston politics, and the city became divided between the Yankees—they were called the Brahmins back then—and the Irish working class. And then, in the 1880s and 1890s, the Italians began to arrive." Veronica waved a hand to indicate not only the house around her but the entire neighborhood.

"The North End had been purely Irish, but in just a handful of years it was transformed. Ten thousand Irish moved out, and fifteen thousand Italians moved in."

Trix studied her eyes, the lines in her face. "And that's why Thomas McGee did what he did."

Veronica nodded. "The Italians were flooding in, and the influence of the Irish began to wane. The Brahmins had never allowed them a seat at the table. But in McGee, the soul of the city had chosen an Irishman as its Oracle. Boston had an Irish spirit in that era, but McGee knew that could change."

"So he wasn't supposed to choose the next Oracle?" Jim asked.

"This isn't science," Veronica said. "I don't know the entire history of all of the Oracles of the Great Cities of the World, but certainly an Oracle can train his or her heir, *if* the Oracle has the best interests of the city at heart. McGee feared that when he died the soul of the city would supersede his choice."

Trix nodded, gesturing for her to move on. "We know this part. McGee splintered the city, so where there was one, now there were three."

"Yes," Veronica said, holding up a hand and counting them on her fingers. "First is this Boston, the one you know. Let's call it Boston A. As far as I know it is unaffected, the city the way it would have been without McGee's botched magic. The other two are the splinters, their realities somewhat weaker for that. In Boston B, the Oracles have been Irish ever since McGee, and the city has developed for the past twelve decades or so under heavy Irish influence. In Boston C, the opposite happened, with the Irish all but absent, and the city developing under the guidance of the Brahmins but without the tempering influences of its immigrant working class."

"You've been there," Jim said eagerly. "To these other Bostons."

"As Oracle, I can never leave my city. My Boston. But I've met those who have traveled from one to the other—"

"Like Jenny and Holly," Trix supplied.

Veronica shook her head. "Not really. Well, perhaps like Holly."

"What do you mean?" Jim asked worriedly.

"Holly is a Unique, of course," Veronica said. "In the other two Bostons, there was no Jim to fall in love with Jenny. In those cities, Holly Banks was never born."

Jim looked as though he might be sick. "And Jenny?"

"No. There are facets of Jenny."

"Facets," Jim murmured, like he was testing the word on his tongue.

"So it doesn't happen often?" Trix prodded. "People like Jenny, who aren't Uniques, crossing over?"

Veronica seemed to consider her words a moment before forging onward. "Think of the cities as all existing in the same location, just slightly out of sync with one another. A kind of membrane separates them, and that is called the In-Between. It's a limbo place, a vast nothing, but it . . . I suppose you could say that it breathes. Better yet, imagine the sea, waves rolling up onto the shore. When there is a storm or some other disturbance, the tide rises higher, sweeps farther inland before it withdraws and pulls things out to sea. The membrane can be like that. It expanded into our Boston for just a moment, and when it drew back it took Jenny and Holly with it. On rare occasions people *have* been pulled across. Where the cities are identical, those people vanish from one Boston and appear in the same spot in the other. But where the cities are different . . . sometimes there are voids, and there have been cases of people being dragged into the In-Between and lost there."

"Jenny and Holly . . . ," Jim began.

"No. That is why I wanted you to take me to the bookstore where they vanished. The store exists in all three Bostons. Jenny and Holly have not been lost in the void. They're in one of those other Bostons right now, probably very confused and very afraid, but alive."

"So, how do we go after them?" Trix asked.

"I'll show you the way," Veronica said. "The existence of a Jenny in each world provides a kind of counter-pressure on that membrane that works to hold each facet in its place. But Uniques have little more than expectation and perception holding them in place. If you know how to look for the other Bostons, how to see the places where they are different, you can walk through in places where others would be lost to the void."

"But which Boston are they in?" Jim asked. "The Irish or the Brahmin?"

"That," Veronica said, "is something the two of you will have to find out for me." She corrected herself. "For *yourselves*."

Trix studied the old woman. "The people this has happened to before—have any of them ever come back?"

Veronica shook her head. "I'm afraid not. But usually they are never missed. Ordinary people, those with facets in the other Bostons, never even know that they've lost someone. The splintered cities change around them. The two of you both remember Jenny and Holly because you're Uniques. The rest of this world has forgotten them. They've been erased."

"Erased," Jim repeated, his voice hollow. "Jesus. That sounds so permanent. What happens when we bring them back? Is it even possible to bring them back?"

Veronica's expression turned darker than ever. She turned to look out the night-black window. "There are thin places where you might get them through. Once I show you how to see properly, you'll be able to tell." She glanced upward to indicate the half-burned study. "But now that you understand, there's something else you need to know."

"What's that?" Jim asked.

"Every time someone is drawn from one Boston to an-other—someone with facets in the other cities—the schism deteriorates more. And if Jenny encounters her other facets, which seems likely, given that she and Holly will be searching for traces of the life they've known, that will exacerbate the situation."

"What do you mean, the schism is deteriorating?" Trix asked.

"I suspect that the three Bostons might be reintegrating."

"Wouldn't that be a good thing?" Jim said. "This is all . . . well, it's unnatural, isn't it? What this McGee did? It's not supposed to be like this, so what's wrong with it all going back to normal? With there being only one Boston?"

"It could be a good thing," Veronica said, glancing away as if distracted, "but there's also a chance that the city would be left in ruins."

Trix stared at her a moment, then reached out and drank her tea down, wishing it was whiskey.

"So, you're saying Jenny and Holly being over there could trigger this thing?" Jim said.

"No," Veronica said, "it's happening already. But they could speed up the process. I may be able to stop the deterioration, but not alone. I need the help of the Oracles of the other Bostons, but I can't pass through into their cities myself. I've written letters to them, intending to find a Unique ally who would carry them for me."

Trix nodded. "That's why you said this was providential, us coming to you."

"It does seem that some greater power is at work here, yes." She smiled, and Trix couldn't help thinking her expression skull-like.

"You want us to deliver these letters to the two other Oracles," Jim said.

"And they will help you locate Jenny and Holly," Veronica replied.

Jim stood. "Come on, Trix. We know all we need to know. We're wasting time." He looked at Veronica. "Show us, please. Show us how to cross over. And give us those letters. We'll deliver them for you."

Veronica exhaled, and Trix saw a flicker of something pass across her face. Fear? She thought not. It was something lighter but deeper.

"Remember to hurry," Veronica said. "And you must not give the letters to *anyone* but the Oracles themselves, and only at the addresses on the envelopes."

"The Oracles don't live in the same building in each Boston?" Jim asked, waving a hand around them.

"Of course not," Veronica said. "Too dangerous. A catastrophe across the In-Between could wipe out this place, and all three of us, at the same time."

"Right," Jim said, uncertain and unsettled.

"And *do not* open the letters yourselves," Veronica continued. "In addition to my warnings and pleas for help, there are incantations that the other Oracles will need to protect our cities. But if an ordinary person were to read them . . . well, without a mastery of such things, you could accidentally trigger an immediate and total integration."

"And destroy the city," Trix said. "Right. Important safety tip."

Jim glanced over at her in surprise at the reference— a quote from *Ghostbusters*—and smiled. "We can do this, right?" he said.

"We have to," Trix replied.

"Or die trying."

Trix grimaced. "Aren't you just a ray of fuckin' sunshine?"

By the time they had returned to McGee's study, the lightness of that single moment had been forgotten. Jim stood in the center of the room, one foot on scorched wood and the other on whole, undamaged floorboards, and felt a dreadful trepidation. Hours ago, the things he had been forced by circumstance to believe would have seemed absolutely absurd. Fantasy. Now, even as he straddled the two sides of that room, he felt torn between the fear that Veronica's story might be the product of an unbalanced mind and the terror that it might all be true. Veronica unsettled him, but he had too much to lose by not doing as she asked.

Splintered cities—the barriers separating them now degrading—in danger of collision? It was daunting enough to think of finding Jenny and Holly in some parallel Boston, especially since they could be anywhere. A hundred anxieties came along with the prospect, not least of which was whether or not he could find them, and how they could all get home again. Would the world realign itself? Was reality truly that malleable? It had undergone a metamorphosis to account for Holly and Jenny no longer existing in this world, so he supposed it could happen.

Jesus, listen to yourself, he thought, staring down at the burn line in the floor, and the half-starburst pattern that—he suspected—marked the explosion that had killed Thomas McGee.

In the end, though, hope must hold sway. Jenny and Holly were the whole of his heart, existing outside of his body, and if they were now somehow elsewhere, then he would have to follow. Any other choice was inconceivable.

"Jim," Trix said, and from her tone he realized she had called his name more than once.

"Sorry," he said, turning to see her and Veronica watching him expectantly. "Were you saying something?"

Trix gave him a knowing look. He saw the pain in her eyes as she took a deep, worried breath and exhaled. Then she glanced at Veronica.

"Okay. We're listening." He patted his back pocket

where he'd folded and stored the two envelopes, unknown names and strangely familiar addresses on their fronts in surprisingly untidy script. "Tell us what we need to do."

The old woman stood at the open doorway, and every shred of her body language screamed that she did not want to be there. In the charred cavern of that half of the room, she looked almost in need of rescue herself.

"You both should be on that side of the room," Veronica said, pointing toward the end opposite her, where the writing desk remained intact and the door to the small bedroom—perhaps once servants' quarters—was tightly shut.

Jim reached out his hand to Trix. She took it, and together they crossed to the desk. They turned their backs to the desk, hands still clasped, and faced Veronica across the length of the room. "What now?" Trix asked.

"Look away from each other," Veronica began. Jim started to turn. "No," Veronica said quickly. "Not like that. Continue to face me, but let your eyes shift to one side. Stare at the wall with only your peripheral vision."

Jim let out a breath, trying to focus. He felt uneasy, until Trix squeezed his hand reassuringly. He glanced at her and nodded, and then both of them followed Veronica's instructions. Jim started by concentrating on Veronica and trying to push out of his mind how absurd the whole thing felt. He had to remind himself that he had accepted all of this, that he believed it. *You have to believe it*, he told himself.

And that was the truth. He didn't have anything else.

Facing Veronica, he glanced to his right, away from Trix, assuming she was doing the same thing. The floral wallpaper was faded, and there were water stains along the seams. He focused on the flowers and those seams.

"Still without turning your head, try to look farther back, into the very edge of your vision," Veronica said. "Your eyes will feel the strain. They may moisten or burn."

Just as she predicted, Jim's eyes hurt. He narrowed them slightly, fighting the urge to close them or to look forward.

"Keep them open. Force yourself," Veronica said. "You may feel dizzy—"

Jim had to shift his feet to maintain his balance.

"—and your vision will start to blur eventually."

"Start?" Trix said. "It's blurry as hell."

"Good," Veronica said, her voice barely a whisper, coating the room like dust. "That's very good."

Good? Jim thought. *This is bullshit. And what is that? Is she* chuckling?

"Concentrate on the blur. There will be two or three variations on what you see, one laid on top of the other, shifting, out of focus."

Jim's eyes were tearing up badly now, but he did think he could see two different variations on the wall to his right, slightly out of sync with each other. One of them had the faded floral paper and water-stained seams, but the other . . . the other blurred version of the wall was just as charred as the far side of the room, where Veronica stood.

"I see them," Trix said, startling him.

Jim's heart began to thunder in his chest. His eyes burned. He wanted to look away. But he couldn't, because this *was* real. *Oh, God, Jenny, it's real. I'm coming to get you—you and our baby girl. Just hold on.*

"Jim, do you see them, too? The variations?" Veronica demanded.

As she spoke, he noticed the third. At first it had been difficult to see, because in that variation the walls were equally scorched. "Yes," he said, hating how small and alone his voice sounded.

Trix squeezed his hand, reminding him that he was not alone after all.

"What now?" Jim asked.

"You've got to separate them visually. Shift your vision to follow only one of the variations that you know is not the image you *should* be seeing. Then begin to turn, slowly."

Jim and Trix both obeyed, still clasping hands, turning together.

"Let your eyes relax slightly. Continue focusing on your peripheral vision, but not so painfully. Uniques can see all three variations, and this should work elsewhere as well, but it will be simpler here. The parallels are more unsettled here than anywhere else in the city. You'll be able to see such places clearly after this— places where the Bostons don't quite match up. Holly is a Unique. You can teach her, as I'm teaching you. In such places, you'll be able to bring Jenny back with you."

"But the void you talked about," Trix said. "The In-Between. People get trapped there."

"You're Uniques," Veronica said, as though it was the simplest thing in the world. "You can guide her through."

As she spoke, Jim and Trix continued to turn. When he'd made it three-quarters of the way around, he could see a badly blurred Veronica in his peripheral vision . . . but there was only one of her. She existed in only one of the variations his strained vision could see.

Veronica grinned, talking again, wishing them luck, cautioning them not to forget to deliver her letters, reminding them that the fate of the city might well be at stake . . . but by then Jim found it difficult to focus on her voice. She seemed to be fading. He kept turning until he and Trix had rotated 360 degrees. The strain on his eyes was great, though he had allowed himself to focus on only one variation of the room around him, with the exception of the distraction of seeing Veronica.

"Do we stop now?" Trix asked.

Jim paused, feeling Trix do the same. They waited for a reply, but none came.

"Veronica?" Jim said. "I need to close my eyes a second."

Still no reply.

Jim ground his teeth together. The need to close his eyes made him grip Trix's hand tighter. Tears began to slide down his face.

"What do we do?" Trix asked him, and from the groan in her voice he knew she was having the same difficulty.

"Veronica?" Jim asked again, but the room felt empty now, except for Trix beside him. He squeezed her hand. "Fuck it." Closing his eyes, he held his free hand over them for a minute. Then he swore again and dropped his hand, blinking.

"Jim, look," Trix said.

He forced himself to focus, wiping the moisture from his eyes. For a second, the room seemed to spin around him. What the hell had happened? The lights were off, the only light coming from behind them. But even in the dim illumination that slipped through the partially open door—which had been closed just moments ago—he saw that the floor and the walls beside them were charred black from fire. The metal light fixture above was twisted and blackened from heat.

"How the hell . . . ," Jim began, trying to make sense of it.

Somehow they had traded places with Veronica. They

were on the scorched side of the room, though they had only turned in a circle where they stood.

"It's backward," Trix said.

Jim retreated toward the door, hitting the lightswitch beside it. The far side of the room was bathed in light from the single intact fixture. On the floor, practically melted into the wood, was half of a desk chair. Jim saw immediately that something was different about it, though it took him a moment to realize precisely what: it was the opposite half of the chair he'd seen before. The missing half.

He turned back to the door. It was narrower than the one on the other side of the room, and he knew where it led. Beside the door, against the wall, was the same writing desk, but now it had been reduced to a charred ruin, the front of it eaten away by fire and the rest blasted black.

"We're here," Trix said quietly.

Jim glanced at her and saw fear and wonder filling her gaze in equal measure. He knew she must see the same in him.

Thomas McGee's spell had gone badly awry. It had scorched the room, scouring the interior with some kind of ritual magic, an enchanted fire that had spared the rest of the house. McGee had vanished. Incinerated? Perhaps. But the room had been just as splintered as the city. In the original Boston, one half of the room had been ravaged and the other remained pristine, as though it had been snapped into place moments after the damage had been done. But in this parallel Boston, the damage was reversed, the opposite side of the room having sustained the fire damage.

Here, the other side of the room—where Veronica had been standing inside the door—was abandoned, the wallpaper badly peeling. Boxes were stacked in both of those far corners, but otherwise the room had been abandoned in this world, just as it had been in their own. Whoever owned this house had left this place alone, perhaps driven by some urge they did not understand.

"Which one are we in?" Trix asked.

"Which what?" Jim said, and then he got it. "Which Boston, you mean?" Trix nodded. "Damn good question."

Jim led the way, pushing the narrow door fully open and stepping into the small bedroom he had entered once before, in another city, in another world. Other than the fact that it still contained a bed, the room was entirely different. The walls were a bright yellow, with hand-painted flowers stretching in a curving line across three of them. The bed had a modern brass frame, with a wooden box at the foot and a handmade lace spread. The photos tucked around the frame of the mirror suggested an older girl or young woman, and the clothes that hung from the open closet door reinforced that impression.

"Shit," Trix said.

"What?"

She looked at him. "We're in someone's house. We've got to get out of here."

Jim laughed softly, more in disbelief than amusement. She was right. He'd been so astonished, his mind full of questions and trying to jump ahead and figure out how they were going to find Jenny and Holly, that he hadn't even thought to worry about what they might say to whoever might live here.

He moved to the opposite door and cracked it open, peering down the narrow steps that he had presumed led to the kitchen or pantry. The bedside lamp was still on, so whoever occupied it was probably at home. But he neither saw nor heard any sign of the residents. "All right," he whispered, turning back toward Trix. "We just have to . . ."

Staring at her, he let his words trail off. Trix had gone to the window and drawn the lace curtain aside. "Jim," she said without turning, "come here."

With a nervous glance down the stairs, he closed the door partway and hurried to her, aware now of the tiny creaks that his footfalls eked from the floorboards. Trix stepped back from the window and turned to him. She tilted her head, urging him to look, holding the curtain back for him.

Hesitating only a moment, he bent and peered out the window. For a few seconds, the view of Hanover Street only looked *off,* as though he'd been away for a while and some enterprising developer had come along and gentrified something, and he couldn't quite put his finger on what. Then he realized that nearly all the shops and restaurants were different, that the Italian flavor of the street had been erased.

But he couldn't keep his focus on the street below. His eyes were drawn higher, to the cityscape rising to the west, to a towering stone cathedral he had never seen before, and to modern skyscrapers with fluid lines and unfamiliar spires.

Not my Boston, he thought. But the cityscape *was* familiar.

Trix leaned in beside him, staring out the window as well, so close that he could feel her breath on his cheek.

"I've painted this," he said, his throat strangely dry. "One of those two *other* Bostons."

"I know," she said. "And I've been here before."

"In dreams," Jim added.

"Nightmares," Trix said, standing up, the motion drawing his gaze. "But this is real."

Jim took one last glance through the window and then let the curtain fall back into place. He hurried quietly back to the door and opened it a crack, checking again to make sure the coast was clear.

He glanced at Trix and said, "Let's go find them."

7

Within a Mile of Home

ONCE, TRIX had woken in the middle of the night to find someone standing at the foot of her bed. It was the most terrifying moment of her adult life. Lured up from dreams by a sense she could not identify, she'd lain awake for a while with her eyes still closed, certain that someone was there. Swimming in that just-woken state, which had the feel of a dream and yet seemed so real, she'd wanted to open her eyes to prove that she was wrong but also to confirm that what she sensed was true. *There's someone waiting for me to wake,* she'd thought, *and I can't open my eyes.*

And then the movement—a shuffling of feet, a rustle of clothing—and she'd opened her eyes and sat up at the same time. Her scream had been one of terror and rage, and the shadowy shape had fled the room, crashing into the door frame and leaving a dent that she had never gotten around to sanding away. *Tooth,* one of the policemen who'd come later that morning had said, examining the indentation. *With any luck it's knocked loose and the asshole will lose it.* She'd slept at Jenny and Jim's for three nights afterward, then mustered the courage to return home. A hundred "what if" scenarios had played through her mind, and sometimes they still did. *In an-*

other world you were raped and murdered, one of her friends had said in the pub one night. That comment had given her three days of nightmares, but even in those she succeeded in chasing the intruder away. It came back to her now as she crept onto the landing of a stranger's house. She knew it was not true. She had woken and scared the intruder away, and that was the *only* truth. Because she was unique.

And now she was the intruder.

She followed Jim out onto the landing and wondered if this was how that unknown man had felt as he'd worked his way through her house—breath held, feet settling lightly in case of creaking floorboards, heart thumping. But she thought not. She had not chosen to be an intruder, and she took no delight in it at all.

The layout of this house was different from Veronica's home. Something about it felt the same—occupying the same space, perhaps, or maybe the general shape and substance echoed the building back in the world they'd just left. But if it *had* once been the same building, someone had spent a lot of time and effort expanding and enlarging it.

The landing cornered around the gallery staircase, and as they reached the head of the stairs Trix paused, listening. She touched Jim's shoulder and he stopped, too, glancing back at her, then down into the hallway below once again. She could see the silvery flicker of a TV screen spilling from one of the rooms down there, and she heard the gentle laughter of someone relaxed at home.

She leaned to her right and looked through a partially open doorway, then froze when she saw the girl—a teenager, maybe fifteen years old, lying back on her bed with one hand behind her head, the other resting on her stomach, fingers tapping gently. Trix saw the wire snaking across the bed to the small device on the table. In the half-light, she could not make out the headphones.

Jim put his finger to his lips and started down the stairs. Trix followed, and as they descended she felt a curious weight growing around them. At first she thought it was caused by her shallow breathing and thumping heart, or the darkness, or the reality of where they were—somewhere different. But as Jim stepped down into the hallway and the girl upstairs started shouting, she realized what it was. The fear of impending discovery was solidifying all around them.

"I'll never . . . see the likes . . . of you . . . again!" the girl screamed from behind them, and as Trix glanced back and up she thought for a surreal moment that the girl meant them. *She sees our strangeness, the fact that we're from somewhere else and don't belong here, and*— But the landing was empty. The teenager was singing.

Jim clasped Trix's arm and squeezed, calling her attention. She looked back at him. He was nodding to the front door, five paces away across the oak-floored hallway. His eyes were wide open, pupils dilated, and she could almost smell the fear coming off him. *Not scared of being caught,* she thought, *but frightened of what that would mean for Jenny and Holly.*

At that moment, Trix vowed that they would *not* be caught here. Whether or not they slipped out without being seen, they would not be caught. She clenched her fists and pressed her lips tight together, and then a voice came from the TV room. "What's the point of a personal stereo if you don't keep your voice to yourself?" the man said, not unkindly. It sounded as if he was smiling as he spoke.

"They call them iPods now, dear."

"Well, forgive me for—"

The girl shouted again, tone-deaf and enjoying every line of whatever she was listening to.

"Go," Jim whispered.

"Jim, we could"—Trix pointed back beneath the gallery staircase. It was dark back there, two doors half-closed on shadowy rooms.

"No," he interrupted. "We need to get out of here."

Somewhere in one of those rooms, a dog growled. *Oh, fuck,* Trix thought, *that's just what we need.*

"Go and ask her to turn it down, sweetness," the man's voice said.

"You go! Lazy bastard."

"I'm watching the game!"

More shouting from upstairs. It was so out of tune that Trix smiled to herself, but then Jim pulled at her, taking his first step across the hallway.

The dog's growls became louder. Soon it would start barking.

Come on! Jim mouthed, taking another step.

The dog barked, the teenager shouted the first line of a new song, and a woman appeared in the living room doorway before them, smiling softly.

Trix wanted to say something to her. Tell her they weren't a threat, they didn't mean any harm, they'd just come through and only wanted to leave the family in peace. But she felt her own jaw drop open in stunned shock, and these words lived only in her mind. Jim's fingers closed tighter on her arm, and she leaned forward, ready to dash to the front door and escape out onto the street.

"Conor!" the woman shouted. "There's someone in the house." Her eyes flickered to the left, and Trix followed her gaze. A dog was emerging from one of the back rooms, still in shadows but glittering eyes and wet, bared teeth visible. It was a terrier, compact and coiled, and she knew she should not let its size deceive her.

The woman looked back at Trix, caught her attention. Trix smiled.

"Otis, sic!" the woman shouted, and the dog came for them.

Jim ran for the door and flipped the catch, and Trix went with him. As he was hauling on the door she turned and lifted her foot, an unconscious defensive gesture, because in her mind's eye the dog was already leaping through the air, teeth bared and ready to sink into her shin.

"What the fuck are you doing in here!" a man shouted, and a shadow suddenly filled the doorway behind the woman. *Holy shit, he's seven feet tall!* Trix thought, and though perhaps panic made him seem taller than he actually was, he was certainly big enough to do them both a lot of damage.

The dog had not pounced. It was hunkered down, hackles bristling, teeth still bared.

"We're not here to cause a problem!" Trix said, and behind her Jim opened the door at last.

The man was stepping past the woman, moving her gently to one side with a protective arm pressed across her chest. His other arm hung at his side, hand fisted into something resembling the head of a sledgehammer.

"Trix," Jim said softly.

"What?" another voice said. The girl stood at the head of the stairs, headphones still on and the music player clasped in her hand. Her mouth hung open in surprise, eyes flickering from Trix and Jim to the dog to her parents, then back again.

"We're leaving," Jim said.

"Damn right you are!" the man shouted, and he darted across the hallway. The dog leapt then, tangling in the man's feet and sending him stumbling toward them, hands outstretched, eyebrows rising in surprise as momentum threw him forward.

Jim tugged Trix through the doorway, and the man's left hand closed around its edge, clasping tight to prevent himself from falling over. Trix saw the dog cowering back against the lowest stair, ears flat against its head, head lowered, eyes staring up at the big man. Behind and above them, the teenager seemed frozen in place.

"Trix, *run*!" Jim said, and he pulled her out into the dark. She turned her attention from the shocked and angry family behind them to the ground beneath her feet, startled by the three steps down to the street that had not been there before. Jim's Mercedes was no longer parked at the curb—of course not—and in its place stood a big station wagon, glittering with droplets of rain.

They hit the sidewalk and turned right, running along the street, listening for sounds of pursuit, and Trix wondered whether Jim was feeling as dislocated as she. There were no obvious differences around them, at least not immediately. But she felt not only that she had not been here before, but never *could* have been. She glanced back at the home they had just left—Veronica's house, in another world—and it was nowhere near the same. The front door still stood open but no one looked out, and she wondered at the scene taking place in there right now. The wife calling the police, perhaps, husband bristling, dog slinking back into one of those dark rooms, the teenager watching from above with a kind of detached surprise. At least they weren't following. At least—

A shadow appeared at the open doorway, big enough to be the man. And he had something in his hand.

"Jim, gun!" Trix said, and they ran faster. Surely he wouldn't fire at them in the street? Would he really shoot at them at all, even though they'd actually done nothing? With every step she expected to hear the sharp report of a pistol and feel the bullet's impact, and by the time they rounded a corner she was panting hard, fear running cold down her back.

"Keep running," Jim said. "Just in case."

"In case he's following?"

"It's not as if we can explain," he said, and it was as close to humor as either of them could find right now.

They ran on, side by side now, and Trix realized what an unlikely pair of joggers they would make. Jim was wearing jeans and a dark button-fronted shirt, having left his jacket in Veronica's living room. And she wore tight black trousers stitched with several zips, a vest top, and a light jacket. Running, they were so obviously fleeing something that they might as well have painted "guilty" on their foreheads.

At the next road junction she grabbed Jim's hand and pulled him left, then leaned against a high timber fence and tried to catch her breath. "Can't keep running," she said, and he nodded his understanding.

"We'd know by now if he was coming after us," Jim said, glancing nervously back the way they had come. He was panting, as was Trix, but she thought it was more out of surprise and fear than exertion.

"So what now?" she asked, though she had already figured where Jim's first instincts would take him. He'd promised to deliver those letters, yes, and they'd both sworn not to open them. But Jim had *not* promised to go directly to this Boston's Oracle. Veronica must have known that he never would, and had not burdened him with the need to break that promise. In Trix's eyes, that gave the old woman more of a human aspect than anything else she'd said or done.

"Now we find Jenny and Holly," Jim said. "My apartment, your place, Jenny's parents'. The first thing she'd do is go somewhere familiar. If this is even the Boston they slipped into."

"If *anywhere's* familiar," Trix said. "Don't you feel . . . ?" She shrugged, because exactly what she felt was difficult to express.

"Yeah," he said, glancing around at the buildings surrounding them. There was nothing too unusual about them, no unique construction methods or materials. But Trix felt totally out of place here. Perhaps it was a combination of many smaller factors—the air carrying an unusual taint, the sky hazed with a different level of pollution, the echoes of unknown voices singing on the breeze—that made her shiver. It was as if they were being watched, and it was not the last time she would imagine that.

That cityscape, she thought, able to dwell on it for the first time. *It's one of those I've had nightmares about— one of those Bostons where I'm now dead—and Jim has painted it, and it's almost like . . .*

As they turned from Prince Street onto Hanover—the smells of the North End's restaurants almost inescapably tempting—a car cruised by, three teenagers inside singing along cheerfully to a song pumping out of the radio speakers. One of the girls looked at Trix and smiled. They sang in English. It surprised Trix, though it shouldn't have. This city might be some kind of parallel world, but it was still Boston.

"We need to get a cab," Jim said.

"Yeah. Carless now." She watched the teens' car drift along the street.

"It's going to be nearly impossible to get one here.

Maybe out on the main road, whatever it is that runs over the Big Dig. Otherwise we can head toward Quincy Market. It'll be easy enough to find a cab there. That's probably better, getting some distance, just in case those people called the cops."

"And if they have?" Trix said. "What would we do? How would we explain who we are?"

"We'd just . . . ," Jim said, voice disappearing into a shrug.

"In this Boston, we're both dead," she said. "Husks in the ground, or dust if our families had us cremated." She shook her head, trying to absorb the strangeness of that truth. *Every breath I take contains molecules I've breathed before in another body.*

"I don't care," he said. His face changed little; there was no dawning realization, only acceptance. "I'm only here for one thing." As he turned from her, she saw him check that the two folded envelopes were still in his back pocket. Each had been marked with a name and an address, and she was keen to check them out right away. But this was all for Jim. For now, she would follow his lead.

Less than ten minutes later they flagged down a cab on North Street. The driver was a big, cheerful Irishman, and he turned down the Celtic-punk CD just enough to be able to shout over it. Something about this comforted Trix, though at first she couldn't quite place what it was. Jim shouted his apartment address, the driver waved a hand and pulled out into traffic, and the music provided a drum-and-fiddle theme to their journey. It was as the Irishman started shouting about roadwork and how the city still wasn't spending enough on road maintenance that she was able to sink back into her seat and relax. *He doesn't see anything different about us,* she thought.

To him we're normal. Clasping Jim's hand, she closed her eyes and rested.

I wonder if Trix is feeling this as well, Jim thought. The sense of being followed was subtle, an itch on the back of his neck and a tightening across his scalp. He did not turn around to look back; all he'd see would be headlights, vague shapes walking along pavements, shadows in this place where he should never be. The feeling was slight. And besides, whoever followed them would be at home in those shadows.

He looked forward past the big driver at the streets unrolling ahead. Trix's hand felt solid and real in his, and he gave her a slight squeeze, smiling when she squeezed back. The driver was speaking, but his words were all but lost in the rush of music blasting from the speakers. Amid such cacophony, Jim found it ironically easy to rest and gather his thoughts.

From what he'd seen of the skyline from the upstairs window in the house they had just fled, this Boston looked quite different from the city where he had been born. How strange that a few significant changes could affect the view so fundamentally, even though ninety-five percent of the city was probably nearly identical.

Yet already he felt so much closer to Jenny and Holly. He and Trix had come through into this reality from another, stepping across the threshold with little more than watery eyes and a sense of shock at their accomplishment, and maybe somewhere in this Boston, Jenny and Holly were breathing, living, striving to discover what had happened to them and waiting for him to find them again. Though this was a strange city, the sense of being an invader here was rapidly fading away.

He could feel the folded letters in his back pocket. Soon they would go to the first of those addresses and look for the first name, but before that he had to see for himself just how different this place was. As Trix had said, both of them had died in this reality and left their loved ones grieving, so his apartment would belong to someone else. But it was the first place Jenny would have checked, and perhaps . . .

"Perhaps she's still there," he muttered.

"What's that?" the driver called.

"Nothing," Jim said, raising a hand. "Turn the music up."

"That I can do!" The driver flicked a dial on the dashboard, and the music roared louder, filling the car and allowing Jim to clear his head.

"She might be," Trix said, leaning into him and resting her head against his shoulder. "But if I know Jenny, she'd have moved on."

"Holly will be her priority. She'll be trying to figure out what the fuck has happened, but she'll be steered by Holly. They'll have to eat, and have somewhere to sleep. And if they can't find anyone who knows them, it'll be a hotel."

"Providing she came through with money."

"Yeah," Jim said. "And providing the currency here is still dollars." He wondered what would happen when it came time to pay the cabdriver. He reckoned he had fifty bucks in his pocket, but would the driver recognize the president on Jim's currency? And beyond that . . . would they have to steal? And if they were arrested, what story could they give? Their names here matched those of long-dead children.

As they left the North End, Jim took more notice of their surroundings, leaving the problems of money and identity until later. The overall impression he'd gleaned from that brief look at this new Boston's skyline was becoming more refined now, and initially he was surprised by how little had really changed. The JFK Federal Building was still there, which told him plenty, and Boston Common was still a welcome oasis of nature within the city. It was across the Common, roughly in the theater district, that the cathedral they'd seen from the house rose toward the night sky. It was well illuminated by display spotlights, proudly flaunting its magnificence over the lower buildings surrounding it.

"That is massive," Trix said, and Jim realized she was leaning across the backseat with him to get a better view.

"What's the cathedral's name?" Jim shouted, taking a risk. The driver glanced curiously at him in the mirror, then grinned again and switched into a new, even more verbose mode. *Tourists,* he must have thought, and Jim vowed to keep an eye on their route.

"That's the world-famous Cathedral of Saint Mary in the Park, and that in front of it is Saint Mary's Park. Green an' lovely, even at night." He turned the music down, and Trix glanced at Jim and raised her eyebrows. *What have you started?* But this was good. They needed information, needed to know what this Boston held for them. And who better to ask than a taxi driver?

"Almost thirty years to build, and fourteen souls taken into the cathedral's bosom," the driver said. "If you visit it on your stay, make sure you take a look at the shrine in there, built to those brave souls. Beautiful, it is." He looked in the mirror again, the smile slipping.

"Where are you from?" Trix asked.

"Well, you're asking me two different things there, young lady," the driver said, his good humor restored. "As to where I was born, that was Cork back in the home country. But where I'm from?" He waved both hands around him, holding the wheel with his knees. "Lived here since I was three years old, and never been back. So anyone asks where I'm from, I say Boston. Who wouldn't, eh?"

"Who indeed," Jim said. A few raindrops speckled the cab's windows, smearing his image of the cathedral, and he wondered whether Jenny and Holly were getting wet in the same shower.

"You're here visiting?" the driver asked.

"Looking for someone," Jim said. Trix tapped his leg, but he moved her hand aside. Why shouldn't he tell the truth?

"Who's that, then? Maybe I can help."

"I doubt it. So . . . I haven't been to Boston before, would you believe? The Irish influence is big?"

"You kiddin' me?" the driver asked. "It's way beyond just influence. Some of them"—he waved both hands again, a gesture that Jim thought perhaps the man used all the time, but which he was sure would wrap them around a lamppost within the next mile—". . . *New Yorkers*. Y'know? There's Irish there, for sure, but none of them are *really* Irish." He looked in the mirror again. "You're not New Yorkers?"

"Baltimore," Trix said, and the driver nodded.

"Knew it. Baltimore. Good city. This one, though, yeah, heavy Irish influences. The best pubs in the States are here, and the best of them are run by guys who've come over from the home country to escape the Troubles."

"The Troubles are"—*over,* Jim wanted to say, but the man was staring at him in the rearview mirror yet again—"terrible," he said.

"Got that right," the man said, voice more cautious now. "Since they started blowin' up planes and trains . . . well, Boston's like the Ireland that should've been. Peaceful. Mainly." They were heading southwest toward Jim's apartment, and as the streets flitted by left and right he found himself growing increasingly nervous rather than excited. He fully expected to find no sign of his wife and daughter at that address, and that should move him on in his search. But there was something else niggling at him.

He glanced over his shoulder into the glaring head-lamps behind them.

"You, too?" Trix asked softly.

"What?"

"Getting the sense we're being followed?"

"Yeah. Ever since . . ."

"We came through."

"Probably the least of our worries. We're dealing with this," Jim said. "Coping. I don't know how, or why, but we are."

"The why is because this is for Jenny and Holly. We've come through to look for them, and that's making us strong."

"So what about them?" Jim asked, and his voice broke. *What about them?* They were dragged through; they didn't come through of their own accord, with their own aims in mind. They didn't understand like he and Trix. They had no inkling of what was going on. What could the trauma of this do to them?

"They'll be fine," Trix said.

"You can't know that."

"No, and I can't say anything else. Just believe it." She glanced behind them, then back at him.

"Unsettled, that's all," he said softly. "With all that's happened, all the weirdness. No one's following us. They *can't* be."

"Right," Trix said, meaning it to sound emphatic. But to Jim she just sounded scared.

They settled close together in the backseat, not quite touching but drawing strength from proximity. And ten minutes later they pulled up outside what should have been Jim's home, and he knew already that things here were very different. Through the rain-speckled windows he could see that Tallulah's still took up the first floor, but above that the floors were dark, several windows boarded up, and it felt nowhere like home.

For a moment Jim wondered whether Miranda was still the restaurant hostess, and what her reaction would be were she to see him. But there would *be* no reaction. Back in the Boston he knew, she had been his friend and, after Jenny's disappearance, apparently his erstwhile lover. But in this Boston he would be unknown. He had never been here before, and to attempt to imprint his memories on this place would be futile. And maybe even dangerous.

"It would have been too strange," Trix said, leaning into Jim to see from his side window.

"Yeah. But this would have been the first place she'd come."

"They've been gone for half a day."

"And I doubt she'd have hung around."

"So where to if you're not getting out here, pal?" the driver asked. There was an edge to his voice now, nervousness or tension, as if he could suddenly sense that things were not quite right.

"Just . . . drive on," Jim said. And he thought, *Where to indeed? Where would Jenny go once she had been here, and seen the differences?* Trying to put himself in her head was just too traumatic, because the confusion and terror she must be feeling were shattering. Instead, he started to analyze her probable approach objectively.

"After here, she'd go to your place," Jim said.

Trix's eyebrows rose in surprise, but then she nodded. "Yeah. But . . . I'm not sure I want to go there myself."

"Right. After that, probably her parents' place. Then following on from that—"

"Oh, shit," Trix said. "Her parents."

"What?"

"She's not Unique, Jim. Somewhere in Boston there's another Jenny."

"Another Jenny," he echoed. It set his head spinning, and he felt suddenly sick.

"Maybe her parents don't live in the same place here," Trix said. "Didn't you help them with their mortgage, back in . . . well, our Boston? So here, maybe they're still living somewhere else. Maybe outside the city. And maybe Jenny will have gone to the cops, realized things were amiss, and maybe—"

"Too many maybes," Jim said. He lifted himself from the seat and took the folded envelopes from his back pocket. He checked them both, and then held up the one he now knew applied to where they were right now. "We go here. Yes?"

"Yes," Trix said, and she sounded relieved. *She wanted to go there right away,* Jim thought, and perhaps that would have been the safest thing to do. He looked across at the building one more time, at the dark windows that he had stood behind a thousand times in another world, another life. He wondered what was behind those windows here . . . but just as quickly realized he did not *want* to know.

"You know O'Brien's Bar?" Jim asked. "It's down on . . . East Broadway."

"Know it?" the driver said. "Sure I know it."

"That's where we need to go," Jim said. Trix sighed and seemed to settle lower in the seat beside him, and he felt a slight sense of relief at having made a more definite plan. They'd go to find the Oracle of this Irish Boston, give him the letter Veronica had sent through with them, and then tell him their problem. They couldn't do this on their own.

"Sure," the driver said softly. "From the second you got in, I knew you needed help." He turned up his music again, even louder than before, and Jim watched the rain-washed streets flit by.

O'Brien's Bar was an innocuous pub nestled among a terrace of houses a couple of blocks from Telegraph Hill. Over the tops of the buildings, they could see the white steeple top of the Dorchester Heights Monument, just a block away. In the other direction was a view of downtown Boston. This part of the city, in Jim's city, had always been Irish, but now the Irish presence was greater than ever. South Boston was truly an old-world Boston neighborhood, mostly residential, with local bars and markets. But in this Boston, where the Irish were the pinnacle of Boston society, Southie was a hell of a lot nicer.

Across the street from the bar was a small park, lit now by streetlights and apparently deserted this late at night. Perhaps shadows moved within the shadows, but Jim could not see, nor did he care. His own safety was not the priority. There were benched tables outside the bar, chained to metal hooks in the pub's front wall so that they didn't walk at night, and even at this late hour lights shone inside. They exited the taxi and Trix paid the cabbie—still dollars, thankfully, and Lincoln was no stranger to him—and Jim could tell that the bar was all but empty. There was faint music playing somewhere in the background, but the usual hubbub of voices was absent, and there was a sense that this place was about to go to sleep for the night. It was a strange way to view it, and disconcerting, but he looked up at the façade and saw tired windows reflecting streetlights; the double doors were a closed mouth, and the building gave the sense that it was something with knowledge and wisdom.

The cab drifted along the street, its engine sounds echoing from silent buildings, and then they were alone.

"Is this one going to be as weird as the old woman?" Jim asked.

"Who knows? What's the name again?"

"Peter O'Brien." Jim looked at the envelope in his hand, the messy lettering, and something ran a cool finger down his back. The hair on his arms bristled, and his senses suddenly became clear and sharp, flooding him with input: the scent of damp soil from the park and spilled beer from the sidewalk, the night sounds of doors closing and car engines ticking as they cooled, the kiss of fine rain against his skin. As he turned around to look across the street at whatever was watching them, Trix was already doing the same.

"It's just the darkness," he said, staring past the street lamps and trying to penetrate the small park. There was a bandstand at its center and a network of pale paths crissing and crossing, and here and there planting beds exploded with the silhouettes of shrubs and small trees.

"No," she said, "not just the darkness."

"Bums, then. Lonely lovers. Drunk teens fucking." But he knew that none of these was true, either. Whoever or whatever watched from over there was more connected to their journey than that. He rubbed the envelope between his fingers and wondered what it contained.

Jim heard the bar door open. He turned away from the dark park and took a step back toward the curb, and the shadow that filled the doorway seemed to swallow the weak light emerging from inside the building.

"Already poured your drinks," the shadow said, and his voice was higher than Jim had expected, and much more welcoming. "It's not cold, and the rain's not too bad. But I'll welcome you in to take shelter from the night."

Take shelter from the night. Jim almost asked if he sensed the watcher as well. But that would be no way to greet the Oracle of this Boston. "Peter O'Brien?" he asked, though he already knew the answer.

"That's me. And you'll be from out of town."

Trix actually laughed, an unconscious reaction to such a mundane observation. "You could say that!" she said.

"Hope you like good beer," O'Brien said. He moved back from the doorway to let them in, and in doing so allowed them to make him out properly for the first time. As Trix stepped into the pub, Jim held back and sized the man up. Smartly dressed in black trousers and shined shoes, a white shirt and black suede waistcoat, he was a barrel of a man, well over two hundred pounds, but he carried the weight well. He was tall and broad, and even before he'd turned a little to fat, Jim knew that he'd been a powerful presence. Yet there was a lightness about him that quelled any unease Jim might normally feel in the company of such a huge stranger. He moved back like a dancer to let them in, graceful and gentle, and his smile lit up his face. His hair was long and tied in a ponytail, and a scruff of graying stubble softened his features more.

"Jim Banks," Jim said, extending his hand as he entered. For a second he saw a flicker of something on O'Brien's face—fear? Discomfort? The smile flexed a little, but it returned just as fresh and welcoming as before. He took Jim's hand and pumped it twice, firm but not too hard. In that touch, Jim felt the warmth of hope.

"Pleased to meet you, Jim."

"And you. I hope you can help me."

"Well, I'll say to you what I say to anyone coming to my bar seeking more than a drink and a pie and a place to rest their feet. I can only do my best." He closed the door behind them but did not lock it. Jim thought perhaps this bar was open every hour of every day, but not always for drinks.

O'Brien showed them to a table in the corner. A candle burned in the mouth of an empty wine bottle, spilling hot wax down the green glass, and three recently pulled pints sat before the chairs. Three chairs. The table was large enough to seat six, at least.

"You knew we were coming," Trix said.

"Not you specifically," O'Brien said. "Just someone."

"We know who you are," Jim said. "And what. And we were sent here by someone like you."

O'Brien raised his eyebrows. Then he held up a hand and nodded at their chairs. The three of them sat, and the process felt almost ceremonial to Jim, a thought given more gravity by O'Brien's nimble manner. He placed both hands flat on the table and seated himself comfortably, spine straight, shoulders loose, before picking up his pint and taking a long draft. He smacked his lips and nodded gently. "Nectar of angels," he said.

"What's the brew?" Trix asked.

"My own. I've a microbrewery in the basement. I call it Old Bastard."

Jim took his first swig. The taste exploded, the alcohol evident but not overpowering, and he felt the rush of its influence spreading through his body. "Certainly well named. And delicious."

"A bartending Oracle," Trix said softly. She was looking at O'Brien with a mix of fascination and wonder.

"Who better to have their fingers on the pulse of a city?" O'Brien said. He took another long drink, swallowing half of his pint in one go, and looking back and forth between them over the edge of the glass. He wiped his mouth and placed the glass gently back on the table.

"So, you're from elsewhere," he said. "That much I know, and I've known it for the last hour. Kicked out the last of my patrons. Pretended I was closing early, when sometimes I don't close at all. 'Cause I figured you'd be along. Sometimes . . ." He looked at the window and sniffed softly.

"You can smell trouble?" Jim asked.

"Is that what you two are, then? Trouble?"

"No," Trix said, shaking her head.

"No," Jim confirmed. He placed the envelope on the table, keeping one finger on it. "We're partly messengers, but mainly . . ." He felt tears threatening, as the weight of events pressed down on him. Sitting here in this ordinary bar with this extraordinary man, he felt control slipping away. By coming through and beginning his search for Jenny and Holly, he had been taking positive action. But now he was about to place himself in the hands of another once again, and he wasn't sure quite what he thought about that.

The only person he knew he could trust for sure was Trix.

"We're looking for Jim's wife and daughter," Trix said. "They've been pulled through from our own Boston into another. Maybe this one."

"Yeah," O'Brien said. He looked back and forth between Jim and Trix, his expression unreadable, eyes twinkling with humor or, perhaps, disbelief. He crossed his arms and sighed heavily, but it was merely the action of a tired man. "And you're Uniques. The both of you. Friends."

He knows, Jim thought.

O'Brien looked at Trix, seeming to see deeper than mere flesh and skin. "*Good* friends. And that"—he nodded down at the envelope, which Jim had placed face-down on the tabletop—"that'll be for me."

"From your counterpart in *our* Boston," Jim said.

O'Brien nodded thoughtfully, drinking the rest of his pint and putting down the glass so gently that it made no sound. He stretched and looked around the bar, glanced at his watch, then focused his attention back on Jim and Trix. "It's been a long day," he said. "You look tired, both of you. And it's been a long day for me, too, what with . . ." He waved one hand, and Jim wondered what wonders O'Brien had performed today, what problems he had solved and lost things he had found. "A couple of hours' sleep will do wonders for us all, and come sunrise I'll be better able to help you."

"You can't help us now?" Jim asked.

"I could," O'Brien said. "I could start. But I can't just"—he clicked his fingers—"out of thin air. I need to talk to you about them. In depth, personally, and a lot of it will be about you as much as them. I need to understand your link to them in order to grab hold of it and pull them in. I need to *know* them so that I can find them. A name's nothing to me without knowledge of who that name belongs to, and it might not be so easy for you, tired as you are. Maybe your Oracle's better at this sort of thing. You understand?"

"Not really," Jim said.

"I do," Trix said, smiling, and Jim thought of her story about her grandfather.

"But—"

"A few hours," O'Brien said. "There's a room made up on the second floor, bathroom attached. It's a double, but . . ." He raised one eyebrow.

"That's fine," Trix said, smiling.

"I thought it would be." O'Brien leaned forward and used one finger to pull the envelope from beneath Jim's hand. For a second Jim wanted to press down, hold it back, but he was not sure why. Insurance? Fear? Or maybe there was no reason at all. O'Brien dragged the envelope across the table to him—it whispered, like a voice in the dark—turned it over, and looked at the writing on the front without expression.

"You'll wake us?" Jim asked.

"Sure. You'll hear me." O'Brien looked up from the envelope. "And Jim . . . Don't worry. We'll find your family, for sure."

Jim nodded, unable to talk because the tears were a pressure behind his eyes once again. He and Trix stood, and he realized how right O'Brien had been. He was exhausted. A couple of hours' sleep would take the edge off his exhaustion, and then tomorrow . . . tomorrow, he would find his wife and daughter.

"Come on," Trix said, grabbing Jim's arm and steering him toward the door O'Brien had pointed out behind the bar.

"Sleep well!" the Oracle called.

As they walked up the curving stairway, Jim heard the sound of paper tearing. And then he heard O'Brien speak again, cursing under his breath. "Oh, you bitch," Peter O'Brien said, anger and resignation in his voice.

What could Veronica have written? Jim wondered. But silence followed, and Jim continued up toward what he hoped would be a moment's peace.

8

The Worst Day Since Yesterday

TRIX PADDED down the corridor of Peter O'Brien's apartment in her bare feet, exhausted but still alert. Her skin prickled with awareness of her dislocation. In college it had not been that unusual for her and Jenny to end up sleeping on sofas and in guest rooms after parties off-campus or even across town. But she was an adult now, and she could not relax in a stranger's home. Knowing that the city around her was foreign to her, that she was an intruder here, only made it worse.

She opened the door to the guest bedroom, the hinges creaking, and stepped inside. Jim glanced up as she closed the door behind her. He sat in a captain's chair by the window, sketching with a pencil he had found in a small drawer in the girl's vanity in the corner. O'Brien might call this a guest room, but it had obviously once been occupied by a young female, and he hadn't changed the décor enough to make it suitably neutral for a guest room.

"Jim," Trix said.

His only answer was the *scritch-scratch* of his pencil on the notepad he'd found in the same drawer.

Trix sighed and unzipped her pants, wriggling out of them and letting them puddle at her feet. She moved to the big queen bed, pushed a bunch of throw pillows onto the floor, and drew back the slightly dusty floral spread before sliding in, clad just in her T-shirt and panties.

Jim hadn't even looked up.

"Mr. Banks," she said. "Earth to Jim."

That got him. He glanced at her, then looked out the window at the cityscape he had been sketching. "Don't you mean parallel Earth to Jim?"

Trix shivered. "This is fucked, right?"

Jim nodded. "Entirely." He put the pad down without even glancing at the art he had been trying to create, then stood up and started to wander the room, not quite pacing. He sighed in frustration. "I mean, what are we doing here?" he said, more to the beamed ceiling than to Trix, or so it seemed to her.

"Taking the most direct approach," Trix replied.

Jim had his fingers pushed into his hair, like he might at any moment attempt to tear his own scalp off. Now he stopped his roaming to turn to her, looking foolish with his hands planted on his head.

"You think?" he asked hopefully.

Trix lay her head back on the pillow and stared at him. "I'm lying in a stranger's bed in a parallel freaking dimension. Yes, I'm totally burned out and I need a rest. Half an hour of shut-eye might be enough to save my sanity. But do you really think I'd be lying here in my undies if I thought for a second that Peter O'Brien wasn't our best bet, our fastest road to Jenny and Holly?"

Jim exhaled loudly and dropped his hands. He came to sit on the side of the bed and took her hand. "If I didn't have you with me, I'd already have totally lost it. I mean . . . if we hadn't caught up with each other—"

"—we'd both still be thinking we were going crazy, and that maybe there had never been a Jenny to begin with."

Jim nodded. "I keep thinking we should have looked longer. I know they had hours on us, and they could be anywhere, but she would've tried the familiar places first, and we didn't cover all of them. We should've gone to her parents' restaurant."

"She'd have figured out something was badly amiss," Trix said. "Felt something wrong. Maybe she saw something that scared her *away* from familiar places."

"But your place? She would have gone looking for you."

"And she wouldn't have found me. The odds of us finding her and Holly standing on the sidewalk in front of my building when we got there are about a kabillion to one." Trix tugged his hand a little, forcing him to meet her gaze. "You heard what Mr. O'Brien said. He's going to find them. But there are preparations to be made, and one of those is for us to rest a little so we can focus."

"You think I can sleep?"

Trix cocked her head. "You think *I* can? Listen, we'll go crazy if we just pace the room while we're waiting for our Irish Oracle friend to get his shit together. It's not doing Jenny and Holly any good. Just lie down with me for a little while. Rest your eyes. Seriously. It's dusty, but it feels good to lie down."

Still, Jim seemed reluctant.

"Show me what you were sketching," Trix said, pointing at the notepad he'd left on his chair.

Finally, given a task to perform, Jim seemed to step back from the frantic edge he had been teetering on. He snatched up the pad and brought it to her, sitting on the edge of the mattress.

Trix stared at the shaded pencil drawing of the view from that window, the row houses across the street from O'Brien's Bar and the taller buildings in the distance, the church steeples, the old stone contrasting strangely with the sleekly modern buildings that the Irish-influenced Boston must have built only in the past decade or two.

Jim kicked off his shoes and slid into bed beside her, sighing as he propped himself up on his elbow to study the drawing with her. "Look familiar?" he asked.

Trix tried to ignore the cold knot forming in her stomach. "You know it does."

She had dreamed this city dozens of times. In her disturbed dreams, she had walked its dark streets. If she went out right now, she thought she might be able to find her way almost anywhere without a map or directions. Those strange journeys had always felt like more to her, as though she had actually traveled, truly explored the intimidating city and learned its secret ways and corners.

"To me, too," Jim said.

Though his dreams were never as clear or memorable as hers, Jim had done his own sleepwalking, taken journeys to this Irish-hued Boston, as well as another. Now, though, he didn't need to paint from the memories of dreams.

Trix stared at the sketch. "Crazy."

"Yeah," Jim agreed.

Trix set the pad on the nightstand and slid farther under the bedclothes, nestling her head on the soft pillow. "Rest," she said.

"What do we have, an hour or so before O'Brien said he'd come get us?"

"About that."

Relenting at last, Jim put his head on the pillow, but

he lay on his back and stared at the ceiling. Trix scooted closer to him and put a hand on his chest, closing her eyes, exhaustion a blanket wrapped warmly around her. Fear and hope chased each other's tails in the back of her mind, but she tried to block them out.

"Do you think—" Jim began.

"Hush," Trix said. "Rest. We'll find them. I promise."

That seemed to mollify him, if only for the moment. She felt him take a deep breath, and when he exhaled he seemed to relax somewhat. The window was open and a cool breeze drifted through, rustling the curtains and carrying the sounds of distant engines. The Banks clan were like a family to her. Holly might as well have been her niece. Trix and Jim were in this together. Lying there with him, she felt closer to him than she ever had before. She could feel his heart pounding in his chest as he tried to calm himself.

"Not exactly the member of the family I would've thought I'd end up sleeping with," Trix mumbled into her pillow.

Jim laughed softly, then a little louder, and then he leaned over to kiss her forehead and pulled her closer. Sharing their warmth—and their hope and fear—they lay together and began to surrender to weariness.

Trix glanced over at the night-darkened window. Somewhere out there, in this foreign Boston, Jenny and Holly were scared and alone. Or were they? The one thing she and Jim had not yet discussed was the possibility that his girls weren't in this Boston at all, but in the other—the third, Brahmin Boston. Trix couldn't even consider it. They were here. They had to be, because though Veronica had shown them the trick to seeing the thin places between cities, she wasn't sure they would really be able to cross over when the need arose.

We're coming, Trix thought, her cheek resting on Jim's chest. *Help is on the way.*

As sleep claimed her, she smiled sadly at the irony.

Jim woke to the sound of shattering glass. The room seemed to tilt for a moment as he battled the dislocation of waking in a strange place. He looked around wildly, saw that the windows were intact, the door still closed, nothing at all out of the ordinary except that he was in a strange bed in a strange room with a half-naked lesbian who happened to be one of his dearest friends.

"What just happened?" Trix murmured sleepily, propping herself up.

Jim shook his head, wondering the same thing. If it had woken her as well, then it hadn't been a dream, which meant the sound had come from nearby. Outside? Maybe. Downstairs? Also maybe.

He crawled out of bed, gesturing for her to remain, and to be quiet.

"Fuck that," Trix whispered. Of course she did. It was Trix. Jim should have known better.

As he slipped his shoes on and Trix dragged on her pants, they heard a muffled shout coming from the bar downstairs. O'Brien's voice, raised in fury. A pounding noise began, like the fist of God knocking on the front door, and the whole building shook in time to that awful rhythm. A crack appeared in the wall, running from the upper edge of the door frame to the corner of the room.

"What the hell is that?" Jim whispered, not sure if Trix would hear him over the noise—not really sure if he was even talking to her.

Trix had one shoe on and the other one in her right hand as she hurried past him to the door.

"Wait," Jim said.

"For what?" Trix asked, spinning on him, eyes wide with fear.

More glass shattered downstairs, and Jim pictured the shelves of hard liquor behind the bar being smashed to the floor. There'd been a big mirror there as well. He glanced at the window, wishing there was a fire escape out there so they could go down and survey the fracas from outside.

"Weapons," he said. "We're not going down there empty-handed."

Trix put on her other shoe. "There's an iron on the top shelf in the bathroom."

Jim picked up the heavy crystal lamp from the bedside table, pulled off the shade, and yanked the cord out of the wall. He glanced at Trix and nodded for her to go ahead, and she turned the knob and swung the door inward.

Out in the corridor, Jim went for the door that led downstairs to the bar. Trix raced into the bathroom and emerged holding the iron Peter O'Brien had probably used for years to take the wrinkles out of his clothes. It seemed all too mundane a detail to exist in the same reality as the shouting and the noises of destruction from below.

A roar of pain rose from the bar, becoming a scream. The pounding stopped in a violent splintering of wood, and Peter O'Brien's voice fell silent.

Trix slipped up beside Jim, reaching out to stop him from opening the door. "What the hell are we doing?" she whispered.

She didn't need to explain. Jim wondered the same thing. From the sound of it, whatever was going on downstairs wasn't some simple bar fight.

"He's our best chance of finding them!" Jim whispered back.

Trix nervously licked her lips, then nodded.

Jim tore the door open and burst through it, running down the stairs, wielding the crystal lamp like a club. Trix came right behind him. He had a moment to wonder if she was thinking what he was thinking—that they were batshit crazy, that these were piss-poor weapons—and then the silence in the bar was broken by a human voice. It might have been O'Brien's, but the big Irishman sounded very small now. "Don't," the voice pleaded. "You'll destroy it all."

As they hit the curve in the stairwell, the words were punctuated with a terrible crash. Jim leaped the last few steps—there was no door, only an archway leading into the bar—and as he stepped into O'Brien's, music started to play. Flogging Molly's "Cruel Mistress." He knew it well.

"Jesus," Trix whispered as she stepped into the bar behind him.

The place was a ruin of overturned tables, broken chairs, and shattered glass, but Jim only got a glimpse of the wreckage—and the blood on the brass bar rail—before he noticed something shift near the huge square saw-toothed space where the plate-glass front window had once been. A figure stood amid the shattered glass, the puzzle of partially painted fragments that had once spelled out O'BRIEN'S in green and gold among them. Taller than a man, it was nevertheless shaped like one. A silver shadow, it seemed to have simply appeared there, standing atop the debris.

No. *It was there,* he thought. *You just didn't see it at first.*

"What are they?" Trix asked, her voice a fearful rasp.

Jim blinked, and he saw that she was right. Beyond the demolished front of the bar, two more of the wraiths stood out in the street, faceless silhouettes who seemed

THE SHADOW MEN   149

somehow still to be looking at him and Trix. Shadows fell upon the smooth slopes of their faces, suggesting eyes and mouth where there were none, only minor ridges that hinted at noses. They were the memories of men, all personality torn away.

Fear clenched at his gut, but Jim took two steps toward the thing still inside the bar, feeling the weight of the crystal lamp in his hand. "Who the hell are you?" he asked, though he thought that Trix's *what* was indeed a better question.

In the distance, sirens wailed, coming nearer. Jim held his breath. For the first time since he had fled a high school keg party where weed and coke had been in plentiful supply, he feared the arrival of the police. In this world, he and Trix didn't even exist. They were the ultimate illegal aliens.

"Why did you do this?" Trix shouted at them.

The music from the jukebox changed to the Von Bondies' "C'mon, C'mon," and Jim glanced toward the source and nearly retched. Peter O'Brien's lower torso and legs stuck out from beneath the heavy machinery, its glass case spiderwebbed with cracks but somehow not caved in.

"Jim!" Trix cried.

He turned, raising the lamp, thinking he had to defend himself, but she hadn't shouted because they were under attack. She'd yelled in surprise.

The wraiths were gone.

"Did you see which way they went?" Jim asked, taking a few steps toward the front of the bar, glass crunching underfoot.

Trix didn't move. "I'm not sure they went anywhere."

Jim glanced over his shoulder at her. "What?"

She gestured with the iron. "They just . . . moved. First the one inside. Like it took a step and just . . . walked out of the world. Then the others went, too. How the hell do we know they're really gone?"

Jim stared at the spot on the partially painted glass fragments where the first wraith had been standing. He moved to the left, trying to look at the space from different angles, but saw nothing. His heart pounded in his chest, full of fear of something he couldn't see.

The sirens grew louder. A dog barked. Inside the bar, liquor dripped from broken bottles and beer from busted taps. The smell of it filled the place. A cold weight settled on his heart. This might not be his Boston, but it was not make-believe. This was a real city, with ordinary people who lived ordinary lives. He would have given anything to be one of them again— anything but the family he had lost. They were worth any sacrifice. "Screw it," he said, dropping the crystal lamp, which broke apart when it hit the floor.

He walked toward O'Brien's broken body. The racks of liquor bottles behind the bar had been decimated. Half of the mirror had fallen away, and the rest clung to the wall like the blade of a guillotine. The brass bar rail was bent and smeared with O'Brien's blood, and red splashes of his life dotted the wooden floor.

"What now?" Trix said, and he heard a thunk behind him as she cast aside the iron. The optimism she had been trying so hard to project had been forgotten. "Jim, we've got to get out of here. We can't afford to be questioned by the cops."

"We're going," Jim said. But he made no move to leave. Instead, he moved closer to the Oracle of this Irish Boston, picturing Peter O'Brien's face, still hearing the amiable bear of a man's voice in his head. A couple of hours, that was all he had said he needed, and then he would have tracked down Jenny and Holly. How many years, even decades, had this man been the Oracle? And then within an hour or two of them showing up he was dead.

Oh, you bitch, Jim had heard him say, and he looked around for the letter, keen to see what it had contained.

O'Brien's legs shifted.

"Jesus!" Jim shouted, staggering backward.

"Did he just move?" Trix asked, freaking out.

"Definitely," Jim said.

O'Brien shifted again. His skull and upper chest had been crushed beneath the jukebox. No way could he survive that. Almost as if Jim had wished him dead, O'Brien's legs settled and went still, and he knew that what they had just seen had been the man's final throes.

Trix grabbed his arm. "Jim. We have to go!"

He nodded, backing away. Together they hurried to the door, only to find it locked from the inside. The wraiths had come in through the plate-glass window, with its painted letters and stylized shamrock. Jim unlocked the door and tugged it open, and he and Trix slipped out of the bar.

Along the street, the first police car sped around the corner.

"Don't run," Trix snapped.

Taking his hand, she led him away from the bar as though they were lovers out for a stroll. But Jim saw faces at windows, and people standing on the opposite sidewalk—it must be near last call by now, but they had spilled out of Dwyer's New Dublin Pub just up the street—and already fingers were being pointed. Some of the spectators were shouting questions at them. A couple of them, wearing Boston Celtics basketball jerseys, started crossing the street.

"We waited too long," Jim said, knowing that every

moment they weren't spending trying to find Jenny and Holly, the trail was getting that much colder.

Trix squeezed his hand. "Okay. Now we run."

And that was when the earthquake hit.

Trix put her hands out as if learning to surf. The street bucked hard beneath their feet, then harder still. This was no mere tremor. Panicked people flooded from Dwyer's New Dublin, across the street. The ground lurched up and then dropped, again and again, as though some wicked toddler had made it his toy and intended to shake it until it broke. The police car skidded to a halt, slewing sideways as a rift opened in the pavement.

Glass shattered all around them. Alarms pealed. Masonry cracked. A fire hydrant less than ten feet from Trix exploded, water spouting upward, showering around them. A piece of the hydrant flew past her head and shattered the rear windshield of a parked car. Jim grabbed her wrist and tugged her back toward O'Brien's.

"No!" she shouted, but her voice was drowned out by the roar and rumble of the earth.

He tried to tell her something, but all she could make out was ". . . outside wall!" Still, she understood. In an earthquake, the safest place inside a building was next to an object that might be crushed—a table or bed—and not beneath it. But outside, in a built-up area, curling against a building's outer wall might prevent them from being injured. Even if the wall fell, it would likely not collapse right down to ground level. And between the fallen wall and what was left of its base, a triangle of life.

Jim tried to pull her toward the building. People screamed. Trix spotted a little yellow dog chasing its tail on the sidewalk up the street. The world continued to buck and crack, so long now that she feared it would never end. A hundred yards along the street, a traffic light toppled onto a swerving minivan, which careened through the front window of a pharmacy.

Beyond where the light had fallen, the three faceless men who had killed O'Brien stood watching her and Jim, motionless, as though the quake could not move them. The moment she noticed them it was as though her perception changed, and she saw others—one standing in front of a hat shop, another crouched on the second-story ledge of an apartment house. The world shook, but the faceless men remained impassive, only watching as Boston tore itself apart . . . again.

Shit, is that what this is? she wondered. *Is it splintering again?*

When part of the street gave way, the sewer cracking open like some ravenous maw, Trix decided Jim had a point. She gave in so abruptly that it was she who pulled him back against O'Brien's. Even the illusion of safety was better than this chaos. A fissure split the sidewalk only feet from where they'd been standing a moment before. Jim held her tight, and Trix pulled him down until they sat, leaning against each other.

The ground heaved up beneath them. Trix struck her head on the masonry; Jim squeezed her hand. The whole world roared, and behind them the ceiling inside O'Brien's gave way, the second-story apartment crashing down into the ruin of the bar, burying the city's Oracle in the rubble of his life.

The shaking eased, the ground steadied, but Trix still listed to one side, staggered by the sudden ending of the quake. The street sang to cries of anguish and the pointless blaring of alarms. Fires bloomed in the distance. She heard several dull thumps and wondered whether they were gas-main explosions.

"Is it over?" Trix asked, standing. Jim held her hand, and they both took a shaky step away from the building.

"Careful," Jim said. "There could be—"

Later, Trix would be sure the next word had been meant to be "aftershocks," but Jim never had a chance to say it.

It felt like a collision. The sidewalk did not buck this time but instead *shifted* to the east with such force that they fell, rolling into the street. Trix scraped her right cheek and both arms on the pavement. The explosion tore the sky apart, deafening thunder followed by a roaring cascade that sounded to Trix's bleeding ears like the whole city coming down around her.

She called Jim's name and looked up to see him on his hands and knees, trying to rise. Screams that sounded distant were actually coming from Dwyer's New Dublin. People had been thrown against the jagged fins of plate glass jutting from the frame of the pub's front window, and a young blond woman hung impaled, staring dumbly at the bloody glass shard sticking out of her chest, her expression not of pain but of sorrow, wondering how and why.

Jim shouted something loud, incoherent—a cry of shock and terror.

Trix sat up and tried to look around. She was shaking, bleeding. A cloud of dust spread across the sky. "What *was* that, at the end?" she said, barely aware that she was shouting. "Was that a fucking *nuke?*"

They were both coughing on the dust that roiled in the street. The ground had stopped moving, but Trix didn't trust it anymore. As she managed to get onto her knees, she kept touching the pavement, expecting to be thrown down again. It took her a few seconds before she realized that Jim hadn't said anything more. She looked up and saw him standing, staring over the tops of buildings, looking even more frightened and anguished than he had when she had first come to him to ask him about Jenny and Holly's disappearance.

Trix tried to see what he was looking at. She narrowed her eyes. They stung and watered with the dust, and she wondered what chemicals she was breathing in from the devastation around her.

On the next block, a silver roof ridge gleamed in the midst of the swirling dust. Trix frowned, staring at it, wondering how she had missed it before. It must be an office building, but the architect had designed it to appear as though the top had been sheared off at an angle. It was made of glass and steel, and now the majority of the windows were broken. She could see emergency lights flickering inside. It was perhaps twenty stories—a tower in this old Boston neighborhood.

And there were others. A modern church stood two blocks down. She blinked as she stared and realized that the street had split around it—and not only the street but the row of shops that had been there before. It looked as though the church had fallen from the sky, like Dorothy's house on Oz.

Sirens wailed in the distance, some growing nearer. Emergency rescue efforts were under way. The fires raged across the city skyline, and as Trix studied it, she remembered her dreams and Jim's paintings, and the sketch he had done only an hour ago, and she understood.

The skyline had changed.

A massive cloud fed by the black smoke from several huge fires began to bloom above the city. It let in faint moonlight, and at last she realized what Jim had seen the second he had struggled to stand. He'd been peering in that direction ever since, as though waiting for confirmation that he had not imagined it.

"That's impossible," Trix said, a terrible numbness spreading through her.

In the distance, the huge, ornate cathedral they had seen upon their arrival in this parallel city had been disastrously altered. At first Trix thought the three towers that thrust up through the roof of the cathedral were separate buildings, but then she realized that their upper stories were joined together, a massive tripod highrise office complex with a revolving restaurant above, capped by a needle spire blinking warning lights to warn air traffic over the city.

Jim shuffled up beside her, cradling his bloody left arm against his chest. "You recognize that building?" he asked.

Trix nodded. It had taken her a moment to remember, but she did know it. She had dreamed it a handful of times, years ago. And she understood now that it had been after her drowning in one reality, and not the others. "It doesn't belong here," she said.

"No," Jim agreed. "It doesn't."

Now the people in the street were screaming and pointing. They had seen it, too. But Trix studied them, and she realized that not all of them had been there before. There were too many. And even here, the buildings were different—weird variations. The pharmacy the van had crashed into had a different sign, now identifying it as an antiquarian bookstore. But the product that had spilled onto the sidewalk belonged to the pharmacy. The façade of Dwyer's New Dublin had been altered completely. Instead of an Irish pub, it had become the Yankee Fish Company.

Trix turned to see that the sign above the shattered

window of O'Brien's Bar hadn't changed at all. *Collision*, she thought. *It is a collision.*

Jim glanced around at the shell-shocked people moving through the streets. Cries for help carried above the sirens and alarms and the sounds of grief-stricken wailing. Many people had died tonight, and many more were still in need. Peter O'Brien might be dead—murdered by those wraiths and buried in the wreckage of his bar—but hundreds, perhaps thousands of others would still be alive, trapped in the rubble.

He couldn't help them.

Injured left arm still held against his rib cage—it wasn't broken, just badly bruised and scraped—he slipped his right arm around Trix's waist. "Come on," he whispered into her ear.

She went along without argument, looking at him with wide eyes. "To where?"

Jim said nothing. He just escorted her along the broken street, survivors of disaster, and made an effort not to meet the eyes of anyone they passed. Together they crossed toward the mouth of an alley, where a wrought-iron fire escape had partially torn away from the building on their left and now leaned precariously against its twin. Trix kept glancing around, her eyes full of fear.

"What are you looking for?" Jim asked.

"Those things from the bar," she said. "The ones that killed O'Brien."

"Wraiths," Jim said.

"You've seen them before?" she asked, misunderstanding.

"No. I just . . . that's how I thought of them. They were there and not there, all at the same time." He didn't see any of them now, but somehow that was no comfort. He feared they might be there, whether he could see them or not.

"During the quake . . . they were watching us," Trix said, a brittle edge to her voice.

"I know," Jim said as he led her into the alley. He glanced around again, but not for the wraiths this time. What he had to say was not something he wanted anyone to overhear.

"The two Bostons," Trix said, searching his eyes for answers. "The two that splintered off . . . they, like, *crashed* back together."

Yeah, Jim thought. *That's the word*.

From what Veronica had told them, he'd had the impression that when McGee caused the schism it had been seamless, unnoticed by the people who had been duplicated in the process. A parting of realities in an otherwise straight, orderly world, like a bubble of possibilities on a single two-dimensional string. But now that the parallel cities and their citizens had been duplicated, they couldn't be erased. Forcing them back together had caused terrible destruction. Buildings that predated the schism—that still existed in both cities—had changed but somehow been merged. But where there were different structures in the two cities, like the cathedral and the tripod building—catastrophe. Metal merged with stone, glass with wood, in an explosive amalgamation.

"I'm afraid, Trix."

Her eyes went wider. "No shit. What if it happens again? What if our Boston . . . Jesus, I can't even think about it. How do we find Jenny and Holly now? How do we get out of here?"

She started back into the street, but he grabbed her and pulled her back. She spun around to stare at him, her face lit with anger.

"You don't get it," he said.

He reached into his back pocket and pulled out the sealed envelope that Veronica had given them to deliver to the Oracle of the Brahmin Boston. He held his breath a second, afraid to open it.

"Wait . . . ," she said.

Jim stared at her, ice clutching at his insides. "We crossed over. We went to the Oracle, and then those wraiths came for him."

Her grief contorted her face, shattering her beauty. "You don't think . . . ? No." She shook her head, then threw out a hand to indicate the devastated city. "You think we caused this?"

"Not us, but I don't think it's a coincidence. How can it be? It's got to be related."

They both stared at the envelope, the name and address of the Oracle of Brahmin Boston scrawled on the front. They had promised they would not open it. Veronica had warned them that disaster could result. But they had not opened the one addressed to Peter O'Brien, and disaster had come just the same.

"Veronica," Trix whispered.

Jim tore it open, careful to preserve the address on the envelope. He pulled out the letter inside—a single sheet of paper—and quickly unfolded it. "Shit," he whispered.

The page was blank apart from a single deep-black spot at its center.

"Oh, no," Trix said, snatching it from him and staring at it. She looked up at him. "It's nothing. No message. Jesus, the wraiths *were* the message. She must have had them following us . . . and we led them right to him."

"But she *knew* his address!"

"Yeah, but . . ." Trix trailed off.

"A message," Jim said. "A . . . something else. I don't

know. I think maybe he knew the moment he opened it."

"She used us," Trix said. "Somehow."

"Yeah." Jim looked around at the crying, bleeding, broken people and the ruin of two Bostons. If they were right, it meant that not only had Veronica betrayed and used them, not only had she arranged for the murder of Peter O'Brien—and the third Oracle as well, if they hadn't figured it out—but it meant that the old bitch had wanted this to happen. She had *planned* for this destruction.

He folded the envelope and almost blank page and stuffed them into his pocket. Then he took Trix's hand. "Come on."

"Why? We've got nowhere to go."

Coughing on the dust of ruined buildings and the smoke from a hundred fires, with cries and sirens still ringing out, he pulled her close. "Jenny and Holly are still out there somewhere."

Trix bit her lip, nodded, and wiped tears from her eyes.

9

Whistles the Wind

As THEY ran, what had happened impressed itself upon Trix with every step. The dislocation she felt should have been aggravated by the earthquake—an event beyond her experience, shoving her farther away from safety and the life she knew so well—but in fact the disaster seemed to have jarred her toward sense and understanding. Maybe it was the sight of her city in ruins, though it was not quite the city she knew. But more likely it was the excruciating sight of human suffering. These people, whichever version of Boston they might have come from, were just like her.

East Broadway was in ruins. The road had been flipped like a giant sheet, coming to rest with bulges and bumps that gaped open to the night sky. Street lamps leaned drunkenly over the undulating road or back against cracked and shattered buildings. The power was out, and the only light came from the half-moon peering between intermittent clouds, car headlamps, and the occasional fires that had sprung up in the ruins. To the north the sky glowed yellow, and Trix could hear the barely audible roar of a massive fire, perhaps as far away as the airport. Already, sparking embers were drifting up from the glow, like fireflies evading the cataclysm. A breeze whispered along the street, like the city gasping in pain.

"How many do you think are dead?" she asked Jim.

"Hundreds. Maybe thousands."

"I wish we could stop and help—"

"We can't," he interrupted. "I'm sorry, Trix, but you know we can't. The only thing keeping me from breaking down here is the thought of finding Holly and Jenny. We know what's going on—about the different Bostons—but they don't. Imagine how terrified they must be. Christ, Trix, I've got to find them. I'm going to lose my *mind*!"

"But which Bostons collided?" she asked, gazing around.

"My guess is the Irish and Brahmin. Veronica said those were the weaker, because they were splintered from the original."

"And you believe her?"

Jim shrugged.

"Well, then," Trix said. "If the Irish Boston and the Brahmin Boston just . . . merged, then there's another Oracle in the city now."

Jim whipped the envelope from his pocket. "Her address is on Harrison Avenue. Sally Bennet. Maybe she'll know. Maybe *she'll* be able to find them!"

Jim's eyes were filled with the desperate knowledge that this was no longer only about them. And Trix understood how heavy that knowledge weighed on him, because she felt it, too. Jenny and Holly's disappearance had led indirectly to this. And what about those things in the bar, those wraiths? *Those things followed us there,* she thought, shivering as she remembered the faceless things standing motionless as the earthquake struck. Watching.

In the distance came the grumbling, earthshaking impact of a building's collapse, and Trix couldn't help thinking, *I'm listening to people die.* She remembered watching the Twin Towers struck by hijacked aircraft, and each time the impact was shown on the news that day—again and again, the blossoming explosions as regular as the country's panicked heartbeat—she'd thought, *I'm seeing hundreds of people die, in that single moment.* It had been unbearable, and hypnotic.

. "Those things," Jim said. He pushed her gently into a shop doorway, feet crunching over shattered glass. Mannequins wearing expensive clothing had toppled into the street, and behind them the ceiling had come down, broken water pipes spraying the shop's interior. "They followed us to O'Brien, then killed him while we were asleep. They needed us to come through—it's like they were waiting for us—and we both felt spooked on our way to O'Brien's. It was them, watching."

"Yeah." Trix nodded.

"So, what if they follow us to Sally Bennet, too? If they kill her, maybe this will happen again."

Trix closed her eyes. Frowned. Opened them again. "Jim, Veronica *gave* you their addresses. She knew where they lived."

"But something in that envelope, or on that note . . . I heard O'Brien's reaction when he opened it." He took the folded sheet from his pocket.

"Just a black dot," Trix said.

"Maybe not to an Oracle."

"Something to let them attack him," Trix said.

"Maybe," Jim said. "She talked about McGee's magicks. Maybe this is some of her own."

"But all this destruction," Trix said. "Could she possibly *want* this?"

Jim shivered. "I think we have to at least consider it.

The timing is too fucking convenient otherwise, don't you think?"

He turned pale, and Trix held his arms and pulled him close. Over his shoulder she saw a family walking along the opposite sidewalk, mother and father on either side of a little girl. They all held hands, and were dressed in smart, dust-covered clothes. The only signs that they had acknowledged the earthquake were the father's coughing and the little girl looking around with eyes wide open. Trix wondered what they'd been doing out so late, or whether they'd dressed and gone for a walk after the quake had struck.

"We have to warn the Oracle," he said. He stepped out into the street and looked around for more of the wraiths, scanning street level, then up at the broken windows and the buildings that should not be there. "I can't see them!" he said to Trix. "Maybe they've gone already."

Trix looked for herself. There was no sign of the wraith-things, but the air was filled with smoke and dust, making a blur of anything more than a hundred steps away.

"Come on," she said. "We might not have much time." So they ran. With a destination in mind, and an aim, she tried in vain to distract herself from some of the sights surrounding them. Because the terrible was merged with the impossible, and that did nothing to detract from the awful reality.

Some of the buildings' façades had tipped outward into the road, exposing the floors and rooms within. Many had collapsed altogether, and the broken roofs of three-story buildings now sat a story above the roadway. Most windows were shattered, and the street was carpeted with glinting glass, smashed tiles, dust, and other debris such as drifting papers, broken bricks, and personal possessions that looked so out of place. *I shouldn't be seeing shoes,* Trix thought. *I shouldn't be seeing someone's bloody nightgown, or a kid's toy gun, or a music system's speaker.*

Beyond the earthquake destruction was the more unlikely damage. Trix could see the difference between the two, and she was sure that Jim did as well, but to other people on the street it must present a bewildering mystery among the chaos. A car showroom had seemingly appeared, straddling one corner of an old market hall and the narrow parking lot beside it, its walls buckled, forecourt cracked, as if dropped from a height. The cars were familiar models, all of them thrown around as though stirred by some angry god. Inside the showroom, where the finest models were kept, two cars were ablaze. The flames spewed across the ceiling and fingered their way up the showroom's front façade, plastic sign bubbling. The only words still visible on the sign were BOSTON'S BEST. Around one edge of the incongruous showroom the older, more attractive market had collapsed, and an avalanche of goods was slewed across the street.

Elsewhere on the street, other buildings had collided in the impact of two worlds coming together. A couple were aflame, some had collapsed, but here and there were structures that remained surprisingly undamaged.

To the south, beyond the ragged outline of collapsed rooftops, Trix could make out the ghostly presence of taller buildings that had not been there before. There was the tripod-like building that had burst from the giant cathedral, but closer to them were other structures. She had the sense that these, too, were new, and that before the cataclysm she would have been able to see open sky where they now stood, and that the buildings' presence here was as invasive as her own. They shimmered through the smoke and reflected firelight from their broken glass and steel façades, giving them the impression of having their own apocalyptic glow. *Like giant faces*, she thought, and the image sent a cold chill through her.

She'd once spent days walking a certain street in Boston and feeling disconcerted for no reason that she could identify. She'd been convinced that something had changed, but the more she walked that street, the more certain she'd become that something within her had altered, not something without. When she'd finally searched the Internet for images and found photos of the same view, she'd realized that an old clock tower in the distance had been taken down. It was the fresh spread of sky that had disturbed her, a space where there should have been no space, and realization had banished the feeling immediately.

Now it was not something missing that made her so unsettled, but something added. They walked through blocks of houses and residential buildings, many of which had been ruined by the clash between the upscale neighborhood of Irish Boston and the forgotten Southie of Brahmin Boston. Others in the street stared in horror and awe at these invading structures. The sense of panic was palpable, its incidental music the screams and cries of those injured or bereaved.

For long blocks they walked, attempting to reach Harrison Avenue, with no chance of any taxi picking them up now. When they reached the intersection at West Fourth Street and Dorchester Avenue, they saw the aftermath of a horrible accident. At least seven cars were involved, and people swarmed over the carnage pulling survivors from the wrecks. Several people sat along the curbside nursing injuries, and in the distance sirens screamed.

"Oh, Jesus Christ," Jim said, and for a moment Trix panicked. *He saw Jenny in one of the cars, she's one of those bodies hanging from that station wagon's windows, and if she's there, then where is Holly?*

But he had not seen his dead wife. When he grabbed her hand and nodded across the road, what they witnessed was altogether more surreal.

Two women stood staring at each other. One must have just emerged from one of the less damaged cars, her right foot still in the footwell, right hand curled around the door frame. She had long blond hair tied in a ponytail and wore a tight-fitting dress and knee-length boots. The other woman stood a dozen paces away, close to the overturned truck that the first woman had crumped into. She, too, had long blond hair, though she wore jeans and a light jacket. Her boots were of slightly darker leather. Her hair was slightly longer.

The women must have been identical twins. Looking from one to the other caused a strange tingling sensation at the nape of Trix's neck. They were equally attractive, but something seemed to draw the beauty from their faces. Something like terror. "They don't know each other," Trix whispered, and Jim's hold on her arm strengthened.

The women stared, utterly motionless while the rescue went on around them. No one else seemed to have noticed this frozen tableau. The woman by the car went to speak; the other woman lifted her arm to point.

"Come on," Jim said.

"Wait, we need to see—"

"Come on." And his voice was so heavy that she could not help but look at him. His eyes were haunted, and she suddenly knew how, and why. Somewhere in the ruins of this city were his wife and child. And somewhere else . . . Jenny's other, her echo, her alter ego.

They moved off, bypassing the accident and the injured people, and Trix kept glancing back at the blond women. Before a drift of smoke hazed them from view, she saw that still neither of them moved. They simply stared.

There were three bodies laid on the pavement outside a collapsed seafood restaurant on Dorchester Avenue. They were lined up as if sleeping side by side, but as they closed on the corpses, Jim saw blood. Before today the only dead body he had ever seen was his mother in the funeral home.

As he approached the bodies, Trix grabbed his shoulder. "Jim?"

"There's something about . . . ," he started, trailing off as they drew closer. One body was covered in a thin net curtain, blurring its features and molding to its skin with blood. For a moment he'd feared it was one of *them*. "Maybe the ghost guys are already ahead of us," he said.

"There's nothing we can do about that," Trix said. "Here." She moved past the bodies and through the restaurant's collapsed façade. Rooting around in the rubble, she pulled out two bottles of water and handed one to Jim.

"That's looting," he said.

"Yeah." She blinked at him a couple of times, then pulled a five-dollar note from her back pocket. She used a small chunk of broken brick to weight it down on the sidewalk before the slumped restaurant. For some reason, that brought tears to Jim's eyes.

"We've got to run," he said. "We can't let anything distract us. Anything like that." He gestured over his shoulder back the way they'd come. *Those women are the same person,* he thought, and he could only think of what would become of Jenny if she met herself. The results could be devastating. What would that do to a person?

Tonight in this city, it must be happening all over.

"How far to Sally Bennet's?" she asked.

"Not far. Across the bridge over the train tracks, under the highway overpass, then a couple of blocks. Not sure how far up Harrison she lives . . ."

"Let's go, then." And they went.

The sights Jim saw that day he knew would stay with him for the rest of his life. There were the stunned people wandering the streets, so many of them that he wondered whether there had been some sort of gas leak that had numbed them all to what had happened. Some of them were crying silently, and others seemed to be attempting to go about their nighttime business, skirting fallen walls or bodies in the street as if they were minor inconveniences. The sight of ruined buildings went from overwhelming to almost unnoticed, and even the structures that were so obviously out of place soon failed to move him. Maybe it was because he was out of place here himself. But the suffering people—the wounded, the bereaved, the confused, and the many bodies he saw in the shadows of ruins or laid out in the street—never failed to touch him. Humanity tonight was suffering more than an earthquake, and he had no idea how they would deal with what was to come. The two blond women could not stare at each other forever.

The sounds of the damaged city pressed in as they ran. Shouting and screaming, the roar of fires, the grumble of falling buildings, the smashing of glass shattering from window openings still under tension, car engines, the throbbing of helicopters passing overhead, sirens, alarms, and somewhere the slow tolling of church bells, mourning the past and solemnly welcoming the future with every chime. And the smells told the same story, the warm aroma of cooked food mixed with the stench of ruptured sewers, the acid tang of fires overlying the sharp sting of dust.

Everything soon became a blur, and he concentrated only on moving. Trix was always by his side, and they swapped frequent glances and strained smiles. He found comfort in his friend, and knew that she felt the same way. She was stronger than he was. He feared losing her.

It was Trix who saw the first wraith, when they were already on Harrison Avenue and headed north. First she was beside Jim, then she'd disappeared, and when he skidded to a halt and looked back, she was staring across the street. A row of five shops had slumped down in the middle, roofs exploded outward by the intrusion of a modern brick church. "It was there," she said when he joined her. "In the arch of the church doorway. Then it was gone."

"You just saw a shadow," Jim said.

"No!" Trix said, frowning at him. "I know what I saw, Jim. They're following us."

"We have no idea how fast they can move," he said, vocalizing what he had only just been thinking. They might have reached Sally already, stepping away from and back into this ruined Boston as he'd seen them do outside O'Brien's. She might already be dead, and the first they'd know about it was when a great, more cataclysmic quake struck.

"That's why we have to move as quickly as *we* can."

They went on, pausing between two parking lots on Herald Street and finding a brief moment of normality until Jim looked to the north. The ruined cathedral was so tall it was visible from this distance, the air between it and them apparently clear of smoke. Fires burned elsewhere across the city, but the cars in the parking lots appeared miraculously untouched. A flock of pigeons hopped from roof to roof, woken from their slumber by helicopters, and sirens, and the sounds of the wounded city.

Jim saw a wraith rushing across the street a hundred feet from them. He saw it again past the next block, keeping pace with them a block away. *Waiting for me to deliver the note,* he thought. And however simple it might seem, disposing of the note seemed far too easy. *There's more to it than that.*

At the corner of Oak Street a building had collapsed. There were scores of people there digging with their bare hands, and Jim felt a tug of guilt as he and Trix sought a way around the destruction.

"Another one," she said. "Keeping pace with us."

"I saw it," Jim confirmed. They paused, waiting for a convoy of police cars and ambulances to pass by. One of the cops, eyes haunted, a smear of dirt across his face, looked out at Jim. "Hid away in a doorway when we turned around. So why not just flit away like they did back at O'Brien's?"

"They don't mind us seeing them."

"Yeah." And if they *could* just step into and out of this world, why not just reappear at Sally Bennet's?

It was a few minutes later when Jim realized where they were. Just a few streets north of here—in his Boston, at least—was Jenny's parents' restaurant. They'd been running the seafood-and-steak place for thirteen years, building a steady reputation for quality food and a comfortable, casual atmosphere. Jim and Jenny had eaten there frequently, and not only because the food was usually free. It was *good.* "Trix, we're close to the restaurant."

"You're thinking we should both go there?"

"No, we can't let Sally down. But I have an idea. You won't like it."

Trix closed her eyes, and he realized how grubby she was. Her pink hair had lost much of its color to the dust. Her clothing was faded, her skin pale, and it was as if the earthquake was doing its best to erase her from the world. That was a concept he did not like. She sighed. "We're going to split up," she said.

"It won't be for long."

"We should go straight to Sally," Trix said, but he could already hear the defeat in her voice.

"It's a distraction. A *good* idea. Their restaurant is half a mile from here, if that. Sally Bennet's address is a handful of blocks away. We go into a building somewhere, hide you away, I leave and race toward the restaurant, the wraith-things follow . . . and you go and warn the Oracle."

"Is your secret name Jason Bourne?"

He smiled again, and this time he meant it. Even in adversity Trix could quip. He wondered where she found the energy, and then thought perhaps such an attitude *gave* it to her. "I'll meet you there in an hour," he said.

"Unless you find them?" And in Trix's eyes he saw fear. She was afraid that she would lose him, run off into this altered, shattered Boston and never see him again.

"Trix, I promise. If I find them, I'll pile them into a car and drive there for you. This is all . . ." He looked around at the damaged city, smelled fire and death on the air, and somewhere in the distance a man was shouting an unidentifiable word again and again. Perhaps it was a name, or maybe an exhalation of pure rage. "It's beyond us," he said. "It's *catastrophic*. But Jenny and Holly are still my whole world."

"I know," she said, but he could still see her disappointment.

"Hey, you're strong."

"Yeah. I don't feel like it." She smiled and ruffled her hair, displacing a cloud of dust and brightening the color a few shades.

"When we get back, keep the pink hair."

"I'm thinking of going for matching collar and cuffs, actually."

"*Too much* information." He took her arm and they walked along the street, passing through a group of people heading in the opposite direction.

"You seen home?" one of the men asked them. "You seen home? 'Cause it's *gone* far as I'm concerned."

"Sorry," Trix said.

"Yeah, well . . ." The man looked Trix up and down, then walked on with the group.

"In here," Jim said. As he dragged open the warped, glassless shop door, he glanced over his shoulder, examining the street behind them, trying not to make it so obvious that he was searching for the wraiths. He saw none, but that meant little. He could feel their eyes on him. He'd heard that some people had a sixth sense that told them when they were being watched, but this was the first time he'd experienced it himself. It turned his skin cold.

As he closed the door, Trix was already rooting around the shop. It sold candles and holders, their smell heavy and sickening on the air even though the window had been smashed. "Here," she said, offering something to him.

He grabbed it, a three-foot-long metal candle stand with a spiked cup on top. Designed to hold a large candle, it would make a formidable weapon.

"Better than a lamp," she said, and in the darkness he heard her nervous giggle.

"Okay," he said, suddenly uncertain. The restaurant

called him, but so did the sense of solidifying guilt that their actions had caused all this. It was unreasonable and untrue, and yet he could not shake the idea.

"I'll see you at Sally's," Trix said. "You go now, or if they're watching they'll figure something's up."

"*Can* they figure?" Jim asked. His fear of the wraiths, their alienness, had barely had time to figure over the past hour. But here and now, their actions and unknown nature suddenly hit home. *Can we really fight them?* he wondered, and his plan suddenly felt weak and point-less. *And Veronica, that dear old lady . . . can we really fight* her?

"What the fuck have we got ourselves mixed up in, eh?" Trix asked.

"Yeah." She came to him and they hugged, then she shoved him at the door.

"I'll hide," she said, "but not for long. Then I'm out the back door and gone."

"Run fast."

"You, too."

Jim nodded in the darkness, and in the distance came another rumble as a weakened building collapsed. He dragged the front door open, smelled fires and dust and fear on the breeze, and then left his friend behind.

Trix counted out a minute, using the counting to try to calm herself. Then she ran like hell. She found the rear door by touch, tugged it open, and emerged onto a wide alleyway behind the row of shops. There was little dam-age here—only the smashed glass that must be common throughout the city—and the area seemed quiet. Weird. The whole city had been shaken awake, and here—

"Hey!" someone shouted, and that was enough for Trix. Jim was going west, and she sprinted north toward Chinatown as fast as she could. *Should've taken the en-*

*velope and sheet from him! Should've arranged some-
where else to meet in case it's too dangerous there!* But
there were so many shoulds, because this was a Boston
of possibilities.

There were two fire engines and a couple of ambulances blocking the street around the next corner, where
a four-story building had collapsed. The structures on
either side of it seemed stable and virtually undamaged—
their architecture slightly off-center, as if built blind—
and she saw the confusion in some of the firefighters'
stances and gestures. *They don't recognize those buildings.* But they were professionals, and by the time she
squeezed by, they were already in action. She glanced
back at the next corner and saw them approaching the
fallen building, ready to do their best even in the face of
mystery.

She ran through the streets of Boston's Chinatown.
Some areas seemed almost untouched but for the familiar scree of shattered glass splashed across the sidewalks
and roads. Others were in ruins. The city had fallen
strangely silent, many routes now blocked to vehicles.
The quiet was broken on occasion by sirens and shouts,
and from some far distance a long, rumbling explosion,
but they were islands of noise in a strange, unsettling
calm. It was as if Boston was in shock, and unable to
speak its usual ebullient language.

Many times over that final block she wanted to stop
and help. There were people in need: bleeding in the
street, pawing at rubble, wandering in a dangerous daze.
But she sensed eyes on her back every step of the way,
and she was scared. She was *terrified*. Lost in a city that
should be familiar and yet that was more alien due to its
occasional familiarity, she craved the company of someone who understood. She hoped that Jim would find
Jenny and Holly, though she doubted it; and she hoped

that she would see him again soon, as they had both vowed. But right now, finding the woman named Sally Bennet was her one true aim.

She did not once look back, because she feared what she would see. As she ran, she tried to analyze the wraiths' capabilities, but laughed at the ridiculousness of what she was doing. Yesterday she was a normal woman in a normal city, with unremarkable concerns and a few personal demons. Now . . .

What was she now? She was no longer sure.

They killed him when we were there. If they are from Veronica, they couldn't just kill him on their own. They needed us. They needed the letter. She couldn't work it out, and her aching muscles and straining lungs distracted her from her thoughts.

At last she reached Beach Street, in the heart of Chinatown, and looked back for the first time. She saw two wraith-things following, though they made some pretense at hiding. They had no faces, yet she knew they were looking her way. The plan had failed—perhaps it had never had a hope of success—and in a display of naked fear, she turned and gave them both the finger. "Fuck you!" she shouted. Her voice echoed emptily along the street.

The road was lined with shops, several of them boarded up, and piles of refuse. There were signs in Chinese and colorful lanterns hanging from lampposts, but they looked as though they had seen better days. Where there ought to have been tailor shops and restaurants, there were mostly dingy apartments and shuttered storefronts. Walls had been sprayed with gang signs, and people were wandering the street in small, threatening groups. Though Chinatown in general seemed more badly damaged than other streets she'd passed down—

which meant that it differed dramatically from one Boston to the next—this particular block seemed to have escaped substantial damage.

Trix slowed to a fast walk, glancing back one more time and wondering if everyone could see the wraiths. *Why not? Why should only I be able to see them?* She had no clue, and not knowing was always more frightening than the truth.

"What the fuck's up with your hair?" a voice said. The kid was taller than her, maybe fourteen years old, pimply skin darkened by a line of tattoo ants crawling around his neck and up one cheek. There were several other youths standing behind him, feigning attitude but exuding fear. Some were Asian.

Here we go, she thought, saying, "Got a problem with pink, Ant Man?"

He scoffed, bristling when a couple of his compatriots chuckled. "Got a mouth on you, bitch!"

"Bitch?" It was Trix's turn to bristle. "Your mother know you talk to women like that?" She took a step forward, the boy's fear apparent, and for a couple of seconds she enjoyed it. "People are dead in Boston tonight, kid. You want to give me shit when a thousand people are buried under rubble?"

He stood taller, glancing left and right—*Can he see them,* can *he?*—then looked down at his feet.

"Your families all okay?" Trix asked.

"Yeah," Ant Man said. "We just dunno what to do."

"Looks like you got off easy," she said, "but you could help me. I'm looking for Sally Bennet."

"You an' everyone else," the boy said. He turned and pointed along the street.

Trix had assumed they were just another milling group. But half a dozen buildings ahead, a line of people snaked down the steps from a front door and twenty feet along the street. There must have been thirty people there.

"They're all seeing Sally?"

"Yeah. Few from round here, some people I've never seen before."

"You give them shit, too?" The boy looked ashamed, and Trix smiled to put him at ease. "Take it easy, kid," she said.

"Name's Marcus."

"It's a good name." She passed them by and hurried along the street, and as she approached the queue she made out the people standing there in more detail. Black, white, Hispanic, men, women, and several children, they stood in silence, shuffling forward slowly as a huge woman exited the building and hurried down the steps.

The number of people here surprised her. Had they all gone through some ritual to find Sally, as she and Jim had done at the traffic island and then the restaurant back in their Boston? She doubted that, given the short time since the quake. And she wondered what that said about Veronica—that she had a greater distance between her and the people and city she was there to protect.

So many missing people, Trix thought. She stopped in the middle of the road, and several people glanced at her. One pointed farther along the sidewalk. "There's a *line,*" the man said.

"Yeah." Trix looked back the way she had come. Ant Man and his hangers-on were walking briskly along the street, and none of them seemed to notice the pale figure crouched atop a two-story house at the far corner. Another hid in shadows across the street. *Just waiting,* she thought. *Watching. At least Jim took one of them with him.* She pressed her hand to her jeans pocket, pretending to touch the letter she did not have, and then stormed up the steps and into the run-down building.

A few voices of protest followed her in, and she heard shock at her lack of respect. But she'd apologize later. If they knew why she was here, they'd say nothing. If they were aware of what had happened, and that their Oracle's life was in danger, they'd have piled in behind her and protected her all the way. Inside the building she smelled cooking vegetables and heard loud, pulsing music, and the line of people led behind the staircase and into a low doorway beneath. *She's in the basement as if she's hiding away.* Hands clasped at Trix as she pushed by, and a few more voices rose in anger, but she forced herself down the darkened staircase. She stumbled, missed a step, and was helped on her way by a shove in the back. She twisted as she fell and saw the angry man glaring down at her. "Wait your turn!" he whispered as she slid down the wooden stairs on her back.

She grunted as she hit the cellar floor, pulling herself to her feet and quickly sensing the different atmosphere down here. She looked sidelong at the walls, expecting to see a thin place, but this was something else.

This was humanity in need, in the presence of a power that might give aid.

"Impatient for bad news?" a voice said. Trix turned slowly and looked to the far end of the basement room.

The girl sitting on a ratty wicker chair couldn't have been much more than eleven years old. She was black, wearing jeans and a grubby Miley Cyrus T-shirt, and holding the hand of a woman kneeling by her side. Trix had never seen a child so haunted and devoid of hope.

"Sally?" she asked. The girl nodded. "Sally, I have something terrible to tell you. I think Veronica wants you dead."

The girl sighed. "I thought as much. C'mere, lady. You better tell me everything."

"First . . ." Trix started shaking. "There are men without faces."

Sally's eyes opened wide. And then, in the building above, people began to scream.

Where four streets met at odd angles, and the traffic island was home to a statue that Jim did not recognize, Jenny's parents' restaurant sat at one prominent corner. Back in Boston it was called Junction 58, and he was thrilled—and a little chilled—to see that it had the same name here. Its ornate glass frontage had shattered to the street, spilling the outdoor tables and chairs that were stacked overnight beneath the awning, but he was still looking at a sight familiar and well loved, and he felt something right itself in his mind. *It's not all madness,* he thought, and then his brief fantasy was blown away.

Jenny's mother stepped out from the restaurant. They lived in the three-story apartment upstairs, and their first reaction after the earthquake must have been to come down to the street, checking the damage on the way. She was waving a menu before her face as if hot, and she was almost the woman Jim had known for so long. Almost, but not quite. Slighter than he remembered, hair longer and darker, face a little more weathered-looking, this was Jenny's mother as she might be five or ten years down the road.

I wonder if Jenny is married, he thought, because he was Unique, and long dead here. A burst of jealousy—of *anger*—swelled through him, and he started across the street. Jenny's other mother saw him and frowned slightly, then looked away.

"Excuse me," Jim said, and then he froze in the middle of the street. What could he possibly say?

"You okay, hon?" the woman asked, and Jim's blood ran cold. *She calls me hon,* he thought, and he searched for any signs of recognition. But there were none. "Hey, mister, anything wrong?"

"Wrong?" Jim asked.

"Aside from the whole world shaking itself apart," she said, looking past him at the glowing horizon and smoke clouds starting to obscure the moonlight.

"I was just wondering . . . ," he started again. But there was no easy way for him to ask about Jenny, and suddenly he hoped that she had not come this way at all. He remembered the two blond women staring at each other back at the traffic pileup—*one* blond woman, really, facets of her existent in two different worlds— and he tried to imagine the terror Jenny and Holly might have felt arriving here and seeing someone who was not quite their mother, not quite their grandmother.

"Wondering what?" she asked, on her guard at last.

"Nothing," Jim said, shaking his head and backing away. *I should have gone with Trix . . . the Oracle, Sally, she'll be able to help, she'll know what to—*

And then someone else emerged from the restaurant's smashed façade.

"Jenny," Jim said. "Jenny!"

And the woman frowned and took one step back, because she did not know him.

10

Don't Let Me Die Still Wondering

CAGED LIGHTBULBS flickered, throwing zoetrope shadows into the basement corners. Trix stared at the young Oracle—her wide eyes, her well-worn sneakers, her faded concert T-shirt, and her skittish body language so reminiscent of an animal used to being beaten. Sally had frozen, half crouched, listening to the screams and running feet from above, as those who had come to her for help were attacked or driven in terror out of the building.

Going tharn, Trix thought. In *Watership Down,* that was what the rabbits called the paralysis they experienced when pinned by the lights of an oncoming car. Sally Bennet had gone tharn.

"Do something!" Trix shouted at the girl.

Sally glanced at her. The power flickered on and off again, and in the moments of darkness, somehow the girl's face was the only thing that Trix could see, despite the dark coffee hue of her skin.

The middle-aged woman who'd been asking for Sally's help when Trix had entered the basement staggered backward toward a corner farther from the stairs, looking around as though for another way out. When Trix glanced at Sally again, she found the girl staring at her.

"Shadow Men," the girl said, voice broken with grief. "You brought them."

Trix felt her heart flutter. The girl was right, but what choice had she had? "I didn't know where else to go. You're the Oracle! I didn't know you were a little girl."

Sally laughed softly but without any trace of humor. Trix noticed that one of her sneakers was untied. The girl shook her braided hair back and knelt on the floor. "It isn't just little girls who get frightened," Sally said.

Trix heard glass shatter upstairs, but the screaming had nearly ceased. The door to the basement shook in its frame. They didn't even need to open the door to pass through it, at least she didn't think so. The wraiths—the things Sally had named Shadow Men—might be mindless things, programmed for this task, but if so, part of their job must be to make themselves terrible. To not merely kill the Oracles, but to destroy everything around them.

"I know! I'm a grown-up, and I'm terrified," Trix said.

The woman who'd backed into the corner of the basement sobbed loudly.

Sally put her palms down on the stone floor of the basement. Her eyes were closed and she breathed deeply and evenly, as though trying to meditate with chaos erupting above her. "The No-Face Men," Sally said.

"Yes," Trix quickly replied. "It has to be them. They killed Peter O'Brien, and we saw them after the earthquake, out on the street."

But Sally seemed not to hear her, and Trix realized that the girl had not been speaking to her. For a second she flashed back to the moment in the bookstore, when she and Jim had watched Veronica testing the edges of reality, her senses touching upon facets of the world around her that others could never reach. *Whatever you're doing,* Trix thought, staring at the girl, *you'd better be quick about it.*

The power went out, plunging the basement into darkness. For several long seconds, Trix could hear nothing but her own heart beating in her ears and the quick, whimpering sobs of the woman in the corner. Then a warm draft of air whipped through the basement and up the stairs, and from above there came an inhuman murmuring, as though the wraiths had finally scented their true prey.

An electric buzz filled the basement, followed by a crackling noise, and the lights flickered back on.

Sally stood in the center of the room, wearing a triumphant grin—a little girl who had just gotten her way. Blood streamed from her nostrils, and she wiped it away with the back of her hand. "Little girl, my ass," she said.

Trix would have replied, but in a moment she was rendered speechless. Arms began to rise up from the floor, ethereal things passing through stone and mortar. They were gray and vague, and Trix opened her mouth to scream a warning before she noticed that they were not attacking Sally. Their faces were weird silver mesh, like fencers' masks, but there were dark ghost faces there as well, things with ancient, hollow eyes, flickering like an old TV trying to lock on to a signal.

These weren't Veronica's Shadow Men. What had Sally whispered? *"No-Face Men"?* They kept rising, taller than humans, thinner, limbs longer. The wails from the woman in the corner altered in tone, rising and falling in a keening song of distress.

Sally pointed toward the stairs. "Go," she said, the triumphant smile gone from her face, leaving only grim determination behind.

The No-Face Men flowed toward the stairs as if driven by storm winds. Trix saw them coming at her and could not help letting out a cry as she threw herself to one side. They flashed past her, buzzing with their own static, and up the stairs. Trix expected more sounds of destruction from above, more cries of fear and despair, but instead there was only silence.

"Martha?" Sally said gently to the wailing woman in the corner, who quieted at once. "Come with me. The friend whose house your son was sleeping at tonight . . . the building collapsed in the quake. Both boys are trapped there, but they're still alive. The city's reacting now. Rescue workers are searching for survivors in the buildings that fell. You need to get over there."

The woman stared at the young Oracle in shock. Sally took her hand and tugged her along toward the stairs. Trix felt frozen—she'd gone tharn herself, listening to the nothing from upstairs.

"You coming, Trix?" the girl asked, looking sweetly innocent.

"I didn't tell you my name," Trix said. She wanted to tie the laces on the Oracle's left sneaker. She felt distant, as though her spirit held on to her flesh only by the slimmest tether. But as Sally and Martha hurried past her, she snapped back into the world as though coming awake from a nightmare. She reached out and grabbed Sally's wrist. "Stop. You can't . . ." She forced the whirlwind of her thoughts to be still. "All of this happened because they killed O'Brien. If they kill you, too, the third Boston might collide with this one . . . these two . . . you know what I'm saying. I won't let that happen."

Sally rolled her eyes. "Duh. Neither will I. You think I wanna die? First thing we do is get our butts out of here."

"But the wraiths . . . the Shadow Men—"

"Can't kill me quite so easily," Sally said. "O'Brien's

guard must have been down if they took him without a fight."

"Veronica gave us—"

"Trix!" Sally snapped. "Do you want to find what you came looking for, or not?" With that, she went up the stairs, Martha following behind her.

Trix stared after them for several seconds, then hustled to catch up. They emerged in a corridor, but half a dozen steps took them into the front of the house, where a silent battle raged in the front rooms and through the open door.

The Shadow Men—the horrible wraiths who had paced her through the devastated city—were locked in combat with the spindle-limbed No-Face Men Sally had summoned. The two sides were at war, grappling in utter silence, tearing at one another with ghostly claws. Their flesh, flayed and ripped, seemed like gray cotton batting but dissipated like smoke in the air. They throttled one another, sailing across the rooms, crashing through walls as though they themselves were solid and the twin collided cities were some haunted ghostland.

Trix faltered, astonished by the scene unfolding around her, but then fear and good sense got her moving and she hurried, praying that she would not be noticed. As thought caught in Sally's wake, several of Veronica's wraiths turned to pursue her, only to be snagged by the long talons of their enemies, whose flickering static faces were brutally blank. One of the No-Face Men opened its mouth—a gaping, saw-toothed maw of oil-black nothing that looked like a hole torn in the curtain of the world, on the other side of which anything might be lurking. It swallowed the Shadow Man's head, biting it off with a silent snap of its jaws. The Shadow Man turned to smoke, drifting and fading in seconds.

There were several dead people on the floor, heads

caved in from being smashed against walls or floors, limbs broken. Despair filled the hollow places inside Trix. These people had come to the Oracle for help in making sense of the collision of the cities, or to find those they had lost in the madness. The others who had come to Sally were gone now, scattered by the bloodshed and the sight of the wraiths. They had run for their lives. But others would come, just as Trix had gone to find Veronica when Jenny and Holly had gone missing. They would be in danger.

Another Shadow Man reached for Sally, and a No-Face Man latched on to it from behind, tearing away strips of its flesh as if it were made of cotton candy.

Sally ran out the door and into the street, pulling Martha behind her. Trix ran out after them, realizing that she had been holding her breath since the basement. She exhaled, turning around in fright. There were Shadow Men and No-Face Men in the street, too, but only a few.

"Go," Sally told Martha, giving her a little shove. "Donnie will be all right if they find him soon. But you've got to hurry."

"Thank you," Martha said, backing away. "Oh, my God, thank you." She fled then, and for a moment Trix wished she could follow.

Sally turned and glared at Trix, one hip cocked. In her sneakers and jeans and Miley Cyrus T-shirt, the little girl would have looked almost adorably precocious, impossible to take seriously, were it not for the pain and wisdom in her eyes. "Now, you," she said. "Come with me. Don't stop for anything."

Sally turned and started to run. Several people who had obviously come looking for her tried to stop her, calling to her, but she ignored them and ran on. Trix kept up, avoiding places where the pavement was cracked or broken, lamenting that she could not stop to help a group of people frantically moving rubble away from a collapsed synagogue.

"Where are we going?" Trix asked, panting, as they rounded a corner, jumping onto the sidewalk to avoid the water that gushed from a broken hydrant and the wreckage of half a dozen cars that were mashed together in the street.

Sally shot her a hard look. "Somewhere they won't be able to follow you."

"Me?" Trix asked. "They're after you."

Sally turned right to avoid the road ahead, where an office building and an old music hall had tried and failed to co-exist, and debris blocked the street. "Yeah, they're after me. But they're *following* you. Veronica marked you with something her Shadow Men can always find, and whatever it is, it broke down the wards and safeguards I'd put on my house. It must have done the same to Peter O'Brien's bar, if they were able to get in there after him. But there must have been more. Did you hand him anything from her?"

"A letter."

Sally nodded. "Hobbling hex. Easily done, if you know how."

"Enabling those things to attack him?"

"O'Brien would have been slowed, his ability to fight back reduced. And he'd have known what was happening."

"So it *is* our fault," Trix said softly, and Sally said nothing to disabuse her of that notion.

Trix's legs hurt from running. Her chest burned from effort and her mind whirled as she tried to make the pieces of the puzzle fit together. She thought of O'Brien opening the envelope, swearing when he found the black-spotted page. He must have known in that moment that danger was approaching.

Trix felt herself swept along in Sally's wake. What could she do now? How was she supposed to find Jenny and Holly? And what about Jim? They were moving farther and farther away from Jenny's parents' restaurant. If Jim went looking for her at Sally Bennet's address, he would find nothing but dead people.

"My friend—"

"Later," Sally said. "First, we get somewhere they can't find us. Then we get that mark off of you."

Trix gasped. "Mark on *me*?"

"The Shadow Men are following you somehow."

"But she never touched me," Trix said, thinking back to her brief time with Veronica, wondering.

"Doesn't matter. Did it somehow, and it needs removing. Then I have to stop that bitch from doing to your Boston what she's done to mine!"

"And killing you," Trix said.

Sally slowed down, out of breath, getting her bearings. She looked at Trix. "That, too," she agreed. She glanced back and Trix followed her gaze. There was no sign of the Shadow Men, but if Trix was really marked, they would find her again as soon as they got away from Sally's No-Face Men.

Her heart ached, but not from exertion. In all of this madness, with the stakes so high, how would she ever find Jenny and Holly?

"Hey," Sally said, reaching out to touch her. "I'll find them. Whoever you and your friend are looking for, I'll find them, and get you out of here. We'll all be safer with you back where you belong."

Trix felt relief wash through her, but then she frowned. She didn't understand why Sally would bother to help her in the midst of all this.

An angry sneer lifted one corner of the little girl's mouth, and suddenly Sally seemed much older, almost cruel. "I'm going to send you back with my own mark on you," she said. "And with my No-Faces on your trail. I won't let them kill Veronica, but they can punish her. Imprison her. Keep her from trying this fucking shit again."

Trix stared at her in wonder. Ten or eleven years old, but so much older than her years, Sally Bennet had it all figured out. She might not be able to turn back time and prevent the horror and devastation that had hit two Bostons tonight, but she knew how to stop Veronica from making it any worse. And Trix and Jim would get Jenny and Holly back in the bargain.

"Just tell me what I need to do," Trix said, hopes soaring.

"For now?" Sally said, grim and dark-eyed. "Just keep up."

She started running again. Trix took a deep breath and ran after her, putting her fate and the fate of those she loved in the hands of a little girl. But she knew she had no choice. Jenny and Holly were out there, somewhere, in the ruin of two cities. The survivors of those two Bostons, and the people of Trix's own city . . . they were all now depending on Sally Bennet.

When he saw Jenny shrink away from him, all of Jim's strength fled. For an instant, hope had raced through him like adrenaline fire, but then he had seen the lack of recognition in her eyes and knew that when she looked at him, she saw a stranger. This wasn't his Jenny.

Exhaustion weighed him down. Thus far, determination had driven him on. He loved his family, but he needed them even more, and that need propelled him through despair and past weariness. But all along, hopelessness had whispered in the back of his mind like some tiny devil seated on his shoulder, and now at last he surrendered to it.

Jim turned his back on the restaurant—on not-his-Jenny and not-his-Jenny's mother—and tried to walk away. He managed three steps before his legs went out from under him and he fell to his knees on the cracked pavement. No tears came. Numb, he felt his whole body sag.

In a moment he would get up. In a moment he would continue his search. In a moment he would catch up with Trix and they would pretend that two cities hadn't just smashed together, that people weren't dead and dying around them, that Bostonians weren't facing their doppelgängers, their reality falling apart. In a moment—

"Do you know me?"

Her voice froze him in place. For a moment he could not breathe, and his chest clenched so tightly that he thought his heart had paused as well. Then she touched him gently on the shoulder and spoke again. "Hey," she said. "Anybody home in there?"

Jim shuddered and smiled at the same time. How many times had she said the same words to him? When he was lost in thought, painting in his mind, she would try to talk to him and it would be like her voice—her presence—was muffled conversation from another room. And then she would touch him, and ask him that same question, in those same words, though rarely with the same sadness.

If he just kept his eyes closed, if he didn't answer, maybe he could pretend for just a little while that she was his Jenny after all.

But he couldn't do that. The sounds of chaos and crisis filled the city, and closing his eyes did not make them go away. There could be no pretending.

Jim turned to look at this woman who was not his wife. She wore a confused and troubled expression, and he wondered what she was seeing on his face—surprise or love or madness, or some combination of all three? "I'm sorry," Jim said, unable to keep himself from searching her eyes for some sign of recognition. "I keep wishing I could wake up and find out it's all a nightmare."

Not-his-Jenny nodded. "Me, too. I think there's going to be a lot of that going around."

Her mother stood on the restaurant's front stoop, gazing worriedly at the two of them. But then something inside the restaurant drew her attention, and after a quick glance, she set aside her broom and went in.

"So, are you going to tell me who you are?" she asked.

Before he could answer, a fire engine roared down the street without its siren, a grim-faced man behind the wheel. They both watched it pass, and Jim saw that a number of people had come out onto the stoops of the apartment buildings on the block. A van pulled up and two burly men got out, staring at the damage to the façade of a music store across the street that had specialized in antique vinyl records. The owners, he figured. The store existed in his Boston, too, and somehow that reassured him.

She was still waiting for an answer.

"I'm Jim," he said, feeling foolish, as though she ought to know. But of course she didn't. "Jim Banks."

"Why don't you come inside, Jim?" she said.

He looked at her, amazed at her tenderness, as he always had been. "You don't even know me."

"No, but I can see you know me. Or you think you do."

"Jenny—" he began.

"Jennifer," she corrected. "No one's called me Jenny since my grandfather died."

Jim nodded, studying her. Jennifer. That would make it easier—at least a little. She had an old scar on her chin that his Jenny had never had and she wore her hair pulled back into a ponytail, revealing three studs in each ear. She was thinner than his Jenny, too, by at least ten pounds. More time at the gym.

"Jennifer," he echoed, finally climbing to his feet. "Why doesn't it freak you out? I mean, yes, I know you, but you're not afraid of me. Why aren't you calling the cops right now, reporting me as a stalker or something?"

"The cops have bigger troubles tonight," she said. "Besides, you showing up here, calling my name, looking at me like that? It's not the weirdest thing to happen to me tonight."

A tremor of excitement went through him, and he could feel his face flush. He glanced at the shattered windows of the restaurant, but from this angle he could only see the ceiling fans and the old tin ceiling. "She came here, didn't she?" he asked, nodding at Jennifer. He smiled. "Is that what you're talking about? You must have thought you were going crazy. And your parents—"

"Who are you talking about?" Jennifer asked.

Jim had to laugh at her tone, and the crinkle of her eyes, and the way one corner of her mouth lifted higher than the other. All so familiar to him. All parts of his Jenny. "The other you," he said. "My Jenny. Your double, or whatever."

But even as he spoke, Jennifer shook her head, backing away from him, broken glass crunching under the soles of her shoes. "Jesus," she said, putting a hand to her temple. "I don't think I can take much more of this."

And Jim knew he was wrong. He wanted to scream in frustration, but knew he would only chase her away. "Jennifer," he said, keeping his voice low and steady enough to draw her attention. "Why don't you tell me what's going on?"

She let loose a frantic little laugh. "You mean other than the earthquake?"

"I'm getting the idea you already know it wasn't just an earthquake," Jim said.

That snapped her out of whatever hysterical slide she'd been in. She looked around the glass-strewn street, glanced over the tops of buildings at the altered cityscape, and then started again for the door to the restaurant. "You'd better come in."

Jennifer used her shoe to brush away some of the glass that her mother's broom had missed, and led the way into what had once been a quaint little restaurant with the best steaks, seafood, and desserts in Boston. Her father, Tad Garland, had been the mastermind behind the desserts. To the amusement of many customers, it was his wife, Rose, who had made it the place to go for steak and seafood. People craving a good meal came to Junction 58.

The interior of the place looked much the same as it had in Jim's Boston—or it would have, if not for the crack in the ceiling and the shattered glasses and bottles behind the bar, and the pictures and other hangings that had fallen off the wall. Junction 58 was some kind of train reference—Tad Garland loved trains—and there were tracks that hung from the ceiling, a whole maze that a pair of model trains and their passenger cars and box-cars steamed through over and over again during lunch and dinner seatings. The track was still there, but the trains had fallen, and lay smashed to pieces on the floor.

Tad Garland sat in a chair, staring at the broken remains of one of his model steam engines, which he had arranged on a table before him.

And a different Tad Garland—slimmer and better

dressed, with round eyeglasses and a long gash on his left cheek—stood over by the bar, gazing wide-eyed at Jennifer's mother, as though Rose Garland might be a ghost.

Jennifer moved toward her father, the Tad who was sitting with his broken train, and glanced meaningfully back at Jim. "Dad," she began.

Both Tads looked up.

Rose Garland went behind the bar, moving past her husband's doppelgänger as though she wanted to pretend he wasn't there, and searched until she had found five glasses that weren't broken. A little more fishing turned up an undamaged bottle of Jack Daniel's. The woman responsible for the best steaks in Boston wasn't going to screw around with wine or margaritas. "I'm pouring myself a drink," Rose said. "Anyone doesn't want one, I'll drink yours for you."

Strangely, it was the other Tad—the one who obviously didn't belong—who first spoke to Jim. "Who might you be?" he asked.

"His name's Jim Banks," Jennifer answered for him.

Her mother and father both looked at her like she'd cussed in church. Rose threw back two fingers of Jack Daniel's, then poured a little more. No one else made a move for the glasses she had set out, at least not at first. But after a few wordless seconds, the other Tad moved down the front of the bar, righting a fallen stool, and picked up a glass of golden brown whiskey. He sipped it, looking at Jim over the top of the glass and touching his cut. "You have any idea how any of this is possible, Mr. Banks?" he asked.

This question got all of their attention. All four Garlands—the ones who belonged here and the one who didn't—narrowed their eyes. Jim studied the two Tads and wondered where the other Rose might be. Was she dead, or had she divorced Tad and left Boston altogether? He decided she must be dead. It would explain the way the other Tad looked at Rose, and there was no way that the Rose Garland he knew would've let her husband keep the restaurant if they'd gotten a divorce. Just the fact that the other Tad had been here when the two Bostons merged meant he still owned the place, at least in his city. And how the hell would that work, now that there were two Tad Garlands in this version of Boston, but only one Junction 58?

"I know a little," Jim admitted.

The Tad who belonged swept the pieces of his train off the table in front of him, and they clattered to the floor. "Well, spit it out, then, buddy. 'Cause my head's splitting in two."

As if realizing what he'd said, Tad flinched and looked over at the other Tad, who laughed and toasted him with glistening whiskey. "Something's splitting in two," the other Tad said. With that, he grabbed another of the glasses Rose had poured and walked across the bar to his double, setting the drink on the table.

Tad looked at the glass for a second, then shook his head with a dubious chuckle and picked it up, sipping the whiskey just like the other Tad.

"Actually, it's not anything splitting in two," Jim said, glancing around the bar, worried about what he ought to say and what he ought to keep to himself. "It's two things coming together that shouldn't."

Jennifer hugged herself. Jim wanted to do it for her, to embrace her and make her feel safe and warm, but she didn't know him.

"You want to explain that?" Rose asked.

"It may be hard to believe—"

"Are you kidding?" Jennifer said. "After the past couple of hours, what could be hard to believe?"

Jim nodded. She was right. No use trying to break it to them gently. "Short version," he said. "A long time ago, an asshole named McGee fucked around with magic and basically broke Boston into three pieces. Not pieces. That's wrong. Three variations. Three possibilities. All three were real, side by side . . . well, in the same space, I guess. And part of the structure that held them apart gave way tonight. Two of the cities crashed into each other. Places where they were the same, like your restaurant, were affected the least. But in other places, where the cities differed the most . . ."

"The cathedral," Jennifer said, her eyes haunted as she glanced out through the shattered windows at the street. "We saw."

Jim gestured at the two Tads. "You guys aren't going to be the only ones dealing with this tonight. My bet? A huge percentage of the city are meeting their twins right now, or they will be soon."

"Not me," Rose said, pouring herself another splash of Jack and staring into the glass. She smiled bitterly. "Turns out I'm dead."

"You're not dead, Mom," Jenny insisted. "You're right here."

"Be glad you don't have to deal with this," her husband said.

"Glad?" the other Tad said, looking at his double in disgust. "Glad that my Rose is dead?"

"That's not what he meant," Jennifer said quickly, trying to stave off an argument.

"How the hell do you know all this?" Rose asked, staring suspiciously at Jim.

He hesitated. No way could he tell them that he had anything to do with this devastation, with crashing their worlds together, with the death and destruction around them. Jim and Trix had been Veronica's pawns, nothing more. He wouldn't take the blame for her madness.

"There's a woman who wants to undo what McGee did. She's screwing with the same kind of magic. But there's no way to undo it, not really. Just by her trying . . . well, you've seen the result. And there's a third Boston out there. If she has her way, that one'll be merged in with all of this, and even more people will die. Maybe a lot more, because I have a feeling that if all three cities are forced into the same space, the quake could be much stronger."

"Jesus," Rose whispered, staring at him.

"Okay," the other Tad said. "But how do you *know*?"

Shit. Think, Jim.

"I'm looking for my wife and daughter. I went to see a man named Peter O'Brien—a guy who knows some of that magic—because I was told he could help me find them. He told me all of this, but he died in the quake."

He hated lying. Jenny had always known when he wasn't telling the truth, and now he looked at Jennifer to see if she could tell, too. But she had something else on her mind. "When you showed up here . . . ," she began. "You were looking for me."

Jim nodded slowly, glancing away for a second and then back. "My wife, Jenny Banks." He smiled weakly. "Jennifer Anne Garland Banks."

Jennifer stared at him for a second, then looked around the room as though searching for something, as though she could see a million possibilities flitting in the air around her head. She strode over to the bar, picked up one of the glasses, and knocked back two fingers of whiskey before staring at him again. She wiped her lips with the back of her hand. "We have a daughter?"

Jim shook his head. "No. Not 'we.'"

Wonder and curiosity and even a glint of happiness had appeared in her eyes as she'd spoken those words, as she entertained the notion of this other version of her life, but his words snuffed out that spark. He regretted them instantly, hating to see the pain of reality settling back into her expression. How could he explain to her that he didn't exist in the Boston she knew, that they couldn't have met? What other questions would that lead to?

"Look, I'm here because I thought Jenny and Holly— my daughter—might have come here, just to be somewhere familiar. Obviously they haven't, or at least they didn't let you see them if they did. I need to get out there and keep looking, so—"

Tad pointed at him but turned to the other Tad. "So this guy is married to *your* Jennifer?"

"No," the other Tad said. "I've never seen him before."

Rose gestured toward him with the Jack Daniel's bottle. "Which means either you're lying, Jim Banks, or you're from the other Boston. The third one."

"Yeah," Jim agreed. "That's right."

"Well, if all this magic stuff is true—" the other Tad started.

"Gotta be," Tad said. "How else do you explain all this shit?"

"Then we get how it is *I'm* here," the other Tad continued. "Our two Bostons crashed, right? But if you're from the third one, the one that's still out there like the iceberg that hit the goddamn *Titanic*, then how did *you* get here? How did your family get here?"

Jim felt like shouting. He fidgeted, looked at Jennifer as if she might rescue him, and then remembered she didn't know him. He couldn't take responsibility for these people. Back in his own life, his own reality, they were his in-laws . . . and Jennifer was his wife. But this wasn't his world, and he needed to find his real family. "Look, I'm sorry," he said. "I've got to find my wife and daughter."

"Jim," Jennifer said. Her tone was soft and kind, and banished any tension from the room. "You were right. If it was me . . . if I was the one lost . . . this is where I would come."

Jim glanced at the door, wanting to run but also knowing she might be right. Jenny and Holly had been here for half a day, at least. They would have had time to come by the Junction already, and maybe they had but had been too weirded out by everything to go inside. Or maybe they'd gotten a glimpse of Jennifer and that had freaked them out even more. But now, in the aftermath of the quake, if she and Holly were still alive—and they had to be—there was a strong possibility they would come here. On the other hand, if he stayed and waited, and they didn't come here, he might never find them.

Had coming here first been a mistake? Being so close to the restaurant, he had been unable to resist the urge to see if Jenny and Holly were there. But he had let Trix go on ahead to the Oracle's address. He had tried to lead the wraiths away, and some of them had followed him, but they had quickly vanished, leaving him alone.

Shit, he thought. *Trix.* He had been so caught up in the shock of seeing Jennifer and her parents, and the presence of the other Tad, that he hadn't been thinking enough about Trix, and the Oracle, and the wraiths.

"Maybe you're right," he said. "I hate the idea of me leaving, only to have them show up here. But I've got a friend with me, helping me search. She's gone to ask for help from someone not far from here, someone else who knows some of this magical crap. I've got to go and get her, and then I'll figure out what happens next. But if Jenny and Holly do come here, and I'm not here—"

"We'll look out for them," Rose said. "I'll make sure they wait." She pushed the whiskey bottle away. Now that she had a purpose, she wasn't interested in drinking herself into oblivion.

Jim looked at her. "Thank you." He looked at the two Tads, and then at Jennifer. "I'll be back."

"Wait," Jennifer called as he started for the door.

Jim prepared himself to argue, focused now on catching up with Trix, making sure she was all right. But Jennifer walked over and kissed her father's cheek, took the whiskey glass he had been sipping at, and drank down the rest.

Then she looked at Jim, eyes gleaming with determination that was so very Jenny. "I'm coming with you," she said.

And as with his Jenny, there was no arguing with her.

Float

BACK AT your house, you knew my name," Trix said, catching up. "How?"

Sally didn't slow down or even look at her. "I'm the Oracle of Boston, honey. I'm the soul of the city. I feel every brick and beam. Every birth and death."

Trix thought about that, about what it must have felt like for Sally when the two cities collided, people dying and buildings crumbling, other people and buildings appearing. "It must be agony," she said.

Sally paused and caught her breath, and for a second Trix saw the pain she had been hiding all along. The girl looked at her without replying, but her eyes were troubled.

"But what about the Irish Boston?" Trix went on. "Parts of this"—she gestured around them as she ran—"it's not your city."

"It is now," Sally said. "It's like waking up with limbs I didn't have before. But I'll learn to use them quick enough." She started running again, darting across an intersection and barely pausing before a tumbled façade. Three stories of the damaged building were revealed, its insides were open to view, and Trix suspected the whole city felt so exposed. She paused to look, but Sally called back over her shoulder, "There's no one left inside."

"Right," Trix muttered as she followed the girl again. "You're the Oracle."

They ran through the shaken city. Trix half expected Sally to be stopped by every wandering, terrified person they saw, but no one seemed to recognize her. But if *everyone* knew the Oracle, the girl would never have time to sleep.

"You had so many people seeing you, so quickly after the quake," Trix said. "With Veronica, there's ritual, and time."

"I don't go with those old-style customs," Sally replied. "If someone knows about me, why make it hard if they need my help?"

"Yeah," Trix said, and they ran on.

A few minutes later, running past a small park where the ghostly lights of mobile phones lit disembodied faces in the darkness, Trix asked, "Have you found them yet?"

"No," Sally said. "But I haven't started looking."

"What? I thought—"

"You need to trust me," Sally said, panting. "Told you, gotta get her mark off you. Her Shadow Men will come after us, following the mark, and when they find us again they'll be expecting more than humans."

"But your No-Face Men, they fought them off, killed them."

Sally chuckled—a terrible knowing laugh. "Element of surprise," she said. "And you can't kill what isn't alive."

"Ghosts?"

"I didn't say that. Now, come on. The less we talk, the quicker we get there."

"Where?"

"You'll see," the girl said.

So Trix ran on in silence, trying to imagine what mark

Veronica might have put on her, and how, and when. And it took only moments for her to realize what this meant. If Sally cleaned her of the mark, there was one other person still lit up like a Christmas tree for the Shadow Men to track.

But for now, Jim was on his own.

The exercise went some way to tempering her shock at what was happening, and her fear of what was to come. She'd had terrible destruction wrought upon the city she so loved, and now the heartache that had brought. But she had also seen people killed by something other than the earthquake. She wasn't sure she would ever forget the image of those bodies, bloodied and deformed by the forces that had destroyed them, strewn around Sally's building and street where they had come in their desperate search for loved ones. She wondered how many of those loved ones were still alive, and what they would think when they saw the manner of their friends' and relatives' deaths.

Muscles burning, chest heaving, she concentrated on matching Sally's surprising pace. *Worse to come,* she thought, and though she had no idea where that had risen from, she couldn't shake it.

Another ten minutes of running, and at last Trix recognized their destination. She'd been to the old Granary Burying Ground once before, walking around on her own, reading the grave inscriptions and admiring the unusual tombs. Leaving the cemetery, she had felt displaced, as if she had just arrived in this city after a very long time away. What she'd thought had been half an hour had really been three, and she'd found a Dunkin' Donuts and sat there for some time, musing over the walk and trying to pin down just why it had felt so weird. She'd lost the memory quickly as life intruded again, and the next day she had barely remembered any of her visit to that place. But it all came flooding back now.

"There's something . . . ," she said, standing at the cemetery gates.

"Come on," Sally said, and grabbed her hand. It elicited a gasp of surprise from Trix, and Sally grinned as she walked them both through the gate.

"I've been here before," Trix said, aware as she spoke that this might not be the *exact* cemetery she had walked around that day several years before.

"Safe," Sally whispered, and she let go of Trix's hand, sank slowly to her knees, and leaned forward until her forehead rested against the ground.

"Sally?" Trix said, and for the first time she was worried for the Oracle. The girl seemed smaller than she had before, and the cemetery seemed to hold its breath at their predicament. From all around came the sounds of chaos—sirens, shouting, and the musical tinkle of falling glass—but the cemetery was quiet, and timeless.

Trix knelt by her side but did not quite touch her. The girl took deep breaths. Trix felt as if they were being watched. Hulking shadows shifted slightly as lights moved out on the road, shivering as if unsure of themselves. "I've been here before," Trix said again, and then she saw movement from the corner of her eye.

"Don't be afraid," Sally said, a curious statement from a girl hugging herself into a ball. But as Trix stood and spun left and right—following shadows that always seemed *just* behind her, *just* out of sight—the girl's words settled and gave her peace.

"The air is thin here," she said. Though Veronica had lied and deceived them, Trix understood the truth of what she'd told her and Jim about thin places, and their ability to perceive them. This was one such place. At first glance she could see no earthquake damage, and she thought she knew why—this cemetery existed in all three Bostons and was the same in each reality. But then along the path from where they'd entered, below the weak glow of a lamp, she saw a bench that had been up-ended, and below it, an old grave. If she'd seen it any other time, she'd have suspected vandals of uprooting the bench from elsewhere and propping it against the gravestone, some pointless amusement that they would have forgotten by the end of the night. But not here, and not today. This was something more.

"Thin enough to see through," Sally said. She was standing slowly now, and she seemed calmer than she had since Trix had first laid eyes on her. A tension had gone from her face, and her pose seemed more relaxed. "So she told you about the crossing points?"

"Veronica? Yeah. She said there were places where Uniques could cross between Bostons. The thin places worried her. Thought they meant the Bostons were rein-tegrating."

"Just what she wants," Sally said.

"She said it was easy for us to see, and she told us how." Trix looked from the corner of her eye, turning in a slow circle, but then shook her head in confusion.

"You won't see the three Bostons here," Sally said. "Well, mostly not. Walk with me, and I'll tell you where we are."

"You said we're safe here?" Trix asked.

Sally smiled, with little humor. "Walk with me."

They moved through the cemetery, away from the en-trance gate and the fence lining the boundary wall. It grew darker as they walked, but never so dark that Trix couldn't see their surroundings. She looked left and right, still trying to catch those shadows that seemed to dance in her peripheral vision. She remembered entering this Boston through Thomas McGee's ruined room, and how she and Jim had seen the three versions of Boston co-existing, once Veronica had told them how.

But this was something different.

"Special place," Sally said, waving her hand to indicate the whole cemetery. "You'll find this cemetery in each Boston, looking the same, with the same people buried here. It's one of the oldest untouched places in all three Bostons—well, in two now. The Shadow Men from your Boston won't be able to track you here. Whatever mark Veronica put on you—and I'll work out exactly what that was soon enough—will be confused. There's static between worlds, and it bleeds through here. It'll confuse them."

"They didn't seem easily confused," Trix said.

"In this form they're drones, that's all, dancing to Veronica's song, but here they won't hear it. I doubt they'll wander within half a mile of here. The cemetery is unique."

"Like me?" Trix asked.

"Not quite," Sally said after a slight pause.

"What do you mean, 'in this form'?"

"Let's save the Q & A until we get you clear of her influence," Sally said, and Trix didn't argue. There was nothing she wanted more.

They passed rows of graves and tombs that cast uncertain shadows. The city was more alive than ever around them as rescue and recovery operations got under way, and that made the silence in the cemetery even more haunting. And when they approached a grave in the center of a path—the tombstone sprouting somewhere it should not have been—Trix felt a chill pass through her, and she asked, "What have you brought me here to see?"

But Sally did not answer that, and as they drew close enough to read the name on the stone, Trix found she could no longer swallow.

"Not you," Sally said quietly. "This place is much older than that." She stopped, hesitated, and then turned to Trix and grasped her hands. "This is the grave of a dead Oracle," Sally said. "A Unique, of course, because we have to be. And it's the only grave in the cemetery that doesn't exist in each Boston." She waved a hand at the bench, then walked past, dismissing the scene.

"So if Oracles can die, why haven't the Bostons collided before today? You haven't been Oracle for long, and there must be more who've died, in this Boston and the others."

"An Oracle always knows when his or her time is coming, and so does the city. They both have time to prepare, look for a replacement."

"But Peter O'Brien was murdered," Trix said, understanding perhaps a little.

"Not only that. Those things Veronica sent . . ." Sally actually shivered, and Trix saw it in the darkness. She remembered the girl summoning her No-Face Men from the basement floor of her home, and her triumphant cry, and she wondered how much that had cost her. "They ripped out his soul and dragged it into the In-Between. Tore out the heart of the city. That was enough."

They hurried on, and Trix wished there was some way she could reach Jim. She needed to talk to him, hear his voice, and tell him what was happening. Her cell phone had been smashed in the quake, and if they hadn't had the sense knocked out of them by events, they would have bought new phones. But shopping had been the last thing on their minds. Besides, she suspected that tonight of all nights, the networks would be jammed.

She hoped that he'd found Jenny and Holly by now. Hoped that they were safe, and uninjured by the cataclysm, and untouched by Veronica's wraiths.

"We're here," the little girl said.

"Where?" Trix glanced around. They were at a corner of the cemetery, bounded by two tall buildings. There was a square paved area with several benches spaced around the edges and a small water fountain at the center. The fountain was not working. Small trees grew here, their shadows cast across the paving stones from weak floodlights fixed to the walls of one of the buildings.

"A focus point," Sally said. "A place where the city's power is at its greatest. It'll help me do what I need to do to you."

"Veronica's mark." Sally nodded. "Will it hurt?"

"I hope not," the girl said, and Trix thought, *You and me both*.

She didn't understand any of this. She'd been made aware of her Boston's Oracle by her grandmother, but that didn't mean that she'd even come close to understanding anything about her. Perhaps understanding would come later.

"So what happens?" she asked.

Sally walked to the center of the small paved square and pointed at her feet. "First, you come and sit here."

It did not hurt.

Trix tried talking to Sally to begin with, asking her about the cemetery and the locus of power, and how it couldn't have been a coincidence that they were in the same place, but the girl seemed unwilling to comment and most of the time did not even appear to listen. So then Trix started thinking about Jim, and Jenny, and Holly, and how likely it was that all of them would make it back to their Boston alive. The reality of what they were going through fucked with her senses, and a voice kept whispering, *Unique, Unique.* She could not decide whether her situation made her someone special, or a freak of nature that allowed what was happening.

Because nature *had* to allow it. Trix was no believer in God, and had always found the whole idea of a supreme being, sin, guilt, and worship troubling. *If He's there, He should let me know* had always been her answer to devout friends. But at the same time, she had always acknowledged the wondrousness of nature, the incredible things that the universe contained and did, and the many facts that humanity, in its arrogance, still did not know. She was a follower of popular science, and well aware that the existence of the multiverse was now considered a valid theory rather than being confined to the realms of science fiction. What was happening here was something familiar to the universe. She and Jim had simply stumbled upon it.

How much more does Sally know? she wondered. The possibilities were chilling. Perhaps, if this was ever over, she'd ask.

"I need to touch you," Sally said. "Your head, your neck. While I'm doing that, think about Veronica. Did *she* touch you at all? Is there a moment you can recall with her when you felt . . . unusual, or unsettled? As if you were experiencing déjà vu, or someone was walking over your grave?"

"After this I might walk over my own, and see how it feels."

"It won't feel good," Sally said, and then she placed her hands on Trix's shoulders.

"What about Jenny and Holly?" Trix asked.

"Soon." For the first time Sally sounded like a little

girl—scared, uncertain, confused. Trix resisted the temptation to look around at the Oracle's face. She was terrified herself, and now that she'd found this girl who seemed to possess some kind of understanding and an ability to counteract what was happening, she wanted to hold on to it.

"Anything?" Sally whispered.

"She gave us tea and cookies."

"Ahh," Sally said, smiling. "Cookies." And she moved her hands from Trix's shoulders down to her stomach.

It was as if she'd swallowed the coldest, sweetest drink imaginable—a blend of liquid nitrogen and chemical sweetener. And yet she'd swallowed nothing at all.

"You might have a bit of an upset stomach for a while," Sally said.

"No kidding," Trix said. She groaned as she stood, and already the girl was walking away. "Hey, where are you going?"

"Away from the static," Sally said. "And I've got to stand on a road. Veronica's Shadow Men can't track you anymore, so now it's time to find the woman and the child."

"But Jim?"

"They can track him, yes."

"Then we have to—"

"The woman and child are the priority," Sally said. She was standing beneath a tree, and she looked like a lost little girl, but Trix knew that was far from the truth.

"So you can send your own mark back with them," she said.

"Both of them, yes. And you, if you'll let me."

"And *how* will you mark us?"

"I have my means. Better than that old bitch's methods. I mean, cookies? Seriously?" She shook her head, glanced at Trix, then nodded into the darkness. "Come on. Lots to do."

Trix could only follow.

When they reached the cemetery gates, Sally paused, remaining in the shadows as she scanned the street.

"I thought you said they couldn't track me anymore?" Trix asked.

"They might have followed, then waited after they lost you."

"Oh, great."

But there were no Shadow Men in the street. It was silent, the buildings dark and still, bearing mute witness to the chaos in the rest of the city. Sirens serenaded the darkness, and Trix wondered how bad it had been, how high the death toll. And she couldn't help thinking of that old lady who had helped her grandmother, and who said she'd help Jim, but who in fact had set the seeds for terrible destruction. How could an Oracle be so brutal? But she looked at Sally and realized that she didn't know the girl at all. Appearances, she had already learned, could be deceptive.

"Their names," Sally said, and she passed through the gate and walked to the center of the road.

Trix glanced left and right for traffic, then stood on the sidewalk.

Sally sighed impatiently. "Roads are the city's arteries. People travel along them. It's the traveling that helps me see, the floating of souls from here to there, the movement of life. I could find them sitting in my dark basement, maybe. But the city's in turmoil tonight."

"But if a car comes—"

"No car is coming. Their names." The girl's voice had lost all trace of childhood, even its timbre and tone bearing the weary cynicism of someone thirty years older.

"Holly and Jenny Banks."

"Come here, hold my hand, and picture them for me." Sally was kneeling, right hand pressed to the road's surface, left hand held up ready for Trix to grasp it. Any other time, Trix might have laughed at how ridiculous this was. But it would take a lot to make her laugh tonight.

So she pictured Jenny and Holly, and concentrating on her lost friends suddenly seemed to drive everything else away. She remembered Holly's soft child's laughter, her innocent beauty, and the way nothing really seemed to bother her. And she remembered beautiful, intelligent Jenny, and how the awkwardness made them closer friends rather than pushing them apart. Her eyes misted, and as she wiped a tear away, Sally sighed in frustration.

"Turmoil," she said. "Fuck it, then—just the mother. I can't concentrate on two. Just think of Jenny Banks."

Trix looked down at the girl and wondered what people would think if they saw them. But no one would see them, she knew, and no traffic would come. This silent street was unnatural in a city so shaken, and perhaps the girl had cast some subtle, strange ward to give herself the time and peace she needed.

She's at war, Trix thought, the idea shocking but fitting. Those No-Faces and Shadow Men had been savage as they'd fought each other. She had no wish to witness more of their efforts. So she thought only of Jenny, and moments later Sally's eyes snapped open.

"I have her," she said. "Leaving a restaurant called—"

"Junction 58," Trix said.

The girl glanced up. "This world's Jenny."

"You're sure?"

"I found her too quickly. Your Jenny will be more . . . fuzzy. Think some more, something about her that's personal to you. You're Unique, so your thoughts will apply only to *your* Jenny."

My Jenny, Trix thought, closing her eyes, and the more she tried to avoid the gentle love she felt for Jenny, the more it came to the fore. So she went with it, remembering uncomfortable stares and glib comments meant as jokes, but hiding something more serious. Jenny and Jim knew, and Trix knew that Jenny was flattered and touched. But she'd always kept secret just how much her feelings sometimes fucked her up inside.

It took longer this time, and at several points Sally squeezed her hand so hard that her finger bones grated together.

"Marlborough Street," the girl breathed, and Trix gasped and let go.

"Where on Marlborough Street?"

"Across from a church . . . in my Boston, before the collision, it was the First Lutheran," Sally said, standing and looking at Trix. "You know that place?"

"My apartment," Trix said, and she was starting to understand. If only she'd listened to Jim and checked other places first, before seeking out the Oracle and dooming that man to death. "She's gone to my apartment, and we can be there in half an hour."

Sally nodded in satisfaction. "Good. Hopefully the girl's with her."

"Of course she's with her!"

Sally shrugged.

"And Jim?" Trix asked. "He was going to the restaurant." Perhaps he'd met Jenny there after all. She closed her eyes and wondered how that would be, remembering the two women staring at each other at the intersection where they'd been involved in the accident, knowing each other and yet unable to believe. The Jenny from Sally's world would not recognize Jim. He would be bereft.

"After we find Jenny—"

"Then you find Jim," Trix said. "If you want us to help you, you have to help us."

"What do you think I'm doing?" the little girl said.

Trix nodded. They started running again, and this time she took the lead. As soon as they left that street, chaos descended once more, and they were returned to the ruins.

Through the streets, across the city, passing sights he hoped to never see again and with Jennifer keeping pace, Jim felt as though they'd known each other forever.

They hurried side by side, and he glanced at her often. Each time he was struck with the strangest realization— *This is not my wife.* It kept hitting him afresh because she looked so much like her and yet subtly different. Sleeker and fitter than his Jenny, Jennifer took their rush through the streets in her stride. Her ponytail bobbed against her back, and her piercings reflected streetlights and the occasional fire. When she sniffed, her nose crinkled in a familiar way, though, and when she looked at him there was the same strength in those familiar blue eyes.

If she had been *exactly* the same, he might have found it easier.

She didn't say much as they hurried into Chinatown, toward the address he'd memorized, the home of the other Boston's Oracle. And Jim had elected not to try explaining everything that had happened and was still happening, because the chaos in the city was enough for both of them to take in. So they moved in relative silence, and it was a comfortable peace that he felt growing between them, seeking acknowledgment. Two people who had never met could never be like this.

"Weird," Jennifer said as they rounded a corner into a busy street. There were lots of people marching this way and that, and a steady stream of cars and emergency vehicles, but other than broken glass, no signs of damage.

"What?" Jim asked, but he knew what she was referring to. The fact that she didn't feel the need to reply meant they were feeling the same way. When they saw a woman covered in blood being helped out of a building, and Jennifer clasped his hand in hers, it felt perfectly natural.

They left the busy area and wound their way along quieter residential streets. There was still activity, but these were not through-routes, and most people out on the streets lived here, in the ruin of what would have been a thriving Chinatown back in his own Boston.

"I'm running through the night with a strange man," Jennifer said.

"Not something you'd usually do, huh?" Jim asked.

"Would Jenny?"

"No. She's married to me."

Jennifer was silent for a while, but Jim could sense her brooding, turning something over and over.

"But there's no me here," he said, "or in the other Boston. There's just . . . me."

"Guess that makes you unique."

"So I'm told."

"You could be anyone," she said, and he heard the smile in her voice.

There was an edge to their conversation that Jim could not avoid or deny. He glanced at Jennifer and recognized the raised left eyebrow, and the way her lips were slightly pouted. They were flirting. He and Jenny often pretended to flirt, enjoying the false loaded air, heavy with potential and the thrum of sexual tension. False, because they often dropped into bed at a nod or a smile. The flirting took them back to their courting days, when love was fresh and sex was perhaps more an exciting adventure than a comfortable journey.

And here he was, taking comfort from someone he almost knew.

"This is so messed up," Jennifer said, and Jim berated himself for ignoring her fear. She was hanging on to him because he seemed to have some idea of what was happening, and he was seeing her familiar sexiness, when she was facing unfamiliar territory.

"You're handling it very well," he said.

"I have no choice. You saw what was happening back at the restaurant. Either everyone I know has twins they forgot to mention, or . . ." She shrugged.

"'Or' is the answer," Jim said. "Come on, we're almost there."

"Jim." Jennifer had stopped on the sidewalk, and for the first time he saw a vulnerability about her. He recognized it, and his heart seemed to drop, his eyes burned, and it took all his effort not to hug Jennifer to him and smell her hair, feel her body beneath the clothes, recognize her and take real comfort. *I can't do that,* he thought, *because she is not my wife.* But Jennifer was so definitely Jenny that his emotions were writhing in confusion.

"Yeah," he said. *She doesn't know me. She's never known me, or anyone like me.* And as he tried his best to imprint that on his mind and absorb it, she went and made everything worse.

"I feel like we've known each other forever," she said. "Isn't that weird? I mean . . . for you, maybe not. But for me, it's just so . . . not me. I've been hurt." She snorted, bitter. "Unlucky in love, Dad says."

"Believe me," he said, turning away so that he did not enfold her in his arms, "it *is* weird for me. Come on, we're almost there."

"Am I going to see her?"

"Yes," Jim said. "Yeah, you're going to see her." He believed that and clung to it, because he could not entertain any other outcome.

He navigated to Sally Bennet's address by memory, and the closer they came, the more unsettled he felt. Part of him wanted to run, desperate to meet up once again with Trix and see what she had discovered. And in that desire was the fleeting thought that, perhaps, Jenny and Holly had already been found, or had already encountered the Oracle.

But countering that instinct was a more basic, animal sense of caution. And what he saw as they turned onto Harrison Avenue inflamed that caution until it began to scream.

This isn't the earthquake, he thought when he saw the scene of devastation farther along the street. He wasn't sure how he knew that, but he did, with as much certainty as he could muster in these uncertain times. Perhaps it was the way that the helpers, hunkered over bodies sprawled across the street, kept glancing around, as if expecting the arrival of someone, or something.

Or maybe it was the blood.

"Jesus Christ," Jennifer said. Jenny would never blaspheme in that way. She held his hand and it felt right, their skin touching was familiar, and when she pressed close he could smell her breath. It stirred memories and blood.

"That must be her house," he said. "They've been here already, and we might be . . ."

Jennifer said something when he trailed off, but Jim didn't hear it. He let go of her hand and touched the folded envelope and paper in his pocket. *I should get rid of this*, he thought, but something told him to keep it. He sensed her following him, but his heart was thudding so hard that he could no longer hear her voice, or the wails of grief that echoed along the street. As he approached he looked at the bodies, desperate not to see . . . *Trix's pink hair*.

He didn't see it, but there was activity in the house as well. Lights flickered behind broken windows.

Jenny's long blond hair, and Holly's . . . Holly's . . .

Jim's throat worked and tears came as he considered the possibility of Holly being here, a victim of those bastard wraith-things that had killed the Irish Oracle. "Too late," he said again, and he turned to one of the living to ask what had happened.

Someone screamed. A woman stood from where she was kneeling by a body and pointed at Jim. Her cry was terrible, and it was taken up by others in the street as they started to flee. *All those people in need,* Jim thought, but for the first time he realized that none of the bodies were moving. "Wait!" he shouted, but behind him Jennifer's voice, broken with fear, turned his blood cold.

"What the *fuck* is *that*?" she said. He looked where she was pointing.

One of them was emerging from the front door of a house back along the street. The door was closed. Another slid down the building's façade, landing gently on the sidewalk and flexing its arms. Two more manifested from shadows as if they had only recently been a part of them.

"Shit," Jim said. One of them appeared damaged, its arm withered and less visible than the other.

Jennifer glanced back at him, mouth open, eyes wide . . . and her eyes grew even wider. "Behind you," she whispered, and Jim wished he *had* held her, just once.

Instead, he turned to face what had arrived.

Trix's ground-floor apartment light was on. Her heart beat, and not only from the exertion. The curtains were drawn, dark and heavy with a Celtic swirl.

I'd have chosen them. She wondered who the hell lived here in this Boston, and whether the building and area could possibly attract like-minded people. The pub on the corner was the same, and perhaps old man O'Reilly still had punk and folk bands on Saturday nights, and open-mic nights on Wednesdays.

"Someone's home," Sally said.

"Then let's knock." Trix crossed the street, thinking, *Let it be both of them, let it be Jenny and Holly,* because she could not imagine how terrible it would be if Holly was lost in this place, at this time.

Jenny would have done anything to keep her daughter safe and sound, whatever weird events had swallowed them up and spat them out in a different place. *I'd die for my daughter,* she'd said once as she, Jim, and Trix were lounging in the Bankses' living room after a big meal. Jim had landed a huge promotional contract with a local brewery, and they were celebrating the following week with a holiday to the Bahamas with their extended family. But that night had been their real celebration, Jenny had told her—a night at home with good food, good wine, and their best friend. And Trix had nodded, looking into the ruby depths of her Merlot, and said, *I'd kill for your daughter.* The room had fallen silent for a while, as they all realized that was one step further.

Up the steps, and she scanned the four nameplates to

see who lived in her apartment. But the paper slips were missing, leaving four mystery bell pushes.

"Try the door," Sally said.

Trix tried. The handle turned and the big glass door opened inward, a waft of musty air emerging from the lobby. *I know that smell!* she thought. No one in her block had ever discovered where the smell came from, and it gave her an intense, welcome feeling of home.

She entered, with Sally close behind, then stood before her apartment door. "Whoever lives here must have taken them in," she said.

"It's a rough night," Sally said. "Something I know more than most is that people are generally good, and usually want to help."

Trix beamed as she rapped on the door. She wondered whether the handle stuck like hers, and the hinges squealed, and whether the oak flooring in the small hallway held the scratched inscription of the man who had laid it decades before. But when the door opened and she saw Jenny standing there, all such thoughts evaporated.

"Jenny!" she shouted, lurching in through the door, arms raised, sweeping the stunned woman into her embrace.

"Wha—?" Jenny said, as if in her terror and delight she could no longer speak.

"Oh, my God, I found you!" Trix said, bursting with tears of giddy relief. "Jim is desperate! Please tell me you've got Holly with you!" She hugged Jenny tight and looked over her shoulder into the apartment. It seemed silent, felt quiet and calm . . . and looked familiar.

Jenny hugged her back. Tight. One hand pulled against the small of Trix's back, the other held her neck, and then Jenny pulled back a little so that they were face-to-face. That was when Trix knew that something was different, because Jenny looked as if she had seen a ghost.

"Whoops," Sally said.

"I don't care if I'm dreaming," Jenny said, "as long as I never wake up." And then she reached up to catch Trix's face between her hands, and kissed her.

12

The Wrong Company

ARE THEY what caused the earthquake?" Jennifer asked. Jim nodded but then thought better of it. There was more to it than that, but now was not the time. Now they had to survive.

Jennifer drew close to him, and once again he was almost overwhelmed by her familiarity. Even catching sight of her from the corner of his eye—her stance, the determined expression, the way she filled her space—flooded him with memories of Jenny. "You've seen them before?" she asked.

"Yeah, but that doesn't help us." Four wraiths were stealing along the street, while, past the scene of ruin outside Sally's house, three more had manifested from smoke and unseen corners. Jim's heart galloped as he tried to think of something to do, some way to escape them. Into Sally's house? But even if they could reach the shattered front door before being caught by the wraiths, they were obviously the cause of the death and chaos apparent in the street. Being inside, even in the Oracle's home, would offer no protection. He'd seen that with Peter O'Brien.

"Are they going to . . . ?" Jennifer asked, fear lowering her voice.

They didn't find Sally! Jim thought, which gave him hope that Trix had made it away with the Oracle. "No," he said, "they won't kill us. But they might take us prisoner."

"Take us where?"

He'd seen them form and melt away again, and the idea of being pulled through with them was terrible. He was Unique, and maybe that would make it possible, but . . .

But Jennifer was *not* Unique. And this place was not a crossing point.

"Jim?" Jennifer asked.

But he could not speak. *What will it do to her to be dragged after them? What will it do to her body, her soul?* He glanced around at the several dead bodies splayed across the street, saw the terrible damage inflicted upon them, and he grabbed Jennifer's hand and pulled her close. "When they come for me," he whispered, "run as fast as you can."

"No!" Her voice was angry and fearful.

"Jennifer," he said, and her face was so close to his that he could smell Jenny's breath.

The wraiths dashed at them, and Jim felt momentary surprise when he heard their footsteps slapping on the pavement. His vision blurred, and he thought that an aftershock was striking the city—buildings shimmered, his stomach lurched, and Jennifer cried out beside him. She hugged him tighter, and her body fit his as well as it always had.

But the ground did not move, and he felt enclosed, his breathing and heartbeat echoing back at him from the wall of air around them. That wall darkened and resolved itself into separate shapes, and he heard Jennifer whimper softly as she pressed her face against his neck. *She doesn't want to see, but I have to,* he thought as the shapes became vaguely humanoid and rushed outward to meet the threat.

The wraiths seemed unconcerned at the appearance of these new things, and unsurprised. They joined in brutal battle without preamble, and the conflict seemed more violent because of its utter silence. One of Veronica's wraiths was flipped around and crushed against the ground, rupturing the concrete paving with a loud *crack!* that gave the fight brief voice. And at last Jim saw the thing that had met the wraith and bettered it. It had a silvered, flickering blank face and long limbs, and its gray shape seemed to flex and shiver as though trying to retain a hold on reality, but that ambiguity detracted nothing from its strength. It stomped down on the floored wraith, driving its foot into the thing's head and twisting, sending glittering shreds across the road. They shriveled and turned black before fading away, and the rest of the wraith melted to nothing.

The faceless man motioned to Jim to follow. Every fiber of his being urged him to grab Jennifer and flee, but while conflict raged around them, this creature seemed the safest ally they had. Still Jim paused, glancing around at the fighting, thrashing things that had come from thin air and belonged. He heard Jennifer gasp, turned around, and the faceless man was so close that Jim could have touched it. His hair stood on end, and his balls tingled. The shape raised an arm and pointed at the house of this Boston's Oracle. And then it signaled once again that he should follow.

They hurried after the shape as it seemed to float across the street, away from the house and the human bodies lying close by. They passed other bodies that were fading away—wraiths and faceless men alike—and Jim wondered if they hurt, and if the shift from living to dead meant anything to them.

"I don't know if I can do this," Jennifer said. "What are they? What is this?"

"It all has to do with the city," Jim said, because he thought he knew where these things came from—from Sally, this Boston's Oracle. Maybe they were constantly on guard outside her home, but he thought not. If they were, why the dead people, the smashed windows, and the sense of something momentous having happened here? The other alternative was that Sally had left them here to wait for him. That seemed more likely, as this thing was guiding them somewhere. And the only way he could figure this out was that Trix had gotten here first.

He only hoped she was all right. And he hoped and prayed that she and Sally had found his wife and child.

The thing led them quickly away from the battle, edging into an alley between buildings, headed west. It passed over a recently tumbled wall, waiting on the other side while Jim and Jennifer climbed the precarious pile. It exuded no impatience but walked on as soon as they were ready, moving unerringly through streets and alleys, across parks, and into the heart of the ruined city. They went through the theater district and kept moving west, crossing streets where buildings had collapsed or fires were raging, passing crowds of onlookers or people trying to help, and no one saw the faceless man. Jim didn't believe for a moment that it was invisible to all but him and Jennifer—how could it be?—but perhaps it had some way of diverting attention, or seeking paths between perception.

Every few minutes the thing held up its hand and turned around, moving past them the way they had come. *It's listening, and watching,* Jim thought. And indeed the phantom seemed to stand for a while breathing in the air and scanning their surroundings. For some reason, that did not make Jim feel safe. He believed the faceless man was just as dangerous, just as *inhuman*, as the wraiths that had killed O'Brien. He was only grateful it was on their side.

"Where's it leading us?" Jennifer asked.

"I think toward Trix's apartment in this Boston. And hopefully Sally."

"Sally?"

"The Oracle. You've heard of her?"

Jennifer frowned, a little unsettled. "I've heard the name Oracle before, yes. A friend of a friend visited her once, so he claims. Helped him find a brother adopted at birth."

"Well, she's the only one who can help me here," Jim said.

"Help you find your wife, Jenny," Jennifer said.

"Yeah," Jim said, and he had to shake himself again. *This isn't Jenny. This is Jennifer.*

"And you believe in all that mystical stuff?"

"Days ago, no, not really. But now . . . if whatever it is works, then yes, I believe in it." He pointed ahead at where the phantom shape had paused at a road junction. "And you've got to account for that."

"Not today," Jennifer said. "I don't need to account for *anything* today. Maybe tomorrow, when all this is . . ." But she trailed off, because what they'd seen of the city proved that this would *never* be all over. Things might improve, people might be rescued, and the injured would recover, but Boston would never be the same again.

As they followed the phantom, Jim started to wonder just what Jennifer-not-Jenny felt about him. Because there was a spark. And however much he tried to smother it, it burned brighter with every passing minute. "Not far now," he said, wondering what they would find upon their arrival. "We're almost there."

*   *   *

Trix leaned back against the wall of what might be her apartment, watching as Sally worked, and she knew that she should be able to control herself. She knew what this was and what it meant, and she was better placed than almost anyone in Boston today to understand what was going on. Yet she was shaking and scared, lonely and feeling shunned by the world she knew, and those worlds she did not.

And she couldn't help feeling jealous. *I need help, too. Sally should be doing that to me.* She hated the self-pity but could not rein it in. Too much had happened for her to beat herself up about how she felt.

Sally was kneeling beside this alternate Jenny and singing a soft song. This Jenny called herself Anne—her middle name—and had been begging Trix to recognize her and love her. *It's Anne. Don't you know me, Trix? Don't you know me?* It must have been Trix's haunted expression that threw Anne into a terrified fit. That, and the fact that she was dead in Anne's world, victim of a car crash three years before.

I'm no ghost, Trix had said, but it was taking the Oracle's ministrations to calm Anne down.

Sally rocked slowly back and forth on her knees, one hand running gentle circles across Anne's stomach, the other seemingly molding the air around her. The song seemed more solid than mere words, heavier than a voice. The air around Sally and Anne danced and flickered, heat haze where there was little heat, and Trix saw distortions that twisted their faces into terrible shapes. Yet she could not look away. Not only was Anne almost identical to Jenny in every way, she had also known Trix before she died in this world.

She knew me, as I've always wanted to know her, she thought. *Knew the heart of me, my deepest secrets, my fondest desires.* Anne had not taken her eyes off Trix since stepping back from that kiss—that wonderful kiss—and she still stared at her now. But her eyes had grown lazy, and her breathing had calmed.

Trix closed her eyes to escape that stare, and found herself staring right back. In her mind's eye she saw herself as she might have been in this world: shorter hair, perhaps heavier-boned, happy and content. And she had died young. In one world she survived, in the others she died, and she knew she should feel lucky and blessed. But she could only feel sad.

"She'll rest for a while," Sally said, and she continued her slow, melancholy song.

"And when do I rest?" Trix asked. But she might as well have been talking to herself. Sally ignored her, rocking and singing, and perhaps somewhere in that song was comfort for the Oracle as well.

Trix could still taste Anne's lips on her own. She had kissed Jenny before, of course, countless friendly pecks on the cheek, and they never meant anything more than that. The real kisses happened only in her mind.

But now, what if I could stay? she thought. *This is Boston, and this is Jenny.* She opened her eyes again and stared at the prone woman, seeing the slight differences but welcoming them. Each difference—the longer hair, the leaner physique—made her love Jenny more. *I can help Jim find Jenny and Holly, see them home, and then . . .*

Sally stopped singing and stood up. She groaned like an old lady, and Trix went to help, thinking that perhaps she'd tired herself out. But when the Oracle turned, Trix was shocked to see tears on her cheeks, her face squeezed as she tried to hold them back.

"Hey," Trix said, opening her arms.

Sally came to her and held her tight, sobbing into her chest. She pulled back and looked up. "Another room," she said. "If she hears . . . me crying . . . the spell might break."

Spell, Trix thought, unsettled. But she nodded, holding Sally and walking her through to where she knew the kitchen would be. When she entered, the room felt so familiar that Trix paused for a moment. But already something in her mind was preparing her for such sights, and she was looking for differences instead of similarities. The wall was a deep ocher color that she would have never chosen, the crockery on a plate rack bore a gaudy pattern, and there were several smoked sausages hanging from a rack above the fridge. Trix hated smoked sausage. Anne must have made this place her own after Trix died, and that planted in her not shock, but an unbearable sadness that threatened tears.

"Anne said she ran," Sally said, voice breaking. "After the collision, when they were both suddenly here. When my city changed. The other woman ran."

"I can hardly blame her." Trix nudged the kitchen door closed with her foot, and then Sally started sobbing for real. It was a shocking sight, because since first meeting her Trix had difficulty viewing the girl as a girl. She'd been an oddity, a child older than her years, wise beyond her age, performing feats that were not possible but were real, and her build and apparent age had meant little. Now she was an upset girl with tears in her eyes and Trix's jacket clenched in her fists.

"Hey," Trix said uncomfortably, unsure of what to do. She'd held Holly like this sometimes when the girl needed someone she regarded as a friend more than a parent—because of issues with friends in school, or sadness over the death of a pet hamster. Now things were different.

"I'm just a kid," Sally said, her tone of voice denying the truth of that. There was no "just" about it. "A kid, and I have to do this all the time, and I can, I can, because that's what the Oracle does. I'm still learning. *Always* learning. But I started . . . started off knowing more than anyone." She leaned back and looked up at Trix with red-rimmed, wet eyes. "Much more than you."

"I know," Trix said.

"But sometimes it's just not fair," she said. "Sometimes I wish it had never happened . . ."

"What *did* happen?" Trix asked, but Sally was saying her own thing. Though she clung to Trix and rested her head against her, she seemed to be talking to herself.

"If it hadn't happened, I wouldn't be here now, and there's so much responsibility. I can do it, normally. You know? Normally, when there's only magic to make and people to find, and the soul of the city to keep safe. *Normally*. But not now. The collision, the damage, those Shadow Men, and the things, the *terrible* things I had to bring across to fight them . . ." She sniffed, then exhaled another heavy sob. "It's all too much!"

"You're doing fine," Trix said, smoothing her hair.

"I'm just getting by," Sally said. She pulled away from Trix and sat back on the small kitchen table, looking around the room as if she could learn something from that place. "But the soul of the city is bruised, and I'm making mistakes." She looked directly at Trix then, and Trix knew what she meant.

"Maybe finding her *wasn't* a mistake," she said.

"No," Sally said, shaking her head. "She's not Jenny."

"No, but—"

"I know all about adult stuff," the Oracle said. "I'm too young to know, but I do. I have to. And I can see into you, Trix. See into your heart." She wiped her eyes and seemed to gather herself, shrugging strength back into her shoulders. Perhaps having something else to talk about—someone else's problem—was shielding her from her own.

"I'm not really thinking anything," Trix said. It was a cruel denial to herself, a stale-tasting lie.

"You've had your time in this world," Sally said. "Do I really have to show you your own grave?"

"I want you to find my friends," Trix said.

Sally nodded, wiped at her eyes again, and then offered a tentative smile. "And if I don't find them, you'll still go back through?"

"No," Trix said. "I won't. I'll stay here until they're found." *I'm her safety net,* she thought. *If she doesn't find them, at least I can go back to Veronica bearing her mark.* She might not have believed a little girl like Sally could scheme like that . . . but she was not really a little girl. The last few minutes had shown that.

"I've promised to find them," Sally said.

"And I thank you for that."

The Oracle sat heavily in a kitchen chair and rested her forehead on her hand, a very adult gesture. She rubbed her head gently, as if to ease away a headache.

"The city is in such pain," Sally whispered. "I *feel* its pain. Every fallen building is an ache in my bones and a fire beneath my skin."

"That's a big burden for such a little girl," Trix said, and the Oracle looked up at her with such gratitude that Trix felt the burn of tears. She wondered when Sally had last been called a little girl, and how she would grow up, never having experienced a childhood. "What happened to you?"

"I was eight," Sally said. "My momma and dadda were killed in a house fire. A black man came and pulled me from the basement window, and carried me away. I wasn't scared, not for a minute. The man was ill. He was my friend."

"Was he . . . ?"

"The last Oracle. I never even knew his name. He took me to the house where you found me, his house."

"And no one missed you? No family, no friends?"

"I *think* they did," she said, frowning as if confused at a nebulous memory. "But the man kept me safe, and I never once feared for myself. Something was happening to me, something wonderful, and it kept everything at bay. The grief over my parents, the weirdness of what was happening. One night I went to sleep with the man singing me songs, and the next morning I woke up as I am now. He was dead, and I buried him in the basement. And that afternoon, the first person came."

"He made you the Oracle?"

"The man? No." She smiled and shook her head. "He just helped me along." She sighed heavily, then sat back in her chair.

Trix blinked at the sudden, shocking change. The tears were gone, Sally's eyes dry as though they had never been wet, and her face was stern once again. Hard, grim, an expression that only an adult should ever wear.

"We should go," Sally said. "I've been wrong once; I won't be again. I'll be precise this time."

"Go where?"

"Just outside, down to the road. I'll find Holly and Jenny, and take you to them."

"What about . . . ?" Trix walked to the kitchen door and looked through the gap into the room beyond. Anne lay where Sally had sung her down, one hand waving slowly at the air before her face, orchestrating her dreams.

"She's under a calming spell, for now. I can strengthen it, leave her so that she wakes up in the morning. That'll be for the best."

"No!" Trix said, remembering Anne's lips against hers. "That's *not* for the best."

"Trix," Sally said, painfully adult, "you're a ghost to her."

"Jenny's stronger than that. She wouldn't want us to leave, not after this. She'd want to *understand*."

"That's not Jenny."

"Yes," Trix said. "Yes, it is." And she meant it. It might not be the Jenny she knew, not quite, and she might be using her middle name. But Anne was a facet of Jenny, and Trix could not bear treating her as anything else.

"You don't want to leave her."

"I think she'll want to come."

"Why?"

"Because she's strong. Imagine if we leave, and she wakes, and for the rest of her life she'll doubt her own sanity. I can't curse her with that. She's had a glimpse of what's going on, and I couldn't live with myself if we didn't show her everything else."

"And she kissed you."

"That's got nothing to do with it," Trix said, but she glanced away. *Maybe it's me who needs to understand as well.*

"Come on, then," the girl said. "I've wasted enough time."

"You're sure you're okay?" Trix asked.

"Of course," Sally said. Her tone was dismissive, but Trix saw that flicker of gratitude once again.

They went back out to Anne, and Trix knelt by her side. Sally started singing softly again, stroking the woman's hair and touching her cheek, and Trix began to explain. Anne did not look at her until she had finished. And then she sat up, holding on to Trix's proffered hand and looking back and forth between her and Sally.

"My bedroom," Anne said. "You're in there." She nodded to what Trix knew was the bedroom door. "You are. Go and see."

Trix went to see. She saw herself right away, because the photograph was large, the centerpiece of a wall display of at least fifty other framed photos of all shapes and sizes. She smiled back at the camera, this face that was hers, and she and Anne sat close together on a park bench, comfortable with each other and so obviously together. In the photo she was wearing a T-shirt that said, WHO THE HELL IS MICHAEL JACKSON? and she laughed. She might not be quite herself, but so much was the same.

The other photos weren't all of her. She saw her mother in a couple, and her cousins, but it was so obvious who was missing—Jim and Jenny. Of course. Because in this world, Trix and Jenny had been a couple, and Jim was long gone.

"I'm so sorry I died," she whispered, staring back at herself for so long that she forgot for a moment which Trix she was, and on which side of the glass she stood.

Back in the living room, shaken and sad, she found Anne sitting on the sofa. She sat beside her.

"I've seen some things since the quake," Anne said. "And maybe they explain this. But it's still . . ."

"Unbelievable," Trix said.

"Yeah. Fucking unbelievable." Anne grinned, and Trix fell in love just a little bit more.

"Jenny!" Jim said, but of course this was not Jenny, either, and he was attuned now to the differences.

"Okay," Jennifer said beside him. "Okay . . . okay . . ." She was looking at the woman who had emerged from the apartment building with Trix and the girl, and Jim saw her legs shaking.

"Jennifer?"

"That's me," she said. "Oh, wait till my folks hear about this."

The strange non-man had slipped from view a block away. Even so, Jim felt them still around, those phantoms following out of sight. He supposed they were still protecting him, though they only made him feel unsettled.

"Trix!" Jim called. Trix saw him and grinned, waiting for a car to pass then dashing across the street. She slowed when she saw Jennifer, blinked a few times, and then her face fell a little.

She hugged him tight. Jim felt her fear and excitement, and something else—a burgeoning sadness. She was still determined, but something subtle had changed.

"Trix, meet Jennifer."

"Hi." Trix shook Jennifer's hand. "And that's Anne," she said, nodding toward where the girl and woman stood on the sidewalk.

"The little girl's the Oracle?" Jim asked.

"Don't let her size and age deceive you," Trix said, chuckling softly. "She's mean as they come when she wants to be, and when the Shadow Men came she conjured up her own version—she calls them No-Face Men—and they fought and—"

"Men with no faces," Jennifer said.

"You've seen them?"

"One of them led us here," Jim said. "And they saved us at the Oracle's house. We got there, some of those wraiths—the Shadow Men—were waiting."

"Just weird," Jennifer said, shivering.

"Sally will need to remove your mark," Trix said. "She's a little . . . strained at the moment, but she's strong as hell."

THE SHADOW MEN 237

"Mark?"

"Veronica. As well as what she sent in the envelopes, she sent something with us, too. So those things of hers could follow."

"How?" Jim asked.

"Cookies."

"Damn. Cookies."

"Oh, I don't like the sound of that," Jennifer said.

Trix smiled and hugged Jim again. It felt good to Jim—she was someone he knew, something he could understand, while everyone else around them right now was either a child Oracle or a facsimile of his lost wife. He needed Trix—brash, dependable, wild Trix. She was his rock, and his connection to the Boston they had left behind. "Oh, this is just all so fucking weird," she said into his neck.

"Tell me about it."

"I don't know where to start!" She pulled back and tried to laugh, but it came out strained and tense.

"Trix?" Something had happened. He waited for her to tell him, but she glanced at Jennifer and turned around.

"Come on. Sally's sure she can find them now."

"Has she said anything about them?" Jim was desperate for news, and his anxiety had been growing by the minute since losing touch with Trix.

"She's promised to find them, that's all," Trix said. And again, there was something she wanted to tell him.

"Trix, I'm here," Jim said. She nodded, her eyes haunted by ghosts he had yet to meet.

They crossed the street, and Jennifer and Anne stood facing each other a dozen steps apart. Trix introduced Jim to Sally, and the girl nodded and looked him up and down. Her gaze was shockingly adult, aged and knowing, and he felt distinctly uncomfortable.

"You can find my wife and daughter?" he asked.

"I can," she said. A shadow passed across her face—exhaustion, he thought, and perhaps a glimmer of fear. But she gathered herself quickly, then looked at the two women who might have been Jenny. "No time for hanging around. We need to get to the street junction, and there I'll trace them. But I'm not so sure it'll be that easy."

"Veronica," Jim said.

The girl nodded. "The bitch had this planned."

"But according to her plan, you should be dead now," Trix said.

"I should. But she'll have backup plans, and other ways to do the deed. You can bet on it."

"How can you know that?" Jim asked.

"Because *I* would." The girl set off along the street, leading the four adults behind her. They walked in a loaded silence, and people parted to let them through. Perhaps some of them knew Sally, or felt the power carried by the girl. But Jim thought it more likely that they were picking up on the strange tension between the two women. Jennifer and Anne, Jenny and Jenny, they walked with Trix and Jim between them but stole frequent glances at each other. They were not the only two people in this tragic city meeting like this, Jim knew. There would be hundreds more, maybe thousands, doppelgängers thrown together through geography, circumstance, or tragedy. But for Jim, these were the only ones who mattered.

They reached the intersection, and Sally paused at the corner, leaning against a garbage can and watching vehicles rumble past. Traffic lights above the road were out of action, and the building on the opposite corner had sustained damage, one wall slumping to the ground to display the tumbled wreck of the rooms within. A man sat on the rubble, drinking steadily from a bottle of whiskey.

A fire engine powered through the intersection, barely pausing. Two ambulances quickly followed. *There are a thousand tragedies today,* Jim thought, but he knew that his own was linked inextricably to what was happening to this city. The more he saw and the less he understood, the more determined he became to fix it all.

Sally stepped into the road. Jim gasped and reached for her, but Trix held his arm and shook her head. "She knows what she's doing."

Jim heard whispering behind him, and he snapped around, terrified that those things had arrived again. But the whispering came from Anne and Jennifer, still maintaining a distance yet starting to communicate in tentative tones.

"It must be so strange," Trix said.

"And yet we're Uniques," Jim said. "*We're* the strange ones here."

Sally had reached the center of the intersection and placed her hands flat against the road. Cars and trucks, emergency vehicles and media vans, they all passed without lifting a strand of her hair or causing a single ripple in her loose dress. It was as if Sally was somewhere else, yet still visible to them all.

"You said I still have the mark?" Jim asked Trix.

"I have a feeling we're being watched," she said. Jim nodded, because he had that feeling as well, stronger than what people commonly called the sixth sense. He not only felt eyes on him, but he could sense the breeze harden across his skin, almost as if holding him in place in this world.

After a couple of minutes Sally stood and walked back to them, passing between lines of traffic that seemed not to slow or notice her at all. And she looked worried. "Need to get that mark from you," she said.

"Tell me you've found them," Jim said as she mounted the sidewalk.

"I *could* tell you that."

"But?" Trix asked.

"I've found Holly." She looked at Anne and Jennifer, and even this Oracle's eyes seemed to glimmer with wonder. "The other Jenny . . . your Jenny . . . not so much."

"No!" Jim gasped. Sally held up one hand.

"I have a sense of her, like an echo around Holly, but nothing solid. She may be with Holly and the collision of the cities is just giving me some kind of interference." She smiled, trying to impart hope.

"What else?" Jim asked.

"Holly is afraid. She's trapped, somehow, but I can't sense her captors at all."

Jim shook his head, frustrated and growing frantic. "What does that mean?"

"Only one possibility that I can think of. Veronica's Shadow Men have her."

"Oh, no!" Trix said. "How did they catch her?"

"I think they may have had her all along," Sally said, and she performed a slow full circle, looking up at the broken windows surrounding them. "These aren't the same Shadow Men who attacked us. *They're* still out there, kept at bay by the No-Face Men who serve me."

"So where is she?" Jim asked. "Where's my little girl?"

Sally told them. And then she reached out to Jim, and he cried as she removed his mark.

13

From the Back of a Broken Dream

EVEN IF they'd had a car or managed to flag down one of the few taxis they saw passing by, they wouldn't have gotten very far in a vehicle. The streets that weren't blocked by rubble or police barricades were jammed with cars driven by people trying to reach loved ones or just get the hell out of Boston. They finally settled on St. James Avenue. Though there were buildings that had merged when the cities collided, spilling debris into the street, the road was passable.

Jim strode with purpose, wanting to break into a run but knowing that the five of them—this impossible gathering of women and him—had to stay together. Sally led the way, and they all seemed to take for granted that she would, despite the fact that she was a child. As the Oracle of Boston, she was both their best guide and their best protection. Jim followed close behind, with Jennifer a few feet to his right. They glanced at each other from time to time, the immediate intimacy they had felt before awkward for both of them. Trix and Anne—that other Jenny—hung back, and Jim felt sure it was partly because Anne and Jennifer did not know how to communicate with each other.

Again and again, they saw examples of this phenomenon as they traveled across the city. Rarely were the twins from parallel Bostons exact copies. They differed in weight and style and clothing. But given what had happened and what was transpiring all over the city, they were impossible to miss. Two old men sat on a stoop, both in gray cardigan sweaters, though one wore a distinguished gray beard and the other looked sickly and had gone nearly bald. They took turns patting the same dog, which perhaps they both now owned. A pair of olive-skinned women shouted at each other in Spanish, both in tears, on the sidewalk in front of a dress shop. One of them held a boy of about eight in front of her, arms wrapped protectively around him, and the boy looked frightened and confused as he listened to the two women—one his mother and one who, in another world, might have been—panic.

Anne reached out to hold Trix's hand. Trix seemed hesitant for a second, then twined her fingers in Anne's. Jim saw the shy way that Anne looked at her—the hopeful gaze in her eyes—and found himself wishing that they had both lived in a world where they could have had their heart's desire. It felt strange but right, and he decided that in a city where reality existed in different facets, everything should be possible.

"It must be so weird for you," Jennifer said, walking along beside him. She had seen the dynamic developing between Trix and Anne as well.

"Weird for all of us," he said.

Jennifer smiled, but her eyes were sad, as if they held a painful secret. "That's for sure."

They had come to the intersection of Berkeley and St. James, where the building on the southeast corner—he thought there'd been a big insurance company headquarters there in his own Boston—had been merged with a tall, gleaming art deco hotel that had to have come from Anne's Brahmin-influenced Boston. What had been there in Jennifer's Boston, with its Irish roots, had been a massive retail space with a Waterford crystal store on the corner. Now broken glass and debris had spilled into the street, and they had to move carefully around it. Sally stumbled a bit, and Jim caught up to her, reaching out, but she recovered without his help.

"I want to thank you," he said.

"For what? I haven't gotten you back to them yet."

"For trying. For removing Veronica's mark from me and Trix. For coming with us now."

The little girl glanced at him, but there were storm clouds in her eyes and her lips pulled up into a grim expression that could not have been called a smile. In that moment, she looked far older than her years—ancient. Whatever part of her was the soul of the city of Boston, that was what looked back at him. "I'm not doing it for you," Sally said. "There are two cities full of frightened people finding their lives crashed together, and now I have a responsibility to *all* of them. I'm not ignoring them just to help you find your family. I'm doing it because of what will happen if *your* Oracle gets her way. The death we've already seen today will just be the start."

Jim glanced away, embarrassed without really knowing why. "I get that," he said. "I know that, of course. But thank you anyway for helping. Not just me . . . all of us."

Now it was Sally's turn to look embarrassed, as if she was ashamed of having snapped at him. "I'm the Oracle," she replied. "It's what I'm *for*."

Jim glanced back to make sure they were all still together. Trix and Anne, hands held tightly, helped each other over the debris. Trix's pink hair gleamed in the city light. Jennifer gazed around at the terrified people they passed, obviously wanting to stop and help but sticking with them—with him—for the sake of yet another of her otherworldly twins, a woman who was her, though they had never met, and a daughter she had never had.

"Tell me about these Shadow Men," Jim said. "How do we fight them?"

"They aren't people . . . not anymore. I mean, they're not solid, right? But they're not really ghosts, either. If they're solid enough to attack you or grab you, then you can grab them back. It's tricky. They kind of fade in and out. It won't help you beat them, but maybe it'll help you get away from them if they try to take you through."

"Through where?" Jim asked.

Sally glanced at him, a bit surprised and disturbed at the same time. "Into the In-Between, of course."

Jim shuddered, mostly because of her tone but also because of the haunted look in her eyes. "What happens if they do?"

Sally glanced back at Trix and the Jennys, then at Jim again. They were making their way around an abandoned Volvo station wagon that had bumped up onto the curb and run over a couple of parking meters. "I know Veronica can't have told you much, but didn't the Irish Oracle—"

"O'Brien."

"Didn't O'Brien explain what she'd done to you, sending you here?"

Jim shook his head. "We weren't there long before the faceless guys . . . the Shadow Men . . . came and killed him."

Sally sighed. "Right. Of course." She gave a small shrug. "Y'know how I just said they're not people anymore? Well, they *were*. The In-Between—the shadow stuff that separates three Bostons, or I guess the two Bostons now—it has tides."

"An ebb and flow," Jim said, nodding. "Veronica said something like that. But she was saying that sometimes the three cities overlapped."

"Yeah, but she didn't tell you about the In-Between. That's what's really flowing. And sometimes it washes into one of the real worlds, and when the wave goes back, it brings people with it. If they're in a place where the cities overlap normally, where the Bostons are the same, then they can slip from one to the other. But if not, and they're dragged out of their world . . . they end up in the In-Between."

Jim felt a little nauseous. "You're saying they get turned into those shadow things?"

"Not right away," Sally said. "It takes time. I've seen them when they're not fully changed, part flesh and blood and part shadow stuff."

"Jesus," Jim muttered.

"Veronica showed you and Trix how to get through at the crossings, the places where the cities overlap, and as long as you're quick and careful, you can do that, because you're Uniques. Holly, too. But Jenny . . ."

Jim stopped, not liking the girl's tone. "Jenny what?"

Sally scuffed her feet on the sidewalk, so much like a little girl. "There are only a couple of places where you can get Jenny through. If you tried anywhere else, she'd get lost in the In-Between."

Jim couldn't help but laugh. "That unbelievable bitch. That was her plan all along, for us to come over here, lead her killer shadows to you and O'Brien, and then lose Jenny on the way back anyway."

"I don't think so," Sally said. "I'd bet that was just her Plan B. Plan A was for *all* of us to die."

Jim gaped in horror and disbelief, a cold edge forming inside him. He had been terrified for Jenny and Holly, determined, but now he was furious. Veronica was going to pay for what she'd already accomplished, and for what she had tried to do. But first he had to get his family back. "So your No-Face Men are . . . ?"

Sally looked up at him, and her smile was almost smug. "My own little victory," she said. "The souls of those yet to be. That's why they have those faces—flitting with potential. And those long limbs, where they stretch for life. And they're eager to serve."

Jim nodded and fell back, suddenly more afraid of this little girl than he thought possible.

Behind him, Trix and Anne spoke in soft voices. He glanced back at them and saw the way Anne looked at Trix when she talked—amazement that Trix was alive, sorrow that this was not the Trix that she knew; yearning for a love she'd lost, and hope that it might be born again. He wasn't watching where he was going, and he caught his foot on a bit of cracked sidewalk and fell to his knees. He skinned his hands trying to catch himself and swore softly, feeling like an idiot.

"Hey," Jennifer said, helping him up. "Are you all right?"

She turned his palms up to examine the scrapes, the contact making him catch his breath. Sensing his sudden tension, Jennifer glanced up at him with inquisitive eyes. They stood like that for several seconds, and Jim understood exactly how Anne must feel when she looked at Trix. But his wife . . . his Jenny . . . wasn't dead. She *wasn't*. "I will be," Jim said. "Thanks."

He withdrew his hands from her grasp, and the two of them caught up to Sally. It seemed to Jim that he and Jennifer were both keenly aware of each other's presence, that there was a magnetism that drew them toward each other even as it pushed them away.

She's not Jenny, he told himself again. But Jennifer looked so much like her that it hurt.

Trix had never been big into drugs, but she had experimented here and there, licking microdots off paper like children's candy at the age of fourteen, smoking pot through high school, and taking a turn at cocaine and Ecstasy in college before deciding that both scared the shit out of her. It had been six or seven years since she'd had anything stronger than a shot of tequila.

But damn if she didn't feel high right now.

Wandering through a devastated city where people faced doppelgängers with whom they would now have to share their worlds and their lives, anyone would have felt lost in the surreal. But it wasn't any of those things that made Trix feel as though she had fallen down the rabbit hole. It was Anne.

Her skin prickled with excitement, and she felt almost giddy. The feelings confused and frightened her, but she could not ignore them. All the daydreams she'd had about Jenny, from musings and sighs to masturbatory fantasies couched in guilt and reservations, had been real in this world, for some other Trix. Anne was not her Jenny. She was not Anne's Trix. And yet . . .

And yet.

Trix knew it couldn't be. Not really. But Anne kept taking her hand, and the way the woman looked at her with those gentle eyes made her want to laugh. It wasn't a time for laughter. Jenny and Holly were still missing, and she loved *her* Jenny and needed to have her back in her life, safe and sound. But maybe there had been three Bostons for a reason. Maybe the whole point of an alternate world was for there to be a place where other fates could unfold, and where broken hearts could find happier endings.

"Hey," Anne said, nudging her. "Are you okay?"

Trix looked at her, tried not to laugh at the absurdity of the question, and then couldn't stop herself. She snickered, attempted to cover up, and failed. Anne blinked, stung for a moment, but then she grinned. "Stupid question, huh?" Anne asked.

"Not at all," Trix said, clutching Anne's hand and swinging her arm like they were lovers on a leisurely stroll. "It's the perfect weather for a walk through Copley Square."

They laughed quietly, and Trix glanced ahead to see Jim looking back at her. She knew that she should cool it with Anne, stop holding her hand, stop whispering with her. She knew for sure that she and this woman shouldn't be laughing together in the middle of chaos, not when Jenny and Holly were presumably in the hands of someone—or something—that meant them harm. As weird as it was for her, she thought, it must be so much worse for Jim. Trix feared for Jenny and Holly. They meant the world to her. But being with Anne made it all feel incredibly dreamlike, and if she didn't laugh a little, she might scream.

Trix would die for Jenny or Holly. *But please let me live,* she thought, looking at Anne. *Let us all live.*

What would happen afterward, when it was time for Trix and the Banks family to go home, she did not know. But for now, she relished the feel of Anne's hand in hers and the knowledge that in this world—in this Boston— they had once been happily in love. "Come on," she said, tugging Anne's hand. "We should catch up."

The two women hurried after Sally, Jim, and Jennifer, making their way past Trinity Church and starting across Copley Square. The park in front of the church had been partly converted into a staging area for rescue efforts at a building on Boylston Street that Trix thought had once been the Globe Bar. City workers and civilians alike were pulling apart the rubble of the collapsed building, looking for survivors. From the looks of it, the bar had been destroyed not by being merged with another structure from its parallel Boston but by the quaking of the city during the collision.

"I wish we had time to help them," Jennifer said.

"So do I," Sally said. "There are three people still alive in there, and one of them not for much longer."

"How do you—" Anne began.

"Are you serious?" Jennifer said. "You know that? You can, whatever . . . sense it? We've got to go and tell them."

Jim looked at her, eyes narrowed in pain. "You can go if you want to, but it won't help them dig any faster. I've got to keep going. My daughter needs me. And my wife, my Jenny. My *you*. She needs me, too."

Jennifer flinched. Trix saw the recognition in her eyes, and wondered if her desire to help everyone else sprang solely from her empathy or if it also came from her fear of what they would find ahead. This Jennifer had never married, never had a daughter. Trix couldn't imagine how the woman felt.

Jennifer held out a hand to Jim. "Let's go. We can always come back and help. After."

They cut across the park, headed for the Boston Public Library, its imposingly beautiful façade with its row of arched windows looking out over Copley Square. The McKim Building, the library's main structure, appeared untouched by the disaster that had shaken the city. Its red tile roof, crested with green copper, had not been disturbed, which mean that the building existed in all three Bostons.

Trix had known that, of course. Sally had told them. The Boston Public Library had been preserved by the people of three cities—with one difference. The Abbey Room, among the best known of the library's features, boasted richly textured mural paintings by Edwin Austin Abbey, including a series entitled *The Quest of the Holy Grail*. In the Boston from which Trix and Jim hailed, the room was sixty or seventy feet in length, but in the Irish Boston, the city's one and only terrorist attack had destroyed half of the room. Instead of restoring it, the architects had decided to separate the unaffected portion of the room with a wall and a door, on the other side of which they designed a new room, filled with paintings by Irish masters. It was meant to be a place of reflection, to honor the seven people who had died that day.

In the heart of the library, the Reflection Room was an island of stability, a place where the parallel cities did not overlap.

That was where the Shadow Men were holding Holly.

Trix took a deep breath, held Anne's hand more tightly, and followed Jim, Sally, and Jennifer up the library's front steps, passing between the statues that represented Art and Science. The middle of the three arched doors stood propped open, inviting them in. Holly awaited within.

As for Jenny . . .

Trix let go of Anne's hand, giving her a soft smile to let her know that she hadn't done anything wrong. But as they passed through the doors, she found clarity returning. Anne was a beautiful fantasy, but Trix could not succumb to that dream. Not yet. Not when the Jenny she had always loved still needed her.

She glanced around anxiously as they walked through the vestibule, the pink marble deceptively warm. There were people moving about in the entrance hall, but she glanced within and saw nothing threatening about them, and no trace of the Shadow Men. Jim went in first, and Trix watched the door through which they had entered, just to make sure they would not be attacked from behind. When she walked into the entrance hall, Trix glanced at the vaulted ceiling, imagining that at any moment the Shadow Men would emerge from the tile mosaic and attack.

"Trix," Jim said, and gestured for her to join them.

The others had gathered a few feet inside the hall and off to the right. The sound of weeping echoed off the walls, and she glanced up to see a grieving woman coming toward the doors, attended by a trio of comforting friends. Moments later, Trix caught sight of a woman who could only be the twin of the one who'd been grieving, and who was apparently following the group but trying not to be seen. She looked bewildered and afraid.

"It's real," Trix told her.

"What?" the woman asked, flinching, as though afraid Trix might try to strike her.

"All of this," Trix said, waving her hand to indicate the women who had just left and the city as a whole. "It isn't your imagination. It's just what is now."

The woman's eyes widened and she hurried out the door, leaving Trix to wonder if the truth had done the woman good or harm.

"Stay with me," Sally told them as Trix came to stand between Jennifer and Anne. Her little-girl face seemed anything but innocent now. She was grim and determined. "Veronica must have Shadow Men holding Holly, so be prepared. If they grab you, shake them off. They've got to partially solidify to hold you, so fight them. But don't try to beat them, because you can't."

"You're going to call some of them up, though, right?" Jennifer asked. "Some of your No-Face Men, the ones who answer to you?"

Uncertainty flashed in Sally's eyes. "I'm going to try. But it takes focus to call them and to command them, and I'm so tired I can barely stand. All of this . . . it drains me."

"You'll do fine," Jim assured her, one hand on the little girl's shoulder.

But Sally was looking at Trix for reassurance. Trix smiled. They had bonded a little in the short time they'd known each other. "You're the Oracle of two Bostons now," Trix reminded her. "If there's magic in all of this, you've got more of it than ever. You'll kick ass."

Sally smiled. "Thanks."

"Okay," Jim said. "You heard her. Sally knows exactly what room Holly's in. We follow her in, get Holly, and let Sally worry about the Shadow Men. And we try not to let them take us into the In-Between."

"What happens if they get one of us?" Anne asked.

"Let's just say it would be bad," Jim replied.

"Bad?" Trix said. "Great. Thanks."

"We'd turn into them," Jim explained. "Shadow Men."

Trix felt sick, a terrible dread spreading like poison in her veins. She tried to shake it off, reaching out to clutch Anne's hand, but it clung to her and would not be dispelled.

"Ready?" Sally asked.

"Not even close," Anne said.

Jennifer glanced at her, their faces mirror images. "In some other world, this girl is your daughter."

Anne shifted uneasily. "I didn't say I wouldn't go. Just that I'm not ready. How could anyone ever be ready for this?"

Trix squeezed her hand and glanced at Sally. "Let's go," she said.

The atmosphere inside the library crackled with static electricity. Jim wondered if he might be the only one who felt it, and if it sprang from the knowledge that his daughter—his little girl—was so close. During the trek across town, he had forced himself not to hope, and now he put it inside an iron box in his heart and turned the key, not to be released until he held Holly in his arms again.

Jaw set, hands clenched, he marched grimly across the entrance hall, his companions nearly forgotten. A glance into the main reading room showed precisely what he had expected—not the quiet studiousness of an ordinary day but the shock and hushed trauma of the aftermath of catastrophe. People sat on the floor, or at reading carrels, faces buried in their hands or laid upon the shoulder of another, who might try to provide comfort in the midst of their own astonishment and horror. The whole city was like this now, and it would take time for them to wake from this shock-trance and try to see how much of their lives remained.

"Upstairs," Sally said, nudging him as she passed by and went through the triumphal arch to the marble staircase.

Jennifer, Anne, and Trix followed, but Jim hesitated a moment. Something wasn't right in the reading room. Something was *off*, a sense that no one there was concentrating on whatever they appeared to be doing. He met the gaze of a white-haired old man who had begun to stare at him and turned away so that the man would not think him some kind of ghoul, entertained by the dozens of little tragedies unfolding in that room. Then he caught sight of a plump black woman standing beside a pale white teenage boy with orange hair. They seemed to sense him looking and turned toward him. Jim felt himself the focus of unsettling attention.

Holly, Jim thought, tearing his gaze from them and hurrying through the arch toward the stairs. The others were already moving up the steps, and Jim hustled to catch up, glancing around warily. At the landing above, where the steps turned before continuing up to the second floor, the marble lions seemed ready to pounce. He couldn't help feeling that the air held a similar threat.

"It's like some kind of weird Roman palazzo in here," Jennifer whispered, her voice echoing off the marble walls and staircase as she stared at the paintings in the arched recesses at the top of the steps.

Jim barely acknowledged that she'd spoken, quickening his pace so that by the time Sally reached the second floor he was only two steps behind her. In the shuffle of echoes that their climb had sent cascading from the walls, he thought he heard something that shouldn't be there, something that didn't match, and it took him a moment to realize that there were footfalls below them on the stairs. He glanced over the balustrade and spotted the plump woman and her ginger-haired teen companion starting up the stairs.

"This way," Sally whispered, spurring him on.

They went through the arcade that separated the stairwell from the second-floor corridor, a gallery named for the artist whose paintings hung there but whose name Jim could not recall. His mural of the Muses of Greek mythology was one of the best-known pieces of art in the library, and two men stood in the corridor staring at it with the casual air of tourists, despite the disaster the city had become. Jim frowned at the sight of them, but now they were so close to Holly he could practically feel the presence of his daughter.

At the southern end of the gallery corridor was the Abbey Room. Jim passed Sally, but the young Oracle grabbed the tail of his shirt and forced him not to rush ahead. The girl glanced back at Trix and Anne. "I'm kind of a wreck. If I have to call up my No-Face Men, I may pass out," Sally said. "Will somebody catch me?"

"I've got you," Anne said.

"Me, too," Jennifer added. She had been lagging behind, the shocks of the day catching up to her, turning her gaze distant and hollow. "Do what you have to do."

They went into the Abbey Room and spread out instantly, Jim taking the lead with Sally and Trix behind him, and Jennifer and Anne coming last. The room rivaled the greatest museums Jim had ever entered, not just because of the paintings but because of the beauty of the room itself, all oak and marble, with thick ornamental rafters on the ceiling. As Sally had told them, the room had been divided by a wall, this portion just over thirty feet to a side. The far end of the room had heavy oak doors set into the dividing wall, and Holly waited on the other side.

There were half a dozen people in the Abbey Room already. Two middle-aged women—European tourists by the look of them—huddled together on a bench, holding each other as though cowering in fear. A sixtyish Asian man in a business suit stood in the center of the room, facing Jim and the others as they rushed in. A young couple, perhaps graduate students, flanked the far door as if they were guarding it.

The sixth person was a dead security guard. He lay on the marble not far from the Asian man, a pool of blood beneath him.

Sally stopped short, glancing anxiously around, and the rest of them followed suit. "I should have realized . . . ,"

Sally said. "I sensed them, but I didn't see them. I never thought she'd risk it."

"Sally?" Jim said warily.

"What the hell is this?" Trix asked.

Jim glanced back the way they'd come and saw the woman and the orange-haired kid from downstairs follow them into the room. The old man who had caught his eye entered a moment later, still staring at Jim. "Who are they, Sally?" Jim asked.

"Not 'who,'" Sally said. "But 'what'? They're Shadow Men."

"But they look normal," Trix whispered, glancing at Anne and Jennifer, the five of them clustering together as the strangers began to close in on them. Only the two terrified women on the bench did not rise—they were ordinary people, trapped here in the midst of the horror.

"They haven't been changed completely yet," Jim told her, glancing at Sally to confirm his suspicion.

Sally nodded. "They're not dead yet."

The white-haired Asian man had remained in the center of the room, but now he glanced at the others, and the strangers all paused. Jim blinked, thinking his vision had begun to blur, but it was the strangers that were blurring. The orange-haired teen's shadow seemed to separate from him, wavering just a few inches to one side like a ghostly conjoined twin. The others all shuddered as the same transformation went through them. Part human and part wraith, they were bodies with living shadows.

One of the women on the bench screamed; the other sobbed hysterically.

Jennifer grabbed Jim's arm. "What do we do?"

Jim glanced at Trix. "We fight."

"What?" Trix asked.

Jim grinned, all his anger and fear swelling up inside

him, fists clenching. "They're solid, Trixie. Let's get Holly. And if they try to stop us, kick the shit out of them."

"Jim . . . ," Anne said.

Sally nodded, reached out, and gave Jim a shove toward the door at the far end of the room. "Go!" she shouted.

Even as her voice echoed off the walls, the Asian man made a single gesture, and the Half Shadows attacked.

14

The Light of a Fading Star

THEY WERE inhumanly fast.

Trix swung a fist at the redheaded kid, but he darted past her blow and grabbed her wrist. He started dragging her toward the wall that separated the Abbey Room from the Reflection Room. She tried to fight her way free, but now he had her by both wrists, and he was strong. She planted her feet, but the soles of her shoes slid across the marble floor.

"No!" Anne shouted. "Let her go!" But as she launched herself at Trix and the redhead, the terror of losing her lover twice in a lifetime clearly making her crazed, the woman who'd come in with the teenager grabbed the back of her neck with one splayed hand and hurled Anne at the ground. Her head struck marble and she cried out. For a second, Trix feared the worst, but then Anne scrambled away from the Half Shadow, who stalked her across the room.

Scuffles and shouts echoed all around. The old man who'd entered last seemed focused on Jim, as did the couple who had been guarding the door to the Reflection Room. Jennifer stood in front of Sally as though to protect her, which seemed strange, considering the girl had more ability to fight back than any of them. The screaming woman had gone silent with fear, and now she got her sobbing friend up from the bench. With one last glance at the dead security guard, they ran for the exit.

The well-dressed man darted toward them, trailing his Shadow Twin like a comet's tail. He grabbed the sobbing woman and drove her head into the wall so hard that her skull cracked, loud as a gunshot, and she slid to the floor, dead. The other woman began screaming again, and she fought him, trying to claw his face and then his Shadow self.

Terror turned Trix's blood to ice. The sobbing woman had died in an instant. They didn't want witnesses, didn't want anyone to come and help, and that told her a great deal. They could be hurt. They could be beaten. And they didn't have any backup.

She shot out a leg, tripped the redheaded kid, and rode him down as he fell. His head bounced off the floor, and she grabbed hold of his ears and started slamming his skull against the marble tile. Someone was screaming, shrill and hysterical, and only when she bared her teeth as she fought his efforts to rise—and the screaming ceased—did she realize it had been her all along.

His orange hair was dark and wet now, and it left bright crimson smears on the tile. His eyes were going out of focus. But then he reached up and struck her in the stomach, took her wrists, and broke her grip. He tossed her away and she hit hard. Trix scrambled up and saw that his Shadow Twin hung even farther out of him. Had it been the Shadow's hands on her, or the human boy's? Did it matter?

He tried to rise but stumbled and hit the floor, too disoriented to attack her.

Jennifer screamed for Jim.

Trix looked up and saw the Asian man looming over

Jennifer. He had a fistful of her pretty hair, and in that moment, she *was* Jenny. Or she might as well have been. Trix ran for her, only to see Sally behind her, drawing symbols on the floor in what must be the girl's own blood. Whatever Sally was up to, Trix knew she had to protect her until it was done.

But then Anne screamed and Trix twisted around to see the buxom woman, Shadow Twin almost entirely outside her flesh, dragging Anne across the floor by one ankle. The thing was taking her toward the Reflection Room, or at least toward that door or wall, just as the redhead had tried to take Trix. There was something to be made of that—something obvious that Trix just wasn't getting—but she didn't have the luxury of thinking.

This chaos would end with them all dead, unless the young Oracle could do something to help them.

Jim saw Trix run past, headed for the door to the Reflection Room, and he prayed she would get through that door, that she would get to Holly. Right now he had trouble of his own. As Trix ran by, the dapper businessman Jim had first seen down in the reading room reached for her and missed, despite his unnatural speed. It gave Jim an instant to act. The other two, the young couple, were grappling with him, trying to stop him from getting to the Oracle.

"Sally!" Jim shouted. "Whatever you're going to do—"

He didn't get to finish. The old businessman punched him in the mouth and Jim reeled backward, breaking the grip of one of the two who still held him. He lunged toward the wall, but what he wanted leaned against it— a wooden captain's chair that had, like the benches, been placed there for older patrons to rest on while touring the library.

Gritting his teeth against its weight, he swung the chair with all the strength he could muster, smashing it into the face and chest of the thing still holding him. The young man let go, flailing as he stumbled back. Blood spurted from his broken nose and dripped down his chin as he sprawled to the floor. He lay with his eyes closed, unconscious and broken, but the shadow part of him created by his time lost in the In-Between—before Veronica had fished him out to make him do her bidding—remained awake, and enraged. It tried to pull itself fully out of him, but it was tethered within him, *was* him, in some fundamental way.

"Sally!" Jim shouted. He faced the other two Half Shadows menacing him, brandishing the captain's chair, which grew heavier with every heartbeat.

"She did it!" Jennifer said, excitement mingling with her fear. "They're here!"

Jim glanced toward the sound of her voice and saw some of Sally's No-Face Men. He counted four, including one grappling with the Asian man who had been attacking Jennifer. A fifth No-Face Man slid up through the floor and darted toward the redheaded kid Trix had beaten the shit out of. The kid had started to stand, limbs moving jerkily, as though his Shadow self was a puppeteer pulling his strings.

Jennifer cradled Sally in her arms. For a moment he thought the girl might be dead, but then Sally stirred, lifting her head weakly and pointing toward the Half Shadows Jim had been fighting. "Destroy them!" she shouted, her commanding tone making her sound much older than her years.

Two No-Face Men sailed across the room and attacked the woman who'd been after Jim. Their hands passed through her flesh and bone, but they weren't interested in her body. Those spectral hands grabbed hold of the shadow stuff, the dusky twin of this woman who had been lost between worlds through no fault of her own, and began to tear it off as though peeling a second skin away from her flesh.

The woman shrieked as though they were gutting her, distracting the other Half Shadows. Another of Sally's No-Face Men careened into the businessman Jim had been fighting and dragged him down, clawing at his body like an animal, though its talons slashed through flesh without damaging the man's body or his clothes. The Shadow Twin within him, though, was eviscerated.

The woman who had been stripped of her Shadow Twin shuffled away on her knees, staggered to her feet, and then stared at her hands as though she had never seen them before. Tears sprang to her eyes, and she touched her face, somehow verifying that she was herself and alive. Then she turned and fled screaming from the Abbey Room, running out into the corridor, and presumably out of the library and into a new world.

The other Half Shadow—the well-dressed older businessman—did not survive the stripping of his Shadow Twin. When the No-Face Men were done scouring the shadow stuff from within him, he lay still, eyes vacant with death.

Jim heard Trix screaming and turned to see her fighting with the black woman, who was dragging Anne toward the Reflection Room. Something was wrong here. Why would the things *want* to take them there?

But it didn't matter now.

He dropped the chair and ran toward Trix but managed to get only a few feet before he felt something grip his ankles. He flailed his arms outward as he fell and hit the marble floor hard, smashing his face on the tile. Dazed, he kicked out to try to free himself, and looked up to see that the one he'd beaten with the captain's chair had regained consciousness. Bloody, face swollen, the thing seemed to be reabsorbing its Shadow Twin. Even as it did, it began to look less solid.

The chair smashed across its back, and the creature fell to the floor again. Jennifer stood over it, staring at him, her eyes brimming with unspoken emotion. She turned back to Sally, who stood shakily beside her.

"Help Trix," Jim told Sally.

But the No-Face Men were already darting through the air, rushing to the aid of Trix and Anne, and the battle was joined again.

The Half Shadow backhanded Trix, and she sprawled on the floor, blood running from her nose. Her face throbbed, starting to swell. She rose again, ignoring the shouts and scuffles elsewhere in the room. The erasing of Jenny from her own Boston had changed Trix, made her stronger and leaner; she had spent a lot more time in the gym in a reality that didn't have Jenny in it. She used that strength and conditioning now.

With a determined snarl, Trix lunged at the Half Shadow. She had tried to trip it up, tried to tackle it, tried to overpower it, but though it had once been an ordinary woman, this thing wasn't human anymore. It was too strong and too single-minded for her to overpower, so her only hope was to hurt it enough to get it to let go of Anne.

Trix leaped on the Half Shadow's back, its ghostly Shadow Twin cold where she passed through it. She wrapped one arm around the woman's neck and, with her free hand, clawed at her eyes. Trix felt her fingers sink into the woman's left eye socket, felt something wet and syrupy spurt onto her hand, and then both the woman's human mouth and the dark void that was the mouth of her Shadow Twin opened in a scream. "Let go of her, you bitch!" Trix shouted, digging her fingers in deeper.

A hand shot out and gripped Trix by the throat. Her eyes bulged as her airway was cut off and the pressure on her windpipe closed like a vise. She stared in astonishment at the wispy gray nothing of the arm that had emerged from the Half Shadow's back. The creature's Shadow Twin had begun to separate from her, at least enough to stop Trix from hurting it any further. Enough to kill Trix if it could.

The shadow hand hoisted her off the ground, her feet dangling above the marble tiles. She battered the wrist, where the dark mist of the thing had turned solid enough to hold her, but could not break its grip. Her vision began to dim, spots dancing at the corners of her eyes as the lack of oxygen made her spasm and kick.

In that moment, it occurred to her that she was going to die. The concept seemed distant. She felt herself jostled as the thing walked forward, still headed for the wall, dragging Anne across the room behind it. The wall was its destination, that much was clear. Trix had thought it meant to take Anne through the door into the Reflection Room, but it did not approach the doorway. Its aim was the ornately carved oak wall that had been put up to bisect the Abbey Room.

Blood rushing to her face, Trix beat the shadowy arm. The Half Shadow turned and glanced at her, one eye ruined, blood and gore smeared on its cheek. It held Anne in its hands, and now it lifted her up and held her out toward the wall. Anne caught Trix's gaze and held it, a terrible sorrow passing between the two women, terror wrought by this moment mixed with grief over moments that might have been.

Then the Half Shadow took a step forward, pushing Anne against the wall.

Through the wall.

Trix began to slip away from consciousness, her brain deprived of oxygen. But her eyes widened as she saw Anne flailing, passing through the wall as if it wasn't even there.

Dark shapes flashed past Trix, filling the edges of her vision, and at first she thought they were in her mind. But they struck the Half Shadow, attacking her viciously, beating at her face and body. One of Sally's No-Face Men slashed through the shadow arm holding Trix, and Trix collapsed to the ground drawing in huge lungfuls of air, her throat raw and ragged with pain. "Anne!" she rasped, scuttling forward on the marble.

But the No-Face Men were there before her. They dragged Anne back through the insubstantial wall, leaving her wide-eyed and shivering as though she had just woken from a nightmare of some frozen hell.

The things fell on the Half Shadow and began stripping the gray shadow stuff from her. In what seemed only seconds they had torn the bits of the In-Between out of her, leaving only that plump woman. She lay on her side and wept and laughed, though whether she was horrified or elated at her rebirth, Trix couldn't tell.

"Anne," Trix said as she knelt by her and laid a hand on her shoulder.

Shuddering, trying to calm herself, Anne looked up at her with wide, searching eyes. Trix blinked in surprise. For just a moment, she had let herself forget that this was the Jenny of another world. In the space of a few hours Anne had become someone real and vital to Trix, not just some doppelgänger.

"You're all right," Trix told her.

Anne reached up, slid a hand behind Trix's head, and pulled her down for a kiss. Trix didn't fight it. Though it lasted only a few seconds, it soothed her heart. When she pulled away, she saw that some of the blood from her damaged nose and bleeding mouth had smeared on Anne's face and lips, and she reached out to wipe it away.

"Trix?" Jim ventured, dropping to his knees beside them. "You okay?"

"Not hardly," Trix said, her voice a rasp from being choked almost to death. She helped Anne to stand.

"What did you see on the other side of the wall?" Jennifer asked, coming up to join them.

Anne shuddered and hugged herself. "Gray mist. Rooms that weren't really there."

Trix saw Jim stiffen and turn on Sally. "Is that what's in the Reflection Room?"

"No," Sally said, her child's eyes innocent. "I told you. Where the worlds don't overlap, they're separated by the In-Between. That's what she saw. The nothing that fills the void between the parallel Bostons. The library is in all three, but here—in both my Boston and O'Brien's—half of this room was destroyed by a terrorist's bomb. The Reflection Room exists because of that."

Sally walked to the wall and pounded on it. Trix flinched, thinking her hand would pass through, but it struck solid wood.

"The Shadow Men can pass through. I know other ways to slip into the In-Between, but it's moving sideways into nothing, which is not the same as going through the door into the next room."

Jim turned and looked at the door to the Reflection Room, where Holly was supposed to be waiting. Trix realized that he no longer saw the rest of them. He had forgotten all about the corpses, not to mention the heavyset black woman who even now climbed to her feet and staggered away. The No-Face Men hovered at the edges of the room, waiting for Sally's instructions.

There were at least two others dead, people who had been Half Shadows but who did not survive the violent removal of the shadow stuff from the In-Between that had infected them. The bloodied redhead still lived. He moaned and put a hand to his temple, frowning in pain, but did not try to rise.

"Are there more inside, Sally?" Trix asked.

Sally glanced at the redhead. "There must be."

"Then you should send your No-Face guys in first," Trix told her.

"Fuck that," Jim said, and he reached for the knob.

Jim pushed open the door into the Reflection Room. The recessed lights were dim, illuminating the many displays on the walls and in glass cases that were meant to educate about the value of human life and the horror of terrorist ideology. In a raised section of the floor the designer had put a Zen rock garden surrounded by a kidney-shaped pool of water with a small burbling fountain. There were comfortable chairs arranged at strange intervals around the thirty-foot-square room. On the opposite side of the Zen garden, one chair had been turned to face the door.

His daughter sat in that chair, her hair a tangled mess, her dirty face streaked with tear stains. "Daddy!" Holly shouted as she spotted him.

She tried to rise, but the Half Shadow who knelt beside the chair held her back. A weasel of a man with oily hair and tiny eyes, he forced her to remain in the chair, his grip on her arm making her wince with pain. Jim wanted to kill him . . . *would* kill him, he vowed.

But there was the other Half Shadow to worry about, the grandmotherly woman with her pearl necklace and wide hips and eyeglasses. She held a knife to Holly's throat.

"Let her go," Jim said, a terrible chill racing through him. "You can't think you'll get away from us." He gestured toward Sally and the three No-Face Men who hovered just behind her as the Oracle came through the door.

The weasel sneered. "This isn't about getting away. The job isn't to beat you. That's not how Veronica wins."

"So, how does she win?" Trix demanded, coming into the dimly lit room with Jennifer and Anne trailing behind her.

"The little girl dies, and Veronica wins," the weasel said.

Then why haven't you killed her already? Jim wanted to ask, but didn't dare for fear of spurring them on.

"Mommy?" Holly shouted, bucking against the weasel's grip. The old woman pressed the knife closer to her throat, and the little girl—his daughter!—whimpered as it drew blood. "Mommy, where did you *go?*" Holly demanded.

Confused, Jim glanced around to see that Jennifer had come up behind him, stepping into enough light that Holly could make out her face. She thought Jennifer was her mother, but Jim knew that now wasn't the time to explain anything. "Sally," Jim whispered. "Help my daughter."

The young Oracle, not even twice Holly's age, nodded once, gently.

"Let her go, now," Jim said to the two Half Shadows who had been left to guard her—to kill her.

The grandmother pointed her free hand at Sally. "Take the Oracle. Break her neck. Finish that job and we'll give you your daughter."

"She's lying," Trix whispered, coming up beside him. "They just said killing Holly was their job."

Jim took a deep breath to steady himself. His face and body ached from the beating the Half Shadows had given him in the other room. His fists opened and closed, wishing for a weapon, for something to attack them with, though he could not risk Holly's life. Powerless and full of fury, he knew there was nothing he could do.

Holly's eyes went wide, then narrowed in confusion and suspicion. "Mommy?" she said again, and he didn't have to turn to realize that she had just gotten a good look at Anne.

Jim had a lot of explaining to do.

"Hollybaby," he said, focusing only on his daughter. "What do you want for breakfast tomorrow?"

Holly began to cry.

"Listen to me," Jim said firmly. "What do you want for breakfast tomorrow?"

"Pancakes with butter and lots of syrup," she said quickly, as though the words had been pushing to be set free.

"You got it, kid," Jim said. "Now, this is important, Holly. Listen closely. I want you to close your eyes and imagine those pancakes, the taste of the syrup, the smell of the bacon I'm going to make to go with them—"

"I don't want bacon."

"Just the smell," Jim went on. "Picture us at the kitchen table. I'll have the newspaper. You can put the Disney Channel on while I'm flipping pancakes and making coffee for your mom."

The weasel looked entirely befuddled. He turned toward the grandmother. "What the fuck is he talking about?"

The grandmother did not reply. Instead, she stared at Jim, head cocked. Her Shadow Twin had partially emerged from her body, and it cocked its head as well, trying to figure out what to make of him, what he might be up to. "He's snapped," the grandmother said. Something in her appeared to soften, and Jim thought he could see the woman she had been before being swept away by a wave that had washed into her world and sucked her into the In-Between.

The knife at Holly's throat dipped slightly.

Jim shot a sidelong glance at Sally, who made the tiniest of gestures with her right hand, as though grabbing a fistful of the air. The No-Face Men who had come in behind her drifted back slightly, as though wishing to be less imposing to the Half Shadows holding Holly. Even more confused, the grandmother and the weasel stared at them.

They didn't even see the ghost hands that thrust up through the floor and pulled them down. The grandmother's eyes went wide, her arms flailing back, and then panic set in and she reached for Holly's chair, but too late. The weasel held on, fighting furiously, spitting and snarling. The hands of his Shadow Twin thrust out, helping as he tried to take hold of something solid, something of this world. One of his smoky gray nothing hands slapped the stones of the raised Zen rock garden. But he could not hold on, and Sally's No-Face Men dragged them both down through the floor and back to the In-Between.

Veronica's creatures had failed.

"Holly!" Jim said, rushing to his daughter.

He ran right through the rock garden, stones shifting underfoot, and nearly toppled into the fountain pond. Holly looked around in confusion, not sure yet that she was actually safe. But then Jim pulled her out of the chair and into his arms. He tried to speak and could not, because emotion had overwhelmed him. He laughed, but every time he tried to speak, tears sprang to his eyes and the words caught in his throat.

"You came, Daddy," Holly said. "I love that you came, crazy Daddy."

"Of course I came," he said, sitting back, holding his little girl in his lap even though she was getting too big for that, pushing her hair away from her eyes and wiping tears from her face, smearing dirt.

"Mommy said you would," Holly said proudly. She frowned and reached up to touch the blood trickling from the slice on her neck. "I'm cut."

"It's okay, honey. It's going to be okay."

"It stings," Holly informed him. And then she turned to look at the others. Her eyes widened as she got her first good look at Jennifer, and then she frowned in confusion when she saw Anne.

"Mommy?" Holly said, hopeful but unsure.

"No, honey," Jim said. "These ladies are . . . they're relatives of Mommy's."

Holly's disappointment seemed mixed with a sort of relief, as if instinct had told her neither of the women was her mother.

Holly studied Sally for a second, and then beckoned to Trix. "Aunt Trixie, c'mere."

Trix went over and knelt down beside them. She hugged them both, and Jim felt such love for her then that he sobbed again. Trix kissed Holly on the top of the head and then, seemingly on impulse, kissed Jim's cheek.

"Aunt Trixie," Holly whispered, looking suspiciously beyond her, toward Jennifer and Anne. "Those ladies who look like my mom are staring at me."

Trix laughed and Jim chuckled softly, shaking his head. He let out a long breath.

"They can see how amazing you are," Trix told Holly.

"Why do you look like my mom?" Holly asked, bending over to peer at them more closely. "She doesn't have any twin sisters or anything, 'cause she would have told me. Unless she didn't know, like that movie with the two girls whose parents never told them they were twins. I can't remember the name."

"Holly, listen to me, baby girl," Jim said, holding her cheeks and forcing her to focus. Sweet and funny as she was, she was definitely in shock. "You need to tell me what happened to your mom. When did you see her last?"

Pain creased his daughter's face, and Jim hated being the cause of that. But they needed to know. "A long time ago," Holly said. "Like, hours. I slept for a while, and then there was the earthquake—did you feel that earthquake, Daddy? I was totally freaked out! After the earthquake, they took Mommy away."

"Where?" Trix asked, gripping Jim's arm to steady him. "Where'd they take her, Holly?"

Holly pointed at the wall. "Right there. Right through the wall, like Mommy was a ghost or something."

Jim felt his insides turn to lead. He turned to look at Sally. "Into the In-Between?"

Sally nodded.

"Oh, Jesus," Jim whispered. He kissed Holly's forehead and then looked up at the Oracle again. "How long? How much time are we talking about for this transformation?"

Trix looked at him. "What transformation?"

Jim stroked Holly's hair, wishing she didn't have to be here for this. "Into one of them," he said. "If she's in there long enough, she's going to turn into one of the Shadow Men."

Jennifer covered her mouth in horror. Trix sank back on her haunches, then sat down hard on the floor.

"So we go in after her," Anne said. "How long do we have?"

They all looked at Sally. The Oracle seemed to have drifted far away in her mind, but now her eyes focused again and she nodded. "It may not be too late," the girl said, looking at Jim and Trix. "But if you're going into the In-Between, you'll have to have an anchor to lead you back, and it must be someone to whom you all have a connection. Someone to stay behind with me."

Jim looked at Jennifer and Anne. "You two . . . you don't even know her. You don't have to—"

Jennifer laughed. "Don't know her? We *are* her!"

Anne stared at him. "It would be like letting myself die."

"Jim," Trix said. "It should be Holly."

"Me?" Holly perked up. "I can help get Mommy back?"

"No," Jim said quickly. "I'm not going to leave her behind now. No way."

"Leave me behind?" Holly said, her eyes going wide. "I don't want to be alone again. Those bad guys might come back!"

But Jim knew, even as she spoke, that there was no other choice. Jennifer and Anne might not be anchor enough to guide them back here.

"Holly, sweetie, I think we need to," he said, and she stared at him, her eyes welling again. "No, no, don't cry. You've been so brave, but you need to be brave a little while longer so we can get Mommy back. We're going to go where they took her, and you're going to stay right here with our friend Sally. She'll protect you."

Dubious, Holly glanced sidelong at Sally. "But she looks like a kid, Daddy. How's she going to protect me if those guys come back?"

Sally smiled. "Holly, do you see those tall ghost guys over there?" she asked, pointing to the No-Face Men lingering in the corner of the room, awaiting her orders. "They take their orders from me. They'll make sure nobody can hurt us."

Holly looked warily at the No-Face Men, as afraid of them as she was of the ones who had held her prisoner. Their faces flickered, fleeting images of a thousand faces they might one day be. "Dad," she said, sounding very grown-up, "this is a terrible idea."

Jim took a breath, sinking down onto his knees in the stones of the Zen garden. He wasn't going to force Holly to do this, but every passing second might mean there would be less and less of Jenny to bring home. Even now, she might be only a shadow of herself. An echo.

Then, in a small voice, Holly spoke up again. "Can you really bring Mommy back, Aunt Trixie?"

Trix nodded. "I think we can. If we hurry."

Holly sighed, stood up, and went to take Sally's hand. "Okay. Hurry, then," she said. "And Aunt Trixie . . . ?"

"Yes?"

Holly grinned. "I like your hair."

Jim laughed. Trix smiled and touched her hair, apparently having forgotten for a while that it was a vivid pink.

"I have a question," Jennifer said, addressing Sally. "If this is happening to . . . to Jim's Jenny . . . what's to stop it from happening to us? I mean, if we go in there, won't we start to be changed, too?"

Sally was a girl older than her years, but from time to time an even deeper wisdom seemed to light her eyes. Jim saw it there now. "There is a way," Sally said. "You won't be the first people to have explored the In-Between. Richard Vernon was the Oracle of Boston—my Boston—before the job landed in my hands. In the short time I knew him, he told me stories. So, yes, there's a way. You might not like it, but if you're careful and quick, it should keep you safe."

"Let's do it," Jim said. "Come on. Time's wasting. Every second counts."

But he saw the troubled expression on Trix's face and knew there was something more. "Why Jenny?" Trix asked.

"What do you mean?" Jim said.

"Why take Jenny into the In-Between and not Holly?" Trix looked at Anne and Jennifer, then at Sally. "Why hold Holly captive? Why not just kill her?"

"Bait for me," Sally said. "When their original plan didn't work, the Shadow Men acted under their own volition and held off killing her. Luring me into the trap. We're here, aren't we?"

"Maybe," Trix said. "But we know *part* of Veronica's plan, right? The Shadow Men follow our marks, we deliver those letters—hexed, cursed, whatever—and then they kill you and O'Brien so the three Bostons collide. You've gotta figure it's all because she wanted to be the one and only Oracle of the one and only Boston, right?"

"Makes sense," Jim said.

"It's the *only* thing that makes sense. But I don't get this thing with Holly. And are we supposed to go after Jenny? Is that all part of Veronica's plan?"

"Does it matter?" Anne asked. "We're going, aren't we?"

"Yes, we're going, no matter what," Trix agreed. "But there's something we're missing here. Something significant. I mean, Holly and Jenny slipped through, the way everyone who's ever gotten lost in the In-Between has. They were lucky to end up in another Boston instead of nowhere at all. So how did Veronica's servants find them so fast?"

"You're saying it was no accident," Jim said, narrowing his eyes, knowing the truth when he heard it. "She *made* it happen. She picked them, and she picked us. She needed us because we're Uniques."

"It's more than that," Trix said. "There are tons of Uniques. You heard what that greasy-looking guy said: they were supposed to kill Holly. Why?"

A shuffling step came from the doorway, and then a soft cough. They all turned, ready for a fight, but it was only the redheaded teenager, bruised and exhausted, blood in his hair, no fight left in him at all. Whoever he had been in the Boston where Jim had come from, he was stuck in this world now, but at least the shadows of the In-Between had been ripped from him.

"I can tell you the answer to that one," he said. "We tossed your wife into the Gray—what you're calling the In-Between—because we didn't need her. We threw her away like trash."

"Son of a bitch," Trix said, starting to rise, fists clenched.

"No," the kid said. "Please. That's not me. I never wanted any of that. Veronica promised she would save us . . . she would get that stuff out of us, give us our lives back, if we did what she wanted. And it was hard to say no anyway. They can command you, y'know? The Oracles."

Jim stared at Sally, wondering if her No-Face Men did her bidding against their will.

"She's all right," the redhead said, seeing his look. "She tries to save the ones she can. That's what someone told me, in the In-Between. But once you're fully gone, there's nothing anyone can do for you. Helping the Oracle, when you're summoned, it's the only time you can feel alive." He turned to Sally. "Thank you. Your guys saved me."

Sally smiled at him, nodding once.

"My wife," Jim urged. "If they threw her away, what did they want with Holly?"

The kid looked at him, then at Holly, pity in his gaze. "Veronica never chose a successor. She doesn't want anyone to replace her. Not ever. But when an Oracle can't choose, or won't, the soul of the city chooses for it-self," he said, turning back to Jim.

"Dude, Veronica wants your daughter dead because she's the next Oracle of Boston."

15

If I Ever Leave This World Alive

THEY COULD have just killed her," Jim said, hugging his daughter to his chest. The redheaded guy had gone, sent away by Sally. The others were milling in a state of shock at the brutal fight they had just survived. Sally sat against the wall recuperating, while her motionless No-Face Men loitered in the shadows, but there was a sense of urgency in the room. They all knew that speed was of the essence. If anyone came in here and saw the bodies and blood, their troubles would have only just begun.

"I would have sensed that," Sally said. "They needed her alive as bait."

"Bait," Jim echoed, and the idea of anyone using his precious little girl like that only increased his fury.

"Like in fishing, Daddy?"

"Yes, honey." He hugged Holly and felt her familiar warmth, and could not avoid imagining that bleeding away.

"Her Shadow Men have been thinking on their own," Sally said. "She must have imbued them with more intelligence than I thought."

"But they didn't figure on us," Anne said. She was

nursing her bruised and bleeding head, but her defiance was unmistakable.

"As if we made much difference," Jennifer said. She was kneeling close to Jim and Holly but not quite close enough to touch. He knew that this must be so difficult for her.

"You made *every* difference," Sally said. Her eyes were closed. She looked reduced, even smaller than the child she was.

"How?" Trix asked.

"You gave them something more to fight. Bought us time to react."

Trix and Anne pulled several of the heavy chairs across to the wide entrance. With the doors closed and chairs propped beneath the handles, it would take a concerted effort to enter the room from that way. And today, they hoped, few people would have browsing works of art on their minds. Art was a luxury, and these were desperate times.

"Honey," Jim whispered into his daughter's ear, and she pulled back slightly and looked up at him.

"I know," she said. "It's time for you to help Mommy."

"And you're going to stay here, be my good little girl." He glanced at Sally, watching him talk to his daughter. "And look after Sally for me. She's very tired, and a little sad."

Holly looked at the Oracle, then sighed. "Daddy," she said, "don't be silly. She's like . . . magic. *She'll* be looking after *me*."

He laughed, and Jennifer smiled at him. "Clever little girl you've got there," she said.

"You don't know the half of it." He wondered what Jennifer must think, knowing that this girl shared her DNA yet was not her daughter. And he realized that after this, nothing would ever be the same again. From this day forward, the merged city of Boston would become the focus of every media outlet, and every scientist. It would be the most famous, most heavily scrutinized place in the world, and thousands of people's lives would be changed. Some of the changes would be obvious and immediately apparent—there would be lots of people vying for the same property, existing in the same space. But many more changes would be hidden away, perhaps forever. There were plenty of bodies in the streets and buried under collapsed buildings, but yesterday's collision must have wiped out many people from reality. Bloodlines had ended, without ever having existed at all.

Across the world, ripples from this incredible, terrible event had changed situations beyond counting.

"You have to go now," Sally said. Her eyes were still closed and she remained seated, but something about her had hardened. Perhaps it was her stronger voice, or the squaring of her shoulders.

Jim stood, still grasping his daughter's hand. The idea of Jenny fading away was terrible, and the thought of her becoming one of those faceless shadow-things was beyond comprehension.

"Are you ready?" Sally asked.

"Are you?" She looked wasted to Jim; he was afraid for her, and of her.

"I can do what I need to do," Sally said. "It's all of you who matter. If you don't get back and stop Veronica, what happened here will be only the beginning. This won't be"—she stood, pushing herself up the wall and shrugging her shoulders—"pleasant."

Jim and Jennifer stood near Holly, and Trix and Anne came to stand with them, facing away from the bodies that Trix and Anne had dragged across to one wall. Smears of blood glistened on the floor. Holly had her back resolutely to the corpses as well, and Jim's heart broke for her. *Even if this all ends well, she's changed forever,* he thought, and his little girl smiled up at him sadly.

"You know what you've gotta do," Sally said, standing before them. "The only way to hide you from the In-Between is to fool it into thinking you're already a part of it. Being turned into a shadow would weaken you pretty badly, even at the beginning. And you'll need *all* your strength in there. So I'm going to lend you souls not yet born."

"So Jenny, now?" Jim asked.

"After this time, I suspect she's in a sort of coma," Sally said. "Which is good, because it will protect her. A little."

Trix exhaled loudly. "Okay. I'm ready. But I've gotta say, it's freaking me out something huge."

Jim nodded. He felt the same way. Sally wanted to merge them with her No-Face Men, masking their humanity with those wraiths' *potential* existence. Hopefully like that, the In-Between would not affect them. At least, not right away. "Are you sure this is going to work?" he asked Sally.

The young Oracle shrugged. "I guess. I mean, it's been done before, but not by me. You should be able to stay merged with them for a little while without it affecting you too much. I'm not sure for how long, but long enough for you to . . ." She waved at the expanse of wall through which the Shadow Men had tried to pull Anne.

"What's 'too much'?" Trix asked.

"I don't know," Sally said. "*I've* never done this before."

"Will we be able to lose them afterward?" Jim asked.

"You will," Sally said. "I'll tell you how. Show you." She was vague, and quiet.

"All right," Trix said. She looked at Anne and they squeezed each other's hands. "If we're going, let's get going. Me first."

Sally shifted her hand by her side, and a No-Face Man came forward, a shadow floating through pools of artificial light. "Try and keep still," Sally said. "And don't fight it."

Trix nodded, then let go of Anne's hand and crossed her arms on her chest.

Jim's first impulse was to shout out and help his friend because he could see that she was in pain. Her face screwed up—but she uttered no sound—as Sally grasped at the amorphous No-Face Man and pressed him to Trix's side. Trix did not move or flinch, but her expression betrayed the discomfort she was feeling as Sally kneaded and pressed, clasping handfuls of shadow and pressing it against her clothing, her skin. The little girl's face was set in concentration, and her lips moved as she muttered some unheard incantation, eyes fluttering, cheeks flushing. She grasped and pushed, and it was almost as if she was trying to mold Trix and the No-Face Man together. As the wraith reduced, so Trix's discomfort seemed to grow.

"You're hurting her," Jim said, but it was Holly's hand squeezing his that silenced him. *My little girl's giving me comfort,* he thought, and a darkness opened in him because of things she had already seen. He hated the idea of Holly becoming as unnaturally precocious as Sally.

Perhaps something about what she was doing became easier, because Sally seemed to speed up. Her hands grasped and pressed, her arms windmilled, and soon she was snatching at the air to retrieve the few dregs of the No-Face Man that remained. At last she stood back, breathing heavily and yet seemingly invigorated by what she had done—eyes glinting, skin flushed and shining.

Trix opened her eyes and looked around. Her pupils were darker than Jim had ever seen them, like pits into nothing.

"Trix?" he asked. She blinked a few times, gathering her personality back to her, finding herself again.

"Fucking hell," she said.

"Okay," Sally said, waving her hand and calling forth another. "Who's next?"

Trix watched Anne, Jennifer, and then Jim go through the process, and all the time she was coming to terms with what she had become. Memories flitted at her like vague recollections of long-ago dreams, and even this distant there was a terrifying alienness to them. She often could not remember what she had dreamed the night before, but a nightmare from when she was four years old—falling from a cliff with her mother, Trix flying, her mother striking the ground and dying—was etched on her memory. These memories felt like second-hand dreams remembered by someone else. They were not only memories that did not belong, but the way they were remembered was all wrong as well. She was recalling someone else's life, long lost to the In-Between.

Trix supposed she should have felt pity, but she was too scared for that. And too determined.

As each of the other three were merged with a No-Face Man, she witnessed them going through the same strange, disconcerting experience. Jennifer cried, reaching for Jim's hand. Anne stood strong, her gaze never diverting from Trix's eyes. And Jim barely seemed to flinch. *He'd go through hell to get his Jenny back*, Trix thought, and she glanced at Anne, thinking that fate had changed everything.

Finally they stood there, altered and yet the same.

"I still see Jim," Trix said. "And Jennifer, and Anne. I see that they're different, but—"

"The In-Between needs no eyes," Sally said. "I can see . . ." She closed her eyes, frowned, and opened them again, muttering under her breath. "I see you all faded away."

Trix shivered and looked down at her hands, turning them over. She knew the backs of her hands, and yet the nails now seemed to seep something blank, like an invisible mist that wiped shreds of reality from view. She blew, but the mist did not disperse.

"Trust me," Sally said. "Don't concern yourself with what's happened, or how different you might be or feel. It's worked, and it'll protect you. And you'll be too busy in there to try to understand."

"Bugs the crap out of me," Anne said, wringing her hands together and then pulling them slowly apart. Trix smiled, her heart quickening.

"Go fast," Holly said. She was holding on to Jim and looking at the other three. "Please go fast."

"We'll be faster than fast," Trix said.

"One more thing," Sally said. "Pass by me; I can do this while you go." She held on to Holly's other hand, and they looked nothing like two little girls.

Jim went first, and Sally muttered strange words as she reached up and touched his face with her free hand. Jennifer and Anne followed, and then Trix grasped the Oracle's hand and gasped softly. For a moment Holly was a part of her—laughing in her mind, giggling as they walked together through Boston, hugged together on a sofa watching her favorite movie, *Lilo & Stitch*. And as Sally let go and her eyes widened just a little, Trix smiled at Holly. "Our bond is already strong," she said. "I'll never let you down, Holly."

"Thanks, Auntie Trix," the girl said.

They stood at the wall, and Trix looked back at the two girls in the center of the ruined room, with blood spattered all about and bodies against the far wall. But she knew more than to ask if they would be all right. "See you soon," she said to both of them, and she was the first to reach for the door handle.

As the door opened, there was a gasp. Trix thought it had come from the other three, but then a waft of air passed her, seemingly drifting *both* ways, and for a moment she became utterly disoriented. She smelled something old and base, her ears sang with unknown whispers, and she was not sure whether her eyes were open or closed.

At first glance, the room around her—the Reflection Room beyond the door—looked quite normal, not part of another world at all. And then she realized that there *was* something strange about it. She stared, closed her eyes and smelled, then tried to just listen, and it took a while to identify what was wrong. *This room is dead,* she thought, and the idea chilled her. Even the wood in the floor had never been part of a living thing. The room was paused, not frozen like a picture, but caught in a gap between moments. It was nowhere a living thing could feel at home.

She walked quickly toward the opposite wall, and before she reached it her surroundings misted away to nothing. As she took several more steps, the floor beneath her changed to something softer. She looked down and saw an uncertain surface, her feet suspended on a vaporous layer. Stamping, she felt no reverberation, and very little impact.

"We're in the In-Between," she said, and though it was muffled, she was pleased that she could hear her own voice. She turned around to see the others coming through the door, and the wall behind her had vanished.

Everything behind her had vanished.

There was mist. Up and down were dictated only by the way she stood, but there was little else to distinguish it. And yet there must have been a firm ground, and some rule of three-dimensional order, because she could see Anne, Jennifer, and Jim, all of them standing in the same plane. They were shadows in the mist, vague shapes that she saw better when she looked to their left or right.

"Trix?" she heard, unsure who was calling.

"Here!" She waved her arms. It felt like someone else waved with her, a shadow echoing her movements. A shape came closer, and Jim emerged from the mist, moisture speckling his unshaven face. Jennifer came next, then Anne hurried to them, footfalls silent, her fearful expression shocking as she emerged into view.

"What is this?" Anne asked.

"The In-Between," Jim said. "The space between worlds."

"How the hell are we supposed to find her in here?" Jennifer asked.

Jim closed the distance between him and Jennifer, standing so close that their arms touched. Trix wasn't sure it was even a conscious movement. "We walk," Jim said. He turned away from them all and looked back the way they had come. Trix knew it was that direction, because she could feel Holly's influence there, like a beacon in the darkness.

"We walk," Trix repeated. "But can you feel . . . ?"

They all nodded, because they knew what she meant. The air of this place was awash with malevolence, and as she inhaled and exhaled, she sensed the shadow inside her settling as it became one with the In-Between again. It smelled of stale cotton candy, and tasted of something rotten.

Without the shadow, the air would be harmful to her. It would start to bleed her of spirit and turn her into one of them, and she'd seen enough to know that their existence was not something to relish. Perhaps there would be no pain, but an unconscious limbo seemed worse than anything she could imagine. In the In-Between, possessing a mind—thoughts, desires, history—seemed the most important thing of all.

"Come on!" Trix said, suddenly desperate for Jenny and fearing that they might already be too late. "We don't walk, we *run*! Hope you've all been keeping in shape." She started running, and the others followed.

There was no concept of distance, other than by counting paces, but from the beginning Trix was certain they were going the right way. Jennifer and Anne passed her and subtly adjusted their direction. Jim followed with Trix, and the two facets of Jenny started moving faster, loping through the mists as something drew them on.

They saw their first Shadow Man, and it shocked Trix to the core. Outside, dragged through into one of the real worlds, these things were horrific enough. But here in the In-Between their monstrousness was more shocking because of its familiarity. In her world they were shapes that barely echoed humanity, but here they were tortured people, naked forms that twisted and writhed through the mists, limbs bending farther than they should, heads twisting and flipping so fast that they were a blur. They moved without walking, their agonies giving them a terrible momentum. And after seeing the first few, she feared that the next one they'd see would be Jenny.

I'll know her, Trix thought, because each of these tortured souls possessed human traits and marks. Some were tattooed, others scarred, and hair color and build were distinguishable even through their pained contortions. As they saw another manifesting from the mists, she dreaded seeing Jenny's hair, her face.

A larger shadow marred the blankness ahead of them, then emerged as a shape with square edges and features she finally recognized. It was Trinity Church, solid across this In-Between because it existed in all three Bostons.

Anne and Jennifer did not even pause. Wherever Jenny was, she drew them on.

Time lost meaning, its only evidence the urgency Trix felt. They passed another building in the distance that seemed solid, and then they entered a park whose plants were barely there, and whose small buildings seemed composed of drifting, shifting structures. Trix's No-Face Man seemed uncomfortable in this place, and her own senses were repulsed by their surroundings. She glanced at Jim and saw that he was equally disturbed.

They did not pause to see what that place was, or why it had such an effect. As they left and entered the nowhere spaces in between, her No-Face Man settled again into the echo he had been. She could never get used to him, but at least this way she felt in control.

"Close," Jennifer called, her voice robbed of its tone by the mist.

"Very," Anne agreed. She looked back at Trix without breaking her stride, and with a burst of speed Trix and Jim drew closer to the two women.

And then Trix heard something in the distance. It was a soft, gentle moan, like wind gusting through an empty woodland. It rose and fell, raising a shiver like ice in her soul. Anne and Jennifer paused, and with their heads cocked they reminded Trix so much of Jenny that she let out a sob.

"We'll save her," Jim said, and it was ridiculous that *he* was comforting *her*.

"I know we will," she said, because any other outcome was unthinkable.

The moaning grew in volume as they ran on again.
Trix felt a tugging inside her, something that set her No-
Face Man squirming, an uncomfortable sensation as if
suddenly her skin could not contain her body. The tugging came from behind her, and she sent a message she
hoped Holly might hear: *We're close, and soon we'll be
back with your mother.*

And then they saw the lonely shape in the mists, and
Trix's heart broke. Anne and Jennifer stopped, sending
shadowy ripples through the heavy air. Jim slowed,
moving past them before coming to a halt. None of
them could take in the pain they saw in the woman they
loved, or the woman they were a part of.

"We can't just fucking stand here," Trix whispered,
and in that silent place it seemed that her words might
travel forever. She approached Jenny and saw how much
had already happened. Naked, writhing, she did not
twist and flex as much as the other changed people she
had seen but rather seemed to swim in the air, limbs
kicking and clawing at the strange misty atmosphere.

"Jenny!" Trix said, grabbing her arms and holding her
still. The recognition in Jenny's eyes was instant and
shocking, because it spoke of such pain.

"H . . . H . . . H . . . ," Jenny said, panting.

Trix nodded, angrily wiping a sudden tear from her
eye. "Holly's fine," she said. "She's waiting for you."

"Can you stand, babe?" Jim said. He was beside Trix
now, touching his wife's arms, her shoulders, wiping a
slick of gray wetness from her stomach and chest.

"I . . . I . . ." Jenny's eyes rolled, her body shook, and
Trix saw shadows flickering from the corners of her
mouth and ears, tendrils flowing inward rather than out.

"She's a long way gone," Trix said. She turned back to

Jennifer and Anne. "Come on. We're going to have to carry her."

Jim lifted his wife beneath her arms and held her against him, taking the hug she could not give. Her body rippled and shook from the forces assaulting it, and shadows manifested from nowhere to flow into her. *How long until she's filled up?* Trix wondered, and she stood beside Jim and offered help.

Jim turned his wife and held her beneath the arms, stepping back and allowing Trix to grab her beneath the knees. Naked, Jenny was on display to all of them, but it was a wretched nakedness—her skin was pale and slick, and things moved inside her. Anne and Jennifer approached on either side, looking down at another version of themselves. "God help her," Jennifer whispered.

"Not unless we do," Trix said. "Come on. You lead the way."

They started running, and it felt like they were being repulsed by the In-Between and forced back to reality. Holly pulled them on, drawing them back to her. Trix relished the exertion, rushing sidelong with her best friend in the world held in her hands, and another version of this best friend racing beside her, her lover in another world. And everything was suddenly starting to feel fine, when Jenny began seizing so violently that she kicked her legs from Trix's hands and twisted herself away from Jim's grasp.

"No!" Jim shouted, and Jenny hit the ground and bounced back up, forced by her flexing limbs, rolling and thrashing like those other tortured Shadow Men they had seen all around.

"Not now!" Trix said. "We've found her, we have her, this isn't fucking *fair*!" As she became angrier and more desperate, the thing within her grew more agitated, and she sensed it thrusting itself out beyond her body's extremes.

Jim was staring at her, aghast . . . and then he came forward and grabbed her shoulders. "We've got to get it out of her," he said, glancing at his hurting wife and turning away again, resting his head on Trix's shoulder.

She held the back of his head and they hugged, two good friends preparing to help the woman they both loved.

"Sally's No-Face Men," Jim said. "One of them could rip the shadows out of her, like back in the library."

Trix nodded, hope igniting within her. Already her thoughts turned inward, feeling for the shadow creature inside her, wondering if it could feel what she felt, if it could know what they needed. "Yes," she said. "It's the only way. If they understand what we want."

Anne and Jennifer stood by with their hands held out but unable to touch her, unable to help. "Will it work?" Anne asked. "If one of us breaks away from the shadow Sally merged us with, we'll be just as vulnerable as Jenny."

"Probably," Trix agreed, a terrible weight on her heart.

"It has to be me," Jim said.

"But what if—" Jennifer began.

"We don't know what if," Jim said, pulling back. "We don't know anything!"

"We could just run," Trix said, but she could already see the folly in that. She hated the idea, and winced when it flashed across her mind . . . but Jenny might be too far gone already. Running would do them no good. They had to act now.

Jim turned, eyes closing as he tried to separate himself from the No-Face Man Sally had put inside of him, but then Jennifer shouted, a wail of emotion rather than words. It said so much. Her eyes were full of pain and denial and anger, and the way she looked at Anne, it seemed the two of them had come to some instant, silent agreement. *No,* Jim thought, because he knew some of what that look meant. Part of it was good-bye. "Jennifer," he warned.

"I didn't get to have a family," Jennifer said, anguish pouring out of her. "But *she* does. It's the life I wished for. One of us has to have it."

Jim started toward her, nearly swimming through the strange atmosphere of the In-Between. Jennifer grasped one of Jenny's waving hands in both of her own, then grimaced and closed her eyes, writhing slowly even as Jenny flipped and thrashed. A gush of darkness flowed from Jennifer's eyes and ears, forming quickly alongside her, an echo of her following a heartbeat behind.

"Jennifer," Jim said, but there was nothing else to say. He could object and push her away, try to break her bond with his poor dying wife. Or he could help.

He went to them, reaching out, trying to remember what he'd seen Sally doing less than an hour before and half a world away. And it took only a second's hesitation before he reached out to the shadow stuff oozing from Jennifer and forming a shape next to her that he recognized so well. He curled his hands in the No-Face Man's stuff, a cool, slick porridge that seemed to tug at every hair on his hand and arm, smoothing against his skin in a sickly, almost sensuous way. Then he thrust his handful down at Jenny and pressed it against her face.

Even though her eyes were closed, he could see the change. Her eyeballs rolled behind their lids, seeing things he had no wish to see but hoped he could ask her about one day. Her skin heaved in movements that her body could never perform by itself, no matter how terrible her fit. He pushed harder, then grabbed another handful and another, and suddenly Jenny stopped moving.

Frozen, arms held out in a crucifixion pose, she opened her eyes and her jaw fell, and she spewed something rotten and black into the shivering mist. It came with a scream, and Jim stumbled back, trying but failing to pull Jennifer with him.

"Jim!" Trix shouted, but she was very far away.

Jennifer's No-Face Man was still emerging, and now it was completing on its own what Jim had begun—flowing into Jenny, expunging the dreadful, dark thing that had made its home there. It gushed like hot tar, a torrent of dried blood, a flood of dead flies, foulness erupting from every orifice and dispersing to the strange air of this In-Between place. When he took in a breath, Jim heaved at the stench and tasted vileness on his tongue.

"Jim!" Trix shouted again.

Driving it out, Jim thought, barely understanding, yet finding hope once again. Jenny looked so slight beneath and behind what was happening, her naked form assaulted and reduced, and he had touched every part of her, loved every inch, and now he was determined that he would do so again.

Jennifer still clasped her hand, bending forward slowly until she went to her knees beside her naked other self.

"Jim, something's happening!" Trix shouted.

I know, Jim thought, but something in her voice made him turn around. And Trix and Anne were looking *away* from Jenny and Jennifer.

In the distance, the looming shape of a building wavered in and out of focus. There was a violence about the huge, slow movement that took his breath away, a malevolence that he was certain had not been there previously, and before he could discern exactly what was happening, Trix made it clear. "Something's here. And it *sees* us," she said.

"No," Anne said, and she looked past Jim. "Something sees Jennifer."

"Not camouflaged anymore," Jim said, realizing what Jennifer had done for Jenny and for him. He went to them both, gathering his wife to him with one arm and Jennifer with the other.

"Jim," Jenny whispered. She was shaking from shock, but when she met his eyes he knew that she was almost completely herself. She looked at Jennifer, concern overcoming her shock.

"Come on," Jim said. He tried to pull them both up, and then Trix and Anne were there to help, hauling Jenny to her feet. Trix hugged her and waved away her confusion.

"Later," she said. "It'll all have to wait until later."

"What have you done?" Jim asked Jennifer.

She looked at him, his wife with another personality behind her eyes, and smiled softly. "Saved myself," she said. "And now I really think we should be running like hell."

Jim nodded, took hold of Jenny's hand with his left hand and Jennifer's with his right, and the five of them ran.

Holly pulled them in, Jim's love for his daughter strong and warm in the distance. And with his wife next to him again, Jim thought perhaps he would find the strength for anything. He felt no tiredness, though he ran faster than he ever had before. Even his fear was slight and remote, though they were crossing an ocean of nothing, a place between worlds where souls were torn apart. Love had brought him this far, and would take him farther.

But the In-Between was no longer passive.

Whatever had seen Jennifer saw her still, and there were stirrings in the mist. The ground rumbled beneath Jim's feet whenever he took a step. The air vibrated, as though something huge was moving in the distance. The mist swirled in patterns he did not know, and complex shapes that no mere mist could make.

"Faster!" Jim said, and somehow they increased their speed. Jenny was gasping and panting beside him. She looked exhausted and terrified, but she was taking strength from these people who had come to find her. He knew that expression of grim determination set on her face—she was hiding her discomfort to do what needed to be done. Physically, she was triumphing, but he had no idea how this would scar her.

Together, that's all that matters, he thought, and the sense of Holly drawing them back was wonderful. But just when he believed it was all going to be all right and that they'd stumble upon the solid Reflection Room at any moment, the ground shook and sent them sprawling.

As he fell, Jim's instinct took over—he had to reach out to shield his fall, and without thinking he unclasped his left hand and held it out before him. He grunted, rolled, and when he came to a stop he and Jenny were still holding hands.

Six feet away, Jennifer slowly stood and faced what was bearing down upon them.

"Keep still!" Anne said. She and Trix were also still holding hands, standing quickly and backing slowly from the shape in the mist.

"Too late," Trix said, and Jim knew that she was right. Camouflaged though they might be by bearing the No-Face Men, whatever was coming for them would have seen through their subterfuge. Jennifer stood before them, a bared human soul in this inhuman world, and now the thing would destroy them all.

The thing was a storm, a riot of mist, and as it approached there were hints of something more solid at its center.

"You can go," Jennifer said. Jim heard her voice clearly, even above the closing chaos.

"No," he said, but she was not making a suggestion.

"You can go," she said again, telling them all that she might be their one chance. As Jim looked from Jennifer—standing tall and straight, and as strong as he had ever seen his wife—and toward the approaching thing, he at last began to appreciate the threat it presented.

Because there was a face. And he had seen that face before.

Trix was by his side then, grabbing his left arm. "That's . . . !" she said, unable to finish. To his right, Jenny hugged his arm, shaking but standing firm.

"That's Thomas McGee," Jim said.

"It doesn't deserve a name," Jenny said. Jim wondered what terrible things she had seen out here, but he could not ask her now. Perhaps he never would.

"Who is he?" Anne asked.

"The reason this place is here. He's the ruination of Boston. The one who splintered it in the first place. I thought he was dead, but instead—"

"He's in the In-Between," Trix said.

"No. Can't you feel it?" Jim said. "I think he *is* the In-Between."

Jenny started shouting, because the shape that was McGee was close now, so close Jim thought perhaps it would reach out and sweep them away. As large as a man, the form at the heart of the mist-storm felt a hundred times more solid, as though its gravity was pulling them in.

"You . . . can . . . go," Jennifer said, and she spared Jim one glance over her shoulder. The shadow stuff of the In-Between was pushing itself into her body, beginning the change that would make her a dead thing, an echo.

He would never forget the look in her eye, because it was the last thing he had expected. He'd have recognized fear, or resignation, or even sadness at the cruel tricks fate could play. But what he saw there was unbridled, uncomplicated love.

She went at McGee, and the re-forming man paused for a moment as if surprised.

"Run!" Jim said.

"We can't just—" Trix began, but he clasped her hand and pulled her after him. There was no time to argue about it now. Later he would tell her, *Jennifer did it for us, and if we'd waited there a second longer, her sacrifice would have been in vain.* And later still, perhaps he and Trix would share quiet, private moments to go over those events again and again, to see what might have been different. But right then they did not have the luxury of time, and when Jim heard the angry shouts behind them—and then those long, terrible screams that would haunt him for the rest of his life—he did not turn around.

Anne and Jenny screamed as well, and for their final few moments in the In-Between they cried tears of unimaginable loss.

Bursting back through the Reflection Room and feeling the weight of reality realigning around them, Jim risked a look at his wife and the woman who could be her twin. They were reduced by what had happened; something was missing from their eyes. As he felt tears blurring his vision, he wondered whether either of them would ever feel fully alive again.

"Mommy!" Holly shouted as they opened the door. *"Mommy!"* The little girl ran across the bloodstained room and hugged her mother tight.

"McGee," Sally said.

"Yes." Jim nodded. Trix was holding Anne as she sobbed. Sally glanced around, then walked slowly across the room and closed the door. She had seen Jennifer's absence and accepted it, and Jim couldn't help hating her for it, just a little. Perhaps that was unfair blame, but right then he had to blame someone.

"Get these fucking things out of us," Jim said.

"Not yet," Sally said. She looked at Holly and Jenny hugging and smiled an unbearable smile. It was a look that said, *That can never be me,* and Jim's anger at her shifted to grudging pity.

"Why?" Jim asked.

"Because it's not over." The Oracle looked at Trix, and Trix looked at Jim.

"Veronica," Trix said.

"Veronica." Sally waved them closer, and Jim realized that it was not yet time to rest.

16

Every Dog Has Its Day

IT WAS daytime. Smoke hung over the city, drifting gently westward and tearing the sunlight into veils of gorgeous color. Jim remembered hearing of similar electromagnetic effects in the atmosphere after other earthquakes. He wondered what more this tragedy might have done, but for now he had his family with him, and he really did not care.

They looked like a party of refugees. Jenny wore a pair of pants and a man's shirt they'd found in a storage room in the library, and she had taken the shoes from the dead woman's body. Jim had been shocked at that, but Jenny had barely blinked as she sat and put them on. Life, death—their distinction was still strong, but now the space In-Between was vaster than ever before. Holly was tired and bedraggled, Trix and Anne leaned on each other for support, and Sally walked ahead of the small group. Some people recognized her and moved aside, almost as if making way for a queen, but most did not. Most of the others they passed in that blighted city had tragedy of their own to contemplate, and their attention was focused inward.

"Can we . . . can we get these things out of us now?"

Jenny asked, shuddering with revulsion at the presence of the No-Face Man still inside her.

Jim had been wondering the same thing. They were out of the In-Between. They didn't need the shadow creatures merged with them anymore. But Sally shook her head again, and Jim saw that old wisdom working behind her eyes. "You'll need them a little while longer," she said.

"But—" Trix began.

"Please," Sally said with a tired sigh. "You've trusted me this long."

Holly took her hand. To her, it was clear Sally wasn't a child at all. At four or five years older, the Oracle was one of the "big kids"—at least in Holly's eyes. "We trust you, Sally," Holly told her, and Jim shuddered, because now there was some of that old wisdom in his daughter's voice, too.

They had another walk ahead of them, in this city where traffic was mainly restricted to emergency vehicles. Not every street was blocked, but there were many more bicycles being used today, and with crowds of people traversing the city in search of something—or perhaps, in some cases, fleeing something—it was a safer bet to walk.

"McGee's house," Sally had said. "That's where she'll be waiting."

"Why can't we just get there through the In-Between?" Anne had asked, shocking Jim, because that was the last place in the world he'd ever want to go again. But Anne's eyes were filled with a fury he had never before seen in his wife. In *his* Jenny.

"No," Sally had replied. "What's left of McGee—whatever he's become—has seen you now."

"I'd fight him." Anne had pursed her lips, her cheeks

glowing red, and even Trix's soft touch had done little to quell her shaking.

"And you'd lose," Sally had said. "He's not our enemy. He's not the threat. His crime happened more than a century ago, and he was its first victim. Whatever he is now, I don't think there's much of Thomas McGee left in him."

So they walked, and Jim wished it was all over. He could not let go of his wife, and he wanted to hold his daughter to him, but it was impossible to walk holding them both. So he gave Holly a piggyback ride and got Jenny to curve her arm through his. Soon Holly was snoring gently on his right shoulder, and he felt the sting of tears at that gentle, innocent sound. "How could she be such a bitch?" he asked out loud, and Jenny shook her head because she didn't know what he meant. But Trix did.

"I can still hardly believe it," Trix said. "After what she did for my family. What she's done for so many."

"You can't purge your sins with good deeds," Sally said.

"So what are we going to do to her?" Jim asked. Before, his desire had been for revenge, payback for what Veronica had done to Jenny and Holly—using them as objects, disregarding their humanity, and causing the disaster he walked through even now. But now, with his family back, gentler emotions had swallowed his rage. He still hated her for what she had done, but the thought of perpetrating violence on the old woman—whoever and whatever she might be—was horrible.

Still, he wasn't the only person here. And Anne's anger glowed like a beacon.

"What happens to her will be her choice as much as my own," Sally said. "But you know I can't go through with you, don't you?"

"Of course," Jim said. "But you Oracles . . . you don't need to be there to get things done."

As they crossed Boston, the closeness of his family—he included Trix in that circle now, and Anne as well—inspired conflicting thoughts. He felt stronger than ever before, and able to face any and all dangers that could be thrown their way. But he also felt incredibly vulnerable. He had gone through so much to save his family, the idea of something happening to them now . . .

He heard Jennifer's screams, and knew he always would. *She knew we were running, knew she was doing it to make time for us, and she'd have done her very best not to scream. How terrible it must have been.*

It took them almost two hours to walk the two miles to Hanover Street. They crossed Boston Common, where thousands of displaced people had set up temporary shelters, and relief agencies were busy erecting tents and treatment areas. There were tears, but there were also children running between the tents playing hide-and-seek, teens playing soccer, and many groups of people had joined forces to prepare and hand out food and water. Spirits were generally high, but Jim knew that would not last longer than a couple of days.

None of them had any true idea about the level of destruction wrought on the city, or the death toll. That was for afterward. For now, they still had more than one world to consider.

Holly snored, and Jim wondered what was going on in her mind. *Veronica wants your daughter dead because she's the next Oracle of Boston,* the redheaded kid had told them. That gave Jim and his family's future a whole new landscape—but it was something else he was desperate not to think about right now.

When they finally found themselves closing on Veronica's house, Sally called a halt and gathered them together in front of a tall townhouse. "Right," she said, and told them what to do.

"I won't let you go. I can't lose you again."

Trix and Anne faced each other. They had spoken at the same time. On any other occasion that might have made them smile, but not now.

"No," Trix said. "Just . . . no. If anything happens to me through there, you'll be stuck, and it's a different world, and—"

"Is it?" Anne asked.

"Yes," Trix said. And it *was* a different world. One where she and Jenny were best friends, but nothing more, except in her own guilty dreams. A world where Anne had never existed and could never live. Over there—back where Trix had come from—she hoped to find that everything was still normal, hoped that bringing Jenny and Holly back would weave them into the fabric of that world again.

And yet . . .

"I'll see you again," Trix said.

Anne's eyes opened wider, and she swallowed hard.

"I'm coming back," Trix said. "I promise you that."

"A promise isn't enough," Anne said. "*Nothing's* enough. I've lost you once already, Trix. I buried you and buried myself in grief, and I can't go through that again."

The others were milling, speaking in low voices while Trix said her good-byes. She caught Sally's gaze over Anne's shoulder, and the little girl nodded. *Maybe she really can read my mind,* Trix thought. Sally crossed the sidewalk and held Anne's hand. "She's right," Sally said, not quite able to sound like a little girl. "You can't go. But Trix is Unique. She can come back."

Anne lowered her gaze, muttering something.

"What's that?" Trix asked.

Anne lifted her eyes and Trix saw the tears streaming down her face. "Will you want to? Once you're back to your old life and everything is normal again, maybe you'll forget all about me. Maybe you'll just be happy things are the way they're supposed to be, and—"

Trix silenced her with a kiss, her own tears falling as she twined her fingers in Anne's hair. Then she broke the kiss, reluctantly. She pressed her forehead against Anne's and looked into her eyes. "You don't get it, do you?" Trix whispered. "This . . . in my heart, this is the way things were always supposed to be."

Anne smiled, wiping her tears. "I bet you say that to all the girls."

Trix could have made a joke out of it, but she didn't even return Anne's smile. "No," she promised. "Never."

Anne took a shuddering breath, then nodded. She would go along with Sally's plan. "You make this work," she told Trix. Then she looked at the others. "All of you. Take care of each other."

Jim put his arms around his wife and daughter. "We always have."

Trix kissed Anne's forehead. "We'll try our best not to die."

Anne hit her. "That's not funny."

"No," Sally agreed. "It's not."

The young Oracle closed her eyes and muttered something, words lost beneath the roar of a police cruiser passing by. Anne's eyes widened in surprise as her No-Face Man slipped from her and flickered in the sunlight, fading quickly to nothing as it obeyed Sally's careful orders. "You won't need him anymore," Sally said.

Trix held Anne as she slumped slightly. Anne sighed as she realized she was only herself again.

"I love you," Trix whispered. And Anne relaxed before letting her go, because that seemed to have made everything all right.

It should have been impossible for her to fall in love so fast—in a single day, only hours, really—but in a fundamental way, she had been in love with this woman for many years. Thomas McGee might have done something monstrous, and become a monster in the process, but the splintering of the city had also given both Trix and Anne second chances at the love they'd always wanted.

"Remember," Sally said, "the only way is to fool her. Holly goes forward. You're offering her."

"She'll never believe that," Jim said.

"It'll confuse her long enough for you to tackle her."

"And then?"

"And then kill her."

They shuffled their feet, none of them wanting to catch another's eye.

"That's just nasty," Holly said at last.

Trix sighed and looked around. The street was relatively undamaged other than smashed glass and a few fallen tiles. People walked here and there with shopping bags, panic-buying food and drink. Others stood on their stoops and watched the world go by, perhaps counting their blessings. What would they think of this strange group of scruffy, serious people?

"Gotta be done," Trix said softly. Though her voice was strong, she had no idea if she could do what Sally asked.

"So these things in us?" Jim asked.

"I've already instructed them," Sally said. "When it's over, they leave. One way or another."

"Thanks for your vote of confidence," Jim said. But Sally's awkward smile made him realize something—she was socially inept, even for a girl of her age. She might be the Oracle, but that meant she would never be normal. Relationships were her work, in many ways, but she could never have one of her own. She was doomed to a life alone. It made him fear for Holly, and wonder whether there had been Oracles in the past who had managed to have love in their lives.

"Good luck," Sally said, and she turned and walked away.

"Sally," Jim said. The girl paused and turned around, and Trix had a sudden, shattering sense of déjà vu. She remembered watching a program once with Jim and Jenny about the discovery of the concentration camps in Germany and Poland. It had been a moment of pure immersion, when the camera had focused on a young girl walking behind a wire fence. She had paused and turned to look at the camera, and even that seventy-year-old footage had done nothing to lessen that girl's haunting, hopeless expression. *Who is she where is she now is she still alive?* Trix had thought, and it had become a preoccupation of hers to find out. She never had, and she often dreamed of that little girl, still standing there staring through a fence, waiting to be discovered. Sally reminded her of that little girl now—eyes deepened by exhaustion, mouth slack, her skin wan and ashy.

"It'll be okay!" Trix said. Sally glanced at her and smiled, and Trix thought perhaps she'd found that little girl at last.

"I'll be watching from here," Sally said, "but you'll be a world away. I don't have to stand *here* and watch." She tapped her foot on the sidewalk and looked down at the tinkle of broken glass. "Besides, I've got plenty to keep me occupied now. So many who need my help."

They watched her leave.

"So, what're you waiting for?" Anne asked. She sat on

a fire hydrant, arms crossed, head tilted to one side. "Get it done, and get your cute ass back here."

Holly giggled. Even Jenny managed a soft laugh and said, "That's not something I ever thought I'd say."

"Don't know what you're missing," Anne said, and winked at her. The two women, facets of each other, smiled conspiratorially.

"So?" Trix said. She looked from Jim to Jenny to Holly and felt a rush of love.

"So," Jim said. And as they walked along the street toward Veronica's house, even Holly was silent, because the unspoken truth hung heavy around them.

If they were successful, today would end with a woman dead by their hands.

"We need to go upstairs to your bedroom," Trix said, and the man's expression barely changed. Behind him in the hallway stood another version of him, slightly plumper, longer-haired, but wearing the same shell-shocked expression. As both wives peered from the living room doorway, Trix began to really understand how fundamentally everything here had changed. *Her* Boston was still safe and sound, ignorant in its single existence of anything so surreal as what she was witnessing right now. But here, everything was different. The earthquake had not only taken lives, it had shattered them as well. The two worlds where these merged Bostons had once been different were forever changed. How would people overcome such a shock? How *could* they?

But then she saw the two teenaged girls coming giggling down the stairs, and she thought maybe it would be fine after all.

"You two again!" one of the girls said.

"You know these people?" the other girl asked.

"Sure. Well. Not really. But they were in our house, and Dad scared them off."

"I like your hair," the other girl said.

"Thanks," Trix said. "Er . . ." This was becoming more surreal by the moment, and when the women started berating their daughters, that only increased.

"Really," Holly said, "we need to do what Auntie Trix says. Otherwise my daddy says it might all happen again, and then there might be three of you. Or maybe there won't be any."

"You need to what?" the man said.

"Upstairs," Jim said over Trix's shoulder.

"Why?" the other man said.

"There's . . ." Trix gave what she hoped was her best smile, unsure how her grubby, bruised face would present it.

"It's something to do with the ghost, isn't it?" the man asked. He nodded wisely. "I knew it the first time I saw you. The ghost."

"What ghost?" Trix asked.

"We've never used the room," he said. He tur\ned to his longer-haired twin. "Have you?"

The man shook his head slowly. "Never liked it. Always felt weird. And smelled."

"Cotton candy," Trix said, and everyone facing her— the four adults, the two girls—knew what she was saying.

The man stood back from the doorway, his motion inviting them to enter. Trix went first, then Holly, and Jim and Jenny followed. "What's happening?" he asked softly as Trix passed. She saw in his eyes the doubt and fear that he had been trying to hide from his family.

"It's okay to be afraid, Conor. But everything's going to work out fine."

They climbed the stairs, reached the landing, and

gathered outside the door. There was nothing to indicate that the room beyond was unused, but Trix had the very real sense that it was not part of the house. *In my world, this place belongs to an evil woman,* she thought, looking around the landing at family pictures showing smiling people and holidays gone by.

"When we go in, hold on to our hands," Jim said to Holly. "We're Uniques, and crossing should be easy for us. But Jenny . . . it might be different for you."

"Different how?" Jenny asked, drawing Holly close to her.

"I don't know," Jim said truthfully.

"You have Sally's No-Face Man still inside you," Trix said. "It might provide a buffer."

"So let's go," Jim said. He reached for the handle and opened the door.

Inside, the room was as they had seen it on their arrival in the Irish Boston. Yellow wallpaper, an antique-style bed, clothes hanging in the closet. But on their arrival they'd believed the room was lived-in. Now they knew otherwise, and Trix saw the signs they'd missed before. The bedroom was like a movie set rather than a real room, arranged to look genuine yet somehow tainted with falseness.

Beyond the bed was the door that led into McGee's terrible room.

She led the way and they all went through. The stench of ash and age hit them as they passed into the ruined room, and she wondered what the family that lived here thought of this place. Perhaps they didn't even know it existed. Maybe this was a ghost room to that family, and that would mean that Trix and the others were now ghosts as well.

She knew that wasn't true, but still it gave her the shivers.

"What now?" Jenny asked.

"I can see," Holly said, her little voice filled with wonder.

"What?" Jenny asked.

"Don't be scared," Trix said. "Jenny, please don't be scared." She held her friend and hugged her tight, and when she breathed in Jenny's hair it was Anne smiling in her mind's eye.

"Come here," Jim said, welcoming them into his embrace. "And you, too, sweetie."

Holly came, too, hugging their waists, stretching as far as she could to embrace the three adults and giggling as she said, "Group hug!"

"You think we need to do the . . . ?" Trix said, swirling her eyes around to imitate the first time they'd perceived the weirdness of this room. But she already knew the answer to that. The thing she carried inside her was already urging her to cross the room. They stood on undamaged flooring right now, and when they crossed they would also pivot around reality—a pivot around which Thomas McGee had twisted Boston. He had created splinter cities primed with the potential for tragedy, but it had taken Veronica to realize that potential.

Jim stared at her grimly, and she tried to smile back. *Sure,* she wanted to say, *I'm ready to kill. Sure I am. For everything she's done, and everything else she'd do.* But she had no wish to speak those words aloud.

It was Jenny who urged them to walk. As a group they crossed the room, and Jenny cried out as they pierced the skin between worlds.

Trix's No-Face Man shivered at the change, a disturbingly sexual sensation.

For just an instant, the whole world seemed to *flex* outward, and a wave of dizziness swept over Trix. Jenny nearly collapsed with the sudden loss of equilibrium,

staggering as though drunk, but her family kept her
from falling. For several seconds, the four of them only
stood and breathed, waiting for the world to right itself
again.

When it did, Trix knew that they were through.

The door stood before them, closed where they had
left it open. Beyond, in the depths of the house they had
just left—a different version of that house, in which
families no longer lived—a voice rose up in fury.

"Veronica's home," Jim said.

"And so are we," Jenny said. "Let's get this finished. I
want my life back."

And the things inside them craved release.

Veronica was in the living room, waiting for them in the
chair where she'd told them about McGee and the In-
Between, setting up the story she wanted them to know
rather than the tale that was true. There was a tea service on the table before her, a plate of cookies, and several
cups steaming with recently poured liquid. Her back
was straight, her hands on her knees. She was every
image the lady, apart from her face.

She had the face of a killer.

Her lips were drawn, her teeth bared, her eyes narrowed and cruel. Her skin was lined now, projecting
every year of her age, and she glared at them with an
anger Jim thought verged on madness. She made him
want to draw back, grab his family, and run, but that
would do them no good. It would do no one any good.
Because while she was alive, Sally and the Bostons were
still in danger.

"Murderer," Jim said, and Veronica's rage exploded.

"How?" she screamed, standing and knocking the
small coffee table with her leg. Tea spilled, a cup broke.

"How did you . . . ?" She stormed at them and Jim grabbed Holly, pulling her behind him.

Veronica sneered. "You think you can protect her behind *flesh* and *blood*?" She waved her hands at the air and screamed, an incoherent outburst that darkened the corners of the room. Shapes parted from the walls— Shadow Men that screamed as they were dragged from the In-Between at Veronica's behest. They swayed a little, and then solidified as they walked to the room's two doors and single window. They were guarding the exits.

"All those people," Jim said. "All those dead people I've seen, and every one of them because of you."

"You don't think she gives a shit, do you, Jim?" Trix asked. He glanced her way, saw her left hand bunched in her pocket. What did she have in there—a knife? A weapon?

"I think maybe once she would have," he said. Sally had told them to offer her Holly, confuse her, then attack, but this Veronica was beyond confusion. Her madness and fury were driving her now.

"You should be dead!" she said, pointing her manicured finger at Holly. "You *will* be dead."

The girl whimpered and hid behind Jim, grasping his right arm. He could *never* offer his daughter, as bait or otherwise. She was far too precious. He had always loved her with an honest devotion, but perhaps it took losing someone and finding her again to make you realize just how powerful love could be. Holly was a vital part of him, more solid and precious than his own heart and soul. He would die for her.

He would *kill* for her.

Jim stepped forward, ignoring Jenny's gasp of surprise and Holly's hands trying to pull him back.

"What?" Veronica said, mocking. "Going to paint me to death, Mr. Artist?"

"In my dreams, I'm sure," Jim said. As he dropped to the floor and reached for a small side table—the only piece of furniture that could be a weapon, and his only hope—he sensed Trix leaping past him to his right, and heard Jenny telling Holly to run.

And then everything froze.

Jim saw the small table before him but could not touch it. Past the table were Veronica's legs, their shadows confused by those of her moving arms and flexing fingers. He could hear the strange words she muttered but could not move his head—or even his eyes—to look up and see what she was doing.

Trapped, he thought, and he could feel the No-Face Man trapped inside him writhing against its confines. *No. God, no.* They carried Sally's mark upon them, enough to allow the No-Face Men into the home that had once belonged to Thomas McGee. The No-Face Men had been the backup plan. If Jim and his family couldn't get to Veronica, then Sally's echo creatures were there to help, to kill her the way the Shadow Men had murdered Peter O'Brien. But the No-Face Man inside Jim was just as paralyzed, just as trapped and helpless, as Jim himself.

From the corner of his eye he could make out Trix, her form impossibly unbalanced where she had been halted in the act of diving at Veronica.

"Stupid people," Veronica said, voice rank with disgust. "You think that defying me bought you the right to come back to attack me. Kill me? Is that what the bitch-girl told you to do?"

Happily, Jim thought, but he could not speak. His blood flowed, his heart thudded in his ears, but his muscles felt like they were made of glass, a fragile skeleton conjured by this woman's mad magic.

"There's only one killing happening here today," the

woman said. Jim heard more of those language-less words, and then a shadow passed him by. A small shadow. Holly, dragging her feet as something drew her forward. Her hand brushed against Jim's cheek as she passed, and he thought, *Is that the last time I'll feel my daughter's warmth?*

Jim struggled and fought and raged, his eyes burning as he defied the spell to lift them. They burned more than when he and Trix had first attempted to see the alternate Bostons, up in that room where Thomas McGee, in his greed and hubris, had split the world asunder. They burned, but he did it, only to see a reality he wished he could instantly forget.

Holly knelt before Veronica, her knees awash in spilled tea. The old woman grinned in delight, reveling in victory, and from behind him Jim heard a faint, desperate whine coming from his wife.

If only we could close our eyes, he thought, because there was nothing he wanted to see less than his daughter's death.

"I'll always be here," Veronica said, "and each Boston will be *my* Boston." She held up one hand and pointed a finger at Holly. A blue light gathered on the end of her finger, dancing like a faraway star. And at one word from Veronica, it leaped forward and struck Holly's face.

"Nnnnn . . . ," was all Jim could say, but he felt his heart crushed and broken, chewed up and spat out, as Holly's head flipped back and her arms went wide, and he saw that terrible light burning from her ears and eyes, nose and mouth. It spilled down her body like the In-Between's mist given form, leaving slick, luminous trails in her hair and on her skin.

"Now, then," Veronica said, turning around as if to deal with the day's next order of business.

"You stupid, stupid bitch," Holly said. It was her voice, but the words . . . the words were Sally's. And suddenly Jim understood that the girl Oracle had never shared with them her true plan.

"What?" Veronica turned back, amazed, to see Holly shake her head slowly, then stand.

"You think a mark is sophisticated?" Holly said. "In *my* Boston, that type of witchery has gone the way of the street-corner card trick. In *my* Boston, I'm so at one with the city that sometimes it loses itself in me, and I have its magic and its history, its soul, at hand. My Boston gives me *real* magic."

"You should be dead," Veronica whispered.

"This?" Holly picked a dreg of the terrible light from her arm and waved it like a string of spit. Then she breathed on it, and it turned into a blade of grass. "How pretty." She dropped the grass, and it fluttered to the ground.

Veronica gathered herself quickly, hissing three words that sent her Shadow Men streaking across the room.

What happened next was so fast that Jim could not make it out. Later, he would put events together from what little he saw, and Holly's few comments about that afternoon, and then the picture would be clear.

He felt a wrench as something inside him burst out. It winded him, shattering Veronica's strange hold over him and jerking him to his feet, and as he gasped he heard Trix and Jenny doing the same. The darkness moved away from him, and he saw, gathering Veronica in its arms, a No-Face Man—not a prisoner after all, now that Sally's real mark, the spells she had hidden inside Holly, had been released.

Veronica screamed, but though her Shadow Men heard, they could do nothing. They were being ripped and shredded by the other two No-Face Men, the violence sudden and intense. And when they had finished, they turned their attentions to Veronica.

"No," Holly said, and Jim could not tell who spoke. Was this his daughter telling those shades not to kill the Oracle? Or was it Sally, through his daughter?

He would never know, and Holly would never say.

Instead, the No-Face Men dragged Veronica from the room and up the stairs. She screamed and railed against them, muttering spells that did not work, incantations that dispersed to the air. And none of them worked because Holly was this Boston's next chosen Oracle, and such violence against her could not be allowed. That was why Veronica had needed the little girl out of *her* Boston—the soul of the city, in this reality, would not allow one Oracle to kill the next.

Jim wanted to watch what happened to the old woman, but Jenny hugged him and held him there, and Trix quietly closed the door. Still, they heard the heavy footsteps upstairs as Veronica was dragged across the small bedroom, and then lighter impacts as her feet fell in the farther room. After that, one long scream, fading, growing distant in space and time, until it was finally cut off by a shattering silence.

Jim turned to his daughter. She was still facing away from them, but her head turned ever so slightly to the left and right, left and right. It was as if she was reading something from the air before her.

Without turning, and in a tone that told Jim he might never hear his daughter's innocent voice again, Holly spoke three words.

"I know everything."

Epilogue

What's Left of the Flag

J IM STOOD in the doorway of their new kitchen, watching Holly coloring at the table. Delicious aromas filled every room. Jenny had decided to make jambalaya, and Holly loved nothing more than to help her mom cook. Sometimes she helped cut vegetables or stir eggs or perform some other task appropriate for a girl who was not quite eight. But most of the time she was content just to be with Jenny. If anything, that inclination had only increased in the six weeks since their ordeal in the other Bostons.

Jim knew how his daughter felt. Ever since they had come back to their own city, he had rarely been parted from his family. At first, he had been unwilling to leave them at all, and had even insisted that Holly sleep in with him and Jenny. He had not worked at all, not a single brushstroke on canvas or anything more intricate than a casual sketch on a napkin, for almost a full month after their return, and had only left them twice to meet with Jonathan. The first time had been to assure himself that the world had returned to normal and that Jonathan was not, in fact, dying of cancer. The second had been to visit a gallery where Jonathan had arranged a display of his work.

Yet the past weeks had been anything but stable. They had put their apartment up for sale and moved into Veronica's house. Thomas McGee's house. With the passage between realities so much easier through that upstairs room, they could not allow it to be sold to some ordinary, unsuspecting family. For weeks they had been redecorating the place, moving in their own furniture, refinishing floors and painting walls, and buying new appliances. No matter what changes they made, though, Jim found it impossible to think he would ever feel at home here.

But what mattered was not what he and Jenny felt. This wasn't really their home, it was Holly's. She was the Oracle, chosen by the city. At first, Jim had feared that there would be many complications in attempting to buy the building from Veronica's estate. When his attorney had done the research, however, he had found that there had been two names on the deed—Veronica Braden and Holly Banks. Holly's name had been added to the deed on the day she was born.

There was no way that Veronica had done such a thing, but somehow, through its influence, the city of Boston had arranged for it to happen. It had chosen its next Oracle that long ago.

Jim felt a familiar sadness engulfing him as he watched his little girl color. Holly sang to herself, a little snippet of a song from some Disney Channel series, and did a little jerky dance movement while kneeling on the chair. He smiled but could not chase away the melancholy in his heart.

"She'll be all right," Jenny whispered, coming up behind him and sliding a hand around to rest on his stomach. She kissed his neck. "She's got us with her. We can do this together."

Jim nodded but couldn't speak. In Sally Bennet, he had seen what happened when a child inherited the role of Oracle. She knew the city intimately, knew the secrets and mysteries of its people, the joy and hatred and despair that seeped into every brick and beam. She had inherited the city's ancient magic, yes, and a profound wisdom far beyond the capacity of a child to wield. In years to come, she would benefit from that wisdom and power, but now she was simply too young to process it all. She knew of murders and infidelity and perversion, and there were months yet before her eighth birthday.

"No child should have such things in her head," he whispered.

"I know," Jenny said, pressing her warm body against his back, kissing his neck again. "But the city chose her. We can't erase that. All we can do is help her carry the weight of it."

"I'll be all right, you know," Holly said.

Jim stiffened and stared at his daughter. She hadn't looked up from her coloring. He didn't think they had spoken loud enough for her to hear.

Now Holly turned to look at her parents, her eyes full of a wisdom beyond her years. "Trust me, Daddy. Everything will be all right."

The doorbell rang. Holly's eyes lit up, and suddenly they were a little girl's again. "Auntie Trix!" she cried, jumping down from the chair and bolting past her parents.

Jenny caught Jim's hand, and as he turned, she kissed him. "We'll be all right. Think of all of the people we'll be helping."

Jim nodded. It would feel good to know that they could do so much good, but he would never feel it had been worth the sacrifice of his daughter's innocence. He vowed to protect her childhood as best he could.

"Without you, this would have broken me," he told Jenny, gazing into her eyes.

"Duh, I know that," she said. "That's why I knew you'd find a way to come after us. Your life would be so boring without me in it. And who would nag you to take out the trash?"

At last, he smiled. Together, they walked along the hall into the foyer, where they heard voices fussing over Holly, telling her how big she'd gotten.

Trix had arrived, but it appeared that their other dinner guest had come at the same time, for Jonathan crouched down in front of Holly and, with a flourish, produced a small gift-wrapped present from inside his coat. "For your new bedroom," he said.

Holly made little excited noises and asked if she could open it immediately. Jonathan insisted, and she tore off the paper and opened the little box to find a small crystal prism inside.

"You hang it in front of your window, and on sunny days, it makes little rainbows all around the room," he explained.

"Uncle Jonathan, I love it! Thank you so much!"

Holly darted to the window to see if she could make the prism throw rainbows, which gave the adults a few moments to exchange greetings. Jonathan shook hands with Jim and kissed both Jenny and Trix. He nudged Trix's overnight bag with his toe. "Spending the night?" he asked, turning to gaze at Jenny in mock admonition. "No one told me it was a sleepover."

Jenny and Trix seemed awkward and at a loss for a reply. Jonathan seemed to sense this, and seemed about to apologize for something he could not possibly understand.

"It's a girls' thing," Jim said, rolling his eyes. "They're all going to camp out in Holly's room tonight."

A lie, of course. But they had all agreed not to tell anyone the tale of the Oracles and the other Bostons. Jonathan might have been able to believe them, but perhaps not. Jim thought that his own life had been better, and simpler, before he had learned the truth of the world, and he didn't think they had a right to spoil that simplicity for anyone else.

Tonight, Trix would be leaving their reality, going to live permanently in the Collided Cities, and they would need to make an excuse to tell Jonathan. The wider worlds of the Collided Cities were still coming to terms with what had happened and the staggering implications, but this world—the place Jim was thinking of as the first Boston—was protected from that. After all they had been through, he was glad.

Through McGee's room upstairs, Trix might visit them from time to time. But she had promised Anne she would return, and wanted very much to find out if fate had allowed her to have her heart's desire. She'd already returned briefly, and told Anne that she had things to finish here before moving over for good. Today's date had almost taken on the importance of a wedding.

It was strange for Jim and Jenny to know that Trix would give up her whole world—her friends and family in this world—for a chance at happiness with Anne, the Jenny of another world. They didn't talk about it much, but Jim could see that Jenny looked at Trix differently, because the two of them loved each other even more deeply now that the depth of Trix's feelings for her had become known.

Anne wasn't the only reason for Trix's decision. The Collided Cities were full of people who needed help, not just to recover from the earthquake but to come to terms with the merging of two realities and what that meant for them—meeting their twins from an alternate Boston, or discovering that in that other world they had led very different lives.

Jonathan smiled at Jenny and Trix. "Next time you have a girls' night, include me, will you? It's not like I have anything else to do."

Jenny touched his arm. "You'll find someone else. Someone who loves you in spite of yourself."

"Gee, thanks," Jonathan said, with a laugh that did not reach his eyes.

"Don't be sad, Uncle Jonathan," Holly said, coming back from the window with the prism clutched in her hand. "You don't need to find someone else. Philip still loves you. He misses you every day, and thinks what you do—that you're both too stubborn to say it."

They all stared at Holly. She had been easing into her role as the Oracle, only helping people who went through the usual ritual to contact Veronica. They were surprised to find a little girl in her place but happily accepted Holly's help. They wanted the Oracle, and Jim supposed it didn't matter to them who the Oracle was. But this was different. Jonathan didn't know anything about the Oracle of Boston.

Jonathan looked at Holly, a range of emotions playing across his face. Finally, he forced a smile.

"That's sweet, Holly darling, but Philip has moved on with his life. It's all right. I'll try not to be sad, okay?"

Holly shook her head, looking almost petulant. "You don't have to pretend you're all right just because I'm a kid, Uncle Jonathan. But I'm trying to tell you . . . you don't need to be sad. If you love Philip, go and see him. He's been sad, too. He doesn't think you'd ever take him back after the things he said, but I know you would."

Jim and Jenny and Trix all shared a look, and Jonathan caught it. He glanced at them in confusion.

"What are you guys not telling me?" he asked. "Did you hear from Philip? Has Holly been talking to him?"

"Jonathan," Jenny began, but Holly interrupted.

"Listen to me, Jonathan," she said—no more "Uncle," and her voice had suddenly become startlingly mature. "Philip is sitting in the café in the big bookstore at Downtown Crossing. He's alone. He's reading and drinking—what is that?—chai tea. The sadness in him is so strong that even the people sitting around him can feel it."

Jonathan stared at her, then looked up—not at Jim, but at Jenny.

Jenny took his hand. "We have a lot of things to talk about," she said. "A lot to tell you. But before we do, maybe you should take a quick drive over to Downtown Crossing. It's so close."

Confused, Jonathan looked at Holly's wise expression and laughed uncertainly, then turned to Jim. He tried to speak but could not. Jim realized that Jenny meant to tell Jonathan everything, despite what they'd agreed, and though he was worried he also felt relieved.

"Go, Jonathan," Jim said. "You'll be glad you did. Come back here after. Bring Philip with you. We won't start dinner until you get back."

"You're serious," Jonathan said, staring at him as if he were insane, and then looking around. "You're all serious?"

Trix tapped his shoulder. Jonathan spun to stare at her. "Dude, seriously," Trix said, grinning. "Go. You won't be sorry."

Jonathan laughed, a smile stealing over his face. Jim could see that he thought they had done something wonderful for him, that they had been in touch with Philip and somehow conspired to arrange a meeting. But that was all right. He would learn soon enough that they had not spoken to Philip at all during the breakup, and then they would have a lot of explaining to do.

"I'll be back," Jonathan said, pulling his keys out of his pocket as he pushed open the door. He paused and looked back at Trix. "By the way, I love the hair."

Trix smiled and thanked him, and then Jonathan was gone.

The four of them stood in the foyer, silently acknowledging the bond that would always exist between them and the secrets that they shared. Jim reached up and touched Trix's hair. When they had brought Jenny and Holly back to Boston and reality had adjusted to their return, Jim and Trix had both found that the changes they had undergone had been reversed. But Trix had liked her body and her look, and scant weeks after their ordeal she had dyed her hair the same bright pink. She was even thinking of piercings.

"It's a good look," Jim told her.

"Come on," Jenny said, taking Trix's hand. "If we're going to be saying good-bye, I'm going to want wine."

Trix allowed herself to be led toward the kitchen. "It's not forever, you know. I'll be back to visit."

Jenny changed the subject, talking about the people who needed help in the Collided Cities, and she and Trix ventured off on that discussion path as they went down the hall to the kitchen.

Jim looked down to see Holly watching him. "Do you think Auntie Trix will be all right over there?" he asked his daughter. But, really, the question was for the Oracle of Boston. "Do you think she'll be happy?"

"Silly Daddy," Holly said, hugging him and staring up

into his eyes. "I know all the secrets from the past, and I can tell you what's going on in the city right now. But I don't know what's going to happen in the future. Nobody does."

That aged wisdom flickered in her eyes.

"That part," Holly said, "is up to us."